CONTENTS

All the King's Bastards	1
Chapter One	5
Chapter Two	17
Chapter Three	22
Chapter Four	28
Chapter Five	35
Chapter Six	46
Chapter Seven	52
Chapter Eight	60
Chapter Nine	67
Chapter Ten	77
Chapter Eleven	83
Chapter Twelve	92
Chapter Thirteen	97
Chapter Fourteen	101
Chapter Fifteen	109
Chapter Sixteen	114
Chapter Seventeen	122
Chapter Eighteen	129
Chapter Nineteen	136
Chapter Twenty	144

Chapter Twenty-One	151
Chapter Twenty-Two	163
Chapter Twenty-Three	168
Chapter Twenty-Four	176
Chapter Twenty-Five	184
Chapter Twenty-Six	190
Chapter Twenty-Seven	195
Chapter Twenty-Eight	199
Chapter Twenty-Nine	210
Chapter Thirty	214
Chapter Thirty-One	218
Chapter Thirty-Two	223
Chapter Thirty-Three	228
Chapter Thirty-Four	238
Chapter Thirty-Five	245
Chapter Thirty-Six	252
Chapter Thirty-Seven	256
Chapter Thirty-Eight	261
Chapter Thirty-Nine	265
Chapter Forty	270
Chapter Forty-One	279
Chapter Forty-Two	286
Chapter Forty-Three	291
Chapter Forty-Four	294
Chapter Forty-Five	301
Chapter Forty-Six	307
Chapter Forty-Seven	312
Chapter Forty-Eight	324

Chapter Forty-Nine	328
Author's Notes	340
Thank You	347
About The Author	348

ALL THE KING'S BASTARDS

Book One of

A Succession of Chaos

By G. Lawrence

Copyright © Gemma Lawrence 2025
All Rights Reserved.
No part of this manuscript may be reproduced without Gemma Lawrence's express consent.
The author's moral rights have been asserted.

No generative AI was used in the production of this manuscript.
The author further expressly and specifically prohibits any entity from using this manuscript to train AI technologies in any way, including to generate text, and including, without limitation, technologies capable of generating works in the same style or genre as this manuscript.

Dedicated to one of my readers who,
during an email conversation,
gave me the idea for this book.
Hopefully, you know who you are.
This hasn't been a painless adventure,
but it is one I am so grateful for.
Thank you.

"There is a tide in the affairs of men,
Which, taken at the flood, leads on to fortune."
William Shakespeare, Julius Caesar.

"It seems to me most strange that men should fear, seeing that death, a necessary end,
will come when it will come."
William Shakespeare, Julius Caesar

"War does not determine who is right, only who is left."
Attributed to Bertrand Russell

CHAPTER ONE

Queen Anne Boleyn

24th of January 1536

Eve of the Feast of the Conversion of St Paul

Greenwich Palace

London

She stared at the blood. Scent of iron filled her nostrils, flooded her psyche. Through her thoughts that blood flowed, pouring as a waterfall in her numbed mind. In there, in her mind, there was so much, an endless tide threatening to carry her away, to drown her, yet when she looked at his body there seemed so little.

A red smear lay on his pale forehead, that skin so very pale, paler than ever she had seen skin appear. She supposed this was what they meant by pale as death, for nothing in life was this shade of white, this white with a touch of grey.

A small stream of blood had dribbled from his mouth. It was dried now, crusting black. Some was on his brow, darkening and hardening the soft strands of that famous red-gold hair. He lay on his back, so she could not see the worst injury, the one the physicians said had killed him. They had cleaned him of course, trying to stem the flow but all the same there seemed so little blood. So little blood, yet blood was all she could see, all she could smell, all she could think. In her head it was, washing back and forth, a crimson, crashing wave, foam curling on a beach, tainted pink.

How could so little blood lead to a death so large?

"Majesty, you must leave him now."

The voice intruded, hurtling rudely, as if from nowhere, into a place most private, into her mind and soul. It had been quiet there a while, the only noise the waves of blood, as she stared upon the crushed body of her husband. She had been alone, just her thoughts, just the numbness of the rushing blood pouring through her, over her, then there was the voice. Why could they not leave her alone?

With the first intrusion there came others, a low murmur of troubled voices not far away, the scent of medicines the doctors had used to try to save him, the perfume of a light breeze of winter, crisp with sunshine and coolness both, rippling through the tent, making canvas sides not fully tied down flap and crack. Suddenly she could hear people milling outside, the nervous crowds there gathered, waiting anxiously to know what had happened to their King. She could feel waning sunshine on her hand, her hand which sat atop his, his familiar flesh under her fingers which was already beginning to cool.

Her dark head bowed over the broken form of her husband; she did not look up.

"Majesty… you must…" The intruder sought to speak again, thinking grief had blocked her ears, but Anne shook her head, pearls on her French hood catching dappled light creeping into the tent from the world outside, from the jousting field where he had fallen, where his heavy horse had rolled on his equally heavily armoured body, crushing him to death. *The weight of his wishes*, she thought, an idle conceit passing through her mind, a mind shocked into stillness by grief and dread. The weight of his fantasy of chivalry and knighthood. That was what had killed him.

"I will not leave him alone; I will not leave him to walk into the arms of death without a friend at his side." Her voice was gentle, but there was steel in it, the noise a sharp sword makes as it is drawn from soft sheath.

The men standing about Queen Anne Boleyn as she knelt beside her husband offered each other weighted glances. She could feel them, those eyes, the heaviness inherent in their gazes. They weighed upon her soul, pressing her as if she were the witch some called her, pressed to death under boards and rocks. They had called her many names, the people of England, over these last years when she had been Queen, before that too when she was called the King's whore, his goggled-eyed jade, usurper of the throne of Katherine. Anne had stood much, and could endure this weight now, though still it pained her.

One tried again. "Majesty... you did not leave him to walk alone. You were here, with him as he passed, that is all a man can ask; that someone is with him at the end, so the passage into death is not done alone. But he is gone now. We must prepare him, look after him. You have matters to attend to."

Did the fool think she did not know this? That there was much to do now? That her husband was dead? The doctors, the physicians had already told her this, that Henry was gone, that the King was dead. The back of his head was crushed, his belly was swollen, full of blood. They had told her this. It did not matter, still she knelt, holding his hand, staring down at him. She needed a moment. In truth she needed all the time in the world that came now and ever after, and even then it would not be enough. But why could she not just have a moment more with him, to accept that Henry was dead?

It was a thing impossible he should be gone. It was too sudden, too quick. It was ridiculous. Everything about this moment felt unreal for never had anyone been as alive as Henry VIII of England. Anne had faced him in enough fights of wills and words to know the furious power of his spirit, shared his bed enough times to understand how he could give himself, heart and soul and body to the woman he loved, and she had been that woman, a long time she had been that woman. Despite his affairs, his infidelities, part of her believed she still was, and always would be the woman he loved. No one had loved her as he had, and no one had loved another as she had loved him. When they fought, when he had strayed, when the world tried to drive them apart, he had always come back to her, always needed her, always heeded her mind, her opinion, sought her out above all others.

But he could not come back to her now.

All the anger of the past year, all the agony of his recent infidelities, the moments when he, in rage, had cried he would not wed her again if he had the choice, the time he told her he could set her down as easily as she had been raised up, all that pain seemed to leave her, replaced by another agony more fierce. It washed over her, this grief, a flickering caress, light as the touch of rain, the spray of a wave. She was flying above silver waves on the sea. The roar of the ocean was in her ears, rushing past her on the wind. The sea was her grief, and somehow she sailed above it, yet at the same time as she was flowing over the top of this ocean, so she was sinking.

The voices, muted and dull about her, seemed to be coming from far away. Even the men speaking with her, trying to reason with her, trying to get her to leave the body of her husband were far away. They could not touch her, could not reach her. They were still at the surface, but a part of her had fallen under the water where all was unclear, dim. The voices, she could not understand them because she was underwater, so they became muffled. They could not understand, these men. They were not where she was, floating, sinking, in and above and a part of the waters of sorrow. They could not reach her, perhaps no one would ever again.

She was alone now.

There were many reasons to be afraid. The moment Anne put down Henry's hand, the moment she ceased to kneel at his side, she would have to face many dangers. The moment she left him, Anne would be standing alone in a world most perilous, trying to shelter not only herself but two souls who could not defend themselves. The protection of the King would be gone. The shield of his personality, the armour of his enigmatic, changeable, sometimes dangerous personality would be hers no more. Bare and raw and naked she would be before the world, alone on a battlefield, facing thousands.

The moment she left him, he would truly be dead, and she would be standing alone.

Anne remembered the Henry she had fallen in love with. The man who had pursued her with word and heart and soul, who had turned the world upside down to possess her as his wife, as his love. The man who had held her hand, courted her above all others, written poetry for her, sung for her, jousted with her colours proud on his lance. They had faced down Emperor, King, Church, Cardinal, Queen and Pope. Together, they had been a force no one could hold back, no one could vanquish, and so many had tried. So many. She remembered the man who had bounced his red-haired daughter up and down in his strong arms, who had held her, his wife, at night, so gently, when times were hard, telling her nothing mattered as long as they were together.

Now they were not together. They would not be again in this life. Her protector was gone. Her enemies were many and her friends few. Anne knew, even then, even while drowning in that first, brittle shock of grief, that there was going to be a fight for the King's throne, a vicious, ugly fight. She, his Queen, mother of his daughter and unborn child, was going to have to hold on to a throne which many would believe she had no right to, on behalf of children many would consider bastards.

When she accepted her husband was dead, when she put down

his hand, that fight was going to begin.

A moment more, her mind murmured. Just a moment to mourn her husband, to remember all he had meant to her. A moment more that was hers, that was his, before the world came slinking as a cat to snatch from her all that had been precious to them both. Anne wanted just a scrap of time that she could cling to in the future when she needed strength. One last moment that was theirs alone. She kissed his cheek, and her tears fell on his skin. There was so much now, times and events, little jests which had passed between only the two of them, and these times only she would remember now. It was a lonely thing, to know she could speak of those times to no one else and have them understand a private jape, a tender moment. The other who understood those memories without explanation was gone.

Slowly, her flesh shaking upon her bones, Anne stood, taking her hand from his, wiping her eyes. Anne took her trembling hands and to steady them, set them on her stomach where the child of the King, his promised boy as they both had hoped, lay within her. Four months. That was how old her unborn child was. A child who would never know his father, but through the stories she would tell.

"My daughter." Anne drew herself upright, willing her swimming eyes to focus on the men of the council and court before her. Her father was there, he she could trust. "Father, you must send guards… no, you take guards yourself and go to Elizabeth at Hatfield, ensure she is protected and bring her to me here, at court. This mission I entrust to you, Father, you and George. Keep my daughter safe."

She looked to the pale face of her handsome brother. Shocked as he was over the death of the King, his friend, he was more worried for her, she knew. George was her closest friend, though a few years apart in age they were as twins of the soul, united in their loves, their passions, their hates. He was the one she would tell anything to, more so than her husband at times, especially over the few last months. George would never let her down. Her brother would die for her.

He bowed to her. "Trust in us, Anne," he whispered. He was about to put his hand on her arm, but she drew herself up stiffly and he nodded, understanding without explanation. She could not show weakness, not now, not at this moment when she had to exert authority over the men who had served the King, and over the country.

"See to it," she commanded, smoothing her gown of purple and cloth of gold. Little gemstones in her sleeves winked in the sunlight. "My daughter is now the Queen of England, until this child is born…" Anne touched her belly, a gentle caress "… and if the King's son lies in my belly, he shall be King, until then, Elizabeth is the Queen. All my children must be protected, all the legitimate children of the King must be sheltered in the dark times coming. It is what he would have wanted. His legacy, the safety of the country, they were everything to him." She choked on the last word and clenched her jaw, trying to control herself.

"It will be done, Majesty." Away her father raced, grey hair at his temples catching the sunlight, shimmering silver, as he reached the throat of the tent, pulling on his cap, calling men to his side. George was with him. They would not fail her. When Elizabeth was here, with her, Anne would feel safer.

She stared at the light a moment, streaming in through the doorway briefly as her brother and father left the tent. Why was the sun still shining? Had not hours, days passed since she came in here to find Henry splayed out on this table as the doctors, surgeons and physicians worked on him? How could it still be day after all that had passed? It seemed crass to think that the sun could still be shining, yet the day had been a glorious one, the sun bright and wind cold, crowds of commoners and nobles alike screaming out for their King as he rode in the lists, until they had screamed for another reason when his great horse had tumbled, when the King had fallen, when the horse had rolled on him, a hundredweight of armour crushing their monarch to death before their eyes.

But they did not know that yet.

Henry had been swiftly carried to the tent which the knights had been using to change their armour in. Doctor Butts, a man she trusted like no other ever since he had saved her and her family from the sweating sickness years ago, had told her Henry had not woken after passing out on the field, that he had died and never again opened his eyes, so perhaps he had known little pain. She hoped so. He should not have been riding in the lists, he was to be forty-five that summer, a birthday he now never would reach. He had been growing older of course, as all men did, but his new weight, gained from hours of reading, sometimes had made such fervent exercise even more taxing. He was still a fine, strong man though not the young prince who had tired ten horses in a day when out hunting, then had come home to win eight games of tennis, but still he ate as if he was that young man. He had not been hale that winter, problems of his country and Katherine weighing on him, but Henry had wanted to compete so much that no one had had the heart to stop him. They should have stopped him. *I should have stopped him,* thought Anne.

Tears rose again; she blinked them away. There would be time to cry later, when she was alone, when none could see her. There were things to be done now, here. If men saw her demonstrating grief, they would think her weak. As she was a woman, they would already suppose this falsehood to be true. If she was to lead, become Regent, she had to show them she was as strong as any man.

Her eyes flashed out, seeking, shifting through the silent crowd inside the tent, looking for one man alone. Next to her kin, she knew him for the most useful man of court. A knave the King had called him often, even making a jest out of it so when he was dealt a knave in cards, Henry had held it up and cried, "I have been dealt a Cromwell!" A smile rose on her face but fell before it could bloom as she thought of her husband, lying dead.

She looked to Cromwell. Troubles they had had of late, particularly over investigations of the monasteries, but he was still the most able of the King's men. "Cromwell," she called quietly and to her he came as fast as his strong, if now portly, legs would carry him. The man was built like a bull but possessed the mind of a snake. She took him aside, her voice low. "Lady Mary must be set under guard. None may hear of the death of the King at this moment. We must have control of England first, and control of Mary, before anything is announced."

Cromwell inclined his head. "The Act of Succession names you Regent, Majesty, in the event of the King's death, supreme governess and protector, set here to reign until your daughter or a son comes of age. The country is yours, and all of us are yours to command. It is law and was the wish…" his eyes wandered to the corpse of the King "… of the King himself."

Anne arched an eyebrow, and Cromwell knew what she was thinking. The people of England had never welcomed her as Queen. Katherine, so recently dead, they had loved and Mary her daughter they adored too, but Anne Boleyn, Nan Boleyn, the goggle-eyed witch, never. Even if it was the wish of the King, even if it were law that she became Regent, that did not mean it would be upheld.

"We need control of Mary," she repeated.

"You suspect rebellion in her favour?" Cromwell's voice was quiet, careful.

Anne nodded. "I do. Gather the Privy Council so we may talk on the best ways to move ahead, and for this moment I want you to send men to take Mary into custody, but do it quietly. Say her father sends for her, say what you wish, but get her somewhere secure and have men watching her."

"The Tower, Majesty?"

Anne felt a sudden chill shriek through her blood. She was unsure why, yet her bones fell to cold, as if Death reached out to caress her. The Tower was the place men had died of late, of course, More and Fisher the year before, Carthusian monks too, who had refused to accept the supremacy of the King over the Church, but it was also a royal palace, a place she had visited many times, the place she had stayed in pomp and glory before her coronation. There was no need for the sense of dread she felt to steal over her.

"Yes," she agreed, pushing aside the creeping sense of foreboding, "but place her in the royal apartments. The ones I used at my coronation. Then it will not be spread about England that she is a prisoner. And no cheering her through London, Cromwell. Whatever barge she is kept on to escort her to the Water Gate, they are to fly no banners of her name or house, and she is not to wave at the common people as she did before when protesting her change of accommodation. Get her there, and do it quietly."

"Fitzroy too should be put under watch," advised Cromwell. Norfolk, the father-in-law of Fitzroy, who was standing not far away, cast a sharp glance at Cromwell.

"Fitzroy is a bastard," interjected Norfolk, striding forth. "He has no claim to the throne, if that is what you are thinking, Master Cromwell. Always he has proved loyal to the King. He will not make issue now with the succession."

"Mary is also a bastard." Anne scowled at her uncle. Never had there been any love lost between them, and she disliked him even more now, for the Duke had been the one to bring the news of the death of the King to her. She had been sewing, making clothes for her baby, lost in idle thoughts of a pleasant future when into her chamber Norfolk had burst to scream news of death and change and grief in her face. He had ripped that gentle future from her hands and handed her instead this unstable one. She knew it was unfair to blame him for that, but part of her did hold him accountable. And quite besides that crime, no care had her uncle taken in telling a pregnant woman that her husband was dead.

His daughter was wed to Fitzroy, perhaps Norfolk *wanted* Anne to miscarry so he might promote his son-in-law as king, despite the young man's bastard status?

Anne set a hand once more on her belly, willing her son to be safe. "Mary is a bastard too, uncle," she continued, "but many will try to name the daughter of Katherine Queen now. Cromwell is right. If we suspect one bastard of the King, then another must be treated the same. Fitzroy must be put under guard too, for now. I have no doubt in time he will prove he is loyal. I have always liked the lad, you know that."

"That *lad* is the King's son, the Lord Admiral of England, Earl of Nottingham, Lord Lieutenant of Ireland and twice a Duke! This would be a disgrace!" Spots of red appeared on Norfolk's sallow cheeks.

Anne drew herself up, trying to ignore the fleck of spittle on her chest, flung there by Norfolk's emphatic, thin lips. "I am certain his detainment will be of short duration. And you will address me as Majesty, uncle, or you will find yourself removed from this place and you yourself detained."

"Majesty." Norfolk bowed in a curt manner. He never welcomed being corrected by anyone, least of all a woman.

Anne wavered a little on her feet, suddenly unsteady as her head waxed light, and Cromwell moved towards her. Anne held up a hand. "No," she said, a note of command entering her voice. "I am the Regent now. I cannot show weakness."

"You are not alone, Majesty," said Cromwell, seeming to see her mind. He ever had a skill in reading people. It was what made him useful, and dangerous. "For love of the King, who always adored you, for love of his true heirs, we stand with you."

"It is true, Majesty," interjected the soft voice of Archbishop Cranmer, his white surplice glimmering in the daylight. Him, she believed without question. "We stand with you."

"England is loyal to you, Majesty," Doctor Butts added.

Anne looked about, her black eyes resting on each man standing with her, encircling the fallen, crushed body of the King. The reign of Henry VIII was done, over in the blink of an eye. *What a foolish way to die,* Anne thought as she glanced down once more at the pale, still face of her husband. What a foolish time to die, when his children were so young, when so much change had happened in his country so fast.

People were still getting used to the notion of the King as Head of the Church, as well as the break from Rome's dominion over the country, and now they were going to have to accept a child or a baby unborn as their link to God? As their monarch and Head of the Church? Spain and Rome were panting for an excuse to invade England's shores and France was a fickle friend. A nephew of the King sat on the throne of Scotland, far too close for comfort, and proposed closures of smaller monasteries, about to be agreed in a month or so, had made the leaders of England deeply unpopular. And she was Regent now, yet the people despised her. *What a time for him to leave us, when it was his will alone which held England together,* she thought.

Anne looked up again. The men about her bowed to her, one by one, in recognition of her new status. They stood with her now, these men, these lords of England rich in power and coin. In the midst of shock and grief, at the edge of a chaos about to fall on them and their world, these men stood with her indeed.

But would they always do so?

CHAPTER TWO

Sir Thomas Wyatt

24th of January 1536

Eve of the Feast of the Conversion of St Paul

Greenwich Palace

London

The man was about to pass by, obviously in a hurry, but Wyatt reached out to grab his sleeve. Any other day this would be a gross insult, an ignorant, impolite gesture never performed at court, but this was not a normal day.

"Cromwell, tell me the truth. Is the King alive?" Wyatt's voice was hushed, hissing from his mouth, a scared whisper. Scared in truth that what he asked would be answered.

"The King is well and hale, Sir Thomas, and will be up and laughing about this soon enough." Cromwell lied smooth as a snake, yet there was something in his eyes which told Wyatt those words were not true.

"God be praised," Wyatt said, a hollow echo. The King was dead, that was what Cromwell was telling him.

"God be praised." Cromwell hesitated. He had been about to announce this news himself, that the King was well and hale and soon would be out of his bed, but the people of court liked Wyatt more than him. They would be willing to believe Wyatt. "Spread this joyous news to all waiting here, please, Sir

Thomas, as I will to the rest of the court inside the palace. The Queen wishes people to move away, so the King may have some peace as he rests and recovers." Cromwell moved away himself then, vanishing into the crowd, which parted for him to pass through.

"Wyatt, what did Cromwell say?" Jane Boleyn, wife of George, was at his side, her bright green eyes on the disappearing dark back of Cromwell.

"You should find your husband, Lady Rochford, stay close to him," Wyatt muttered, his eyes also fixed on the space where Cromwell had been. His mind was racing, all thoughts and none at all whipping past him in a moment.

Jane put her hand on his arm, turning his eyes to her. "What did Cromwell say?"

"That the King is well and soon will be up and jesting about this matter."

Jane narrowed her piercing eyes on him, green gimlets in her pale face. When she spoke, it was a whisper. "You do not believe him."

"I believe fully that is what he wanted me to tell others."

She nodded gently, though her lips looked paler as blood was drawn from her face to support her heart. She understood too, a lifetime at court had taught Jane how to read men's faces and not pay heed to their words. "Then that is what will be told; that the King is fine."

Others pressed about them, seeing that Wyatt had spoken to Cromwell, and to them Jane and Wyatt told their lies, spreading them far and wide. People believed them with ease, for people always believe most firmly in what they want to believe. If the King was well, all was well. If not, then all was not. Believing the lie made them safe, in their hearts and minds, so believe it they did. Soon enough there was laughter as people spoke proudly of the feats of their King, his strength, the other victories and accidents they had seen him and others undertake. Wyatt swallowed as he heard chuckles and saw smiles, a hard lump of guilt in his throat. Soon enough all this laughter and safety would be ripped from these people, as it had been ripped from him. They thought the world one way, and soon it would turn another and they would find all they knew was upside down. He had done that to them, yet also he had been the cause of this present relief and happiness. They had a moment more of peace than he and Jane had. Perhaps one day these people would be grateful for that gift.

"I should go to the Queen," Jane whispered eventually as the crowds began to disperse, just as they had been told to. People moved like lambs, thought Wyatt, shifting in safe little clusters, glad to have been given a task to help the King, that of moving away so they would not disturb his rest. They fell in together, a herd. Whoever claimed that man was a predator? En masse, man had more in common with sheep.

No doubt Queen Anne had actually wanted them gone so her men might move the body.

He nodded. "Go to the Queen. I will find your husband."

"He left, I saw him, with his father."

Wyatt did not doubt her. Jane always had an eye on George. Their marriage was often rumoured unhappy, yet he was sure she loved him as well as a woman with a heart might ever love a man. He had never understood why George did not love her back. Jane was a beauty, and a clever one at that. Women of court were selected for their blood and for their looks and Jane, with her fair hair carrying a trace of red, her green eyes and pale skin, was a highly attractive woman. Had Wyatt not always been distracted by another Boleyn and been friends with the brother of that Boleyn too, Wyatt might well have sought Jane out as a mistress.

"I think they have gone to protect Elizabeth," Jane said quietly.

It was a reasonable conclusion, and an intelligent, perceptive one, but he had always thought her quick. "Go to the Queen. I will see what more I can find." He pressed his hand to hers. "And fear not, whatever storms come, we can see them through."

Jane took back her hand and lifted the hem of her gown from the dusty ground. "Let us hope that is true, Sir Thomas."

As Jane spoke to the guard on the door of the tent and was ushered inside, Wyatt walked out onto the jousting ring. Servants were here and there, buzzing as bees amongst the stalls, picking up items discarded by their masters in haste when the King had fallen. Distantly he could hear the common people who had come to see the jousts that day. They had been ushered out of the tiltyard gates but had thronged not far away. Someone was talking to them, telling them all was well. Cromwell, he suspected, or one of his men.

Wyatt stopped wandering as he came to the centre of the tournament ground. The towers stood before him; their tall shadows cast long upon the earth, like dark fingers spreading over the skin of the world. A bird sang somewhere, a blackbird by the tune. It sounded so bright and cheerful, as if nothing ill had occurred. The happy song jarred in his mind, rupturing sense and reason as he realised anew that some did not know what had happened here today, that some did not understand the moment of the occasion. The world would continue on, the beasts of the bracken and the birds of the skies would continue to wander, to fly, and yet for them, for the people of England, all had altered.

He had not known why he had wandered there, but as he saw it, he knew.

There, on the dust of the ground, was the blood of the King. Splayed out, a pattern strange, just as a horse falling on a man will tend to make upon earth, shone in the light of the crisp sun. The gloaming would be fast upon them, in winter sun retreated swift from sky, but it was morning then still and there was light, and that little light shone on the blood of the King, making what still was wet twinkle, as into the earth of England it seeped gently, as if the country which had born Henry of England into the world was claiming him back.

First blood had been spilt, but Wyatt knew as he looked upon it, it would not be the last.

CHAPTER THREE

Henry Fitzroy, Duke of Richmond and Somerset

24th of January 1536

Eve of the Feast of the Conversion of St Paul

Greenwich Palace

London

"Leave it, Surrey. Unhand him."

Henry Fitzroy, bastard son of the King, the most titled man in England under the King himself, put his hand on his friend's arm, trying to steady him, to stop violence erupting. There was a scent of sweat on the chamber mingled with perfume. The guards had rushed there evidently, their cheeks were flushed, their brows wet. He and his friend were sweating too now, now that men had marched there and told them they were not to leave, as if they were under arrest. Fitzroy could smell the musk and rose on the skin of his friend, mingled with perspiration born of indignation, as well as the rising scent of the ale they had drunk the night before, leeching from pores now open in rising fear.

The man bristling at the guard, one hand on the guard's chest to stop him advancing, was the Earl of Surrey, Henry Howard. Surrey was the son of the Duke of Norfolk as well as governor of Fitzroy's household, his mentor and his good friend. Surrey was a poet, a gentleman who ran a temper hot as fever and mean as a boar when the mood struck him, as it did now. His face was red, and his eyes burned as he perceived an insult and possible threat to himself and his friend, Fitzroy. Surrey's other hand was on his sword, the very sword these men had just demanded he hand over, just as they had demanded Fitzroy's.

Fitzroy felt the same anger and confusion, but he was more prone to thinking before throwing himself at men in a fury. He was of course smaller in stature and a little younger than Surrey, so caution was only sensible, but it was also a trait of personality. As he matured, Fitzroy could feel the weight of his titles on his shoulders increasing every year, and even if he was not destined for the throne – although sometimes he wondered on his father's thoughts on that matter – he was destined for great power. Yet all he had, his riches, titles, estates, even the very recognition of his birth, relied on but one man, the King.

His father had recognised him as his son, had heaped titles on him, Duke of Somerset, Duke of Richmond, Earl of Nottingham, Lord Lieutenant of Ireland. Never prince was Henry Fitzroy called, but a bastard prince he was. Never in line for the throne was he, yet beloved of the King he was. It was a delicate position, that of a bastard, his father the highest of the land but his mother never a queen. Though guilty of the sin of pride as a child, Fitzroy had learned confidence without arrogance as he had grown, for he knew he could not afford arrogance as a real prince could. Real princes can afford anything, but bastards must always have an eye on their purse. He had learned to pay respect to men lower than him, especially the other Dukes, like Norfolk, Surrey's father, for they resented him being placed higher. He had taught himself caution.

But Surrey was right to feel the threat, the danger, for Fitzroy did too. Something ill was clearly going on this morning.

They had been at court since Christmastide, the King welcoming him to Greenwich for the festivities, then for New Year. Just as these guards had marched into the chamber, Fitzroy and Surrey had been about to make their way to the lists to watch the jousting. It was an event set up to, unofficially, celebrate that Katherine of Spain, Henry Tudor's first wife was dead, so now peace, friendship and increased trade with Spain and the Holy Roman Empire were possible.

"Thank God we are freed from the threat of war!" his father had rejoiced upon hearing Katherine, a woman he had lived with for twenty years and had many times sworn he had loved, had died at her sorry, lonely and neglected house of Kimbolton on the edge of the wild fens. No one said outright the jousts were a celebration of her death, but it was clear that was what they were. Fitzroy had attended all days, watching his friends ride, watching his father. He was not to compete a great deal, not yet, being still young, too precious for the King to risk. The obsessive protection of his father was one of the reasons Fitzroy knew the King loved him. Though in truth, his father never had been mean with words of affection, always he professed love for Fitzroy.

Surrey was due to ride that afternoon as one of the answerers, and they normally would have gone and watched the morning events, but Surrey had wanted to tarry a while inside that morn, having drunk too deep the night before from his cups. Fitzroy, always wanting to do as Surrey did, since his mentor and friend was well-beloved to his heart, had agreed.

He had wondered fleetingly why the din of the tourney had stilled somewhat over the last hour, and had idly thought the knights must have not been as impressive as the day wore on. Frequently men did tire, the weight of mail or armour making them weary, the events of lance and sword sapping their stamina. Then the noise had ceased for a long time, and a strange hush had fallen, and now there were men here, the King's own yeomen guards, telling him he was not to leave his chambers in the palace. Something had happened and whatever it was, it was serious.

But still, even if he was not willing to lose his temper as Surrey was so happy to, as the men failed to grant a reason for this apparent house arrest, he was willing to try again to gain information. "For what am I being detained, and why? Do you not know you must bring a sheet of charges to me, with the seal of the King, if I am to be arrested in this manner?"

His voice sounded bolder than he felt. Seventeen Fitzroy was, almost. Another few months and he would turn that many years. He had been on the cusp of being sent to Ireland with an army to govern that land just as once, when he was a child, he had been sent to govern the north of England. Of course, back then, lords with greater experience and years had governed in his name but soon he was to get his chance to show the King what he could do as a true leader, as an adult, as a son Henry VIII could be proud of. This bastard son was one of the most powerful men in the country, high in the favour of his father, the King, married to the daughter of a Duke, and yet it seemed as if he was about to be arrested, by men who claimed to come from the King.

From behind them there came a rustling in the corridor. A tall shadow stepped out, one Fitzroy knew well. "Your Grace," Fitzroy said, addressing Norfolk, bowing his head.

"Your Grace," Norfolk responded, dipping his head in response.

"Father, what goes on here?" Surrey asked, stepping forth again.

Norfolk waved the guards back. "Go, to the doors with you, knaves. You can see the Duke and my son the Earl are not about to take flight out of the chamber. They are men of honour, not rats set to race out of an ale butt. Go to!"

The men stepped backwards, stood at post at the door. They set their eyes on the wall in submission. Norfolk was feared by many at court, he had power, an ancient name and a cruel temperament, as his wife was only too aware. He was also Fitzroy's father-in-law and a man who had done much to support and tutor him over the last two years. His interests and those of his son-in-law were aligned.

Fitzroy did not always like Norfolk – which was only to be expected, he was not a likeable man – but Fitzroy trusted that whilst he was wed to his daughter, though the match still was unconsummated, making it potentially not binding, Norfolk would promote his interests.

"What goes on?" Fitzroy asked, edging closer to his father-in-law. "What is this?"

Norfolk looked to the guards, now standing at the door. Some outside in the corridor, some inside. They were still gazing away from them. He grunted in satisfaction, although you could never be sure with Norfolk, since he constantly made many noises, his digestion troubling him more than conscience or kindness ever had. "I am not supposed to say," he whispered swiftly. "The Queen ordered it, but you must know. You *should* know, it is your right." He sighed. "The King, your father, is dead. Earlier this morning it happened, an accident on the jousting field. You are being placed under guard whilst the Queen gains control of the council, of Mary and of England."

Those gabbled words, slipped out from an almost silent tongue, altered Fitzroy's world forever. A shadow slipped inside his heart, and something of chaos fell into his soul. His father was dead?

All colour drained from Fitzroy's face and Norfolk grabbed his arm. "You must not show sorrow… they must not know that I told you!" His whisper was harsh, hushed, and pained.

Fitzroy nodded, straightening his back, swallowing hard. "Of what does the Queen suspect me?"

"Of being the only son of the King who is now dead," Norfolk hissed. "And that is enough."

CHAPTER FOUR

Lady Mary Tudor
24th of January 1536
Eve of the Feast of the Conversion of St Paul
Hatfield House
Hertfordshire

"Why will you not tell me where I am to go?"

Her voice rose shrill, so unlike her usual deep tone. For good reason. She long had feared this moment.

Since the day her father had separated from her mother, since the day Anne Boleyn became Queen, Mary had expected this; something inside her had known that one day men would come and they would take her somewhere, a somewhere from which she would disappear, never to be seen again. She knew well the tales of her royal great-uncles, Edward and Richard. Where would her secret grave be? An unmarked, un-consecrated mound of cold earth perhaps, that people would one day come across and suppose a pauper's grave, never knowing there was a princess hid therein, her skeleton slouched, its mouth open in a last, silent scream, the last noise ever she made on this earth before someone decided she should be silent for the rest of time.

"My lady asks only what is reasonable." Her maid stood at her side, bristling with indignation just as Mary was with fear. But she would not show that. *My mother was brave, my mother had courage*, Mary's mind told her. Over and over that call sounded in her mind, like a prayer.

"My lady, our orders are from the King himself. You are to be brought to him. You are to meet with your father. Will you defy the orders of the King?" Chancellor Audley looked grim as he ignored her maid and directed his commands to Mary alone.

"Your father commanded this indeed, Lady Mary." A sound of skirts brushing the floor rushes was heard, and Mary turned. Lady Shelton had come into the room, her watchful eyes only more intent. "The order carries the seal of the King." She walked to Mary, held it out so Mary could see it.

Mary took the paper silently to examine it. Lady Shelton pursed her lips at Mary's rudeness in failing to acknowledge her, and yet to Mary's eyes her behaviour was not rude. She needed not to show deference to a woman whose titles ranked below hers as Princess. The trouble was, Lady Shelton believed they were closer in rank than Mary did, since Mary's father had named her a bastard and disinherited her.

There to oversee the household of Elizabeth, Mary's half-sister, Lady Shelton carried a name Mary loathed, for she was another Anne Boleyn, the sister of the concubine's father, Thomas Boleyn. For many months now, Mary had been forced to be part of her sister Elizabeth's household, sent there as a servant, a new, humiliating position thrust upon her to make her understand her new station in life, to make clear that she was a bastard, named and known and her sister Elizabeth had supplanted her in the succession. Lady Shelton, it was true, had tried to be kind at first, but increasingly aggressive orders from court all sent, Mary was sure, by the concubine and not by her father, had come and had been carried out by Lady Shelton. All these orders about where Mary was to sit in the great hall at dinner, whether she was allowed to ride out by herself, what she was allowed to do with her day, were intended to make Mary submit and accept her reduced position in life, to honour Elizabeth and recognise Anne Boleyn as Queen, to admit her mother and the King had never been married. They wanted her to name her dead mother a whore who had lived illegally and knowingly with her father in incest. They wanted Mary to deny her own titles and ignore her destiny. They wanted her to honour her father as Head of the English Church, ignoring the sanctity of the united Catholic Church and the august position of the Pope. They wanted her to go against all her mother had believed, to soil her mother's memory and betray her own interests. All this was the plan of the whore, Anne Boleyn, and Mary would have no part in it. Mary's defiance in the face of all these measures had led to harsher treatment as the King and his wife tried to get her to submit.

But for all that Mary suspected, for all concerning which she defied her father, if it was his command that she come to him, she would obey. These men had a document, the one Lady Shelton had handed her. True, it was signed with the dry stamp, but clearly it was a royal command. It did not say where she was to go, only that Mary was commanded to come to her father. Mary quaked, wondering what her father meant to do to her. Half of her hoped, as ever she had, that he had at last come to his senses, would restore her and set Anne Boleyn aside. Half of her feared she might be about to be arrested for high treason.

Yet would they dare? Her cousin was the Emperor of the Holy Roman Empire and also the King of Spain, she had support amongst the people and some, although few had stepped forward boldly for her, amongst the nobles. Her mother was gone to God, the long fight Katherine had endured too much in the end for her body. Katherine's will had always been strong, but there was only so much ill treatment a person could put up with before the body succumbed. Mary was alone in many ways now her mother was dead, but she was not without support. Tepid and unsure it might be, but some believed as she did, as her mother had, that Mary Tudor was the true Princess of England and the only legitimate heir of the King.

"Wherever His Majesty wishes for me to go, I will go." Mary stood tall, putting a hand to the sleeve of her maid to stop her saying more. She could tell by the expressions on the faces of Audley and his guards that she was not going to get anywhere by being difficult, but fear still sounded in her heart as a drum beating in the shadows of night. "My maids, they will come with me?"

She had no household anymore. Her father had dissolved it, sent away Margaret Pole, her mother's old friend and Mary's long-time governess. Mary had two maids left to her.

Margaret Pole, the Countess of Salisbury, had offered to stay on without a wage, but her father or rather her step-mother, the Boleyn whore, didn't want that. Anne Boleyn wanted Mary isolated and alone. Anyone left friendless is easier to destroy. Separate the weak member of the herd and it can be hunted down with little effort.

Mary was certain it had been the Queen's order that her household be dissolved, and she be sent to wait upon her sister Elizabeth. All these lessons in humiliation had not worked; Mary never had and never would accept that she was illegitimate. Her mother, who had died not two weeks ago and was due to be buried in four days' time, had been the true wife of the King and always would be. Had the Boleyn whore not come along and bewitched the King, her mother might still be Queen, might still be alive, and Mary would still be the heir to the throne.

But Mary never had had the heart, or perhaps lack of heart, to unleash her pain and misery on Elizabeth. Mary had thought she would resent the child, but even from the first, when she had been brought to Hatfield and had looked into that cradle, had seen the red-haired baby with the crooked, gummy smile and black eyes, she had not done so. The child was innocent of this, and no matter who her mother was, Elizabeth was Mary's half-sister. Growing up alone, Mary had often wished for a sibling, someone to play with, someone to protect and cherish as her mother had cherished her. She had always loved children, wanted one of her own, and somewhere in her heart as she played with Elizabeth, as she held her, it seemed as if the child *was* her own. No, try as she might, Mary could not hate her. She loved her sister.

"Your maid may come."

Mary nodded. "Where are you taking my sister, the Lady Elizabeth?"

They were both housed in Hatfield House, so it was impossible to hide the fact that the young Elizabeth too was being moved. Were it not for the fact that these men were wearing her father's livery Mary might have thought this a plot to kidnap the royal children. But Mary had also seen Thomas and George Boleyn at a distance, commanding men who were packing the goods and household of her sister into wagons. Elizabeth's grandfather and uncle would not harm her, so both of the King's daughters were being moved, although perhaps not to the same place. What was going on? The order gave no reason, no further information. Perhaps there was a sickness close by, and their father wanted them away from it? But why not just say that if it were the case?

"The Princess..." Audley's tone was heavy with emphasis that *Elizabeth* was the princess, the royal heir, whereas Mary was not anymore "... is to go to her mother at court for a visit. That is not your concern, my lady. We must leave now."

Mary blinked. "May I not have time to gather my belongings?"

"What you need will be brought to you. There is no more time to delay, my lady, the King's commands were to be exacted immediately."

She had time to put a cloak on, that was all. To a horse she was marched, as if under arrest, thence to a barge. As they sailed upriver, heading for London, Mary thought they might take her to Greenwich or Richmond, but they went the wrong way on the river for Richmond, and never to Greenwich did they go. As they came before the Tower of London and turned for the Water Gate, she turned to Audley in puzzlement. "But, my father rarely stays here," she said to the man. "He never has liked this place, my lord, his mother died here."

"Here he will meet you, my lady." Audley would not look in her eyes and Mary felt a chill not born of the river's breath nor of the season of winter steal upon her soul.

"In all things, I am the King's daughter and will obey," she said.

Audley cast her a look as if to say that hardly was true, given her outspoken resistance to the King's will over many a matter of late. Mary stuck her chin in the air, her deep blue eyes daring him to challenge her statement. Audley did not. He was not one for confrontation, unless Cromwell commanded it.

As the boat stopped at the steps, Mary took hands with a guard on the slipway and stepped carefully from the barge onto the stone walkway, slippery with green weed which spread, its tendrils floating in the water slopping against the side of the boat. It was growing dark, the guards carried torches, and the scent of the river here, under the arch of the Water Gate was ill, fishy and dank. She paused, looking up at the towers within the outer wall of the Tower of London that she could see. The walls were high and built thick in the Tower, the towers that marked the wall were tall too. In the centre shone the White Tower, its roof she could just see from the Water Gate if she ducked her head, as she had to when emerging. Mary shivered as she walked within the Tower confines, her blood cold for a moment as she thought on Bishop Fisher, on Thomas More. They had been prisoners here, until they were executed last year for denying the supremacy. She knew not why she thought only of them. The Tower had been a prison in the past, it was true, but it also had been the seat of kings, the place royal monarchs stayed before their coronation. It was not only a prison.

It is not a prison, she told herself. *It is not a prison.*

And yet, as she was welcomed by the Lord Lieutenant and Constable of the Tower, as she was marched by torchlight to the royal apartments, those hated apartments renovated three years ago for the coronation of Anne Boleyn, Mary felt like a prisoner. Even before she walked into her rooms, she knew.

She had not been brought here to meet with her father. Something else was going on, and without even the slightest resistance she had become a prisoner of the Crown.

CHAPTER FIVE

Queen Anne Boleyn

The evening of the 24th of January 1536
Eve of the Feast of the Conversion of St Paul
Greenwich Palace
London

"You are... were the King's most trusted men," Anne announced to the gaggle of hastily assembled lords packed into the council chamber. Her eyes were captured by one in the throng. One man in dark robes shone somehow, stood out, almost as bright as the many gold chains of office illuminated in the light of the torches and candles placed about the chamber. Dukes, Norfolk, Suffolk, Earls like Oxford and Sussex, their clothes were finer, rich fur and bright colours. Cromwell looked like a raven amongst peacocks, yet his robes seemed to stand out the most. As a shadow so he stood.

It was night, the gloaming having fallen then darkness racing fast upon its footsteps. The palace was busy still, courtiers being told to keep to their chambers were rebelling, heading to those of others to discuss the day. Guards were patrolling the corridors, hangers-on to court were lounging about, as usual, making trouble. In the King's Privy Chamber, it was still, quiet. Candles were placed on the long table which stood between all the men gathered about it, Anne at their head. Lamplight and candlelight guttered from table, from wall, casting dappled radiance. It was so like the sunlight of that morning which had rained upon the face of the dead King and now lit upon the faces of the men there, watching her. This link between that awful morning and this awful evening made a part of her heart ache. Just as it ached when she spoke as if Henry were alive still.

Anne's mistake of tense tore at her insides, cruel fingers of grief dipped into her belly, pulled her intestines as if she was being executed as a traitor. She winced, then regretted it, hoping the lords there gathered had not seen. Men could show emotion, anger especially, but as soon as a woman did, she was feeble. Of course, demonstrate no emotion and she would be named unnatural for failing to grieve for her lord. Anne already knew there were few ways to win this game, yet win she must, to safeguard her children.

She looked up at the lords before her, trying not to be seen swallowing a lump in her throat formed of fear, hard and dry. It is taxing to the spirits, and hers already were strained, to find yourself in a room, supposed to be the commander of all within, and know that many, if not all, were expecting her to fail, and some were hoping with all their hearts that she would. Some would relish seeing Anne on the ground, thrashed by all life could whip her with, gazing up at them with those famous dark eyes humbled. Some would no doubt love to see her disgraced, and dead would appease more than one. But Anne Boleyn had never been daunted by the expectations of men or the world. If she had, never would she have become Queen. It did not matter what they thought of her, what mattered was that they obeyed her.

For that, she would need at least some of them on her side.

But they needed her too.

The King had made it law, in the year previous, that when a king of England died it was in the power of the next ruler to reinstate the powers of the bishops of England. The same was true of the whitestaffs, the great officers of the court and household. The council too was now hers to arrange. The authority of all these men had been bound to the King, to the throne, and now was tied to her. Anne had already decided to widen the council. She would offer more men power and thereby, she hoped, gain more support, but it was also up to her now, as Regent, to reinstate the powers of the high-ranking officials, the Great Officers of State, and the bishops of England. She was dependant on them, and they on her.

Faces gazed at her, a myriad of emotions laid bare, some grave, sympathetic, some contemplative, critical. Many lords of the council had been rushed there from town houses and chambers about the palace. Some had been at the joust so had seen what had happened, yet all had been told the lie the King was alive, and then as they had filed into the chamber, the truth had come out. She had told them of the death of the King and yet still, despite all that had happened, despite all this telling others the tale of Henry's death, she kept slipping, speaking as if Henry were alive. Every time she had to correct herself, he died again, right before her eyes. She could still feel his hand in hers, the last warmth of his skin.

People think death is one moment, and perhaps for the person who has died this is so, but for those left behind, death never ends. The dead die, and the living live with death then always in their lives. It is the space left behind when a loved one leaves, the shadow always missing at one's side. It is the gap in heart, in mind, in the daylight and night that a person leaves behind. It is the silence when their voice might have answered. Never does it leave, never does it go.

Death becomes for the living a series of moments of remembering, of forgetting the dead are gone and of losing them all over again when memory rises, recalling what the mind never wants to recall. Grief becomes a cruel sprite, anxious to hide in the heart and leap forth at times when it is expected least, to rob joy from the day.

It hurt so greatly, this cruel remembering, that it stole Anne's breath and claimed her heart. There was an extra beat in the chambers of her chest, an unsteady, shaky pulse, which sounded every time she thought of Henry's pale face, his closed eyes, the blood drying on his forehead. Every time that beat echoed in her heart she felt the closeness of Death, a presence lingering near, perhaps waiting, intent on seeing if Death, that wraith of wretchedness, would only claim one life that day, or if another would be served up, another sacrifice of this fragile, flailing Tudor line.

He will not take my children, Anne thought. He would not take her either; Elizabeth needed her, so did her unborn child.

"Our son, Anne!" the King had crowed only the day before. "What a man he will be, our little imp!"

A man Henry would never see.

She had to stop thinking of him. Thinking of Henry crippled her. She had to put her children forth in her mind, they would grant her strength.

"Now you will be the leading lights of my child's reign." Anne set a hand to her belly. "Until this child is born, a child your master believed to be a male heir, my daughter is to be named the Queen of England and I, under the edicts of His Majesty, Queen Regent."

She had to mention that the child unborn might be a boy, had to. It would gain her and Elizabeth more support. Anne did not like it, but that was the way the world was; men ruled and women did not. If these lords thought a legitimate male Tudor heir could still be born, they might give her time to rule, to prepare and to plan in case a boy was *not* born, in case another girl came and she had to convince the council and people of England to do as they never had, and uphold a Queen Regnant of England, to support Elizabeth as their next monarch.

Even had Elizabeth been a boy, this would have been a

dangerous time. An infant on the throne was never good for a country, and many all over the world thought her offspring were bastards and Anne was merely the mistress of the English King. Oh yes, even with a boy there would have been trouble, but with a girl, Anne's claims for her own rights as Regent and for her children as future rulers were even more likely to be challenged.

And there were others to set in her place, Mary and Fitzroy. Those who wanted Catholicism back might support Mary. Those who wanted a male on the throne might uphold Fitzroy. A claim by the Poles or Courtenays even, might arise. They owned royal blood, Norfolk did too. Suffolk's children, although all girls, were the children also of Princess Mary Tudor, the King's dead sister. There were possible claimants everywhere. Anne had to have the council on her side. Men of power, wealth, they could command men. Without them she was lost.

She glanced again up and down the room, trying to gauge the mood. There had been nods as there were scowls about the dim chamber as Anne made announcement of her new position. She was not universally liked, Anne knew this, but by the Act of Succession, which they all had sworn, she was named Regent, she had the right to rule, although without them her title was meaningless. Power is never inherited, even by a king, it is bestowed by others, by people who believe that one man, that one sovereign has the right to rule above all others. In so many ways all the pomp and ceremony of the throne was an act put on to ever confuse the people, so they would look on the King and say, "See his clothes and the band of gold upon his head, that man must be powerful. We should obey him!"

Now, in this moment, Anne was only too aware of the fragility of power, the illusion of it. Like confidence, it was a mask made of brittle paper, only too willing to crumble and fly away in the wind.

"I was not born to the seat in which I am now placed by destiny, by God and accident of fate," she admitted. "That I know, but the King raised me up, decided I, a mere woman born of ancient but not the highest nobility, was worthy and the King made our children, children born into this world through my body, royal heirs of his house. God, in His wisdom, granted us children. The King is gone, my lords, nothing I can do will bring him back, but his blood, his children, one alive and one resting under my heart, they are still here. You know his wishes, his decrees on who should follow him. You signed the Act of Succession and agreed to uphold it. Elizabeth and this child within me are the legitimate heirs of the King, his chosen successors. They are young, innocents in need of the protection of good, honest men, of knights of this realm, but they are of the royal line. They require your support, my lords, as I do. I mean to be guided by the men my husband trusted, by you, so that we may together take care of our lands, our people, our *England*, and of the children of the King until they come of an age to rule."

"It is said you have placed his Grace the Duke of Richmond under arrest." Audley, the Lord Chancellor, lifted his voice. He looked weary after a day of riding miles to fetch Mary then back again to court. Anne's brother and father looked likewise fatigued. "Is this true, Majesty?" His tone was a touch hostile, but not overly so. Audley was Cromwell's pet, under his control and influence. If Cromwell was on her side, the Chancellor would be too. The man had no backbone of his own, Cromwell's arm was Audley's spine.

Anne inclined her head. "Under guard, my lord, but not under arrest and only for the immediate moment, this most fragile time." She turned to glance into the eyes of other men about the chamber who had not heard this news. "If, in time, Lady Mary, who has been taken to the Tower and Fitzroy who has been confined to his chambers here in Greenwich, prove their loyalty to my children, they shall be freed. I have no doubt

Fitzroy will be the first to stand and proclaim Elizabeth as Queen when he is able, he always has loved his sister."

Loved more the fact she was a girl, Anne thought. Fitzroy had always seemed receptive to Anne, that was true enough, and she did harbour affection for the lad. Katherine had despised his very existence, but Anne had accepted Fitzroy and made friends with him, in part because his father adored him and in part because she had liked the noble bastard's company. Perhaps it was only reciprocal, polite friendship, but it was something, and he had seemed delighted with his half-sister, Elizabeth, when he had met her upon coming home from France. But Anne had indeed suspected many times that Henry Fitzroy warmed most especially to Elizabeth because she was not a male heir. Before Anne and the King had married there had been talk of Fitzroy being legitimised or even married to the Lady Mary with a papal dispensation, so he and she could inherit the throne. Anne knew not if Fitzroy had heard of this plan mooted so long ago, but it was probable. He had friends and supporters; he was a male, therefore desirable as a ruler, and he was almost of an age to rule independently. Some might call it providence or fate, in truth. King Henry, his father, had been seventeen when he had come to the throne. His grandmother, Margaret Beaufort, had been Regent for a matter of a few months or so before Henry VIII achieved his majority. That Fitzroy was almost the same age, well, some might name it destiny or serendipity indeed, a sign that his rule might become as a mirror of his father's.

Anne's marriage to the King, the prospect of sons coming from it, had put a stopper in Fitzroy's plans, if plans he had, to become named heir to the throne. There had still been talk about court after her marriage on the matter though, and especially after Elizabeth was born, and Anne knew that there were men willing to support the young man. With the King dead, with only a girl, an infant at that, in line for accession, Fitzroy might make a play for the throne. He might have loved

Elizabeth as a sister in times of peace, but war and ambition can turn many a good virtue to ill vice.

"The Lady Mary is but a girl," William Paulet, another friend of Cromwell's and old servant of the King's, chimed in, breaking through Anne's thoughts. "Surely, Majesty, she can pose no threat?"

"The Lady Mary might be young, but a woman she is, my lord, not a girl," Anne replied, setting her hands to the small bump on her front. She had to keep reminding them of the line of the King within her. "And surely you can understand she poses a threat, no matter how unintentional that might be, to the will of your master, the King, in whom should succeed him?"

"The Queen Regent is correct, my lord. When news of the King's death comes out, this will become a fragile time, with so many emotions frayed, and there is danger of rebellion from the common people, with Mary as their figurehead," Cromwell interjected bluntly. "Many common people would support her, and older families of this land, dedicated to papism rather than the King's will on religion and godly reform of the Church, might too. It was only sensible of Her Majesty to move Mary to the Tower. The Lady may become, *unwittingly*, of course, I am sure..." Cromwell sounded entirely unconvinced about this statement "... embroiled in the plots of others. She may have no wish to be used as a figurehead yet might be used so, against her own kin no less, and if she is free about the world how are we to know if she is innocent or not? This way, we know, do we not, my lords? For any plan hatched which involves the Lady Mary will be formed independently of her. If the King's bastard daughter is locked away, we know she has had no part in any whisper or otherwise of rebellion. The Queen Regent is, in fact, *protecting* the Lady Mary by this action."

Several men were obviously highly dubious about the merit of this statement, but others nodded as Cromwell continued. "I have no doubt, as Her Majesty says, that in time the Lady

Mary may be released. This shift of houses is, however, at the moment as much for the safety of the Lady Mary herself as that of our present Queen, Elizabeth, and the Queen Regent."

"And the safety of the country." Anne spoke loud, so she could be heard by all, but cast grateful eyes at Cromwell. "Rebellion aids no people of a kingdom, particularly the poor. We move with care, my lords, so we do not ignite the common people of our blessed land who will soon be consumed with the fire of grief. A small spark may a mighty fire start in the right conditions. There are people who might do something rash now, inspired by mourning their prince. We must temper their sorrow, lest it become perilous to us. I want us to escape unburned from this sorrow." She looked away, her eyes filling with tears. "Or, as unburned as it is possible to be."

The men there looked uncomfortable. Their own grief at the King's passing they held inside them, of course, but the grief of a woman was always so unpredictable. *That is why they should not rule*, thought Norfolk, *their brains are too weak with all the emotion flooding through them to be rational creatures.*

"Is the Princess Elizabeth to be announced as Queen?" Oxford asked, "or are we to wait for any such announcement until your child is born, Majesty?"

"Is it not confusing to announce a Queen when another may supplant the Princess in a matter of months?" Sussex interjected.

Anne collected herself swiftly before they fell to argument. "Here is a document," she announced, sweeping out a hand as men who worked for Cromwell came to the table from the edges of the room, a large sheet, a document, in hand. They laid it on the table. Clearly this was a prepared move, or so Norfolk suspected. "You are all to sign this, or I shall know the reasons why."

"What is this document?" asked Paulet as the lords rose to gather about it.

"It is an oath, which you will also speak aloud, before the others gathered here and witnesses of my household, in which you swear to uphold my daughter, Princess Elizabeth, at present, as Queen Elizabeth I of England and if my unborn child should be a boy, you will uphold him as King Henry IX of England."

Some eyes, belonging to men who had truly loved the King, glistened to hear that Anne was to name her unborn son for him. It was fitting.

"Surely, Majesty, we have already sworn this, with the Oath of Succession?" Charles Brandon, Duke of Suffolk, her husband's greatest, longest standing friend, asked the question. He was one of the men whose eyes had glistened to hear the name of the new King.

"You have, Your Grace," Anne agreed. "But in such a time as this, I would have you swear it again. The document also holds you to be bound by honour to an oath to uphold me as Regent, governess and protectress of England until the King's heir comes of age. I would have you swear these two things today, my lords, and sign to them, then we shall move forward with the business of the realm and the funeral of the King."

"Majesty," Cranmer's voice rang over the others, peaceful it ever was when he was not speaking in passion of the faith. "I am sure we all wish, at this difficult time and every moment after, to assure you that we stand with you, as Regent of England. As the King chose you to be his wife and chose you to rule as Regent in the event of his death, so he chose with the hand of God guiding him."

Anne saw a barely disguised flicker of contempt pass over Norfolk's face. Cleary, he did not think her chosen by God for anything. Norfolk thought women good for breeding, bedding and beating, that was all, although he had, at times, demonstrated grudging respect for her predecessor, Queen Katherine. Anne suspected that was only because Katherine had been a most conservative Catholic, as Norfolk was. Anne, Catholic though she was, believed in reform. As an evangelical she was less than human to Norfolk, a heretic and nothing more. "Thank you, Eminence," she said to Cranmer. "Your loyalty and devotion to the Crown and to England is something we wish all men possessed."

She glanced to the edges of the chamber where her men, her bishops, created and elevated at her request, stood. Latimer, Shaxton, Hilsey, Foxe, as well as her chaplain Parker and almoner Skip, they would stand with her. When Cranmer had called, the bishops had come straight to court. The Church as a whole might still be divided over her, not knowing if she was the one defending them whilst Cromwell attacked or vice versa, but some men of the faith of England were dogs with good, sharp teeth and would stand on her side in this fight.

"The paper is before you," she said. "Will you sign and uphold the wishes of your master the King, or will you not, and tell me why?"

The men of the council were trapped and they knew it. Even to ask to take the document away and examine it would mark them, here and now, as enemies to the Queen Regent.

To a man they signed their names, they stood and swore their oaths, but Anne was more than aware that to some these were but hollow words.

Still, if they went back on them now, she could name them twice a traitor and arrest them.

CHAPTER SIX

Henry Fitzroy, Duke of Richmond and Somerset

25th of January 1536
Feast of the Conversion of Saint Paul
Greenwich Palace
London

"And if I sign this, I will be released? God's blood! I am no danger to the Queen Regent. Let me see her, let me to her, man, for she and I have always had an understanding of temperament and nature!"

Fitzroy was starting to lose his temper, might shortly become as Surrey, who soon, he was sure, would erupt as an enraged boar in the forests. Fitzroy's friend was becoming only more and more restless as the hours rolled on and they were not allowed out. Fitzroy had sworn many times that morning already, using God's eyebrows, a curse which reminded him of his father, God's blood and other parts of the Almighty to curse, but Surrey had gone further, attacked a guard that morn with his fist and thrown a bowl of pottage at another. Both guards had backed away, although the one Surrey had attacked with the pottage clearly had thought of fighting back, then thought better of assaulting an earl.

Fitzroy's anger simmered, not so bold and obvious on the surface as that of Surrey, but it still was there. A more carefully concealed animal it was but exist it did.

It was hard for a young man of so few years in truth, but who felt as if he was aged and wise, as all young people who have small experience of the world do, to be so locked away as the world as he knew it shifted and rocked on its axis, as all that was once truth was turned upside down. The world was altering, and swift, great, significant change was on its way, and he was stuck here, unable to experience it. His father was dead, but how could he believe that until he had stood before his body? How could he grieve until he was free? His poet friend might well have said it with more flair, but Fitzroy felt that without freedom he could neither love nor hate, grieve nor experience joy. Everything was muted by his imprisonment. He could not feel for he had been separated from life. He could not experience anything fully, for he was not part of the world. Everything about him, his life and emotions felt cut off, numbed. When he thought of the death of his father, he felt nothing but hollowness. He was not sure if this was grief or shock. Blaming his captivity was easier than thinking he might well be experiencing sorrow so deep he could not grant it a name.

But he hated his captivity, that he knew for certain. Fitzroy felt like an animal in the Tower menagerie, once wild, now contained, a growling, pacing lion swinging a head of useless, sharp teeth about, encased in boredom so deep, so suffocating it threatened his sanity, his true nature being so suppressed that his mind might shatter under the pressure, a thousand shards of brittle ice cascading as a boot stamped upon a frozen pond.

Although, he had to admit, the Queen Regent sent fine wine and good food. Cards and chess, books too had been sent, to entertain them. He had hesitated a moment over the first meal sent before taking up the food, a dish of good rabbit in a heavy-spiced sauce, on his jewelled eating knife and setting it into his mouth. Usually there was a man to test his food. His father had insisted on it ever since he was a little boy, the King not wanting a poisoner to steal away the life of his 'precious jewel'. He did not have such a servant here. Only a few servants were about Fitzroy now, his taster not amongst them. Did that make him vulnerable?

It would be easy for the Boleyn Queen to remove Fitzroy here and now by covert means. Perhaps that was why he had been locked away. A little potion in a drink, some subtle powders in his meat, and he might be gone by the morrow. A problem erased. He could vanish, and all the potential trouble he might cause for his sister the Princess Elizabeth, or their unborn sibling, would be done. It would be a safe way to be rid of him.

It had been rumoured the Boleyns were not above using poison; when Bishop Fisher and Thomas More had been alive, they had sat down to a dinner one night as Queen Katherine's case had been fought in court. They had almost never risen from their chairs as poison had been slipped into their pottage by their cook. People said the cook knew not what he had done, had been told the powders someone had given him were a joke because they were a laxative, but he never had revealed who gave him those 'jest' powders and why would he not reveal the name if it had been a jest? The only reason not to reveal the name was if that name belonged to someone rich and powerful, someone who could harm not only the people at that feast, but people the cook loved. He had gone to his death, boiled alive, without ever mentioning a name, and it had been widely rumoured the Boleyns had been behind the poisoning, trying to do away with all the men who supported Queen Katherine, so they might better the cause of Anne. If the Boleyns had done such a thing to make Anne Queen, would they not do the same to keep her Queen?

Fitzroy had not believed the rumours of poison which had floated around the Boleyns at the time like a poor smell. His father had not believed them culpable, and Fitzroy had followed the will of the King in most matters. But now that it was his life in the balance, he had cause to pause, to wonder.

Would not the Queen do anything to protect herself, and her daughter? Fierce Anne was about Elizabeth. Fitzroy had admired, even envied the love he had witnessed radiating from Anne towards her daughter. It was brighter than the sun, blinding to gaze upon. He had been taken from his mother at a young age, put into a household of his own. Ever he had been surrounded by people, yet always he was set apart a little, by his position, by his birth. Not quite one of the higher nobility, not quite one of the lower and in truth he owned no full family at all. His father was his father, his mother was his mother, but his father was married to another. No true place, that was how it felt to be a bastard. You ever were present and yet never were quite accepted. Still he remembered the heartbreak and loneliness he had felt when he had been told his mother was no more to be with him every day. Elizabeth Blount, Lady Tailboys as was, Lady Clinton now she had wed again, always showed affection when they met after that first moment of separation, but there was always a distance between them. She had married twice, had other children and his half-brothers and sisters he loved, some were even in his household now, but he had missed his mother's love as a child, especially when he was sent far away to govern the north. Never had he been allowed to express that loss, boys were not supposed to hang on their mother's apron strings, as the saying went, yet still he had missed her. Many nights he had cried quietly as a young child when no one else was awake, wishing his mother was there to hold him.

Anne had always been there for her child.

Anne had tried to breastfeed her daughter, had brought a cushion into court when Elizabeth was a baby, and only the horrified command of the King had stopped her from placing her child at her side on that cushion, at the side of her throne, as she went about her daily business as Queen. Elizabeth had been sent by the King to her own household, away from court, but Anne had often gone to her, ridden out so she could spend time with her daughter, and now, at this time of crisis, he heard Elizabeth had been brought to court, no doubt so Anne could protect her. Anne, he sometimes felt, had loved her daughter more than his mother had loved him. Anne would do anything for Elizabeth.

Would that *anything* go as far as murder? Fitzroy thought it possible.

Yet, for all that, Fitzroy could not see Anne as a poisoner. She was no coward, and she had a sense of morals, unlike many at court. That did not mean, of course, that her ambitious brother or underhanded father might not consider doing something, but in the Queen, oddly perhaps, Fitzroy had a fair amount of faith.

He glanced at the window. Rain was beating the panes, the good weather of the day before gone, just as his father was. The heavens now were ill tempered and ominous. The King had been talking of removing feast days and saints' days that the old Church held to, since they were popish and also, Fitzroy suspected, so he might get more days of work out of the common people and thereby more taxes, but this had not gone ahead yet and Fitzroy, born a Catholic, knew well that

that day, the 25th of January, was the Feast of the Conversion of Saint Paul. It was a day, as common people held, on which the weather and perhaps the mood of the year to come was decided. "If Paul's day be fair and clear, we shall have a happy year," he remembered his mother singing to him when he was small. "But if it bring both wind and rain, dear will cost all God's grain. If the winds do blow aloft, then wars will trouble this realm full oft. If clouds or mist do dark the sky, great store of birds and beasts shall die."

Fitzroy tried to repress a shiver as a savage gust of wind, fierce and true, blustered against the panes, making the window rattle.

"Give me the document, man, I will sign," he said to Audley, who stood there holding it limply like the ineffectual milksop the Chancellor was. "I will show the Queen she has nothing to fear from me." Fitzroy swept his elegant signature across the page.

For now, said a voice in his mind.

CHAPTER SEVEN

George Boleyn, Viscount Rochford

25th of January 1536

The Feast of the Conversion of St Paul

Greenwich Palace

London

Anne held out her arms and ducked to one knee, not caring for the dust of the floor rushes upon her glorious gown as her daughter entered the hall, carried by Lady Shelton, flanked by maids and guards, with Lady Margaret Bryan, and George and Thomas Boleyn all trooping in, escorting Elizabeth to the arms of her mother. George and Thomas had been chosen to guard Elizabeth when not needed in council. To Anne, it was the most important of tasks she could think of.

"Elizabeth!" Anne cried and from Elizabeth there came a throaty, wet giggle as she was set down and on unsteady legs ran to her mother. Anne swept the tiny girl into her arms, lifting her into the air as Elizabeth screamed with happiness.

George stood at the back of the hall, smiling, leaning on a pillar adorned with false leaves and flowers made of silk, still there in celebration, decorations for the King's tournament. It was supposed to be a welcome to spring, the tournament, though spring was still far off in truth. Servants were quietly taking the decorations down, the royal households had been informed of the King's demise, and informed that news was to go no further than the walls of Greenwich, on pain of death. Soon black banners and hangings would go up in place of the leaves and the flowers. Mirrors would be covered for a time. He was glad there still was colour, even though to some eyes it might well look gaudy, inappropriate. George did not think so; life should be celebrated as death mourned. They were but two ends of one story, after all.

He leaned on his pillar, watching, the smile remaining on his face. There was nothing, George Boleyn had frequently thought, more endearing than the sound of his sister's voice when she saw her child. It was a sound of pure joy, unadulterated, untouched by the world. Anne became a thing of light when with her daughter. As much as any poetic passage of the Bible, as much as any time he had marvelled at the beauty of a church or vivid scene concocted by nature, so George felt awe when he looked on Elizabeth and Anne together, contained in their love, safe in their joy. It was one of the proofs of God's existence, he felt, love such as this enduring in a world such as ours.

No child of his own had George, yet when he heard the depth of love in Anne's voice as she saw Elizabeth, there was nothing he wanted more. The King had kept mother and daughter often apart. It was true the scandalous halls of court were no place for a child, and the ill airs of London, frequently carrying pestilence, could be dangerous too, but sometimes George had thought it more than that. He thought it had been envy.

The King had never liked Anne's attention being bestowed too greatly on another. He had strayed often, but he never welcomed her gaze straying, even if only to their daughter. Anne's entire focus should be on the King, that was how Henry had thought. Sometimes, when the King had been in company with his daughter and wife, he had seemed jealous of the little babe who claimed the eyes and heart of Anne with such idle, charming ease. Even when they had argued, when it had seemed he liked Anne not, even though he had taken mistresses and flaunted them in her face at court, still the King did not like Anne spending time with others. His was a possessive, obsessive love, and even when it seemed he did not love still he did not want to relinquish his property, and Anne was his, or had been. George thought one of the reasons Elizabeth had been sent to her own household with such speed was so the King could have Anne as he wanted, to himself. *What a thing,* he thought, *for a man to envy his own child, because of the love her mother offers to her.* Did the King suspect Anne loved Elizabeth more than him? It was possible, and probably it was true.

George watched as Anne set Elizabeth on the ground again, on her chubby, wobbling legs. The Queen took hands with the Princess, though she had to stoop to walk, and Elizabeth gabbled at her mother in her broken, haphazard speech, which, although frequently intelligible as words were always in a rush to escape Elizabeth's mouth, was a great deal more advanced than other children her age. Happening to glance sideways for a moment, to the ladies who surrounded the Queen, George caught a haunted expression on his wife's face, one that could break any heart.

He sighed at her look of love, of yearning, of a gentle kind of jealousy, not marred by vicious intent, but which stirred deep the soul within. His wife was watching Anne and Elizabeth. Jane had experienced carrying a child, but never for long. Three babes, or was it four? They had died in his wife and emerged, no form to bury, just blood, broken tissue, the sorrowful, torn remnants of a life never lived. Every time, Jane had been crushed. Every time, George had tried to ignore what had happened, to not speak of it. He knew this pained his wife, having no one to talk to of her suffering, but he could not endure it. It gave him guilt, thinking God was punishing not Jane but him, and the guilt made him run from a wife he already had chosen to neglect. That caused more guilt, until all that ill feeling compounded upon his soul, leaving George having difficulty looking on the face of his wife at all, so painful was the experience.

Yet it was not Jane's fault, and that he knew.

His father had been pressing him to seek an annulment from Jane on grounds of infertility for more than a year now, but oddly, though they had often not got along, although often he had said in one argument or another that he wanted rid of her, as soon as an opportunity to separate had come, he had found he did not want to leave Jane. She had been a steady part of his life for so long, he wasn't sure he could cope with a new woman in his household. In his bed, well, that was a different matter, there were plenty of temporary women, but his house was another issue.

Of late, though, George had been thinking perhaps there was more to his unwillingness to separate from Jane.

Fiercely loyal was she, that was not something to cast aside with ease. In all that had happened, through times of her being banished from court for defending Anne, through all the times he had been unfaithful and she had discovered it, for all the times he had been cruel enough to mock her love for him, Jane had never wavered, had never stopped loving him. Often George saw himself as the sinner he was, his faults so many and varied he wondered how people endured him. His pride, so overbearing and puffed up, was upon him sometimes so heavy it was like a disguise he wore for a pageant, and when he looked in a mirror he knew not who this fool was that he had become, prattling in front of men so much older and wiser than him, as if he had anything of worth to say, strutting about court, drinking and whoring all night then stumbling into a council meeting in the day, getting by only because his mind, even with all he made it suffer, was quick as a fox who spies a hound at his tail. Sometimes George looked in the mirror and had no idea who this prancing, pathetic peacock was.

No, sometimes he knew not who this fool was, this cloak of a person he was wearing over his true self. Oh, he knew he had many good qualities, he was clever, his tongue sharp and easily as witty as that of his sister Anne. He held a fine tune with his strong voice, could joust and swing his sword with skill so men thought him manly, he made a skilled ambassador, unscrupulous, multilingual and canny, had become a poet of no small measure, and he was handsome which smoothed many a way to his liking, but his sins, they weighed on him in the early hours when he woke and stared up at the curtains about his bed, wondering who the woman was who was snoring away next to him, the scent of old wine as a fug about him. With his head ringing from the drink and din of the night before and his soul berating him for once more setting it in jeopardy because he could not control his impulses, he would lie there feeling dirty, soiled, and alone.

Oddly, at such times, he missed Jane. When he slept beside her, he never woke in the night, never had bad dreams. Sometimes when he woke, he would find himself wrapped about her, and she nestled into him as if he was protecting her and she him, as if in sleep and dreams they knew this solid truth of mutual protection, of the worth of being cherished and could find one another, true souls touching. It was as if she sheltered him from all the demons chasing him in the night. There was in him at such times an understanding that when he was with her, he was where he was supposed to be. Something about Jane felt like home. He did not want to lose that, and yet he never seemed able to treat her well.

She knew everything about him, the good and the bad, and she loved him. He had once thought it pathetic, this acceptance of him just as he was, but he was starting to wonder if it was not the highest of virtues. He had loved her once, when he was a lad, before they were promised to one another. He could not remember why he had fallen out of love with her, but it was probably something to do with the chase. He had ever wanted a woman who didn't want him, and Jane so clearly did want him, so she was no challenge. Yet was that reason enough to dislike a wife... because she loved him? Because she loved him when he was clearly unworthy of love? Because she offered love freely, honestly, rather than teasing him and playing courtly games, never offering affection without something in return?

George had begun to suspect that it was not Jane he despised, it was himself. He could not understand someone loving him. He had thought her unworthy for she loved someone truly unworthy like him. It had also come to his attention that perhaps he feared her *because* she loved him, he feared to be in love, though he had sworn himself so many times. Never had he truly loved for never had he allowed anyone that close to him, even his family were always kept a little at a distance.

Whilst he feared to lose his heart to anyone, something inside him did not want Jane to stop loving him. He had a feeling that if that day came, he would indeed be beyond help, a sinner lost for all time in the darkness, groping his way only further into an expanse of blackness where there was no light, no hand waiting to aid him, no hope. His pride would overrun him, chase away all that was good. His drinking would kill his wit, his whoring would strip away his soul. In honest moments he knew it was not the women he lay with that were the problem, it was him, the way he approached them, selling them love and pretty poems, charming them into bed with his tongue then becoming cold and distant the next day, turning his back on faces that fell with disappointment and towards new ones who lit up to be honoured by his attention. It was like a drug, like drink, this endless chase, but it was eating away at him, bite by little bite. That was what stripped his soul, treating other people as if they were not people, using love as a weapon, wasting all that was good within him so it fell as soot to the earth, and from that soil only evil would grow from the wasted ashes of virtue.

Something whispered to George that as long as Jane loved

him, there was hope for him. That was why he could not separate from her, could not do as his father wanted and seek an annulment. If he lost Jane, he lost hope. Though he could explain it to none, he knew it was the truth.

"Have you been a good girl?" Anne was chattering away to her daughter. He could see, however, in between the smiles, the tears that were trying to fight through his sister's black eyes. At some stage Anne was going to have to explain to Elizabeth that her father the King was dead, that he was gone and never would return. How does one say this to an infant? Elizabeth was not yet three. Would she even understand her father was dead, or what that meant? George chided himself, she would not understand what it meant, of course, that was beyond her comprehension. Even they, adults though they were, did not know what might happen next. They hoped for Heaven, of course, but would God allow any of them to enter?

He glanced at Jane again and thought how beautiful she looked. She was smiling at Anne, watching as the Queen held her daughter. Jane's face was pale, her bright green eyes lit with tears, making them shimmer like the emeralds on her throat. Jane always had been one of the beauties of court, which was another reason he did not want to be rid of her, a shallower one in some respects. She was pleasing to look at. Another wife, chosen by his father, might be selected for money or titles, not how she appeared. Beauty was important to George, he found it inspiring, and it too gave him hope. Beauty was a sign, he thought, that God still loved this world. Beauty was a gift the Almighty had offered humankind.

A movement distracted him. To one side of the hall, past Jane, he saw the Seymour brothers and their sister, another Jane. They were whispering together as everyone else talked. He frowned. Anne had said she would send an order that Jane Seymour was to be removed from court, so what was she still doing here? He wondered if his sister had rescinded it, deciding to keep the Seymour girl close. Jane had been the mistress of the King, and what if she was with child? Perhaps Anne wanted to check.

Her other ladies, Madge and Mary Shelton, Margery Horsham, Mary Howard, Margaret Douglas, Margaret Lee, Nan Gainsford and Jane his wife all stood to one side, watching Anne and Elizabeth. *This child, this tiny child who is my niece is now the Queen of England,* George thought, at least until the child four months gone in Anne's belly was born. If a boy, he would be King, this soul not even alive yet, with no idea he was to be born into a world so insecure. If a girl, Elizabeth would remain Queen, and she had no idea, either, what a dangerous position that was. How long could it be kept from a child? Not only the danger but this weight of destiny?

Watching Elizabeth giggling, once more wrapped in her mother's arms, George hoped it would be some time. If he could protect his niece from the weight of the world set to fall upon those tiny shoulders, he would, and by the look on his wife's face, she felt the same.

CHAPTER EIGHT

Queen Anne Boleyn

January 1536

Richmond Palace

London

"It is a good day to announce it, the weather will prevent unrest."

Her father was perhaps attempting to be kind, sometimes it was hard to tell with Thomas Boleyn, but Anne felt only more uneasy as he spoke. She stared out of the window, watching a mixture of snow and sleet fall. Snow was pretty and graceful, but this ungainly mixture seemed to slump from the skies, falling in messy, wet, hopeless puddles, slopping down the window's diamond-shaped glass. It was cold, the good weather of a few days ago having vanished, as fine days often did in England – which was why they were cherished so dearly when they made an appearance – and following rain and wind, a storm of wet, slick snow and ice had come pouring from the skies. Unattractive in this half-formed state though it was, her father was right, the weather would prevent unrest, perhaps. For now.

It was true there would be few people out in the street to hear the announcements being called out in the city of London, as well as in towns and villages about London where royal heralds had been sent. The rest of the country was to follow soon, when royal messengers on fast horses made it to each place designated for unveiling the ill news of the King's death. Parliament had been informed, and now the people followed. It had been enough days, they had control of the government, the council, Fitzroy, Mary and Elizabeth. That was all they could hope for. All they could do was now to wait, to watch, to bury the King. There would be no coronation to follow funeral, as usually there was. Anne worried this might cause more unrest, for usually grief of one king passing could be mitigated by another rising, keep the people's eyes on the dawning sun rather than setting moon and all was well. But Elizabeth would not be crowned for two reasons, the first that a boy child might yet come of Anne's womb, of course, and the second because Elizabeth was too young. An infant could not take on the mantle of kingship, as so many people had told Anne. Henry VI, the only other babe sovereign of England, had been seven when crowned.

"Other countries must have crowned infants," she had protested, but the truth was, this was an unusual situation. No one wanted to crown a girl when there might be a boy available in a few months and many thought a baby or infant could not possibly understand the coronation oath, to which they would have to swear.

This left the crown unsecured in truth. Without an anointed one on the throne, that throne was at risk. When before a woman had been left as claimant to the throne, the Empress Matilda, her cousin Stephen had taken advantage of the fact she could not immediately travel to England to take up her crown, being then in Normandy and heavy with child, and had had himself crowned. Since he was anointed, he was the chosen of God, so he claimed. Matilda had rightfully objected, since she was the heir of Henry I, and the country had been plunged into war for more than a decade until her son came to the throne. Not immediately crowning an heir could have heavy ramifications, ones Anne did not want to face, especially considering everything else she presently had before her eyes.

Cranmer had observed that a ceremony of sorts could be done, even a coronation, when Anne's son was born, to secure the throne as his, but many lords of the council thought it too much to ask a babe with no knowledge of the world to take on the responsibility of the Crown. A sovereign made promises to their people at a coronation, just as the people made promises to them. If the sovereign did not understand, could not even properly respond, these oaths could not be made.

They had to wait, and the people had to wait too, for their King.

Anne had insisted however, privately to Cranmer and to Cromwell, ordering them to gather support, so her son would be crowned, or Elizabeth if a daughter was born. Even if England was to crown an infant, Anne wanted that to go ahead. There could be another coronation later, when her child was old enough to fully understand the ceremony, to swear to all their responsibilities, but a crowning, a coronation, some definite recognition of the next ruler of England had to occur, for the safety of the country.

"We must secure the thought that this *is* their King," she told Cromwell and Cranmer, her hand indicating to her stomach. "If there is no ceremony, the people will always be able to choose another ruler, to protest they may support another claimant as God has not shown His approval of my child."

"We will garner support, Majesty, fear not." Cromwell played with a ring on his finger, gold with a great ruby set into it. The King had given it to him, Anne remembered. "Lords who protest people of the past waited with Henry VI fail to understand this situation is most different. There was no other true claimant then as everyone supported the child of Henry V for the throne, when he was a child at least. You are right, for the security of England, your child will be crowned."

But her child needed to be born first.

Today, however, there would be other thoughts in the minds of England's people. Once grief had made its first pass upon the common people, questions would follow.

She was no fool, she knew the people of England were going to struggle to accept this. The King dead and Anne Boleyn was Queen Regent? Elizabeth *might* be Queen? England had never had a Queen Regnant before, nor a Queen Regent running the country for perhaps sixteen years as her baby daughter grew up. The son Anne swore was in her belly was no certain promise. There was a lot that was new to accept here.

Had it been Katherine ruling for Mary the people might have accepted it, might even have rallied behind her. Many had thought Katherine a saint, after all, but Anne Boleyn they would not rally behind. Indeed, they were fortunate it was January and the weather was foul. Her father was right when he said this might stop the people from rioting today, but what of tomorrow and the next day? What of when the weather cleared, and spring came? It was, to Anne's mind, entirely possible that the winter might simply give people time to prepare so when the thaw arrived revolution would erupt in many parts of England.

But if it gave the people time to prepare, it gave her time too. And no one was going to hurt her children.

"You have sent word to Mary in Calais?" Anne asked her father. She watched as his face stiffened. "I commanded it," she reminded him.

"Word has been sent," he replied, his tone rigid as a corpse.

"There is danger for her, Father," Anne reminded him. "She is a member of our family, though her marriage we approved of not, and she may be at risk there, in Calais, her children too." Anne thought of one of Mary's children not in Calais. Henry Carey was Anne's ward and he was housed at Syon Abbey, learning much under the tutelage of Nicholas Bourbon, the renowned French scholar Anne had brought to England the year before, after Marguerite of Navarre had petitioned her to help him escape France, where he might have been persecuted for his faith. Anne had the better end of the bargain, she thought, for Bourbon was a wit, a poet and a fine tutor for her ward, Carey. The son of Henry Norris, Groom of the Stool, was also there, being educated by Bourbon.

Anne had thought of bringing them to court, but Bourbon assured her Syon was safe and the Abbess, Agnes Jordan, had promised it would remain so. Anne believed Agnes. Not long ago she had met with the Abbess and by negotiating with her had secured Syon, had protected it from Cromwell's over-enthusiastic investigators, by persuading the Abbess to have the nuns of Syon agree that the King was Head of the Church. Anne remembered the light of Agnes's pale blue eyes when Anne had said she considered Syon one of the shining beacons of the faith in England, one that could not be permitted to fade away. Anne and the Abbess had an understanding now, and Agnes knew Anne wanted Syon to survive. The Abbess would care for Anne's ward for she knew Anne would work to preserve religious houses which kept to their vows, like Syon.

All the same, Anne had sent guards to Bourbon, just in case.

"You, too, disapproved of her union with the soldier." Her father's voice called Anne back to the present.

"I did, and yet later I softened, and I sent to her money without anyone knowing."

Her father looked astonished. "But… you were as angry as I was."

"I was, but in time my anger left me, and I remembered she was my sister. Mary remains my sister, and your daughter, and no Boleyn should be left alone in the world now." She sighed. "Mary named her daughter after me, did you know?"

Her father nodded. "I knew."

"Mother is to come here too? To court?"

"She will be here this evening, though she has not been well. She wanted to stay at Hever, but Hever is not a place we can easily defend if there is unrest. It was built in the thought that the troubled days of civil war were behind us."

Anne's eyes flashed to his face. "Then you do think there will be trouble?"

"I think we should act as if there will be, then if it breaks we are prepared and if not, all is well too."

"You speak of it as a storm." Anne stared out into the world again. "Leave me now, Father. I wish to go to my chapel and pray for the soul of my husband."

As he left, Anne thought on her words. *No Boleyn should be alone now.*

"I am here, you are not alone," she whispered to the child in her belly later, when she was kneeling in her private chapel, and Anne wondered if those were the words she thought her child wanted to hear, or if they were words she herself longed to hear.

That night she walked in a dream she had wandered in before. There was a tower standing in a desert, its sides of stone awash with blood. As Anne looked to one side, she saw Katherine, the old Queen, beside her. "The stones bleed," Anne said.

"They have done, and will so again," Katherine replied. "Do you remember the prophecy?"

"Of the tower?"

Katherine smiled. "When the Tower is white, and another place green, then shall be burned two or three bishops and a Queen, and after all this be passed, we shall have a merry world again."

"The Abbot of Garadon," Anne said, shaking her head. "I remember hearing it. What of it? Many a fool makes as if he can see the future."

"Look to the tower," Katherine said, her hand lifting to point.

Anne looked and saw the blood was gone. The desert was gone too and the tower shone bright white. No longer a lone, single tower was it, but instead the Tower of London, and about it, the city was burning.

"I am your death," said Katherine. "As you are mine."

CHAPTER NINE

Magpye Grey
January 1536
The King's Arms Inn
Southwark
London

The wishes of the Regent and her father came somewhat true, for in the streets of London there was unrest indeed, yet quickly did it retreat inside. Shock caused the people of England to freeze rather than fight that day. News of the King's death had been proclaimed in town squares by royal heralds, their robes and hats sodden with the weight of icy water slipping from grey skies above, and that water was already freezing on the cobbles as dusk fell upon daylight like a wolf baring teeth to a doe. The King was dead. The Princess Elizabeth was proclaimed Queen, for now. The Regent of England, Queen Anne Boleyn, was to rule with the benefit of a regency council until the Princess came of age to rule alone, or until a son, born to the Regent, arrived safe into the world and came of age.

Some thought Norfolk or Suffolk, Fitzroy even, should have been named Regent, or Lord Protector. Few supported a woman in the role, still less a woman like Anne Boleyn.

Stricter, earlier curfews were put in place immediately, the Night Watch called to duty. Booted feet tramped the streets as the gloaming fell. Blazing torchlight shimmered on cobblestones slaked with ice and wetness as men patrolled, shouts rang, telling people to get indoors and stay there. Doors closed fast against the night, the wind, the snow still falling. Men of the watch and royal guards walked the streets continuously it seemed, ensuring none were out after dark. The sound of feet sloshing though heaped, wet snow and puddles echoed against the whitewashed walls of the homes of London's people.

But before curfew had fallen that night, shocked citizens of London gathered together to talk in homes and barns, in inns and taverns. They came to converse, to mourn, to worry as one. In some homes, neighbours gathered about a fire; they could slip back easily enough to their own homes next door without being seen when the time came. This wasn't a night to be alone. There was much to discuss, after all, and sitting about fires and by the light of rush lamps many did discuss much, many worries, many troubles. Some said a prayer for the King's soul.

Those in inns where heavy doors were closed fast against the night, where beds of hay could be bought for a coin or two and shared with others – often many bodies lining a long, attic floor – lifted a cup of ale to the King.

Some wept, talking of the bold, bright, young man who had come to the throne, of the prince everyone had adored for he had been so handsome and learned, strong and loyal. Darkly his ill deeds were spoken of, but blamed on those about him, Cromwell, Cranmer, Anne, Wiltshire, they had been the ones to blame for the split from Rome, for the monasteries being investigated, for the casting-off of good Queen Katherine and her daughter the innocent, brave and beautiful Princess Mary. The King, now dead, could do even less wrong than before in the eyes of some, for whilst some will ever blame the sins of a powerful and feared man on those about him, on those who influence him, there are many more who never will wish to speak ill of the dead. Quite why is a mystery. The dead are no more innocent than the living. Perhaps people feel they have been punished enough by dying, yet those same people would tell you the afterlife is preferable to this one and to go there is an honour.

But what is true is that when we lose a person, no matter how many wrongs they have done us, we tend to remember the good about them and forget the ill. Since death is the greatest loss, the greatest separation any of us will experience, it is the one loss which, then, will swifter than any other wipe the ills a person has done from memory, and leave us to retain only the good, the sweet, the cherished remembrances of them. Death, in so many ways, becomes our most intense expression of love, one so deep we may drown in it, embracing the very waters which suffocate us, stealing our breath.

No one had known for sure the King was dead until now. Oh, there had been rumours, of course. The walls of court were thin in truth and words had leaked from the palace by mouths which were not supposed to talk, by gossip spread by tongues which others, fearful of this news, had proclaimed as lies. People had been willing to believe it was a lie the King was dead, that this tale was mere hysteria spread by those who wanted to shock and impress, become important, their reputations bolstered by these false tales designed to grab the attention of fools. They liked to be the centre of attention and would say or do anything to gain that attention, people had said, looking on scornfully as those peddling whispers of the King being dead had whispered on. Most had hoped their monarch was simply ill after his fall in the joust. They had not known that all this time, this long week, he had been already with God.

The child, as everyone in the inn called her, walked from table to table in her father's establishment, picking up mugs and spent trenchers of bread, moist from the serve of mutton stew sold earlier in the evening. The trenchers she threw to the pig and the chickens in the back garden of the inn, good food for them. Her ma's stew was popular, so was the ale her pa served, which in truth was also brewed by Ma. Ma made the inn work, so said her father. He was there to keep order, prevent drunk people from brawling. It was Ma who made almost everything they sold. Pa bought in beer, it was true, because with the hops included in the drink it lasted longer than ale, but many customers preferred ale, and Ma's in particular, for it was sweet, not bitter like beer was, and often she flavoured it with herbs.

"Without your ma, I'd have nothing," Pa said often enough. "People think I own this place and for sure it's my name on the door, and yet without your ma, Magpye, I'd just be a man standing here behind a counter with a club in my hands!"

Margaret, or Magpye as her ma and pa called her, had worked in the inn her parents owned since she was old enough to walk and carry something at the same time. She couldn't remember a time she hadn't worked. Ma cooked and brewed ale and Pa served the customers and kept the peace. Magpye fetched, she carried, she helped. If she stood on a stool, she could aid the kitchen maid, Jane, in washing up the rough mugs they used for customers. Sometimes, if there was a wealthier person staying, they would have a dish rather than a trencher for their serve of stew, or pottage, as rich people called it and she'd help wash that too. Magpye spent most of her time out with the people, however, but they rarely noted her. Regulars gave her a smile, asked how she was. Most men knew to keep wandering hands off her tiny body since her pa was handy with that club he kept behind the bar for emergencies, and he was a burly man who had served in the King's wars in France so few wanted to cross him, or his daughter. For the most part though, Magpye, ignored because she was so little, wandered and she cleared, and she listened.

"That's why she's like a Pye," her mother had said. "Look at those bright, black eyes and tell me there's not a mind like those tricksters with their trailing black and white feathers behind it. She gathers gossip as the other Mag-Pyes gather shiny things."

Magpye was fairly sure that the birds she shared a name with mostly gathered flesh, titbits from a dead mouse here, the body of a songbird there, the smashed remains of an egg to be sucked out and drained down a gullet, egg and yolk and blood flowing over a tongue tingling with stolen pleasure, gaining life from death. They weren't sentimental beasts, the birds she'd been named for, they took, and they ate, and they lived, but they were survivors, they were tough, resilient and could be cruel when they needed to. She wasn't sure how much she was like them, but the gathering of gossip was true enough. She wasn't even sure where it had started, but it had become a habit. Her ma and pa liked to hear what she found out. It was good to know what was going on in the neighbourhood and beyond and Magpye's little ears were keen, as her mind was sharp and good at remembering.

"Another word for the Pye is talebearer," her mother told her. "You are your name, my Magpye."

Magpye was gathering much to tell this night.

Her father's inn had once been called The Angel, but as the King's position on faith became known, Magpye's father, along with others, had changed the name of his business from something which might be thought popish to a name which demonstrated allegiance to the King. The King's Arms was named to show the world that her pa supported the King and his new religious reforms. Pa was a reformer himself, a man who could read too, which was a thing most unusual considering his position in society. He had showed Magpye some words, and now she could read her prayers in English, as her father said they should be read, so the people of God's world could be close to God.

Magpye had learned her catechism, of course, how to recite

a Pater Noster, an Ave Maria and the Credo in Latin, as well as the Ten Commandments, as was taught in the petty school near the church, but she learnt there by reciting what she was told to recite. They didn't teach reading to girls, only boys were accepted into higher classes.

So Magpye's pa had taught her those prayers in English, so she understood what they meant, and he had shown her how to read them too. Pa said God didn't need people to speak in Latin in order for the Almighty to understand them. "He made all people, and all languages, did He not?" Pa said with a laugh. "Men who think God only understands Latin, they are fools, and they dishonour the Lord for God is all powerful and all knowing, and if that doesn't include knowing all languages, Magpye, so He can hear us speak to Him, I know not what it means."

But she was not to say he had taught her to read, and not only because she was a girl and some thought that wrong, to teach women, their minds being too weak to take on knowledge as some men claimed. Her pa didn't believe that, but he did warn her about telling others what he taught her. She was not to say about the English Bible, a Tyndale New Testament, Pa owned – their most precious and expensive, and hidden asset – nor about being closer to God, as not everyone agreed; some thought common men should derive all knowledge from priests and not be close to God at all. Others thought men, especially common men, should not read prayers or the Bible in English. Pa believed they should, and he believed other things, such as the bread at Mass not being truly the body of Christ but simply a symbol of the Last Supper. Not even the King agreed with all Pa believed. "But he will come to," her pa had said one night when she was in her bed, soft with hay and fragrant with the ladies' bedstraw and meadowsweet she and Ma had gathered that summer just passed. They had said a prayer together, Magpye and her pa, and she had asked questions. Pa liked her to ask questions.

"With his good Queen, Anne Boleyn, at his side," Pa went on, "the King uncovers much of the truth, and he will go on to find more. It is like a puzzle, learning. You find one thing, then another, and before you know it, Magpye, you're on a path and every way-marker is a new piece of the puzzle."

"Is that not frustrating, Pa?" she had asked, and he chuckled.

"No, Mag. It's the truest joy of life, a gift from God. The only frustration is when we can't find what we need to find, but God will send all that we need eventually, show us what we must learn, and it is our job to learn it when find it we do."

Pa had thought the King had learnt much, especially from Anne Boleyn and Archbishop Cranmer, who Pa called an angel sent to guide England. He had travelled, her pa, picked up ideas from other men. His father had been a merchant who came of money, and Pa had gone to school as a young boy, but he said never did he learn more than when he learnt of the truth of how the faith should be upheld. When he was a boy he and his father had gone to Saxony and there he had learned much from men in favour of reform. In the King's army he had met others like him. When the King had taken an interest in the cause of reform, and when he had become Head of the Church, Pa had rejoiced.

"Man should have a closer link to God," he had told her. "The Church, they want us separate, so the priests and the bishops, and the Pope worst of all, can have power over us, power of knowledge for they speak and read Latin and the common man can't, so the common man remains ignorant because he can't read the Word of God for himself. But God wants us close, He wants us reading the words of the Scripture in our language, so we understand His Word fully, in our hearts and our souls. Some close to the King want that too, so they persuade our King away from ignorance and darkness, and slowly he comes to the light, but not all want matters of faith to change, so we must be careful, we who have the same ideas as the good people of court, careful of what we say. It's easy to be accused of being a heretic these days."

"I do not want to burn, Pa," Magpye had said, her eyes wide.

"They won't get you, my Magpye, you're too quick and clever for them," he told her with a chuckle. "But fear not, for the Queen and Cranmer, Latimer too, he is a good man, they will teach the King, and he will lead us, you'll see, to a better time."

But the King would not, not now. The King could not lead anything for the King was gone. The Queen was Regent and not everyone was as full of praise for her as Magpye's father was.

"And now the whore is to rule in the King's place," whispered one man to his friends as Magpye passed by, collecting cups. He was not the only one saying such in the inn that night, she had heard insults directed at the Queen many times that hour. Usually there was gambling at some of the tables, cards or dice, sometimes a musician would come and play, but this night there was nothing but the low hum of conversation. The King's death was on everyone's lips. "She did well out of this."

"Think you... it was no accident?" His companion leaned in, foul breath rising from rotten teeth made no sweeter by the liberal application of ale steamed in the air between them. The fire let out a pop, air stored in slightly damp wood somewhere, and the people huddled about this man as if he was a sage, which to them he was, jumped a little. Shivering, they crossed themselves.

The sage swirled the ale in his tankard as Magpye stepped close, pretending to be as busy with her hands as she was with her ears. "Poison is a woman's weapon, friend. Everyone says it, so true it must be. And the King never was unsure of himself on a horse, was he? Never faltered, yet that day he did and that day he died. What if it was indeed not an accident, but was done on purpose? People said he was tiring of the Boleyn witch. What if she knew that?"

"But she is pregnant with his child."

The sage turned savagely on the commentator. "Think, fool. What if it was not his child? She has men about her all the time, everyone speaks of how she flirts and teases them, Thomas More said as much, did he not? Before she convinced the King to kill More, his friend. And she and the King were struggling to have a boy child a long time. What if the whore went elsewhere for seed? What if the King found out that lump on her front was not his babe, and was about to do something about it, so she killed him? It was said he was mighty fond of this new one, the Seymour girl."

"Seymour, the poxy whore!" shouted one, far drowned already in his cups. There had been songs of late, in the streets, deriding Jane Seymour as a jade.

"Lift your skirts then lift them more!" another chimed in with the next verse and there was laughter from all around them.

"Hush, cretin." The sage was angry, not liking his attention being stolen. "What if he was planning to be rid of the Boleyn Queen, and make a Seymour one instead? The good, true Queen Katherine is gone to God, poor lady…" With that, many formed the sign of the cross again upon chests and foreheads "… With her gone, many would see the King as a bachelor again, able to wed whom he wanted if his marriage to the Boleyn whore was not recognised. Perhaps she knew that. Perhaps she got rid of him before he could get rid of her."

There was silence a moment. Magpye held her breath, wondering if in this silence any would notice her hovering.

"That is wild talk, treason." It was a harsh whisper that came eventually from one of the women. She was young, still had fresh skin and all her teeth, quite remarkable even at her tender age. She bounced a babe on her hip as it burped and grizzled. The baby seemed to consider crying then decided there was small point, so went to sleep.

The sage chuckled. "Wilder than a mere knight's daughter, as her father was before the King elevated him, supplanting the good, Christian Queen we had had ruling over us for twenty years? Wilder than England breaking ties with Rome? Wilder than a bastard being named Queen as our Lady Mary, the true princess, is cast aside? And where is the Princess Mary? I hear she was seen on a boat some days ago, headed for the Tower. She is England's true heir. Is she to vanish, as the princes, her great-uncles, did before her because bad King Richard wanted them out of the way?"

The night grew long, and people did not break the curfew set in place. They stayed inside. There were beds upstairs in the attic paid for, but few made their way there to sleep in rows on the soft straw Magpye's pa had laid out fresh that afternoon, mixed with a little bracken to keep the fleas and other creatures that might bite away. The customers didn't care what pains Pa had gone to for their bedding. They were too busy talking, a thousand plots or more grew in feral mouths, born of grief and fear, and as the wind rose outside so inside a fever broke upon the people of London. By the time the grey light of dawn was rising Magpye knew many there were certain of two things; the King had been murdered and the Princess Mary, the one true heir of England, was in danger of her life.

CHAPTER TEN

Queen Anne Boleyn

30th of January 1536

Greenwich Palace

London

"I like not they are buried on the same day," Anne murmured, staring out of the window at the grey river, the skies obscured by sleet. "It is as if they are bonded, Norris, as if she has claimed him back. I have lost my husband to death, and that I can stand, just about, but to lose him to Katherine again…"

Henry Norris, former gentleman of the Privy Chamber and Groom of the Stool, former great friend to the King, stood beside Anne. He made as if he would put a hand to her shoulder but stopped himself. She was a widow as she was the Queen Regent, and on both counts not his to touch. She never had been, though many times he had wished she could be.

They were not alone, that would not be wise in such troubled times. Anne's ladies, Margaret Lee, Elizabeth Browne and Nan Gainsford were on the other side of the room, along with George Constantine, Norris's man, but they knew to keep a discreet distance, so Norris and Anne could talk.

"The people will not note the one for the other, Majesty. Katherine's burial goes ahead quietly, whilst the King's is attended by all," he said.

"All but me," Anne replied sadly.

"That is but tradition, Majesty."

It was true. The spouse of a dead person did not attend the funeral but sent someone instead in their place. Royalty often did not attend funerals; it might make people imagine the death of the monarch and thereby commit treason. Anne was being represented by the Duchess of Suffolk, Katherine Willoughby, as the King was buried in Westminster. Lady Eleanor, daughter of the Duke of Suffolk, had been sent to be chief mourner, although not to represent Anne, at Katherine's funeral. Bishop Hilsey was officiating in Peterborough, Cranmer at Westminster. Anne knew she could trust both men to preach in a way that would support her and her children.

Yet Anne carried a sense of having betrayed Henry, for he had wanted to be interred at Windsor, but she could not allow it in the end. It was too far from London and the people needed to see the procession, needed somewhere they could go, as if on pilgrimage, to mourn their lord. His heart she had sent to Windsor, to lie in the tomb he had stolen from Wolsey and captured for himself. His body she had sent to Westminster Abbey, so he could remain forever in the heart of the city which had loved him, and he had loved. She felt guilt over it, but she hoped Henry would understand.

Others had not.

"It is not as the King would have wished!" Suffolk had almost shouted at her when she relayed the plan to the council.

"The people need their King close to them, Suffolk," Anne had explained, as gently as she could. Her voice cracked as she spoke, and the blaze of his brown eyes had died down. Swiftly he had excused himself.

The people needed to know the King was gone, too, to be sure of it. If he was buried far away, people might talk, call it a plot, talk of his body being hidden, talk of poison. She could not allow that. There was so much to be careful about now.

On this same day as the King was buried, Katherine's body, which could wait no more, was being interred in Peterborough Cathedral. Word had been sent to Anne that when Katherine's body had been opened to prepare it for burial, the former Queen's heart had been found to be black. Some who had heard this whispered it was proof the Queen had died of a broken heart.

Anne had sometimes doubted whether Katherine truly loved Henry, or perhaps that she had loved him at the end of their relationship, but Katherine's last letter, sent to court from her deathbed, had convinced Anne that the former Queen had indeed loved her husband. Anne was sorry if, in truth, Katherine had died of a broken heart, but Anne had loved Henry too and he had loved her. The urge to be together had proved stronger than any guilt over the severing of a relationship which had lasted decades. Katherine had had much time with Henry, Anne much less, especially as his wife.

Was it not fair that she, who had loved Henry too, should have been permitted some time as his wife, after he and Katherine separated? Perhaps, or perhaps not. Only God could tell them who was right in this matter which had consumed so many hearts, so many lives.

Anne had hoped that, as Norris said, Katherine's funeral would be forgotten as the King's went on, that few would pay attention. That had been the plan, and a good one, but she wondered now if it was wrong to bury them on the same day, wondered if she was enacting some design of destiny by doing so, obeying some call from another world, linking Katherine and Henry together. When they all came to Heaven, would she be Henry's wife, or would Katherine? Would they all be at peace there, at last, or would war rage between them even before the spirit of God?

If any did note Katherine's funeral, there was a message to

be found in its ceremony, in its pomp. The arms of Spain and Wales were to be quartered on Katherine's tomb that day, banners hung in the cathedral were those of Spain and Wales too. Katherine was being buried as the Princess Dowager of Wales, the wife of Arthur Tudor. It was to be made clear by Hilsey in the ceremony that she never had been married to the King, that her daughter was illegitimate. Katherine's funeral was a political pageant. This was not even Anne's command, not the way she would have had it happen; the King had made clear to his men as soon as Katherine died that this was as he wanted it, his former wife's funeral to be used as a way to hammer her reduced status into the minds of the country. Anne had followed all of Henry's instructions, sending Richard Rich and Thomas Wriothesley along with Bishop Hilsey to ensure what the King had wanted was carried out. She had stood by his wishes, but still, Anne hoped all eyes would be on the King's funeral, all minds too.

Mary was not permitted to go to her mother's funeral. Anne did not trust her outside of the Tower, and thought the funeral might rouse the public to the cause of the daughter of Katherine of Aragon.

Even now, the funeral procession of the King would be wending through London, paupers carrying torches leading the way past houses draped with black cloth, until they reached the Abbey of Westminster which Anne had ordered to be illuminated by thousands of candles. There were crowds of people out, even in the snow and sleet, the bitter cold, lining Henry's route to his tomb with tears, with their prayers.

It would have comforted you to know how greatly you were loved by your people, Anne thought. Sometimes of late, after all the changes to the faith and in marriage, Henry had doubted his people still loved him as once they did, she knew that, doubted the common folk of England supported or respected him. Sometimes Henry had called them ungrateful, dishonest, but never had he really believed that. He had loved his people, and as any heart deep in love yearns for that love to be returned so the King's had.

She hoped he could see them now, mourning for him. Death might lose its sting a little, if Henry could feel the sorrow of his people.

Norris had chosen to stay with Anne on this terrible day. Others had too. Many of the King's former men, Weston, George Boleyn, Norris, had offered to be the Regent's personal guard for the day, just in case trouble should arise. It was of greater comfort too, so Norris hoped, to Anne, that men she knew were with her rather than just palace guards. She needed to talk, so he thought, though in truth she had said little until that point.

Anne put a hand to the glass, cold under her skin. "It still seems like fate, Norris, that Katherine died then Henry, and now they are on the same day buried. I thought once she put a curse on me, so I could not bear his child but perhaps that was not the curse. Perhaps she cursed Henry, so he would never see our son. Perhaps that is why he died now. Katherine took him to death with her, so he never would know his son. What did she write in that letter before she died? *Mine eyes desire to see you above all other things.* Perhaps that was her, calling him to her side. I feel she has stolen him from me."

Norris sighed. "Majesty, you are lost to grief, and it makes you imagine fell things. The King's death was an accident, not a curse. Many of us had said to him over the years that he should ride no more in the lists. He was not as young as he once was and sometimes his reactions were slower. You know this, I know that you too hesitated when he announced he would ride in these tournaments."

"Tournaments put on to celebrate our freedom, *because* Katherine was gone," she argued, shaking her head. Her hair, so dark and long, he could see a glimpse of under her French hood. Not just black shone there, glimmering in the light of the window, but the deepest blue, too, like the wing of a raven. "Do you not see? This was her revenge on us. We should have mourned, should not have acted as we did, wearing yellow on the day we heard of her death, ordering dances and feasts and celebrating. We mocked her death, and we were repaid in cruel kind. God granted Katherine a wish, and her wish was to see her husband again, in Heaven."

"He was not her husband, Majesty, he was yours."

Anne turned dark, sombre eyes on him, her face pinched. "In her eyes, in the eyes of many, my friend, he was her husband, and I was nothing but his mistress, Elizabeth and this child I carry nothing but bastards. Katherine's eyes might be closed now but her vision of us, the way she saw Elizabeth and me and my unborn child, that remains. Katherine's curse does not end with the death of the King." Anne's voice fell to a whisper. "I think it out there, in the world, as if it escaped. Sometimes I think I hear it, a voice on the wind, a breath on my neck, something coming for me, for us."

Norris fell to one knee before her. "Majesty…" he took her hand "… I swear to you, neither I nor any of our loyal men will allow any harm to come to you."

Anne nodded, putting her hand on his shoulder as she tried to smile at him. It felt odd, unnatural, but the edges of her lips lifted.

That was how one smiled, she remembered, but she did not feel it in her heart, that flooding of sunshine across shadow which had once accompanied a smile. The sunshine was there no more, all there was, as there was creeping across the world, was a veil of shadow, all the time growing darker, growing stronger.

CHAPTER ELEVEN

Queen Anne Boleyn
Late January 1536
Greenwich Palace
London

"It must be permitted; this delay is unconscionable! The Lady Mary has lost her mother and father in a short space of time as well as her rightful position as heir of this country and now is made a prisoner. I must be allowed to see her for the sake of decency and friendship, and to ensure the Emperor can be assured that his beloved cousin is still alive."

The ambassador was close to incandescent fury. Clearly one word the wrong way or spoken in the wrong timbre might push him over the edge. Gazing at him, Anne wondered if he might burst into flame. If so, the white spittle flying free of his mouth might well extinguish any fire.

"Ambassador Chapuys," Anne said, holding up a hand. "That is enough, my Lord Ambassador. You accuse us of much, rashly and without cause. Let us also not forget my daughter has lost a father of late, and I have lost a husband. England has lost her King, and yet we all are capable of expressing our grief without lashing out at others with unfounded accusation and wild gossip."

"The Lady Mary has been taken prisoner, Majesty, so the accusations are not unfounded." How unwillingly did he say the word, *Majesty*. It sneered as it slid from his usually so politic tongue.

Anne stared at this man. In truth, she could hardly believe he was standing in front of her. Chapuys had tried so hard to avoid her for so long. Barely had they been seen in the same place since Chapuys had come to England so many years ago to become ambassador to the court, as well as the champion of Katherine and Mary, to represent their kinsman, Charles V, King of Spain and Holy Roman Emperor.

Refusing to accept her as the wife of the King or as England's Queen, Ambassador Chapuys had stayed far away from Anne, so he never had to officially recognise her as Queen. Katherine, to his eyes, had always been Queen and Anne never, but now he had no choice but to appear before her. Anne was the Queen Regent. Mary was in her custody. If he wanted to see his charge, he had to petition the Queen directly. He had tried going through Cromwell, Cranmer, Norfolk, but none had the authority to grant him access to Mary, only Anne did, and from a distance she would not give him what he wanted, and for good reason. She wanted something too, only more important now was it for Chapuys, and through him the Emperor, to recognise her title. So, necessity had finally forced Ambassador Chapuys to present himself before Anne Boleyn for the first time since he had come to England, and that meant recognising her as Queen and the present ruler of the country. Chapuys had never intended to do such a thing. Anne could almost see him silently praying to the ghost of Katherine, to the soul of Mary still living, for forgiveness in carrying out this heinous act of publicly acknowledging Anne's status.

Henry tried for so long to get you to acknowledge me, Ambassador, Anne thought idly, her heart, stunned by all the agony and fear of late, still managing to pain her. How could an organ so numb do such a thing? *And now by his death, Henry has finally succeeded.*

Grim mirth rose in her, but she could not laugh. Not only because it would hardly help the situation, but because she did not truly find it amusing. There was little which moved her now. Elizabeth was one of those little things, but besides that, to merriment or to grief she felt deadened. Except when with Elizabeth, Anne had not laughed since the King died; her soul too heavy to allow her heart to experience joy unhindered. There was a weight upon her not only of sorrow but of worry almost incapacitating in its strength, worry for the future, for her children. Once, not long ago, she had laughed, she remembered that. She had listened to musicians play, had encouraged her husband to chuckle at her jests and japes. Anne had danced, once. She could barely remember now the woman who had done all those things. How had she laughed? The mechanics of it seemed lost to her.

The only time she truly had smiled of late, smiled with her eyes and heart, had been when Elizabeth was with her. Elizabeth could touch the Anne which this new woman, the Queen Regent, sometimes thought lost. Whilst Elizabeth was there, Anne was lost no more.

Her daughter was housed here in the palace now. Men kept telling Anne it was not safe, her uncle of Norfolk most especially, who always had an opinion about everything. He and others declared that Elizabeth should be sent away again to the country for court always carried a risk of sickness, but Anne would have none of it. She wanted her daughter here, where she could see her, where she knew she could gather her in her arms within but a few moments. Anne needed the strength Elizabeth granted to her.

Besides, house Elizabeth too far away and Anne would be distracted, wondering if her child was safe. She had never liked her daughter being in a separate household in any case, even when Elizabeth was born Anne had tried to keep her with her, to breastfeed her, to have her on a bed in court, by her side. The King had not allowed it, thinking it a scandal she should act in such a way, as if she was a lowly peasant carrying her child to the fields, swaddled on her back, keeping her daughter with her as she worked, but to Anne love for her child was nothing of lowness, it was the highest virtue she contained.

At this moment, as she struggled with a feeling of numb sorrow over Henry's death, with fear of the future and the people she ruled, even with the man before her showing eyes afire with hatred, Anne knew Elizabeth was the only thing in all the world that could save her from falling into a pit of lowness; she was Anne's tether to this earth.

And you, my child, her mind murmured to her babe. *You too are what will save me.*

Grief has such power, fear too, so strong they are we can forget, can think they are stronger than anything. But love, when it is true, may hold up the world so it might sing amongst the stars.

Anne lifted her chin and stared into the ambassador's brown eyes. "The Lady Mary has been taken to the Tower, not under arrest, but for her own safety. She is housed in my own royal apartments."

"Her own *safety*!" Chapuys spluttered.

Anne continued with what she believed was remarkable restraint and coolness. *Finally, Henry, I have learnt to control my temper, are you proud?* she thought. "Indeed, my lord, for we have concerns that some villains may think to assert Mary's old title, even her once-claim to the throne, revoked by the King, our lost beloved lord, and by Parliament and law. Many once thought the Lady Mary, bastard though she now is proved, to be England's heir before she was disinherited by her own father. If some rebellious factions of the country thought to make trouble, Lord Ambassador, they could place her as a figurehead in front of a foul rebel army and march out, making trouble for England itself, which I know the Lady Mary, a daughter of England, never would want. The lady herself might be entirely in ignorance of their aims, and innocent of leading a rebellion yet she could be seen as the leader if irresponsible persons make her appear as such. We do not want that. Therefore, you may tell your master the Emperor that his bastard cousin has been taken to a place of safety and there she will stay until we are assured the populace is at rest and fully understands and accepts our changes of government and ruler in the wake of the tragedy we all have experienced. Once we are assured she will not be used, no doubt against her will, by those who would cause trouble, Lady Mary will be released and will be brought to court to serve in my household."

"*Your* household, Majesty?"

Anne smiled. It did not touch her heart. "Indeed. You are right when you say she has lost much, and I, who have also lost almost all that was dear to me in this world, understand her heart well. Perhaps now that her mother has gone to God, Mary will not be so determined, so adversely influenced by those who wish her nothing but ill will, to continue demonstrating the foolish and rebellious behaviour which caused so much pain to her late father. It is sad to my heart that they never had a chance to reconcile, but Mary and I still have that chance. I would offer her a place in my household for whilst she is a bastard she is of royal blood and should be within the household of the Queen Regent." *And because I do not trust her in the household of my daughter anymore,* Anne thought. Mary had entirely too much to gain if Elizabeth should become ill or die.

"You are right when you say the Emperor is her cousin, Lord Ambassador, and England values his friendship," Anne went on, "but Mary has family here in England, too. Her cousin Lady Margaret Douglas serves me..." Anne held out a hand to indicate a pretty, elegant lady at her side, one Chapuys and all at court knew well, and Margaret ducked her head and heel in recognition "... which will comfort her for the two ever were close, I am told, and Mary's half-sister, my daughter, is also Mary's blood, her kin. I am sure she will wish to be by Elizabeth's side at this time and in the future, to protect and keep safe the one who is not only her sister, but, at present, her Queen."

Chapuys narrowed his large eyes and Anne thought, not for the first time, how like a hare he looked. It was her pet name for him, granted as much for his old habit of scampering away every time she appeared like a hare over a hilltop as for the way he looked. The hapless hare, that was what she had named him in happier days. Henry had laughed at that. A vision of her husband's face alight with mirth, his blue eyes sparkling with admiration at her wit, flashed into her mind. Anne almost looked about for him, then stopped herself. She cursed her mind. Still sometimes she forgot he was gone. It kept happening. Every time she forgot and remembered he was gone it was as if her heart had been pummelled flat with a butcher's hammer. Anne swallowed, the pain making her nauseous. *Why did you leave me?* her mind asked Henry, but his ghost did not answer.

"If you say that England values the friendship of the Emperor then let me see the Lady Mary so I might assure my master that his cousin is still alive." Chapuys drew himself up. "Majesty," he added at the end, an afterthought, apparently, but she knew it was not. Chapuys was a clever man; he knew how to place a well thought out insult. The delay this time, like the sneer the last, was intended to demonstrate he did not recognise her as Queen, let alone Regent.

"If you will not believe my word, then certainly you may have an audience, Lord Ambassador, but you must assure me that you will remember all I have said. Lady Mary is in the Tower for her own safety. Any other suspicions you or she nurtures are false, and if such notions should spread out from behind these walls or those of the Tower and seep into the ears of the very people I am trying to calm, console and contain in the aftermath of the King's tragic death, I shall prevent further meetings between the two of you. Have I made myself clear?"

The King's tragic death, Chapuys' mind scoffed in the silence of his thoughts as he bowed his head to Anne. A tragedy indeed! The Boleyn whore was now in control of the country, free and unrestrained without a master and her daughter, the little bastard she always had doted upon, would be Queen. All this postulating about a boy in her belly was fantasy, he was sure, for women in Anne's chambers had told him, in return for a purse of gold, that there were many signs she carried another girl, and considering her past record of miscarriages, a girl that might not even live. There had been rumours until this late pregnancy that the King would cast her off because she could not provide a son. A tragedy late events may be for others, but not for her. The King's death had granted her power, power beyond all imagining for the mere daughter of a noble.

That thought pulled him up short. When someone is murdered the culprit is often the one who had the most to gain. The one who had benefited most was in truth Elizabeth. No infant could have engineered the death of the King, yet what of her mother? Anne was now sovereign in all but name until her child grew up, and how long would that take? A decade or more? The King had been tiring of her, her influence had waned so Cromwell had informed him, and were it not for the babe in her belly it had been rumoured the King might well have looked elsewhere for a new bride. One inconvenient wife had been removed, why not another? And with the death of Katherine of Aragon there was no longer the possibility that if the King set Anne aside he would have to return to Katherine and his first marriage. That was what many had said, that if he left Anne, Henry of England would have to admit his first marriage was the true one and return to it.

But ever since Katherine had died, Anne could have been set aside and a new wife chosen. Many had never accepted the legality of the King's second marriage. Easy it would be to dissolve. It was ironic in a way that in truth the first, the true

Queen, had been keeping the second, false one, safe.

People had whispered of marriage alliances with France or Spain, a few had even mentioned that the King seemed most fond of his new interest at court, Jane Seymour. Chapuys had considered approaching the Seymours of late, making friends, helping Jane to gain power as the mistress of the King. Had Anne Boleyn not been with child, her husband could very well have seriously considered setting Anne aside. Had she known that? The Boleyn witch knew most things that went on at court. If she had known, had she been threatened?

Could she had found a way to bring this death about, in order to protect herself and assure her daughter's future?

But surely, it had been an accident, and yet... there were herbs that might make a man dizzy, might impair judgment or make a man overly bold. Plants could cause a man to fall unconscious. The King had been with Anne just before he came to the lists. Chapuys had been told so by his spies in Anne's chambers. The King had gone to her that morning to ask if she was coming to attend the foul jousts set up to celebrate the death of one of the finest women Chapuys had ever known. Was it possible Anne had dosed him with something? Nothing had been said of foul play, but the doctors had not been looking for evidence the King had been tampered with by poison or narcotic, why would they? They had seen his horse fall on him, and that was enough to kill a man. But the King had been a champion jouster all his life, had only once before taken a fall that was in any way perilous, and that time he had accidently ridden into the lists with his visor raised and received a face full of splinters from Suffolk. That was the only time he had been beaten before, and whilst it was true that some men would allow their King to win *because* he was the King, Henry VIII had not needed men to pretend to lose to him. His skill had been admired and feared.

Was it possible, then, that someone who stood to benefit

the most had given him something, some subtle powder or potion slipped into his drink, which had impaired his vision, or competence, which had made him pass out, perhaps, which had led to this accident? It was clever if so, and Anne Boleyn was a clever woman.

"You have our permission to visit the Lady Mary," Anne announced, breaking through his torrent of suspicious thought. "For a short while. As long as there is no conversation between you which we find abhorrent, you will be permitted to visit each week."

She smiled again, a pained, hollow line it cut across her face. "England does not wish to lose the good will of the Emperor just at a moment when it is finally possible that we can indeed, and without hindrance, become great friends."

"Indeed, Majesty." Chapuys bowed. *Friends?* His mind screamed. *Never!*

CHAPTER TWELVE

Queen Anne Boleyn
2nd of February 1536
Candlemas
Greenwich Palace
London

"The Duke has signed the papers and sworn the oath, he must be released from house arrest, Majesty."

William Paulet, Comptroller of the Household, the King's Lord Chamberlain and Master of the Wards, had a kind face, Anne thought, if it was at this moment set hard and resolute. What was more annoying was, he was right.

"I still feel there is a risk," she said.

Anne thought of the ceremony of that morning, Candlemas. It was supposed to be a moment of light and hope as winter drew to an end. The purification of the Virgin after the birth of Christ, that was what Candlemas celebrated. She and her ladies, all dressed in white, had processed to the altar of the chapel at Greenwich, carrying candles. Blessed at the altar, they had then carried those candles in procession about the palace, courtiers bowing to them along the way. Her bishops, Latimer and Cranmer the most outspoken, had not welcomed the ritual, thinking it too much a sign of the old faith, but Anne had convinced them to uphold it this year at least. The people, the court, they needed something of hope and that was what Candlemas had always meant to her, a turning point in the dark of winter, looking to the light and hope of spring.

Paulet nodded. "I understand, and perhaps there always will be a risk, Majesty, but unlike the Lady Mary, the Duke of Richmond has signed his name, has sworn before other men an oath to uphold you and the Queen Elizabeth, or a King born of your body. We can ask no more of him than this and the fact is, Majesty, we need him. There is word there may be unrest arising in Ireland and he is Lord Lieutenant of that isle. The King was on the verge of sending him to Ireland to regain proper control of that often troublesome country. Fitzroy is also the Lord High Admiral and therefore should be in at least nominal control of the fleet if trouble seems likely from abroad. He may be young, but he is a Duke and blood of the King's blood even if he be a bastard, and the longer you keep him a prisoner, even one held only in his rooms, the more likely it is he will emerge not as your friend but as your enemy."

"What if he is already my enemy?"

Paulet breathed in and let it out slowly. "Then, if proved, we can re-arrest him, but in that case we would be acting with legitimate charges which might be used against a man. At the moment the only charge against him is that he is the King's natural son, and no matter if that does potentially make him a danger it is not something which is, in truth, a crime. A crime against marriage, perhaps, but not the law, and since the King and Katherine of Aragon were not wed, as we have found since, then perhaps his crime of being born is not even a sin against marriage."

Anne stared at Paulet a long time, so long the silence stretched, awkward and tense in the air. "I hope you are not going to suggest the boy could be considered legitimate? Bessie Blount and the King were not wed either."

It might be easy for someone to legitimize Fitzroy, using that idea,

Anne thought. She had not considered such before Paulet said it, that someone might claim a promise had perhaps been spoken between Bessie and Henry. A promise or calling each other husband and wife followed by consummation was good enough for the Catholic Church to name a union a marriage, and what if someone claimed such about the King and his former mistress? Turned up fake witnesses? It might even be that Fitzroy could be legitimized without any lie of marriage between the Blount woman and the King being made up, if the King was considered a free bachelor at the time of Fitzroy's conception, and his mother had too been unwed, unbonded to another. It would take a dispensation, or Act of Parliament, but it was possible. There had been cases before where, considering the two who had made a child were both unmarried, their child was considered born in honesty and had been legitimized.

Realising he had potentially made a mistake, Paulet hurried on. "I simply mean he has done nothing, Majesty, and the people know that. Majesty, Fitzroy is beloved of the common people, and we need them on our side. In the north he is well respected as he was once their Lord Lieutenant and people remember his council well, even if he truly did little and his men much, since he was a child when in post. The French love him, after he spent time at their court, and the English people will not stand for him being locked away for long, Majesty, he is popular with commoners and at court. King François liked the lad too. Fitzroy has never shown interest in rising above his position and always attended to anything his father asked of him with loyalty and devotion. Over and over he has proved himself true to the throne and to his family. He was to give up Collyweston for you, soon, was he not? Under order from the King, and never did he object to losing one of his best houses to give to you."

"He was to receive Baynard's Castle and another London house in return, my lord, he was hardly sacrificing much." Anne's heart was hammering. The thought of what men might do with Fitzroy, what a weapon they might make him into, frightening her so deeply her bones seemed to shiver.

Paulet frowned. "It is a risk to trust, but it is no less a risk to keep him imprisoned. You must give him freedom of the court at least, Majesty, no more guards on his doors, no more restriction to his movements about the palace. If needs be, you can keep him here and not allow him to travel anywhere, such as his estates, or Ireland."

Anne put her hands behind her back, folded them, so the men there would not see them shaking. Thankfully, her voice remained calm, betraying nothing. "You think I risk incurring the wrath of the world, merely for holding a lad I suspect may cause trouble for me in the future?"

"I do, and we have his word now. If he breaks it the world will see he is no kind of man, and you will be just for moving against him then. At the moment, Majesty, you are seen as the unjust one for you lock a man away before he has done anything."

"It is treason to think treason, Sir William," Anne reminded him.

Paulet inclined his head. "But you have no evidence he ever has considered it, Majesty. Always he has been loyal to his father, to the country. He has sworn to be loyal now to you and to his siblings, your children. Lady Mary refuses the oath still, but he signed it and swore it immediately when it was handed to him."

She sighed. "What say you, Cromwell? And you, Cranmer?"

It was likely to be the same opinion just from different lips, she knew. Paulet and Cromwell were friends and allies, and though Cranmer often would take a slightly different line from those men, he concurred with them often enough.

"I would say if you consider him to be a risk, Majesty, keep him under watch." Cromwell smoothed his habitually dark robes. "I have men in his household already and we can have others watching him. But, Majesty, I agree with the Lord Chamberlain. There will be unrest if Fitzroy is not released, particularly now he has sworn the oath, and we need him. If he turns out to be loyal, all the better for us, for his support as the highest titled man in England will be valuable. If he turns out to be a threat, we shall deal with him as such."

There was such coldness expressed as Cromwell said that last part. All the shivers in the long dark of the earth of a graveyard could not have been colder than his tone.

"Our royal guards are sworn to you and your children, Majesty," Cranmer added. "We will see you are well protected."

There was a pause as Anne thought.

"Release him, but he is not to leave court," Anne surrendered. "And I want eyes on him, ears in his chamber." She narrowed her eyes at her men. "The truth is, my lords, that many people consider my daughter a bastard, Mary has been named as such and Fitzroy certainly is one, but if it comes to a choice between three children and one of those children is a boy, how many will ignore the accident of Fitzroy's birth and think a man preferable even if illegitimate, to any girl who is legitimate?"

"Fitzroy may not have any such ambitions," said Paulet.

Anne laughed without mirth. "Half his blood is Tudor, my lord. Believe me, he has ambition."

CHAPTER THIRTEEN

Henry Fitzroy, Duke of Richmond and Somerset
February 1536
Greenwich Palace
London

"You're lunatic, Brereton, I just was released, and by such plans you would have me back in captivity, and in worse a state than before, too." Fitzroy's voice hissed into the ear of William Brereton.

Fitzroy sat at the table in his chambers. The guards had finally left his doors, he was free, although he was not certain exactly how free he was. Whilst eventually, after he signed the paper supporting Elizabeth as Queen, Fitzroy had been set at liberty in most ways one could think of, he had still been politely asked to stay within the palace walls, and he was fairly certain he was being watched. He had gone out little, in truth, only a walk here and there to greet people in the gardens or the halls of court to demonstrate that he was indeed a prisoner no more. He had been invited to the next council meeting in his position as Lord High Admiral and Lord Lieutenant of Ireland, but he could feel eyes on him everywhere he went. That was why, when Brereton had whispered this radical suggestion into his ear, he had replied with care, and in a murmur.

"We cannot talk of this here," he went on, his breath heating the skin of Brereton's rough face, grizzled by years spent under sun and sky, as a rider on the King's business and, many said and quite rightly, as a pirate upon his seas. Brereton was a member of Fitzroy's household, took care of his affairs in Wales, where he had estates. Fitzroy had always liked the wily old wolf, had trusted him, but at present he was not sure whether to trust anyone anymore. Were the things Brereton was saying being suggested out of loyalty, or as a trap?

"I am being watched, Brereton."

"There are ways to speak without being heard, and I do not hear you say you are averse to the idea, Your Grace, only to being found out." Brereton spoke no louder than a heartbeat in his master's ear. Long had pirate served bastard prince, teaching Fitzroy much about the world that his father might not have appreciated, and now Brereton appeared to have moved on to greater plans, instilling some ideas in Fitzroy which the Queen Regent and her supporters certainly would not welcome.

But was it possible? These things he suggested, would others support them?

"I am illegitimate, no one would support me for the throne."

"But a male heir you are, all the same, Your Grace. The King's marriages have both been contested by various factions, does that not make all his children bastards? And if all are, then why not choose the male from amongst the King's bastards as the next King? Why not take the highest titled man of England and place him on the throne? At the very least you should be regent, Your Grace, rather than the Queen. Much as I admire her, she is not the one to hold this country together. The people despise her, but you they have always loved. And at most… I think you know your father had plans for you. What if this child in the belly of the Queen should be another girl? A female cannot hold England together, an infant certainly cannot. Are we to allow England to fall to rebellion and revolt, invasion too, all because a female baby has been left upon the throne by accident of fate? Your father never wanted a girl to hold his throne, you know that. That was why he left Katherine, why he married Anne, why he turned the world upside down. It was not the woman he wanted, delectable though she might be, but the heir. That he died without a legitimate male heir is a travesty, but you, Your Grace, can be the son he wanted, the one to lead England, to unite us all."

Fitzroy paused, wondering still about Brereton. Had Cromwell sent Brereton to trap him? But Brereton and Cromwell did not get on. They had struggled over lands and men in Wales, Cromwell resenting the authority Brereton had because of Fitzroy. Brereton had been close to the Queen, though. One of her admirers. She even had a hound he had given her, named for his brother, Urion. Never had Fitzroy had reason to distrust the man before, but still the Duke paused. "And if the Queen's child should be a boy?"

"He would still be a baby, even younger than the Princess Elizabeth. You *must* contest the regency of the Queen, my lord, and only you have the right to do so. At least you must be our Lord Protector, but I am not alone in thinking you should be named King."

"The Queen would have my head if she should hear of this, and yours, Brereton." Would the man go so far as to say all this if he did not believe it?

Brereton sat back and smiled. "I note you do not say nay to what I propose, my lord."

Fitzroy stared at him for a moment, his mind working fast. If he said anything now that later might be used against him, he could protest he had only said such to discover a plot, to aid the Queen. "I do not say no," he said. "But I do not say yes either, and nothing can be done whilst I am here."

"That is why we must get the Queen to support your move to

Ireland, to maintain control over that country, as your father wished," still Brereton spoke low. "There is likely to be unrest in many areas of the country now she has been announced as Regent. Ireland is a volatile country and were a foreign army to head to England, Ireland is an ideal stopping place, a good base for an all-out invasion of the English mainland. She needs a good man there, holding the country for her. Who better than the Lord Lieutenant?"

"The Queen wants me on the minority council for my sister Elizabeth, I think she would not let me leave London."

"You can still accept that post, but all council members must also be ready and willing to be used where they are valuable. Others will support your move to Ireland, Your Grace, some because they think like me and others because they will want you gone so they can move higher up in court. We do not even have to go to Ireland; Wales has many good men you could use, or the north of England where you used to hold power as Lord Lieutenant. Once you are free of this place, and are in post elsewhere, secure in your personal power, we can move on the next stage of the plan, whatever you decide it to be."

"Whatever *I* decide it to be?" There was a question in Fitzroy's voice.

"Indeed, my lord. You are my master, and I will follow where you lead. I think at this time, however, it is hard to see what should be done for you are so close to court. It is hard to see what options there may be. Seeing things at a distance often makes men aware of and appreciative of the larger picture."

Fitzroy nodded. "I see sense in that, and I think you are right, Brereton. I need time and space to consider what is next for me, and for England."

"Of course, Majesty." The old dog winked at the young Duke of Richmond.

Fitzroy could not help but smile.

CHAPTER FOURTEEN

Henry Fitzroy, Duke of Richmond and Somerset
February 1536
Greenwich Palace
London

His steps sounded, hard echoes slamming on the rushes laced along the floor of the corridor, bouncing from cold walls of stone as he marched to the Queen Regent's Privy Chamber. His men were at his heel, trooping behind him. Most were there to guard the son of the King, and some as he had no doubt were there also because they were being paid by Cromwell to watch him. But Fitzroy was about to prove to the Queen that he was no threat, at least for now. If all went well, he would also lose the men Cromwell had placed to watch him by carrying out this action.

Cromwell and Cranmer were at the ornate outer doors, waiting for him. Gilt paint on the door behind them almost seemed to dance before Fitzroy's eyes in the light from the window, curving in flourishes surrounding images of lions and roses. "You sent word, Your Grace, that you needed to see the Regent and us?" Cranmer asked politely, eyes flickering to the men at Fitzroy's back.

Fitzroy bowed his head. "It is urgent, and it must be

understood there can only be the four of us inside the room. My men will wait outside."

Cromwell and Cranmer exchanged glances, clearly worried by a notion that Fitzroy might attempt assassination. Royal guards were there, on the doors, but the young Duke had brought men too. If it came to a fight, they looked to be even in number. Was this part of the plan?

"I know you question my loyalty," he whispered, leaning in to them, "I understand the Queen suspects me, but by this proof you shall find I am the Queen's man. There is a plot afoot, and she must know of it before the conspirators strike."

Cromwell narrowed his eyes, those sharp, dark orbs locking with Fitzroy's a moment. Cromwell was not a man to betray emotion but there was a flicker of surprise in the depths of his eyes. Cleary his spies planted in Fitzroy's household had not got wind of what had occurred most recently. Another thing that was clear was that Cromwell was thinking those men would be in trouble now, for failing him. "Come then, Your Grace," he said. "We will do as you say."

The doors opened at Cromwell's knock. Queen Anne was within the chamber, her women with her, a flock of colourful birds about the Queen who was dressed in white, for mourning. It suited Anne, Fitzroy thought, making her skin illuminate, like sunlight upon snow.

Fitzroy smiled somewhat shyly at his beautiful, clever wife, Mary Howard, as he entered and bowed his head in greeting to her, then bowed to the Queen. Mary fell back, but her eyes never left the face of her husband. When would they ever be allowed to live together, she wondered? The King had always said it was too soon, his son too young to be risked in the fever that might come of the marriage bed, but the King was gone, and both of them were older now.

"The Duke of Richmond and Somerset would speak to you alone, Majesty," Cromwell said. "He has urgent news, but

Cranmer and I may stay to hear it."

"Wait in the next chamber," Anne told her ladies.

"The guards too, Majesty," Fitzroy said in a low tone.

Anne lifted her eyebrows and glanced at Cromwell, but when he nodded, she waved her hand. "Wait outside the doors," she instructed her men.

As the palace guards stole from the chamber, their leather breastplates creaking, halberds rapping on the floor as they marched, Anne turned to her husband's son. "What is this news so important that none but us can hear?"

She looked nervous, he realised. A touch of fire in her eyes, like a torch carried on a black night of winter. *She is scared of me*, he thought, and the notion gave him a thrill of pleasure just as it offered him a touch of guilt. There was a power in fear, something he could almost taste. He liked it and at the same time did not welcome that he liked it. It felt unworthy.

And yet he was here to take away that fear, of him at least. Here to prove himself loyal. Perhaps she was right to fear him, however. This one plot men had brought to him he was to unveil before her, an act which hopefully would bring him greater liberty and trust. Yet the words of Brereton still echoed in his ears, whispering to him by night, telling him he could have more than ever he, or his father, dreamed for him.

Fitzroy bowed again. "Majesty. I know you have cause to question my loyalty, but let it be plain understood between us that I am no threat to you or to your children and to prove this I shall share something. Men came to me within this hour, men who wish you harm."

"What men, and what harm?" Anne's voice was calm, but he saw fear lift its head more boldly in her eyes.

"Sussex was the man who came to me. He tells me Westmorland, Worcester, Oxford, and Lord Sandys are with him as well as Richard Rich. There may be others."

"All those earls and lords were close friends of my late husband, your father," she said, narrowing her eyes.

"But no friend to you, Majesty."

"I thought Rich was your man, Cromwell?" she asked, turning to him.

"So did I, Majesty." Cromwell breathed in through generous, flared nostrils. This news infuriated him, Fitzroy could see it. "The man has ambition. It is possible he has seen a way to quicker advancement and taken it."

"And this slipped by you?" Anne asked. "I thought you missed nothing."

"Sadly, no man is capable of such, Majesty, and Rich is… slippery when he wants to be."

That was true enough, thought Fitzroy. Common gossip held that Rich had perjured himself over the Thomas More case, declaring that More had told him that the King could not be Head of the Church, and thus condemning More to death. Rich had few scruples. If he had changed sides and was working against Cromwell, his former master, it was not a great shock.

Anne smoothed her skirts. This white dress was a gown she had recently had made, though she never thought to wear it for mourning. Anne had intended to wear it with both sleeves and a kirtle bright of colour, but in mourning she had adapted. White was the colour the French court adopted when a loved one died, and Anne, who had spent so much time there, thought it fitting. She knew it looked well on her. That had been the point. Trying to get her husband to attend upon her rather than Jane Seymour had been the point of many of her new clothes, a point now wasted. "Just what kind of unfriendly gesture are we talking of, Fitzroy?"

The lad took a breath. "Sussex whispered in my ear that the regent of England should not be you, Majesty, but another, and he suggested me. They mean to attempt a coup, Majesty.

Sussex has had control of the dry stamp of the King, I know not how he obtained it. They have forged a will, making it clear that England, during the minority of Elizabeth and any other child you might bear, is left subject to the rule of a regency council headed by me, and comprised of the men I have mentioned. They think it would be a simple matter to convince others that the King, my father, never meant to leave England in the hands of a female ruler, even as regent, and they will claim you usurped the throne. In a council meeting a few days hence, the accusation will be brought up, the will produced and they will arrest you. Of course, they will ensure that the babe in your belly is left unharmed, lest it be a boy, but you will be taken to the Tower until the birth and afterwards will have no contact with your children. They will assume control of the country, placing me, as the highest titled man of this conspiracy, as Regent, but England will be governed by the whole council, each with a vote on how power should be used. If you do not bear a boy, Elizabeth would be betrothed now and married as soon as possible to a man of their choosing, and he would be King, holding greater powers than your daughter."

"I see." Anne had turned a little pale. "What of Suffolk and Norfolk? They hold higher titles than any of the men you have mentioned. Should they not be on this council?"

Fitzroy shook his head. "At present, they are not involved. Sussex wanted me to bring Norfolk in, since he is my father-in-law, and they are unsure of Suffolk, for he would surely know the King's will had been forged, being so close to my father. Sussex thinks Suffolk would try to be Regent, over me, whereas they think Norfolk would accept my position, given our relationship."

"Because Norfolk would consider himself the power behind the throne, or behind the Regent, in this case," said Cromwell thoughtfully.

"Indeed, although I suspect Sussex wishes for that role in

truth," Fitzroy replied with a wry lift of the eyebrows before he went on. "They think to place Suffolk under arrest too, claim he aided you, Majesty, in your plot to steal the throne." He looked at Cromwell and Cranmer. "You too, Cromwell," he said. "You would be arrested immediately."

Back to Anne came his eyes. For a fleeting moment she thought how like his father's they were, blue as the sky on a cold day. "In truth, I think they do not want another lord with such power of influence left free," Fitzroy went on. "Norfolk, they think they can win to them, through me, but they do not want Cromwell or Suffolk loose about England, for they know those men could reduce the power of the new regency council. Your brother and father would also be arrested, Majesty, sent to the Tower for treason."

"What of Cranmer?" Anne asked indicating to the silent Archbishop who was regarding Fitzroy with grave eyes.

"The regency council, as was explained to me, wishes less change in religion and the powers of all bishops who are in favour of reform would be reduced. Sussex and the other conspirators believe that with Katherine dead, the King would have eventually returned the authority of the English Church to Rome, so they mean to carry this out. I have not heard they mean to imprison the bishops and Archbishop Cranmer, but it is possible."

"With the papacy still hesitating over recognising your title, Majesty, this could indeed be dangerous in many ways. They could have support from Rome to take the entire country." Cromwell looked ill at ease, as well he might. News from Richard Pate, England's Ambassador in Rome, had come, saying the papacy was to investigate Anne's lawful right to act as Regent, as well as the claim that Mary could be the rightful Queen. It was clear what the outcome of that investigation would be. England was no more under the heel of Rome, but that did not mean the Pope rejecting Anne's title was not a threat.

"If the papacy backs Mary or this new, apparently conservative, regency council, and if the Pope persuades other countries to as well, these conspirators could well have great military support," Cranmer agreed.

There was silence a moment.

"I think, in truth, they would need little support from Rome or anyone else," Anne said. "With all of us in their custody, locked away, it would be over." She gazed at Cromwell, and eventually he nodded in agreement.

Anne rocked back on her heels, regarding Fitzroy. "And you come to me with this? Why not accept? You could be made Regent and rule England."

Fitzroy smiled but shook his head. "Majesty, my father honoured me with titles and position, and I am ever grateful, but I do not think he ever intended me to reign. This coup would place my half-sister, you and your unborn child in hostile hands and hand the government of England to a group of men my father never intended to rule." *And no doubt they would find a way, in time, to be rid of me, too,* he thought.

Brereton had urged him to go ahead with the plot, but Fitzroy thought it both premature, and a mistake. If he was to rule, if he decided to press a claim, he would do so on his own impetus, wielding his own power, not as a puppet of other lords, like Sussex.

"They want to make you Governor and Protector of the realm?" Cromwell asked slowly, "as Gloucester was for Henry VI, perhaps?"

"Indeed, until such a time as the King's heir is old enough to be crowned and to take on the governance of the realm."

"And in the, perhaps fifteen or eighteen years until a child of the King reached their majority, these lords would rule England?"

"They would."

Cromwell nodded. "How many guards do they have in their pay to bring this about?"

"I know not, but I know it is to happen in two days, and that means two days to prepare and to bring in your own men, Majesty," he said, turning on the last word towards Anne, "men you can trust. I can offer my own, too. They are entirely loyal to me."

"And they mean to announce this in the council chamber, whilst in session?" she asked.

Fitzroy nodded.

"Then we must be ready for them." She looked at Cromwell. "I need men you can trust, ones that cannot possibly have been bought by Sussex and his allies."

"I will have them ready," he said.

Anne turned to Fitzroy. "I did suspect you," she confessed. "But by this action, should we succeed and prevail, you will have proved yourself a friend to me and my children. If I remain on this throne, you shall ever be close to me, and I will name you both friend, and son."

Fitzroy, quite astonished at himself, felt tears start in his eyes. Genuinely her words touched him. Always he had wanted to be accepted by Katherine of Aragon, and never had it come to pass. Anne had always been kind and welcoming, but this was more than that. He had his own mother, of course, a woman he loved dearly and respected, but a part of him had always wanted to be accepted by the wife of his father, as if by that acceptance there would be something fulfilled he never thought complete, that he would be part of this family he always had felt separate from.

"My loyalty is yours, Majesty," he said, stooping to one knee.

In that moment at least, he meant it.

CHAPTER FIFTEEN

Queen Anne Boleyn
February 1536
Greenwich Palace
London

Nobody moved.

"Arrest her!" Sussex shouted again, a high-pitched screech which resounded loudly from all four walls and yet sounded fulsomely less certain of success than the first time he had shouted it, after brandishing the forged will at Anne in council, after accusing her of usurping the throne.

Seeing no support emerging from the guardsmen about the room, the ones on the door Fitzroy had sworn were all men who were loyal to him, Sussex himself leapt for Anne. Quite what he intended to achieve with this reckless, desperate charge no one ever would know as a fist came up, crashing straight into his nose and thwarting his purpose.

Blinded by sudden tears, swearing like a fishwife, Sussex stumbled backwards as Cromwell, owner of the fist, advanced. "Take my lord the Earl of Sussex into custody, along with Worcester, Westmorland, Lord Sandys and the Earl of Oxford," he barked, then pointed a finger at Richard Rich. "That knave too," he added.

The named men backed away from the table, hands flying to swords as the guards advanced on them. Richard Rich, at the edge of the room, made to race from a side door but a guard stepped in front of him, and Rich fell back. George and Thomas Boleyn drew their swords, flanking the Regent.

Sussex just had time to see Fitzroy motion too to his men to step forth and arrest the conspirators, just had time to gape in amazement at the betrayal of the Duke, before another hand caught Sussex in the face, a palm striking up at his already broken nose. This second strike floored him. As he hit the floor, through a sea of tears he stared up into the face of the Regent herself. Anne stood over him, a tower of rage, yet cold and controlled as a frozen sea.

"You thought to arrest me, to steal this throne from my guardianship, to take my children, even one as yet unborn from me?" she said, her voice all the more deadly because of how very calm it was. "You thought to wrest me from this chair, in which my husband, your late lord and King, and a man you called friend, set me?"

There was a scuffle as Westmorland tried to fight, but the press of guards was too great, and he was overcome. Worcester simply handed over his sword, knowing there was no point in trying to escape. Oxford scowled at Anne, and at Fitzroy. "Traitor!" he shouted.

Fitzroy simply smiled. "I think you are the one who owns that title, my lord Earl," he said smoothly.

Anne looked about at the lords, some struggling, some resigned, their daggers and swords taken from them, their arms behind their backs, held tight by Fitzroy's guards and Cromwell's. Suffolk and Norfolk were gazing about in confusion, their hands on their own swords, clearly baffled by the commotion, although obviously relieved to still be at liberty. "His Grace of Richmond and Somerset came to us a few days ago, and informed us of your plotting, Sussex. You thought he was your man, but he has proved himself a loyal friend to the Crown, and to my children. You, however, have proved you cannot be trusted. Chambers are already prepared for you, in the Tower."

"Take them away!" shouted Fitzroy.

"You'll pay for this, Fitzroy, you bastard son of a whore!" shouted Sussex as they dragged him from the chamber.

"What the Devil goes on here?" Norfolk shouted, banging his fist on the table.

Anne turned to the confused Dukes. "Your Graces of Norfolk and Suffolk, I apologise that I could not inform you ahead of time of this attempted coup, so you had time to prepare yourselves. The truth is, the plotters intended to involve you, uncle, by increasing and then most likely threatening the future power of your son-in-law…" she gestured to Fitzroy "…who they intended to make Regent in my place, for a time at least, and Suffolk, they intended to take you prisoner, knowing you would not accept the false will of the late King, my beloved husband and your friend, for you would know he never signed his name to the document they had produced. The fewer people who knew of the plot, the more chance we had to foil it, but know that I understand you were not involved. His Grace of Richmond informed us of your innocence even as he brought the plot before us."

Norfolk swallowed, his throat dry. "What will you do with them, Majesty?" There was a note of respect in his voice, little enough used when it came to her. Foiling a plot to unseat her was worthy of admiration, she presumed.

"They will be taken to the Tower, and we will try them for high treason." She nodded to her uncle. "You will assume your traditional position of Lord High Steward of England for the trial, uncle, since they will need to be tried by their peers."

"Should I not do so?" asked Fitzroy. "Be the one to try them?"

"We will require you, my lord, to give evidence, and that would mean you would have to question yourself, were you Lord

Steward." She smiled and touched his arm. "But we understand our debt to you, Your Grace. Only too well do I understand that."

"I still think we should have been told, Majesty," Suffolk chimed in.

"Her Majesty, though certain of your loyalty, my lord of Suffolk, was not sure what men of what lords these vile plotters might have got to with their promises and wiles," Cromwell interjected. "As you see, even I lost one of my servants to their machinations. We could not risk it, in case any of your men were compromised. They could have gone to Sussex and revealed that we knew of the plot, then it might have unfolded at a different time, when we were unprepared." *And you are such a dullard you might have unveiled the plot yourself, Suffolk dull-of-brain, to all of court and country,* Cromwell thought, adding a charming smile so the Duke would not see the contempt hiding in his eyes.

Suffolk nodded. "As you say. They intended to imprison me?"

"They knew you would question the validity of the will, being so close to the King he would have told you had he created a new one which could supersede the Act of Succession, Your Grace," Anne told him.

Suffolk nodded slowly. "I was going to ask to read it."

"And had you, and had we known nothing of this plot, you would be on your way to the Tower now, my lord, along with me, had they succeeded. They meant to take Elizabeth and lock me away until my boy was born, then take him from me too."

"An ungodly plan," Cranmer noted in a scathing tone.

"An unchivalrous one too," Suffolk added.

"Majesty…" Her brother's voice. "Your child is unharmed?"

Anne smiled. "He rests easy, I think he did not even wake when I struck Sussex." She massaged her wrist. "Although it hurt me a little."

"It was a fine strike, well deserved," Cromwell said, and Anne noted that as he spoke her brother cast an eye glinting with suspicion over Cromwell. George had been doing that much of late. Long he had harboured thoughts that Cromwell might be moving to work against them, and Cromwell certainly had overstepped his authority a few times with matters George was charged to deal with. But, as she had told George of late, the past was done with, and Cromwell now was their man in full and in truth again. She needed him.

"No man will steal the rights of my grandchild, whilst their lioness of a mother is here to protect them," said her father, pride ringing in his voice like the bells of chapel on a Sunday.

Anne stared at the door. The shouts of the lords could still be heard, wending down the corridors of court. "Indeed, Father, they will not."

CHAPTER SIXTEEN

Archbishop Thomas Cranmer

February 1536

Westminster Abbey

London

Candlelight broke upon the tomb of the King, a gentle illumination. Darkness was spread as a cloak beyond in the abbey, making it appear as if the King's tomb was the only monument left to the world. Soft scuffle of footsteps sounded far away, as monks serving the abbey passed through long corridors of ornately carved stone. Scent of incense billowed, smoke rising as silver snakes from braziers burning softly, dissipating into the shadows. Cranmer gazed up. The effigy of the King was still upon the tomb, a carved likeness in wood which in time would become one of stone, as the Queen had promised. It was being carved with care by masons handpicked from the many talented men of that trade in London, and soon would be ready to place in the abbey.

Cranmer knelt before the tomb, praying. He did not believe in the old ways, that a soul needed to be prayed for in order for it to reach Heaven, that was not how God decided who would enter the Kingdom of eternity, he was sure, but the old King had asked once, should he die before Cranmer, that Cranmer would ensure Masses were sung for the King's soul, that prayers would be spoken, so Cranmer had ordered the Masses he thought unneeded, spoke the prayers the King had wanted.

He did it to honour his King, a man he had called friend, though he was certain the King was already in Heaven, already welcomed there, one of God's people.

As he prayed for the King, he prayed too for Henry's children, for his wife. Those on earth had more need of the gentle kindness of God than the dead ever would. Cranmer had always admired the Queen, her wit and intelligence, her grace in times of pain and hurt, many caused by the King himself, as well as her faith, curious and questioning, and her openness of soul. It was a rare thing to find a frank woman in this world, so many were encouraged never to be themselves, were taught instead to hide much in case of condemnation, but the Queen was always herself, straightforward where she could be, kind where it was deserved, and to her foes she was wrath incarnate, though Cranmer had never seen her make an enemy where it was unwarranted. Even to the Lady Mary, Anne had tried to be kind, though the girl had frequently contested the Queen's position and that of Elizabeth.

Cranmer had faith in the Queen. Anne was the one who would see them through this time of insecurity, and England had done this before, had it not? Henry VI had been a child-king, and it was not until later, when his sanity deserted him as an adult, that troubles amongst the old families had broken out. Richard II, too, had been young when presented with his crown. There had been trouble in his reign too, but only when he grew up, when the intense indulgence of his youth produced an adult unworthy of the throne.

Cranmer had no intention of allowing the mistakes of any past kings to bear upon the children of the Queen, and he knew Anne would not either.

If enough men rallied behind the Queen, England could emerge unscathed from this time, become better than before, stronger, wiser. With a child to become King or Queen, there was potential, if people could see it, for greatness. If the future sovereign was not indulged or pampered, but prepared, so much could be done. A child could be intensely trained from infancy for the role, could be nurtured as no other babe, even a royal heir, ever had been before. They could be taught to uphold the Church, the new Church, to be Defender of the Faith all their lives. Much Henry of England had done for his country as his eyes had come unbound from the lies of Rome, but much too could his children do, and his wife. Queen Anne had the loyalty of Cranmer, and he would see to it the Church stood firm on her side too.

Eventually Cranmer rose to his feet, dusting down his white surplice with his hands. A shawl of wool, simple and black, lay over his shoulders to protect them from the draughts winding their way through the abbey that night.

As he turned, a shadow shifted before him, making him jump a little. "Cromwell," he breathed.

"I did not want to disturb your prayers," the man explained, stepping from the deeper shadow. He need not have bothered, in a way. With his habitual dark robes, his dark colouring, his pale skin, bleached by so much time spent inside, casting eyes over books of figures and facts, Cromwell was a creature born to dwell between the spaces of darkness and light.

Cranmer smiled. "In that you succeeded, old friend, but you disturbed me after. I thought… well, no man, even one as prepared to meet the Almighty as I am, wishes to find a person unknown at his back."

"For that, I am sorry."

"You were waiting for me?"

Cromwell dipped his head in agreement, stepping forwards. "The Queen wishes us to act for Master Tyndale, still under arrest in the Low Countries. The King was recently persuaded to ask the Emperor if Tyndale might be released and sent to England to be tried here, in his native country, for the charges of heresy laid against him. The Queen, who needs no persuading as to the worth of Tyndale returning to England and has no intention of trying the man for anything, wishes us to approach the Emperor on the matter, quietly and with care."

Cranmer breathed in and frowned. "I doubt he will agree, though I am more than willing to try again. Tyndale is a valuable reformer, a great thinker who would be a boon to England."

"The Emperor's cousin, Mary, is in our power. He may agree to negotiate, in return for a promise to release her."

Cranmer smiled. "She is detained for her own protection, as I have many times informed Ambassador Chapuys when he comes running to me to complain."

"Indeed, yet since the Emperor and his ambassador obviously do not believe us, they may be willing to haggle over Tyndale, in order to secure Mary's release."

"Which the Queen intends to carry out anyway, at some stage?" Cranmer asked.

"Whether our Queen intends to or not, we must at some stage release the King's daughter."

"I see. Well, I am more than willing to try, my friend. I did before, at the King's request, but the Emperor thinks I am the Antichrist, so was not particularly open to my overtures."

Cromwell laughed. The idea of Cranmer, this gentle man, so soft spoken, unless in the pulpit, being such a creature was comical, and yet knowing all that the Archbishop had brought about in England, Cromwell supposed by reputation alone it might be easy for strangers to think thus of him.

"I will approach Chapuys." Cranmer said, smoothing his surplice and moving as if to end the conversation.

"There is another matter." Cromwell stopped the Archbishop with his words.

"Oh?" Cranmer tried not to smile. This was just like Cromwell. The man thought he was subtle, and to many he might seem so, but Cranmer had long ago learned to read him. The man would approach with a minor issue he wanted support on, a favour he knew might be easy to secure. Once he had that, Cromwell would slip in another, potentially a riskier favour. Yet often such wiles he would succeed for having gained support in one matter by seeming to be on the same side or holding the same values as the one he was asking boons of, Cromwell was more likely to secure the second too.

He was a clever fox, there was no denying that.

"The Queen wishes to delay the Act to suppress the smaller houses of religion, the first bill of dissolution," Cromwell said. "She thinks the country is not stable enough, that people will object, and she fears that whilst her husband, God rest his soul, could have carried this Act through with the sheer weight of his personality, she will not succeed in the same way."

"I see. And you have come merely to inform me of this?" Cranmer had a way of teasing men, it was a charming part of his personality, this idle playfulness often missing in the higher ranks of the Church where so many took themselves so seriously.

Cromwell smiled. "I think you know why I have come to you with this, Eminence. The Queen respects and loves you. There is no one she trusts more. If you stand with me on this, she will agree too."

Cranmer sighed, turning serious. "If Her Majesty believes to pause would be the correct course of action, we must obey."

"If we pause now, the momentum will be lost. You have seen the reports, Eminence, you know the issues at hand and the scale of the problem. If we pause now, monastic houses in dire need of closure or correction will have time to mend their ways, on the surface at least, but perhaps well enough that they may be known abroad by men of England as good and true, and that would be a false picture painted. My investigations turned up much, my lord Archbishop, much that I think you also understand requires correction."

Cranmer folded his hands before his body. "I agree, many of the houses are in dire need of closure, and as Vicar-General of England it was nothing more than your duty to investigate and report on such matters. I have spoken to many leaders of the larger houses who can absorb monks or nuns evicted from the smaller. There are many eager to take on such people, desiring to reinstruct them that they might become better servants of the Lord." He paused. "I agree there is a need, Cromwell, but…"

"Then aid me in persuading the Queen to go ahead with the reading of the bill and the vote on it." Cromwell cut across the Archbishop before he could protest that the Regent should be obeyed without question on this matter. "I can bring the Act through the Commons and the Lords. I have enough men on my side for that. The people, we can deal with them later, but the truth is that the Crown needs that money, the money from the lesser houses, *now*. There are many threats, domestic and foreign, to this regency. We will have need of the money from those monasteries soon enough."

Cranmer frowned. "The Queen wanted much to go back to the people, to enhance education and to promote the formation and upkeep of better religious houses."

"That can be done in time. The treasury is all but empty, the old King, God rest him, spent much and thought not much about the future. We need that money, my lord Archbishop. What if the Emperor were to launch an invasion on behalf of his cousin, Lady Mary? What if the Scots start peering at England with covetous eyes? We may soon have need of soldiers and defences. For the protection of the Queen and her children, for the safety of England, the Crown must be richer than it is. We have, after all, of late seen how eagerly men close to the Queen, men who once were loyal friends of the King, will work against her. Others will follow. Money is the best protection in the world, old friend. Better even than loyalty, because loyalty can be bought with enough coin."

Cranmer narrowed his eyes. "But in time, the money of the lesser houses will be used to support charitable causes, and further reform of England?"

"We can set plans for that out, of course, and I have no doubt the Queen will push for it in any case, but for now, that money is needed to ensure there *is* an England left that it might support charitable causes."

Cranmer nodded. "I will speak to her."

Cromwell looked relieved, yet there was something else in his eyes Cranmer saw; a twinkle of greed. His friend always had liked money, that he knew. Cromwell had started out as a mercenary and once a thought of money in return for life takes root, it is hard to dig out of a soul. If money can be paid to take life, money becomes more important *than* life, after all. But Cranmer knew there were other passions inside Cromwell, and he hoped, hoped greatly, those virtues would win out over the vices. All men, after all, are subject to sin and some men manage to rise victorious over it. Cromwell had been in many a battle, he could win this one too, if he chose to.

Cromwell went on. "The monks and nuns are to be sent to larger houses, as you say, so there will not be as much outcry as the Queen thinks. We have made provision for most of them, and those whose sins are such they should not continue in any godly position will be sent back to their families."

Cranmer played with a thick band of gold on his right ring finger, his episcopal ring. A sapphire was set in its centre, twinkling in the gloom. "If they have them, old friend. Many people are placed in the Church for the precise reason that their families cannot care for them."

"Which also should be an abhorrent practice set to an end,

think you not? Should people enter the Church because their families cannot support them, or because they have a true vocation? Should the Church not be full of those dedicated to the service of God rather than those merely trying to avoid the hardships of poverty?"

"Of course," said Cranmer. "It does hold, however, that at present this is not true, and therefore some not welcomed at home may become as vagabonds."

"Perhaps that is God's wish for those who did not respect the teachings and laws of the calling in which they served."

"I believe God to be a kinder ruler than to think thus of Him," said Cranmer, "but this is not the time for intense theological discussion, and I do agree with you in many ways. I will speak to the Queen."

"Thank you, my friend." Cromwell looked to the tomb. "Poor Harry," he said, his eyes fixed on the King's effigy. "To think he never got to see his son, for whom so much was done."

"We all will meet again, one day," said Cranmer.

CHAPTER SEVENTEEN

Sir Henry Norris
February 1536
Whitehall Palace
London

"You must cheer yourself, Majesty, the King would not want to see you thus."

Norris was walking beside Anne, their steps echoing in the long gallery of the royal apartments, apartments she and the King had designed. Long enough had the court spent at Greenwich. It had been time to move on, so Greenwich could be cleansed with vinegar and wine, the floors scrubbed, jakes emptied, the halls purified with smoke of incense. Anne had ordered they move to Whitehall, perhaps because of the memories it held for her.

When this was York Place, the Cardinal's great residence, it had not been as it was now, this sumptuous, sprawling mass of a palace. Anne and the King had worked hard on it, the palace, the design, the fittings and architecture had been a passion shared, an outward expression of their love for one another. The King was gone, yet echoes of him, of him and Anne and all they had meant to each other, done for one another, remained. Sometimes, when he woke in the night bathed in sweat after dreams of fear came, portents of future disaster, Norris could swear he still could hear the King breathing beside him. Many nights he had been his master's bedfellow, there to protect him, to keep the King warm. Now when he woke, it was as if the King was there still, a ghost at his side. Sometimes he felt as if he could hear the slightest note of reproach on the breath of his ghostly master, as if the King had known, or now in death knew for certain, how Norris felt about Anne Boleyn.

Despite any ghostly recriminations, Norris would not have been anywhere else that morn but with Anne. Even the melancholy of his Queen could not deter him from seeking her company. To be beside Anne was his favourite place to be, it had been since long before this present moment where she needed him so much more than before. The King had remarked on it once, spoken of his servant's habit of drifting to Anne. Once Henry had noted aloud before others that if Norris was not serving him then always he was to be found in the chambers of the Queen.

In truth, that observation had frightened Norris. He had always thought that in life at least his master had not noticed that Norris harboured affection for his wife, and despite all who had claimed Anne's influence over the King had waned, it never truly had. The King had loved no woman besides her. All others were distractions, passing fancies there to massage his self-image or insecurity, his heart never offered to one of them, even if his body freely was. And the King had not been a man to share the heart of his wife with any man, even his best friend, even in friendship, even though Norris had never had the slightest intention of doing anything about his feelings for her.

His emotions were his secret, and he was determined they would remain that way. Anne needed a friend now, not some knave using her time of grief to offer himself to her.

The King had often treated Anne as if she was a possession,

as if she should exist only to serve him. Norris did not think the same. Officially, Norris had been the King's best friend and most trusted servant. Unofficially, he was rather glad his demanding, crude and increasingly cruel master had died before fully noticing Norris's secret, and whilst she mourned the King now, perhaps it was better for Anne too that he was gone.

Norris wanted what was best for Anne. Painfully, hopelessly, that was all he wanted, her happiness.

No matter if the situation was impossible. No matter if she had never looked at him in such a way, Norris was in love with Queen Anne Boleyn. It had been that way for years, since first he met her, and had never changed. *No*, he thought, it *had* changed. It had grown deeper, more hopeless, increasingly doomed, and oddly, the more he knew it to be doomed the more he had affection for his ridiculous love.

Yet was it so ridiculous now? The King was gone, most recently gone it was true, so this was indeed no time to offer his heart to the woman he loved, such would be crass, and Norris was a gentleman, perhaps one of the few still left in the world. The Queen was waiting to bear the child of the lost King, so it was hardly the time in that respect either, but was it so impossible to think that she might, one day, be free to wed again? The council might not want her to, of course. If Anne took a husband, there might well be confusion over what part he would play in England. Would he be a mere consort to the Dowager, or partner to the Regent? Would he have power merely as her husband, or as a king? Would it be suspected Norris was making a play for the throne if he dared tell Anne how he felt, and what would she think? Would Anne believe he was honest or suspect he was using her to gain power? It was a situation unprecedented, and he had no wish to make trouble for the woman he loved. The opposite was true, he wanted to make life easier for her.

But it had occurred to him that perhaps he was of low enough rank to be considered not a problem in this fragile game of such massive stakes being played out at court, and in England. The council might think he had no designs on the throne, which was the truth, and consider him less a danger because he was not a rich, powerful man. All Norris wanted was to sweep up the woman he loved in his arms and keep her safe. That was something he could not do now, but in the future, perhaps there was hope.

There was also another sticky matter in the way, as he was engaged to Mary Shelton, Anne's cousin. He had been putting off the match for some time and had not really known why he was doing so for the lady was fair and sweet, with a good mind, fair dimples and pretty chestnut hair. True, she had been the mistress of the King, Norris was well aware of that, but he was also aware Mary had taken on the role because Anne had asked her to. Worried by the rise of Mary Perrot, another former mistress of the King who supported Katherine and Mary, Anne had asked her Shelton cousin to infiltrate the King's bed, oust the Parrot, as some had called Mary Perrot, and speak well of Anne. It had been a dark time for Anne, Norris knew, a time after losing a child during which she had worried that another woman might supplant her. Mary Shelton had agreed to become mistress to the King so that Anne had someone speaking for her within the King's bed. Norris judged this action commendable, honourable even. There were in truth many reasons to push ahead with marriage, but something had always stopped him.

Now he was sure it had been fate, holding him back. Had he married and bedded Mary, Anne would have become as his own kinswoman by law and anything between them would have become incest, and whilst cousins had married and no doubt would again, it required dispensation. At the moment he was still free, if he could put off marriage with Mary, to offer his heart one day to the woman who already held that heart in her hands.

"The only thing that cheers me, Norris, is when I am with my daughter," Anne said as they walked, not noting his racing thoughts. She had enough of her own to contend with. "With Elizabeth, I am sated, but at all other times I am afraid, ill at ease. I hear rumours of unrest, people talking of revolt in favour of Mary. The council are biting at me all the time, and half of them are now in the Tower awaiting trial. I am surrounded by enemies, my friend, and I have just lost the man I loved, dearly, for so many years that it feels as if I never knew a time when I was not with him. Seven years trying to be wed as man and wife, Norris, then less than three married and he is gone. What could we have done with all that time that Katherine and her daughter and the Pope wasted?"

She set a hand on her belly, she was doing that a lot these days, he noticed, and he noticed everything about Anne. It was as if she was trying not only to protect the child inside her from the events of the times, but from what they might hear. Sometimes her cupping hand looked as if it was trying to cover the ears of a very small head.

If only it were possible, thought Norris, *to so shield children from the world*, that we could stop them hearing words said against them, that we could make it so the world was always as sweet a place as the womb of a mother, so they were surrounded by nothing but love, by the protection of another person so complete that it became flesh about their flesh.

"I hear tales that on the night before Katherine was buried, there was a bright light seen about the church where her body lay," Anne went on. "People gathered, though they were not permitted to enter. They say the church was lit up as if the sun itself was caught within the stones of the walls. They are calling it a miracle, the common people, a sign Katherine was blessed by Christ." She breathed in and let it out slowly. "And at the same time, I am told that before the King was buried, a dog was seen at his coffin, licking up blood that had spilt from inside the coffin itself. What are we to make of these portents, Norris? For I tell you, the country makes much of them, declaring Katherine was godly, perhaps even a saint, and the King was as Ahab of the Bible, the tyrant foretold whose blood the dogs would feed upon. And what does that make me? Many speak against me. My men, preachers sent out by Latimer and Cranmer, they hear it in the streets. We arrest those who speak out, but how can one silence thoughts which spread as whispers through the country?"

He crossed his arms behind his back. "The country will settle, and there are many who support you and your children, Majesty. You have more supporters than you think, and your bishops are firm behind you. Their men go out preaching every day in your name, and that of the true heirs to the throne."

Anne smiled – she was proud of her bishops and made small attempt to hide it. They were *her* men, it was true, nurtured and protected by her, in some cases by Cromwell too, they had risen in the Church of England because she wanted men like them there, reformers and free thinkers. They were radical, no doubt about it, and to varying degrees which sometimes caused heated arguments betwixt them, but they were united in one thing: their Queen. Anne possessed their loyalty, a loyalty strong and devoted, such as few people would ever know in life. Latimer in particular was a man who breathed fire when he preached, and he was inspiring many to her cause. Cranmer too was a great orator, talented with his words and true in his heart. They were a comfort indeed.

She put her hand on his arm. "You are right, I should not give way to my fears." Anne smiled, but Norris moved away, just a little, so her hand fell from his arm. Anne's eyes widened and he thought he caught a light of dismay in them.

But perhaps he saw what he wanted to see.

"Majesty, I would not have those with tongues of evil say

anything untrue of you," Norris explained, glancing about. "Such a gesture, even between friends, might well be misconstrued."

She swallowed and briefly, almost imperceptibly, shook her head. "Evil times indeed," she agreed. "And evil times breed evil tongues. You are right, my friend. My behaviour must be beyond reproach or question now and always, until my daughter or my son are safe on their thrones, perhaps beyond. I can no more play like a child or merely think of the lighter side of court as once I revelled in. It is my place to be Queen now, but also King."

There was a haunted look in her eyes as she thanked him for his care for her reputation. It was times like this, when he thought she wanted to say more and did not, which troubled Norris the most. For he was sure in such times that she felt the same as he did, that her heart reached out for his and that was why he could feel a bond between them, because somewhere her soul had found his, a fragment of it, and had wrapped about it, tight, so it would never be lost for she held it.

And he was just as afraid that he was imagining all this, and should he one day muster the courage to tell Anne how he felt, he would see nothing but amazement in her eyes, formed because never had she thought of him in such a way, and never would she.

CHAPTER EIGHTEEN

Lady Mary Tudor

11th of March 1536

Shrove Tuesday

The Tower of London

"My lady, you must not despair."

"I am far from despair, Lord Ambassador. If there were a word to describe my feelings, I think incandescent fury would come closest to the myriad of emotions fighting within me."

The King's eldest daughter was pacing the chamber. Rushes and herbs under her feet were releasing a sweet smell of rosemary, meadowsweet and lavender as her heels pounded leaves and stems dried and bound in bundle and mat, over and over. Chapuys observed her nervous energy. Though she said she was furious, he knew Mary was scared.

Mary had been unable to sit still for days. She was supposed to, she knew, Lent was almost upon them and Lent was a time for prayer and reflection and yet, imprisoned, she was consumed by relentless restlessness, so much that she knew not what to do with it. Fervent prayer could only take up some of her energy, fasting could only slake a little. Shrove Tuesday was in truth a traditional time for the people to run a little wild before

Lent, and wild was how she felt.

"I wonder how many will experience any happiness today," Mary said as she paced, giving voice to her thoughts. "This day is usually a time for celebration, games, feasts. I suspect this year I am not the only one spending it in contemplation, or agitation."

That was true enough, Chapuys thought. In England, Shrove Tuesday was a day many took to the streets. Revels were held, brothels sometimes were attacked, although plenty of men probably lingered after invading them, to *comfort* the women there. Football had been often played on that day between villages, although the King had grown to dislike the game and had banned it in favour of archery. Plenty of men did end up injured in the traditional fight that took place after the match. It never was announced, the fight, and Chapuys did not understand why it always happened, but always it did occur. For some years he had thought it part of the game itself, until it was explained to him a football match did not, in fact, end that way.

Shrove Tuesday boasted other diversions. Children would be out playing games of tipcat and stoolball in the streets, and cockfights would be taking place everywhere, perhaps the odd pancake race or two as well. It was usually a day of high merriment before the long season of introspection and meditation that was Lent began. But Mary was right, there were not so many feeling merry this year.

"Can you not go outside, my lady?"

Mary shook her head. "They have forbidden me, Lord Ambassador."

Although she had been taken out into the privy gardens of the royal apartments in the first days of her captivity by Lady Kingston, the Constable's wife, so she might walk and exercise, this had ceased abruptly when it had been rumoured that common people of London were planning to find a way to get to Mary to aid her to escape. That was what she had been told, in any case, when she asked to walk out one day and found the activity not available to her anymore. Quite how this rescue was to come to pass, Mary had no idea. Did people of London mean to scale the high, strong walls of the Tower? Fight the numerous well-armed guards who patrolled on top of those walls, and avoid being shot or stabbed with a spear? Did they mean to storm the gates? They first would have to navigate the great moat about the walls or find a way to pluck her from the gardens and fly her to the river by magic.

A slightly more reasonable notion was that plenty of people lived and worked in the Tower of London, and perhaps those who meant to speed her from her doleful prison intended to find their way into the Tower en masse, but with care, concealed amongst those who worked here, eventually overthrowing the garrison and springing her from her comfortable prison and away to safety.

In all honesty, when the command had come that she was to cease to use the gardens for exercise, she had thought of the princes in the Tower again. One of the last places they had been seen was the gardens of the Tower. Was the same thing to happen to her, she would be here one day and simply gone the next? Would she become a mystery which people throughout time would seek to unravel?

Whose would be the mind behind the hand that came to throttle her in the dark? Whose intentions would tip the palm of the one who held the poison? If history came to think on her sudden disappearance, she hoped they would know there was only one true suspect: the Boleyn whore.

Mary would not stoop to name her Queen nor yet Queen Regent as she now called herself, and now that she knew the tale of her father's sudden death, Mary wondered if he had not only been bewitched by this woman but had been murdered by her. Mary certainly believed Anne Boleyn was a witch, there was no other way a woman of such paltry charms, such gaudy, insubstantial character could have lured her father away from a good, pious and wise woman such as Queen Katherine, daughter of Castile and Aragon, without some influence of dark magic and witchcraft. To so bemuse him so that he not only left his lawful wife and beloved daughter behind at the whim of this woman but had left the Church, had started to plan to dissolve smaller monasteries, had turned his back on God.

Mary had heard that plans on that front had stalled somewhat, since her father's death. Some said Anne Boleyn herself was against the wholesale closure of all smaller monasteries, but Mary could not believe so wild a lie. Cromwell was responsible for much of it, Cranmer too, but the idea had been Anne's, she was sure of it. Her father had been a devoted son, a valiant knight of the true Church until the Boleyn harridan had started poisoning his mind with her heretical books and ideas.

Perhaps this had always been her ultimate aim, Mary thought, to rise to become Queen of this nation, to birth an heir then kill the King and have herself named Regent. Perhaps Anne Boleyn had planned this from the very beginning. After all, the one secret of power is that one can never have too much, so perhaps the King had been simply getting in her way, slowing her plans. Would Elizabeth even make it to the throne with this witch in power or would Anne sit on the throne until the day she died? Perhaps she would stoop even so low as to murder her own child if that child stood in her way, if that child thought to take her crown.

On, on Mary's imaginings ran, that if Anne Boleyn could murder not only her husband and perhaps even her daughter to remain in power then what was she to do with Mary, a girl she never had liked? What would the witch do to someone who had a true claim to the English throne? Mary had many thoughts and none of them had a happy ending. For her, at least.

From her window she had seen men of the council marched into the Tower confines some days before, Oxford, Westmorland, Lord Sandys, Sussex, all friends of her father. There had been more, but their faces she had not caught in the commotion surrounding them, the guards marching before and after. Into the towers they had gone, separated, the earls to the Beauchamp Tower, the others to the Martin and Bell Towers, or so Mary thought. She had lost sight of them after a time. People said they had tried to overthrow the Regent, but Mary suspected this was not true, or was only a partial truth. Anne Boleyn was ridding the country of people who would oppose her, that was the truth. Those men were here for the same reason Mary was; they posed a threat to Anne's power.

"The people cry out for your release, Your Highness. You will not be here long." Chapuys stood, his normal calm and control clearly ruffled, and that scared her more.

"I suspect, Lord Ambassador, I may well be here eternally, as bones buried in the chapel, if something is not done for me soon. What can the Emperor do? You must write to him again, tell him how I am treated here and what danger I am in. My royal cousin must put pressure on the witch to make her see she cannot act like this, against me or others, with impunity. There are laws and rules to this world, and she is bound to them as any of us are! What of my mother's friends here in England and about the world? Someone must put pressure on the council to release me or I fear, my lord, I fear that soon either I shall find myself on trial for treason imagined by the woman who now calls herself Regent of this country, or I shall simply vanish, and the world will forget my name."

"No one will forget you, Highness."

Mary laughed, but there was no mirth in it. She waved a hand airily above her head. "Oh, you are right, perhaps they will say of me there was once another daughter of the Tudor line, but we have forgot her name... Margaret, was it? Oh, but it was a great mystery, her vanishing, and then they will go on with their day and that will be all that is said until the next time someone remembers I disappeared." Mary scowled at her friend, her active hand dropping from the air to clench as a fist at her side. "My lord, my friend, please hear me. I am not destined to become some footnote of history that people wonder over. My father was Henry VIII, King of England and my mother Queen Katherine, daughter of Isabella of Castile and Ferdinand of Aragon, the most Catholic Monarchs. I will not slide into the darkness of obscurity without a fight, my lord. You must find people to bear upon this false Regent. You must find a way to free me."

Chapuys stared at her for a moment, and she saw tears in his eyes. "You fear for me so greatly you would weep now, here?" she asked.

Chapuys shook his head. "You are so like your mother, and your father," he murmured. "Your mother's courage was quieter, but she knew when she had to speak loudly, and your father was a lion sadly never tested truly in war. In you I saw both of them just now, the best of both of them." He drew himself up, pushing his shoulders back. "My lady, I have written to my master, I did so the very moment I heard your father was dead and you had been arrested, to appraise him of the situation, and he has sent word to court demanding your release. At the moment, there has been no answer I can send to my master except the same lie I am told over and over by the Regent and her men, that you have been taken into custody for your own protection, in case the people think to rise and set you at the head of a rebellion, using you against your will."

"Pah!" Mary exhaled as she hissed. "It would not be against my will; I am the one true heir to England's throne."

"Take care and do not say such even as a whisper in my ear," warned Chapuys through gritted teeth as he glanced nervously at the door. "It may only take one lie dreamed up by your enemies to send you to trial and to the block, my lady, but one truth spoken by you will achieve the same destiny. Speak that sentiment aloud and the Queen has means and just cause, according to the laws of England, to arrest you in truth for treason."

"I say it to no other but you."

"And me you can trust, but not all who listen in. The walls of the Tower have ears, my lady. Take care. As most of England loves you so some untrue souls love the Queen and her daughter just as much. Reformers and heretics are all over England now, many more have flocked here since the religious changes, for they want the kind of country the King was trying to build, one lost to sin and divided from the true Church."

She marched to him, taking his hands. "That is why you must get me released from here, not only for me but for England. I can save this land, Chapuys, you know I can. I can return us to Rome, to the true faith. I can pull England out of this pit of heresy we have fallen into."

"I am doing all I can, Highness, and I have plans. I can say little about them, but be ready, always, to leave if you are given the word."

"And what would the word be?"

Chapuys smiled. "Pomegranate."

Mary almost wept. Her mother's sigel had been a pomegranate. "Granada," she whispered. "It would not be said accidently in conversation," she noted.

"And it shall not be said by accident, but with intent," said her friend.

CHAPTER NINETEEN

Lady Margaret Douglas

12th of March 1536

Ash Wednesday

Whitehall Palace

London

There was a soft sound of feet on the floor of the chamber, which told her he was close. "We cannot meet, Thomas, not here, it is too risky," Margaret Douglas whispered as from behind her an arm slipped about her waist. There was no conviction in her tone, and Thomas Howard knew it, so he pulled his secret wife to him, making her giggle softly.

She felt naughty for it. Today was Ash Wednesday, first day of Lent. A solemn, more solemn than ever before, start to Lent this year had been, marked by a long ceremony in the chapel at Whitehall, Cranmer talking with gravity and care about the King, about this Lent being a time to reflect on the past more than ever, but also to plan for the future and all they wanted to achieve. Margaret knew she should be solemn that day, her forehead still marked with the cross of ashes Cranmer himself had drawn on her. "Remember that thou art dust," he had said, "and to dust thou shalt return."

Cranmer had not wanted to go ahead with the traditional ceremonies, Margaret knew, but Queen Anne had told him he must, for the sake of the country, one last Lent done in the old manner and they would talk of changes to come in the future.

But with Thomas, her Thomas, Margaret often forgot the troubles of the world. When he was with her, there seemed trouble no more, but only light and laughter and hope.

Margaret turned in his arms, touched the side of his handsome face, her finger tracing the line of his jaw, a light caress which made his bones, and other parts of him, quiver. The half-brother of another Thomas Howard, the Duke of Norfolk, Margaret's Thomas was younger than old, brittle Norfolk, more handsome, more charming, he wrote her poetry and sang her songs. They could dance together before court sometimes, but only a little, only as much as they dared so none discovered their secret. She wondered now if it was such a risk. Queen Anne Boleyn, whom Margaret had served for several years as a lady-in-waiting, had always seemed as if she knew the couple secretly had feelings for one another, and had seemed to approve their match. Anne had hinted that with time the King could be made to agree, then Margaret and Thomas might wed. No one knew they had already done so, almost two years ago in a secret ceremony. None knew they had already consummated the match many times.

None knew she carried a child in her belly.

That was now the main worry she had about confessing her relationship to the Queen. The King, Margaret's uncle, would not have approved of a younger Howard becoming Margaret's husband, and King Henry would have been furious, had he lived, to find out she had secretly married, had failed to ask his permission, had chosen her own husband, one lower born than she, instead of marrying where she was told. He might have locked the couple away, separately of course, or even taken the head of her husband.

But now there was another life to think about, besides those of herself and Thomas.

Margaret was in the line of succession, as the daughter of Margaret Tudor and Archibald Douglas, she was of the Tudor line, as would her child be. Though not as close, obviously, to the throne as the child the Queen carried or as Elizabeth was, Margaret and her child still bore a claim and what if the Queen should have another miscarriage or birth another girl and what if then Margaret should bear a son? If that happened the Queen Regent might well not look with favour on this match already made between Margaret and Lord Thomas Howard, even though Thomas was another of the Regent's uncles. Anne Boleyn might in fact come to view Margaret and her child as a direct threat to her own children, and although Margaret believed Anne had affection for her, she also knew well that nothing on earth meant more to the Queen than her children.

This was a dangerous time, and Margaret was in a position most perilous. Relying on the friendship of the Queen was not something she felt entirely secure in doing, but what else to do and who else to tell? She knew not.

Thomas kissed her lips, such a light and sweet caress. He was always thus with her, gentle, kind, caring. It had been why she had fallen for him. So many men at court were full of bluster, pretended to be kind to maids and then were cruel when they got what they wanted. It was not so with Thomas, gently and passionately he loved her, and he was a fine man, a good rider in the jousts, a talented swordsman. The two sides of his character, that he could be strong when needed, gentle when he wanted, appealed equally to her, they always had. "The time will come when we can announce our union," he said, "and we must do so soon, must we not? The King is gone, and you have always said the Queen loved you well and was understanding of your love for me."

"But I fear, with so much at stake with her own belly, she will not look kindly on mine." Margaret glanced about, standing back from her love just a little. Her gaze was caught by the decorations of bulls, lions, greyhounds and roses carved on the ceiling, surrounded by globes painted gilt. These chambers, how well she knew them. Whitehall always felt like coming home, though it had altered much over the years.

For two years this had been one of her houses. When her father had sent her to England as he struggled with James V of Scotland, she had been brought here, as well as other houses owned by her godfather, Cardinal Wolsey. She had joined his household for protection. The King had, at that time, trusted Wolsey like no other man, and Margaret had been fond of him too. The Cardinal had a taste for the finer things in life, it was true, and many were his flaws as a man and as a servant of the Church, but in truth she had thought him clever and to her he had been kind. Moderate he had been in terms of religious fervour; fewer men had burned for heresy in his reign as Chancellor than during others. Sometimes, when she was here at Whitehall, once York Place, she could still hear his laughter, still see the red robes of his office vanishing about a doorway or fluttering at the edge of a corridor. Quick on his feet Wolsey had been, for a large man. Sometimes she could see those eyes, twinkling with a merry jape as often he had ready for her. Sometimes she missed Wolsey. He had been as close to her as any member of her family, perhaps closer, more a grandfather than godfather.

After Wolsey's fall and death, she had entered the household of the then Princess Mary, her cousin, and three years ago she had come to the household of Queen Anne, a woman she had been prepared to dislike for the sake of her cousin Mary, and for the sake of Wolsey since Anne had all but brought about his fall, but to her surprise she had come to like and respect the Queen.

And then she had met Anne's uncle, had fallen in love.

"We must tell someone, at some point," he said. "How long can you hide our child?"

"I am but two months gone, the child not even quickened yet," she said. "We have time to consider, but you are right, we have to tell someone, at some point."

"Do you still think the Queen the best person? You seem more unsure than before."

"Who else can we tell? Your brother Norfolk would never be an ally to us. I am in the line of succession. Our child might well be seen as a threat to a child of the Queen, but certainly it will be a threat to any child of Mary and Richmond, and people whisper that Norfolk is hoping the Queen will bear another girl so his son-in-law might be raised up to supplant Elizabeth. But if I, the King's niece, his *legitimate* niece, bear a boy child, we might jeopardise Richmond's future, and that of his children with Mary."

"Richmond has proved he is loyal to the Queen, and Norfolk stood with him, so I hear. Also, my love, there are no children of Mary and Richmond for still they have not lain together as man and wife. The Regent has said the King instructed this was not to happen until Richmond was eighteen, so he would not become overtaxed by the strains of the marriage bed. I have heard it said the King feared this was what had happened to his brother, Arthur, so wanted his son to hold off, until he was older and stronger."

"I admit that is true, perhaps the talk about Norfolk is but gossip, yet all the same, I worry." She chewed her lip. "I just hope the Queen does not see me as a threat. I think I can say to her I have no ambition, besides to be with you."

"So, you do wish to tell her first?"

"I think so, but still I fear what she will think of me."

"The Queen loves you."

She nodded. "I think that to be true, and I just hope she does not believe, when we tell her, that I designed this."

Thomas smiled in a wry, crooked fashion. "You would have picked a husband higher than me, surely, my lady wife, were you making a play for the throne."

She laughed a little, reaching out for his cheek again. "Thomas," she whispered. "There is no one higher than you in my heart."

"None may rival you in mine either." He stole her hand to kiss the palm. She shivered with pleasure, remembering many times when he had kissed every part of her skin, held her close, the sweat of their bodies mingling as perfume in the air. That was how this baby had been created, in love, in their joining within her as one.

There was a noise at the end of the corridor – a gang of young men, always roving the halls of court, were on their way. "I will away," he said, seeing her face turn pale at the thought of being caught. "But soon, we will be together, and all men will know I am yours and you mine." He touched her belly. "We will care for this child together, Margaret, all our days, together."

"Together," she swore as he kissed her palm anew then vanished through the second door of the chamber, just as the Queen strode in through the first, the noise of her arrival having been masked by the young men out in the hallway. Beside her were Margaret Lee, Wyatt's sister, and Nan Cobham. Both smiled at Margaret as they entered. Margaret's breath stole from her chest to think how close she had come to being caught.

"Margaret," Anne said with obvious affection. "I was looking for you."

Margaret swooped to a graceful curtsey; skirts of pale blue slashed with crimson fanning out under her. Soon she would have to panel her dresses, she thought, start wearing her gowns looser little by little. It would be better to start now, so it was not so suspect later. "Majesty," she said. "What can I do to serve?"

Anne looked pale and there were dark circles under her eyes. She had not slept well since the King died. Margaret had been worried for the Queen. Anne was a creature made for joy, and she had been full of sorrow of late, about the King's death to be sure, but before that too, as he dallied with others and treated her ill. It had pained Margaret to see it, and whilst she had always been a favourite of the King's, she had often not loved him as it was perhaps her duty to do. Too cruel and mean was he to the people she truly loved, too harsh and changeable to fully trust. But Anne, Anne was a different matter.

Margaret was not lying to anyone, least of all herself, when she said she loved her. Without reason, without any need to do so, the Queen had welcomed Margaret and tried to make her feel at home. The Queen had always been good to her, and whilst Margaret had many reasons to dislike her for the sake of Mary and Katherine whom Margaret respected and had been close to, she did not. That was another reason she paused, besides fear of the Queen, about revealing her secret. For love of the Queen and the thought that she might hurt Anne when Anne had been hurt enough, Margaret shied away from telling her of her marriage, of her child.

"I was looking for someone to sit with me and sew perhaps, or cards?" The Queen smiled. "I am a little restless, anxious, since the King left us, since all this fell upon me. I would have someone calm my nerves."

"Of course, Majesty."

Margaret brought out cards, better for nerves to play than try to sew, she thought. They would not bet, of course, it being Lent, but they could play. Common people were not allowed, but the higher nobility, anyone with an income over £100 per year, were permitted. Queen Anne sometimes did not approve of such things, she liked her ladies to be beyond reproach, and sewing or embroidery, accompanied by a woman reading from the Bible might be something she would have supported at other times, thinking it more pious, but that day Anne looked relieved. The trouble with embroidery was, with the fingers occupied the mind had the space to race on, ignore even biblical verse being read and instead concentrate on horrors born of the imagination. Cards consumed the mind, and that was what the Queen needed then.

As Margaret dealt on a small table near the window, she looked on the slight lines about the eyes of the Queen and in them could read the fears assailing her mistress. Of course she could read them well, they were mirrors of her own fears.

CHAPTER TWENTY

Magpye Grey

March 1536

Lent

Southwark

London

The people in the square were agitated, Magpye thought. They jostled, murmured in a restless fashion. Her mother looked nervous too, her hand wrapped about that of Magpye was clammy, and she kept her daughter close but she did not move away from the square. There were many people gathered there, their feet making a noise like distant thunder on the cobblestones. Magpye and her ma, Joan, were in the good part of town, near the market. A preacher was speaking.

"The one, true Queen, Elizabeth of the house of Tudor, daughter to his Majesty King Henry VIII now sadly gone of our lives…"

The man preaching was standing on a barrel so more could see him as he droned on about the ancient bloodline of the Tudors, the rights of the Lady Elizabeth, Princess of the realm, and those of the child still carried in the womb of the Queen Regent. Magpye couldn't see the man, she was too short, so she could hear him only and even that was dim. There were too many people muttering around her. All she could see was her mother, at her side, hanging on to Magpye's hand with a death grip, a basket hooked on her other arm. All else Magpye could see were backs and bums, coats and gowns. She was too little, she mourned. If Pa were here, he would have set her on his shoulders so she could see. Ma did not do things like that; it wasn't seemly for women. Magpye liked Ma's hand in hers, though. Ma's hands were delicate and soft despite all the work she did. Every night she bathed them in a mixture of grease and herbs she made herself, and it healed any cuts and kept her skin soft. It also made her smell like burdock, dog rose petals and chamomile, which she and Ma gathered from the waysides and fields outside Southwark each year, just to make the balm.

The press of people was a little unnerving, that was another reason she liked Ma's hand, it felt safe. The smell too, of so many people, was off-putting. Ma's herbal perfume could not compete with the stench of sweat and ale, the scent of baked fish pies, since it was Lent, wafting in the air, being sold out of baskets by wandering maids. The far-off pong of the busy river, too, intruded. Here and there came a whiff of spices from a stall not far away, selling cinnamon and nutmeg, black pepper and mace. But that sweet smell could not compete with the odorous perfume of the bodies near her. It was winter still; many people had not bathed since autumn, just washed their hands and faces each day. It was considered dangerous to open the pores in the winter months when so many wandering spirits of sickness were abroad, just waiting to do ill. Magpye could often smell people a little when she was close to them, but here, in the middle of the crowd, the scent was intense. She could smell bodies and crevices and cooking, garlic, onions and herbs, old bread and bad teeth. Ma insisted they not only wash faces and hands but change their linen undergarments every day, and use the herbal balm on their skin, but clearly others were not as fastidious as her ma.

Ma's basket was empty. They had not even got to the stalls Ma wanted to visit to gather a few ingredients for the inn's food that night. In Lent, whilst the inn did not have to close it did have to observe certain customs, and although the King's laws had been altering over the years as reform had taken hold, the King had continued to support the practice of not eating meat in Lent. Some said it was less to do with faith and more to do with finance, for England's fishmongers and fishermen were some of the best in the world and encouraging the trade was good for England. Serving fish stew night after night could become tiresome, however, so Ma liked to have many herbs and spices so she could make each new pot different from the last, for a little variety. Some herbs she grew herself, marjoram did well in their garden, but it was not quite up yet. Magpye would pick wild garlic from the woodland not far away, which was just starting to emerge now, and they had dried herbs from the year before. Spices like mace, cinnamon and nutmeg, though, they could not grow. They grew in hot places far away and had to be bought. Those, if they were a good price, and some honey to make a sweet fish stew for the night, was what Ma was looking for.

They had come along the river, for Ma liked to see the boats. There were always many on the Thames; merchant vessels carrying silk or pottery, copper, lumber or fruits, and smaller boats which shipped people from one side of the river to the other. It was quicker to use the river than to try to navigate London Bridge, which, with all its shops piled on top of one another and all the people visiting those shops, was a slow way to cross from Southwark to the rest of London. Pa said there were more than a hundred shops on London Bridge, a mighty number Magpye could barely comprehend. London Bridge was too crowded and noisy, but Magpye liked the river. Sometimes when they walked out on the streets which all sloped towards the river, Ma would point to a sail and tell Magpye where that ship had come from or was going to. She knew by the colours of the sail, or the pictures painted on them.

A cutpurse, much the size of Magpye, came past and took a peek in her ma's basket, then winked at Magpye when he saw her watching him. She stuck her chin out sharply at him, flashed her eyes to say he was to go away, or she would tell he was there, and he vanished into the crowd, brown eyes shining with amusement. He gave her a wide grin before he slipped into the mass of people. She felt a little sad for a moment that he had gone. He had a nice smile, even if he was missing some teeth. His new ones were probably yet to grow. He was about the same age as her, seven.

There were many like him about London. People called them the undeserving poor for they did not seek work. The deserving poor, those who were too aged or ill or had been disabled by losing a limb in times of war were registered by the Justices of the Peace and provided for by the local parish through a weekly tax. The monasteries helped people too, but there was never enough to give relief to all people in need and many people believed the vast majority of the poor were undeserving, were lazy and were poor simply because they did not want to work. Vagabonds and beggars could be whipped or have their ears burnt with a hot poker if caught, but some begged all the same, as some stole and some pretended to have licences to beg. True beggars had their licence from the Justices and were permitted to ask passers-by for a coin or some bread. Ma said many people whom others called the undeserving poor could not work either, for they could not find work or were too small or weak or old or had lost a limb or an eye yet had not been registered or not believed about their conditions. She said people ought to be kinder to the poor, for it was not as if anyone wanted to be without money or a safe place to live. Some people just ended up in hard times and could not find their way out. The cutpurse was most likely an orphan. Pa sometimes said there were as many orphans running loose in the city as there were stray dogs.

But it was a good thing the cutpurse had gone. Her ma had a small pouch of coins hung at her girdle, and Magpye didn't want her losing them to the sharp knife of a thief.

"Who is he?" One man nudged another near her in the crowd, indicting to the preacher who now was speaking of the child in the Queen's belly, calling the unborn son, as he declared it was, a second Josiah. Magpye remembered Josiah from Church and from her pa telling her stories of the Bible. Josiah had been a child-king, come to his throne after his father Amon died, assassinated. Josiah had brought about great reform, taking his country of Judah away from worship of pagan deities so his people only worshipped the one true God.

"One of Latimer's," replied a pox-scarred man near her, folding his arms and squinting against the sun. It was overcast, yet still the day seemed too bright.

The other man shuffled in beside him, approval riding his features as he craned his neck to see better. "I like Latimer, a good speaker."

"And a good troublemaker. He had Bristol up in riots before he came here to serve Cromwell and the Queen, my cousin told me of it."

"The King liked him; that's enough for me."

"Tell us of the Lady Mary!" someone on the other side of the crowd shouted, interrupting the preacher just as he started to get a good, strong rhythm to his speech going. "Where is she?"

"Yes!" screamed a woman, possibly a little drunk. She wasn't wearing an apron and Magpye knew that meant she was probably a woman who sold her body. Magpye looked at her own apron, at Ma's. They were a faded blue, marking them as good, honest women. The woman might be one of the Winchester Geese, prostitutes who worked in stewhouses about Southwark and were licensed and taxed by the Bishop of Winchester, who held great power in Southwark. "Where is our Lady Mary?"

"The Lady Mary has, by order of the Queen, entered protective custody so none shall, in this time of trouble, try to steal her from these lands." The preacher puffed his chest out, as if daring the people to challenge him.

He didn't sound very sure, however, even Magpye could hear the tremor in his voice. The crowd didn't believe him either. They started shouting, demanding to know where she was. "She was taken to the Tower, as Fisher and More were!" someone shouted. "They mean to kill our Princess!"

"Time to move," her mother whispered. Joan had worked in an inn for many years. She knew when trouble was set to erupt.

They just got out of the crowd, had barely reached an alleyway on the other side of the square when the surge happened. It was like watching water, Magpye thought calmly as she saw the crowd press forwards, flowing as one, towards the man preaching. The Queen's guards were about him, holding them back but it was as when waves surged on the shores of the Thames when the thaw arrived in spring. A wave cannot be held back, even if a rock blocks one part of it another swell will rush about, crash upon the shore.

"Back, Magpye," her ma whispered, pushing Magpye behind her, deeper into the alleyway. "Don't be afraid." Her mother stood guard over her, watching for a way to escape. Ma's hands shook as she adjusted her linen coif, rumpled in the rush to get out of the way of the crowds. "Don't be afraid," Ma said again.

But Magpye wasn't afraid.

Perhaps it was odd for her ma clearly was, but Magpye knew how to run for home, how to hide in the streets, under stalls or in alleyways. She was so small people rarely saw her. When older children had tried to take things from her, on her way home from the market when sent to get something for Ma, or from the church where she had learnt to say her prayers in Latin, that was what she'd done. She hadn't been afraid then either, she ran because she didn't want them to get her, but she hadn't felt fear. Perhaps she wasn't afraid because she'd never been caught, so she didn't know what happened if someone 'got their hands on her' as often the older children had yelled.

Her ma seemed to know, however. Joan's face was white as the ghosts who walked on All Saint's night as she, seeing no way through the trouble in the street, turned and led Magpye deftly down the alleyway at a fast walk, away from the square and the beginning of a small riot which, although put down fast by the Queen's guards, was only the first of many.

CHAPTER TWENTY-ONE

Queen Anne Boleyn

March 1536

Lent

Whitehall Palace

London

"We need more guards with the preachers if they are to go out again, Majesty," Latimer said.

"*If* they go out, Bishop Latimer? They must." Anne was pacing the chamber. She stopped and looked at him. "I would have thought you the last, Latimer, to turn squeamish in the sight of our mission here."

The bishop smoothed his plain robes. A devoted reformer, some said a Lutheran heretic, Latimer was always one for plain clothes, not adorned. He wore his faith on his sleeve, as it were. "Not squeamish, Majesty, sensible. If crowds riot as they did today in Southwark, then our men need more protection to spread your word. If there is trouble, it is a good thing in any case to have men there, ready to take control of the populace. We cannot send men out and merely hope for the best. There are too many supporters of Mary and the corrupt Church she stands for out there."

Anne turned to another man in the chamber. "What say you, Cranmer?"

"I say the same, Majesty. Sadly, many are in support of Lady Mary and Chapuys is doing us no good there, either. He made it plain to half of London he was off to see the King's bastard in the Tower the first time he went and has done the same every time after, so anyone who did not know Mary was in the Tower will have heard of his visits by now."

Anne grimaced. Chapuys had done it before, of course, when he went to see Katherine, trying to make it plain to the people of England that sainted Katherine was a prisoner of the King. He had done it to rouse sympathy for her, and to shame the King. That time he had paraded all through London so all witnessed him, his gentlemen or, as many suspected, servants dressed up to appear like gentlemen, chatting loudly about the former Queen as through London's streets they rode. They had even handed out alms as they went, so people would remember them well.

This time he had been warned not to ride through the streets as he had before. Chapuys, however, slippery little tick that he was, had simply chosen to take this literally and instead of riding had taken a barge to the Tower each time he had gone to Mary, stopping at all points along the way that he could manage, and at all of those many points his men had tarried to chat with every ferryman and passenger to discuss the holding of the Lady Mary as well as lauding every virtue she possessed to them. They had even pulled alongside other boats to tell them where they were going. The King's water pageants where ships had fired at each other and cannon had exploded from the Tower of London itself had been quieter than Chapuys on his jaunts to see Mary.

So now all of London was speaking of poor Mary and most knew she was in the Tower. Many did not believe she was there for her own good. They also knew the Emperor's ambassador had been there, indicating support for Mary from Spain, the Holy Roman Empire and possibly the papacy if people strung together the Emperor and his oft-ally the Pope, though there had been a little contention between Rome and Spain of late as the papacy increased its independence, struggling out from under the boot of the Emperor. After the sack of Rome some years ago, the Pope had been entirely the Emperor's creature, and prisoner, but now there was a new Pope and the Vatican was determined not to be ruled by anyone else again.

The papacy still might unite with Spain against England, however, that remained a danger.

Anne was sure that had been partly behind the riot this afternoon, not only word spreading that Mary was in the Tower, but that the former Princess might well have support from foreign powers. It made people bold on her behalf, the idea that a foreign lord might come and rescue her, a fairy-tale princess from a tower, *the* Tower, no less! And her rescuers could place her on a throne, and the people might well support it. The rioters certainly could have been inflamed by love for Mary, but they had been emboldened by confidence handed to them by Chapuys.

Anne shook her head in anger. People always wanted to believe in such tales, ones of romance where there was a wicked villain and a good soul and, in this tale, she was the evil step-mother. It was easier, she supposed, than the truth, less messy than reality.

"Perhaps we should move Mary to court," Cranmer suggested, glancing at Latimer and the Queen in turn.

Anne shook her head. "When she signs the oath and swears, as Fitzroy has, then I shall consider freeing her. Until that time, I will not. If she signs and swears not, her intentions are plain."

"At the moment she claims she cannot sign without legal counsel, sent by her cousin, the Emperor."

"That is just a method to delay. If it was true, would Chapuys not do? He was trained in law, was he not? No, this is a tactic. She defied her father, refused to stop calling herself Princess or her mother the Queen, so why should she obey me?"

Cromwell, sitting in a corner of the room, lifted his hand, an indication that he wished for the attention of the room. "The Poles, Baron Montagu prominent amongst them, as well as the Courtenays, are all about court, speaking on behalf of Mary, rousing sympathy for her," he said. "I have word that Reginald Pole is in Rome, petitioning the Pope to make a stand for the daughter of Katherine of Aragon, and the Emperor is to send men to support Chapuys here at court, demanding her release."

"You think too, then, she should be moved to court soon?" Cranmer asked.

"I do not. I think we are far safer with her in the Tower, as her Majesty has said..." here, Cromwell inclined his head respectfully to Anne who received his gesture with a nod "... and yet, I think we must have some plan about how to deal with this troublesome girl. The crux of it is, she has not committed treason, as far as we know, so holding her indefinitely on the mere idea that she might will get us into trouble with the common people and with many of the most powerful people in the world. She was taken into custody so fast upon the death of her father than nothing which has happened since can be blamed on her. Releasing her might well see her become the focus of rebellion or it might lead to her rebelling. If that were to happen, we would have just cause to arrest and punish her, but at the moment, with nothing to accuse her or her supporters of..." He spread his hands.

"You want to release her just to see if she will do something, and have then an excuse to arrest her?" Anne asked, incredulous. "Everyone knows Mary stands for the old faith. Everyone who has a vested interest in maintaining Rome instead of the King's supremacy over the Church will flock to

Mary."

"And if that happens, we will know our enemies' faces, Majesty, they will be no more in the shadow, but revealed by the light," said Cromwell.

Cranmer chimed in. "We have good men, good generals who will stand for you, Majesty, and your daughter. Fitzroy has proved himself loyal, let him go to gather the army he was promised for Ireland. If there is trouble, he can bring those men here to defend London."

"We cannot pay for so many men to eat for so long," Cromwell objected. "A standing army is not something we can support, but the Duke could indeed see how long it would take to gather those men, or others, to arms."

Anne clenched her jaw. "Fitzroy may well have proved himself for now, but although his father wished to send him at the head of an army, that was to test the lad. Fitzroy has never seen actual combat or command."

"Then send one who has with him. Norfolk has seen many a war, or Suffolk, he fought in France."

She stared at Cromwell a while. "Do you not think there is a danger in putting Norfolk and Fitzroy together, and with an army, no less?" she asked. "He is the lad's father-in-law, has been his mentor in many ways these past few years since he came to court. Should Fitzroy decide to acquire designs on the throne, would it not benefit Norfolk to support him?"

"Fitzroy has recently demonstrated he has no designs on the throne. He could be Regent by now, Majesty, yet by his own choice he is not," Latimer pointed out.

"And Norfolk would never support a bastard for the throne, Majesty," said Cromwell. "It would be putting common blood on the throne, and he never would support that, even if the bastard be wed to his daughter. Your daughter is also his blood, true blood, legitimate royal blood and she is his great-niece as the child you carry might be his great-nephew. If you wish to truly secure him, talk of promising Elizabeth to a Howard. That way he has a possibility of a great-grandchild with a place in the succession."

"What Howard?"

Cromwell shrugged, the gold chain of office on his chest glittering in reflected light from the window. "The Earl of Surrey and his wife had a son and heir not ten days ago. Elizabeth would be a few years older than he, but they would make a fair match, all the same."

"Elizabeth is potentially a queen, at the least is a princess, and should be married to a king." Anne's jaw was clenched tight now. "Even if she were to drop lower in the succession, under a boy child, still she would deserve a higher match than the son of an earl."

"Betrothals are not marriages, Majesty, as well you know." Cromwell stood carefully; his knees had been paining him of late, too much time spent with them bent for hours under a desk. "It only has to be an offer, for now. Nothing formal, and even if Norfolk insists on something formal it can be broken at a later stage, when the country is secure and all is in place. Queen Elizabeth is, after all, a mere babe in arms and far too young to consider anything like consummation which would secure the match legally. Even some kind of proxy ceremony could be broken by the Church." He glanced at Cranmer for confirmation, and the man nodded.

Anne let out a long breath. "You mean, bribe my uncle with this now, and retract it later?"

"If it is to our advantage, and, Majesty, should the child you carry turn out to be a girl, then she could marry into England. Duchess of Norfolk is a mighty title and one which has connections to your own house, therefore would not be a low place to set a second daughter of the royal line. It would also keep your daughters close to you, one of them at least, in England, where you are. Many royal mothers lose their daughters to other lands and never see them again. You would have a chance here to keep one or both daughters with you, by your side."

Anne paused, thinking on that. It was a good point. "Any child of mine and Surrey's heir would be second cousins."

"The Church could grant dispensation, if needed, Majesty," said Cranmer, "and Cromwell is right, it might not be needed. The offer alone might be enough to secure Norfolk."

Anne nodded slowly. "Make alliances now, to secure the realm, but do not think to hold to them?"

Cromwell spread his hands. "You *can* hold to them, if the deal still is of advantage to you, Majesty. Let us leave a space for fate, accident and imagination in our planning. Deal with today's problems today and whilst we can certainly consider problems of the future, let us not try to solve them all now. It leads to hesitation and headaches, trying to solve that which has not yet occurred."

She gave a short laugh. It was, Cromwell thought, a pretty sound. He had not heard it since before the King died. He always had admired the Queen, liked to see her merry. He too had a side which enjoyed wit and comedy, as she did.

Of late, before the King's fatal fall from his horse, he had worried they were heading to opposite sides of power; the Queen had been starting to oppose him over the monasteries, demanding that his men show evidence for all the corruption they had uncovered, and admittedly some had been exaggerated. He had urged his commissioners to turn up plenty of corruption to convince the King to close the houses, so the wealth of the lesser monasteries could flow into the royal treasury. It was needed; the King had spent coin as if he had an endless supply, and one of Cromwell's jobs was to keep the King happy, which meant finding more money for him to spend, and money to keep the country afloat. The

King had wasted so much coin, almost all left to him by his father, paying for wars and entertainments, for his armed charge against the Church, as well as his ships, tapestries and pageants.

Anne Boleyn, sadly for Cromwell's plans, had morals and a less flexible notion of faith than her husband had possessed. The Queen had seemed to uncover Cromwell's plotting, his attempt to make the monasteries *all* appear as if they were woefully corrupt and beyond redemption, and had made trouble for him, or had started to, which had led to the King checking and double checking all Cromwell set before him. It had been tiresome, but that had ended as the King died and Anne's concerns had switched to control of the country.

Cromwell's investigations had continued since unhindered, and he hoped when the issue of the smaller monastic houses was brought before parliament soon he would have the Queen's support. She needed friends and he was a talented friend to have. The Court of Augmentations would be set up after the Act was passed, which would be responsible for directing and managing the wealth stripped from monasteries, and Cromwell was determined to be in charge of it. The truth was, England needed that money more than ever. The treasury was depleted. The Queen wanted to save some houses, but he hoped many would be closed. It was the only way to ensure they had the money they might well need not only for the future, not only for Cromwell's pocket, tipped at just the right angle to receive much but never so much as to alert anyone too greatly to his thievery, but also in case they needed money for armies, mercenaries, bribes, for war within England itself, or invasion from without.

Someone, Cromwell thought, had to think of money over morals. Morals were all very well, but they were not going to change the world as money could. Besides, they could uphold morality when they could afford it.

"The idea of Norfolk is interesting and may be useful," Anne said. "But I want Bishop Gardiner to talk to King François too. Gardiner may not like me, but he is our ambassador to the French court, and I want to see if the French would be open to an alliance. They have not been good friends to me of late either, it is true, mainly due to their King's recent dislike of reformers, but circumstances in England have altered. My daughter could become Queen and if the Dauphin married her, he could become King or King consort of England, or I will have a son whom a princess of France could marry. I harbour doubts the Emperor will truly become our friend, especially whilst we hold Mary, but the French could become allies. They want support for their claim on Milan and Marguerite of Navarre, sister to François, is somewhat in my debt since I aided her in bringing Nicholas Bourbon to England. If Gardiner were to approach the French King through Marguerite, François's beloved sister, we might see success. If I have a son, I might be willing to talk of marriage between him and Marguerite's daughter, Jeanne, as well."

"The last negotiation with the French matched the Princess Elizabeth to the Duc de Angoulême, I believe, rather than the Dauphin," Cranmer pointed out.

"The husband of Elizabeth could become King. The stakes are higher for England, therefore the groom should be of higher title."

"I will send word to Gardiner and inform him not to share this news with any in England," Cranmer replied, "but, Majesty, I assume Norfolk would hear of it eventually, and if he comes to understand you are negotiating the same deal with the French as with him..."

"I have two children, Eminence, or soon will have. One may marry into Norfolk's house, and one may marry into France.

I wish to explore our options. We need the Duke loyal, but alliance with France would bring greater rewards still, especially if we are to resist any effort the Emperor may make on behalf of his cousin."

Cranmer sniffed. "The Emperor has ever made much noise about Mary, and Katherine when she was alive, and always has done nothing in truth for them, Majesty."

"That may change if he thinks he could invade England and place his cousin on the throne. Mary would be ever in his debt, and England would be ruled by Spain, just another part of the Hapsburg Empire."

"If the Emperor thinks England and France are poised to unite, he may become more conciliatory," Cranmer said thoughtfully. "He seemed quite willing to break a path to friendship with us when Katherine died, even before that, when she was ill."

"There is another way to neutralise the threat of Lady Mary," Cromwell interjected.

"How is that, Cromwell?" asked the Queen.

"Marry her to a supporter, one who can hold her in check," he said. "One who is not a high noble, so he does not get ideas about the throne."

"Someone suited to her bastard birth," mused Anne. "I like the idea, but she will never agree to it. We cannot force her to the altar."

"If she thought it was the way to freedom, she might take it," he said.

"Who would you suggest as this husband?"

"I would have said Edward Seymour, he sought an annulment of his first marriage and has been granted it since it seemed his wife had two sons fathered by Edward's own father, making these sons in truth Edward's brothers. He is not too high, but a good servant to the Crown. Sadly he has recently married again, but his brother Thomas remains unwed. Thomas is a little wild, but Edward may be able to tame him enough that Mary could be under our control."

Anne frowned, resuming her pacing. "I think he is too low. She would not accept that. I also do not trust the Seymours. True, Edward seems a devoted reformer, and he, too, is a cousin of mine, which you would think would put him and possibly his brother on our side, but he was busily thrusting his sister Jane into the King's lap before Henry died, causing trouble between the King and me. There were rumours the Seymours were going to try and make her the King's premier mistress." *Or even his wife*, she thought, her hand straying again to her belly, *if my child died before birth, as my last two did.*

Anne looked up to see that Cranmer had been staring at Cromwell. "*You* would be the obvious choice, Master Cromwell," Cranmer said. "And I think you know that but do not wish to say it aloud, for you know how it will look."

Cromwell shrugged. "I had the thought, but I doubt she would agree to me either. I am not even of lesser nobility, by blood."

"Her Majesty, the Regent, could decide to elevate you," Cranmer pointed out.

Anne gazed at Cromwell. For years she had thought him her man, her most dedicated servant, a friend, even. A year ago, had this happened, had this suggestion been made, she would have trusted him implicitly, but during their troubles over the monasteries it had become clear that Cromwell was not dedicated to the faith as she was, but instead to finances. He had been in the King's ear, trying to persuade Henry to keep all the wealth of the smaller monastic houses for the Crown. Cromwell wanted reform for the gold it brought to his pockets, not the godly service it did to the faith. Due to this realisation, her own faith in him had been shaken, just a little, just enough.

But Cranmer had a point; married to Cromwell Mary would be a lesser threat. The common people did not like Cromwell. If

Mary was wed to him, it might take her out of the running for the throne. If she had a child, it would come half of common stock, half of bastard. She would be wed to someone in Anne's faction, to a reformer who might well bring her to see the light of all they were trying to achieve in religion. True, she had doubts about his faith in some ways, but officially, a reformer was what he was, and he had served her well of late. Others had turned on her, Cromwell had not.

But could she trust he would not use Mary to make a play for the throne himself? Could she trust him with a title and all the benefits that title might bring? George had many reservations about Cromwell's loyalty. He had spoken of them at length, but it was doubtful people would accept Cromwell as king. The nobles certainly would not, Norfolk would have a fit of apoplexy if Cromwell attempted such a thing. Even if Cromwell's ambition was that way inclined, he would not achieve it. Such a match, arranged by Anne, might well be incentive for Cromwell to remain loyal, too, if he was wavering.

"Let us send a marriage proposal to the Tower," Anne said. "You will take it, Cromwell, offer your hand to the girl. We can talk of titles at a later stage." She lifted her eyebrows. "If, as I assume, you are not averse to the notion?"

"If you wish me to try, I am willing, Majesty," he said, sweeping to a bow.

CHAPTER TWENTY-TWO

Lady Mary Tudor
March 1536
Lent
The Tower of London

"He was here, Chapuys! Offering his hand to me, during Lent no less, as if I were some common woman of Putney!"

Mary could not sit still, and this time Chapuys could hardly blame her. Her news, shocking though it was, he had partly expected, although the bridegroom offered staggered even him. He had long expected the old King or his whore would try to sell Mary off to a supporter, a safe man of England, a loyalist, someone they could control. Such had been done as the Tudors rose to power at the end of the second phase of the long civil war. Queen Katherine had told him how Margaret Plantagenet, later the Countess of Salisbury, had been married off to John Pole, a loyal supporter of King Henry VII, so her royal blood would not cause the new King any concern. The same had been done with the last unmarried sisters of Elizabeth of York, the threat of their claims to the succession neutralised by the men they married, in theory at least, so yes, he had expected they would try to marry Mary lower than her blood deserved, had expected they would wed her to someone loyal to their regime.

He had not, however, expected it to be Cromwell.

The man was not even slightly noble, had been born of an innkeeper and once had served as a mere mercenary, and was certainly no match for Mary who had the blood of the highest of England, Spain and the Holy Roman Empire flowing in her veins.

"He said if I agreed to this, the Regent would set me free of this place." She paced past him, her hands in the air. "This means it is a condition of my release, does it not? Without agreement to this, I will find myself ever trapped here, until or unless they find a way to murder me."

"We will not allow that," he said quietly and as she came to a stop before him, he took her hands and leaned in close to her ear. "I cannot say much here, now, there are ears on us, but I will find a way to aid you, Your Highness. Be ready, always ready."

"For what?" she whispered.

"For the moment of pomegranate."

She stood back, nodding. She understood. He would find a way to get her out.

When Chapuys left, Mary still could not settle. Her nervous hands fingered a gold collar at her throat. It had been her mother's and the golden cross upon it held a sliver of the True Cross within it. Only just before she came to the Tower had it been sent to her. Katherine had left it to Mary in her will, and a servant had brought it straight to her. Cromwell had been making demands to examine it, no doubt because he wanted to steal it from her, but they had ceased as she was placed in the Tower. Mary prayed her mother's necklace would bring her clarity, solace. Little of either did she feel she possessed, at present.

The ambassador had promised to find a way to free her, but what if his way failed or he was found out? What if she was left truly without friends in England and he was sent away by the Boleyn fishwife? Mary walked the chamber, staring at the furnishings left there. Of course, much had been taken away after Anne's coronation. Royal apartments were frequently not merely left as they were; chairs and beds, hangings, cushions and other items were shipped, from palace to palace. Even on progress the chambers of the King and Queen were dismantled and their furniture brought along by creaking wagon, set up in each new residence they were to stay a few days so that each place felt like home. When Mary had arrived, there had been little here. A bed had been shipped from one of the palaces, chairs too and cushions so she could sit beside the fire. There was a Bible, thankfully in Latin, for her to read. Mary's mother had believed there was small harm in translating the Bible, as long as if only the nobility were to read it, and Mary had been in agreement, for a time. The thought was, the nobility were better educated and therefore could understand the word of the Lord if it was translated, but common people were not well educated and required priests and other officers of the Church to explain the parables and passages of the Holy Book to them.

Mary had agreed with her mother until her father had started to make changes to the Church, then she had seen that once one thought of reform entered a mind, so that mind became corrupted, only too open to all kind of heresies. Since then, she had rejected the progressive thought of her mother and decided the only safe way was to worship as the true Church had decreed was proper. They had been right, had they not? The Pope and his cardinals and all who had called for no alterations to be made to the way the faith was worshipped and performed. They had said there were dangers in allowing men to read the Bible in their own language, dangers that schisms would form in the Church as men, able to read the Bible in their own tongue, misunderstood the teachings of the Lord, or even chose to wilfully misunderstand them to bring chaos into the world. They had been right, for even a godly man like her father had been perverted, turned from the true path when reform had first entered his life.

She stared at the tapestry. That had been here when she arrived, probably was the same that had surrounded the Boleyn woman when she used these chambers for her fake coronation. Was this a kind of torture, sending Mary here, to this place which had held her father's mistress safe, her belly swollen with child with Elizabeth, before that false coronation three years ago? Mary remembered the day only too well. She and her mother had been separated by then of course, and tales had come racing from London telling of how glorious the event was, how the people rejoiced at the sight of the new Queen, how Anne had been honoured more than her mother, Queen Katherine, had when she had been crowned, because Anne had been crowned using the rites reserved for kings and not those employed for queens.

Mary had wept that day, fallen ill not long after, lost in misery and tortured by shame on behalf of her mother. The public humiliation of what her father had done to her mother had stolen her breath. But after, she had heard other tales. How people had mocked the entwined initials of H and A, painted on hangings for the occasion to signify the union of Henry and Anne, calling out "Ha!" upon seeing them. She had heard how some common men had to be forced to doff their caps when the Queen sailed past them in her carriage, all dressed up in white and silver, as if Anne was some being of purity rather than wickedness. She had heard of her mother's defiance, and how Katherine continued, with great courage and pride, to use her true title of Queen of England, and Mary had followed suit, calling her mother Queen and herself Princess.

Even separated, she and her mother had been as one in mind and heart and resolution. Mary had felt at times as if her mother was the courage she felt inside her, that when dark times came and Mary felt like cowering, there inside her rose courage, an actual person, and that person was Katherine of

Aragon.

When her mother had died, she had thought that courage might die too, but it had not. Then her father had died too, and as Mary had found herself standing almost alone in the world, a child no more, something of both her parents seemed to rise in Mary. There was a sense in her soul that she carried them now; a weight of grief and love she never would mind bearing. United, as they should have been in life, so they were in death, and they lived in her, their child. And she would not let them down, not now and not ever. To the last, just as her mother had fought, Mary would fight and she would show her father, even if now he would have to see it from Heaven, that she, his daughter could rule, could unite England, could take the throne and hold it.

But first, she had to get out of this place and escape the man the Boleyn Queen wanted her to marry.

CHAPTER TWENTY-THREE

Eustace Chapuys, Imperial Ambassador

March 1536

Lent

Le Herber

London

Chapuys hurried along the streets which led from the river and into the cramped innards of London, a cowl over his head. His clothes were plain, to avoid detection. Houses seemed to hang over the streets, the extended upper floors of the timber-framed buildings poking out into the air above like a belly protruding after a good meal. The English called it jettying, this practice of building out from a house. Sometimes houseowners would be reported because the projecting storeys were too low and caused an obstruction for those on horses, or even those walking the streets. A street with too many could feel close, suffocating. They cast shadows on the road too, and those shadows Chapuys stuck to as he hastened past a pungent sight. Horse dung had been swept and shovelled into one great pile, letting off a fragrant pong of digested hay and grass, waiting for the night soil men to come and collect it. Birds of different sizes, all dressed in black feathers, were pecking at it, and at each other when one tried for a tasty treat another wanted. Cawing, they fluttered and flounced at each other with wing and claw and beak.

The best dung went to the gardens of the King, and the rich. Poorer folk had to make do with the waste of their own animals, a pig or goat kept in the back garden. Sometimes they used human waste too, mixed in with animal dung. It fed small sections of crops grown in many a backyard, providing herbs and vegetables for a family. Most houses in London, poor or rich, had a garden, even if some only held the jakes, what the English called the latrine.

But this was the better end of town. Here there were grand houses with parks, walled vegetable gardens, orchards and stewponds. The gardens here smelt of flowers in the spring and summer, as well as horse dung, incense, and the ever-present scent of the river.

Past a burbling, fast-flowing gutter filled with dirty water, still sharp with a touch of ice, the Ambassador marched, his men at his back. The scents of the long-running gutter and of the river were strong and high on the air that morn and he held an orange stuffed with cloves to his nose, the fruit covered with a strip of cloth. The orange was a sign of great wealth, not commonly found outside of court in England. Whilst he hardly wanted to be accosted by guards, suspected as being a poor man or vagrant in this part of town, he did not either wish to announce his status too loudly, his identity at all, and his purpose to no man.

They turned a slight bend in the road. The cobbles here were good, well laid and almost straight and flat, a rare thing in London. Most streets were mud, sometimes grit, fresh layers thrown down when the King and his men travelled through and not at other times. At least here there were no fish stalls or tanners, the stink of fish guts and the piss and shit the tanners used to cure hides rising as a fug in the air, sticking in nose and throat. Sometimes you could taste the scent of London. Here the gardens of the houses were large, the buildings well made, built for the wealthy. Not so cramped here were the houses, where the rich lived, but still London always felt claustrophobic to Chapuys, so many people packed in such a small space. Many places he had lived, but England would never be a favourite, the climate, the way his people were treated, and the cramped living to be had in the towns were all things he wanted never to experience again. If not for Katherine and her daughter, he would have requested to leave his post here many years ago. But once he had become devoted to Katherine's cause, and through her, Mary, he had no choice but to stay. It was not only his master's wishes he carried out, it was his own. Never had he admired women more than the true Queen and her daughter, and now Mary was alone in the world and at risk. His master, the Emperor, could never truly be trusted to do anything for Mary, Chapuys knew that only too well. Much did Charles V promise, often did he shout and bluster about the treatment of his aunt and cousin and little did he do to alter anything. Katherine and her daughter were pawns to Charles of Spain, but not to Chapuys. To the ambassador they were people, and they were people he loved.

His cloak tried to slip backwards, and he pulled it up deeper over his head. A guard at the gates of one of the houses looked up with a slight amount of interest, anything passing by to break up the dull monotony of his day he would pay attention to, and Chapuys nodded, and continued on before the man could note his face. Hopefully he would say nothing, would not recognise the ambassador. Possibly the guard might belong to a family who sympathised, and therefore even if Chapuys was seen here, on his way to a house he had no business in going to, nothing might be said. He hoped that would be the case.

He had come on an unmarked boat, just another of the wherries which offered rides along the River Thames, from one side or mooring to another or one quay to a second. He had two men with him for protection but otherwise was trying to travel without being seen. Chapuys had made a fuss, plenty of noise and show when off to see Mary in the Tower to make it obvious she was being held prisoner there, but he did not want now to make a show.

It could cost a head if the Regent found out what he was up to.

He turned another corner, came to gates leading into gardens and the long path wending to the house, Le Herber. Once the seat of the Earl of Warwick, it belonged now to his descendant, a woman Chapuys was hoping would help him with the cause of Lady Mary. There was no reason she would not. Margaret Pole was Mary's kinswoman; she had also been Mary's governess and Katherine's most devoted friend.

A man at the gate let him in without question when the ambassador announced his name. The guards had been informed of his arrival, obviously. There had been trouble in London, so the guards were watchful, but he was welcomed in with speed, taken to the house, and within, to find the Countess of Salisbury waiting for him.

"Ambassador." She walked to him and offered up a dignified curtsey. "I hope you were careful on the way here?"

He bowed low, catching the scent of a peppermint lozenge on her breath and rosemary rushing up from the floor mats. "All care was taken, my lady, I was not followed."

"Let us hope that is indeed the case. This could lead to the end, for all of us."

"*Us*, my lady?"

She indicated to a side chamber and as he walked in, Chapuys found himself in company with Margaret's son, Lord Montagu, as well as his brother, Geoffrey Pole, Henry Courtenay the Earl of Devon and his wife Gertrude. There was also Nicholas Carew, the King's former Master of Horse, and Elizabeth Grey, the Dowager Countess of Kildare, a cousin of the late King.

"You may trust these people, as you trust me," Margaret said.

"All of us wish to have the Princess released and restored to her true position."

Chapuys gazed about with some nervousness. The more people who knew the more danger there was, but he had to admit, most of them he knew to be avid loathers of the Boleyn Queen.

"You said you had dire news of Mary," said the Countess, walking to the fire and setting a hand on the mantelpiece. "I hope you are not to tell us the snakes of court have contrived a way to harm the Princess?"

"In a way, Your Grace. They mean to make her marry as a condition of her release, to Cromwell."

Gertrude Blount looked as if she might burst into flame at his words, the Countess herself looked sickened. "This will not come to be," said Margaret stoutly. "We will not allow our Princess, the true ruler of England, to be so insulted or diminished."

"The Emperor would never stand for it either, madam, and has sent word to me that I am to aid his cousin in taking the throne, and in achieving her freedom in order to do so in any way I see fit. I have formulated a plan, but I will need aid to bring it together."

The Countess nodded. The English gable hood she wore concealed much, yet Chapuys could see some hair come loose at her temple, dark auburn flecked with silver strands which shone bright as the fire reflected upon them. "We have already thought that if we could speed Mary from the Tower she could be brought here, first, then we could ride for the north. Warwick Castle is one of the best and most impregnable in England and is under my command. It would provide a base for her, so she might rouse an army to take London. I believe not only common people will rise to her cause, but nobles will too. Carefully, each of us has been reaching out, to test the loyalties of those we know."

Chapuys felt that worry steal upon him again. "A fine plan, my lady, although I would exercise caution in the extreme. If any one person approached talks, the whole plan may unravel."

"We have spoken only to those we are sure of, for now, Lord Ambassador," Montagu interjected, an irritated look on his face, as if Chapuys daring to be there at all was an insult, let alone offering advice. Chapuys had never liked Montagu, there was an inherited sense of arrogance in him the ambassador liked not, something of a man who believed he should have been more important than he was. It was a frustrated high-handedness, which made him only more unlikable and grating.

"But how are we to get her from the Tower? The place is impenetrable." Gertrude Courtenay, née Blount, actually a distant kinswoman of Bessie Blount, Fitzroy's mother, folded her hands before her as if to present herself as modest and humble. Chapuys knew she was nothing of the kind. Of all the people there, bar the Countess of Salisbury, Gertrude had the most steel in her. She also had the most ambition, even more than Carew who was a grasping climber if ever there was one. He was a good jouster, though, Chapuys had to admit, and was handy with a sword, like the Pole brothers. In a fight they would be most useful. Geoffrey Pole, however, worried him more than a little, since the young man tended to gabble at the best of times and spill secrets as a drunk spills his ale. Geoffrey never seemed to take life seriously, whereas his brother, Montagu, took everything seriously enough for the both of them. Perhaps that was why Geoffrey had so little gravity, his brother had inherited it all.

Chapuys smiled. "Not so, my lady. I have studied your histories. The Tower was breached once before."

"In Wat Tyler's Rebellion you mean? The Great Rising? But there were circumstances there not open to us now, my lord. The guards on the Tower walls left the gates and portcullis open so the King could ride back in with ease during the time he went out to meet the rebels. That was how they gained entrance."

"Circumstances may always be open, if one knows where the keys to the hearts of people are kept," Chapuys said. "And the people of England love Mary. Many small riots have already broken out in London in her favour. I would ask that you find a way to break more, to encourage more riots, so a great rising might begin, here, in the very heart of London. When London is risen, we will get Mary from here so she may go to Warwick and gather her army."

"Why not stay here, fight with the people who will rise in London?" Carew asked.

"I do not think a rising of commoners, ungoverned by leaders, will last long in London," Chapuys replied, turning to him. "Others will fight back, the Watch, the royal guards, the guilds, the people, and London, vast though it is, is a contained space, where those rising in Mary's favour may be trapped and enclosed. We need a more structured assembly of forces to overtake the royal palaces, and we will need a greater force than is presently in London to take the country entire. Warwick Castle is a good plan, my lord, we just have to get the Lady Mary there."

Carew nodded. "You may have a point," he said. "I have heard of Norfolk and Fitzroy being sent soon to see to the navy and forces that were supposed to go to Ireland. Were they to join in anything against the common people, the people would not stand a chance."

"You do not think they could be persuaded to join us?" Montagu turned to Carew. "Norfolk loathes the Boleyn witch, though she be his niece. I am sure he, like many of us are aware she only got upon that throne by seducing the King with sorcery."

"They are offering the little bastard Elizabeth to Norfolk's grandson, the one just born to Surrey, as a bride," Elizabeth Grey interjected. "Norfolk has a chance for a grandson as King. He will not support Mary."

"Fitzroy would be just another complication in any case," said Geoffrey Pole. "The lad, many are saying, holds a claim to the throne."

"He is a bastard," said Carew, narrowing his eyes.

Geoffrey rushed on, that eagerness to explain himself which Chapuys feared aflame in his eyes, quick on his tongue. "Yet if the marriage between Katherine and the King was not valid, then the King was a bachelor when Fitzroy was born, and in many cases such children have been legitimized."

"But we know the King and Katherine *were* married, do we not?" the stern voice of his mother broke over him. Geoffrey almost winced. "Princess Mary is our rightful Queen, because her parents were, indeed, married."

"Of course, lady mother, I was but repeating what some are saying. Mary is indeed our Queen, but we should know what might occur should Fitzroy attempt to make a claim or if men seek to support him."

"Would Norfolk support Fitzroy?" asked Henry Courtenay. "Whilst he despises common blood, his daughter is married to the lad. Support the Queen and he would have a grandson on the throne sharing it with Elizabeth, then perhaps, in a decade or two, a great-grandson ruling England alone, but support Fitzroy and he would have a daughter on the throne as Queen now."

"Either way, we cannot trust him, that much is clear," said Margaret, cutting through the theories and chatter with an admirably curt knife. "We must look to our plans, not his. Mary must be freed of the Tower." She turned to Chapuys. "Now, Ambassador, tell us your plan, and tell us what you need us to do."

CHAPTER TWENTY-FOUR

Queen Anne Boleyn
March 1536
Lent
Westminster Palace
London

"I still think we should have waited, Cromwell," Anne said as they entered her apartments in the old palace of Westminster. Much of the old palace had been destroyed by fire years ago. Part of the palace was suitable for use by the royal family still however, and since they had been at Parliament that hour, it was a convenient place to talk afterwards.

The bill for the dissolution of the smaller monastic houses had been passed, just. Cromwell had leaned on the necks and no doubt other body parts of the members of both houses to bring it about. It had been the King's wish, Henry's last order to his parliament, and Anne suspected that was also why it had been passed, the men there present believed they were appeasing the ghost of a king they had feared, certainly, but also loved.

They had not wanted to sit, had not wanted to pass such a bill during Lent, either, but Parliament was not forbidden from sitting in Lent and Cromwell and Cranmer had leaned on Anne, telling her not only was the money needed now, but also that this was a holy mission and therefore Lent was a suitable time to go ahead with it. A purging of past sins was a mighty signal to send, demonstrating that the past was done with, and a new light would dawn upon England, so Cranmer had said.

It was the smaller houses, not the larger ones, which were under attack, as many would see it, but there was a caveat within the Act that any houses the King, or now the Regent, wished to save could be excluded from closure. This reassured Anne, but it was also true, as Cromwell had said to her, that the Crown needed the money that would come from closures, and that many of the smaller houses were corrupt – but still, Anne was uneasy. She was already unpopular; this would make her even more so. The King was no more here to lecture his people on the righteousness of his claim to be Head of the Church. They might have respected his right to issue such commands, but would the people respect hers? Anne was not Head of the Church. Technically, Elizabeth, a baby, or the babe in her womb now was. Many thought that notion lunatic as it was, and some had never even accepted the King as supreme leader of the English faith. Anne was to act in stead for her daughter, and perhaps some thought that even more ludicrous, seeing as they had always thought her a heretic whore. The regency council was to support her, but as the figurehead of England, Anne would be blamed for all that occurred that the people did not welcome.

In truth, Cranmer was the acting Head of the Church at the moment, and reforms of the faith would be guided by him, but even Cranmer she worried about at times. Though she trusted him more than any man, already he had been pressing for radical reforms she knew the King would never have approved of, ones which took the still most Catholic, in practice if not in leader, Church that Henry had formed away from traditional ways and closer to Lutheranism. Cranmer wanted to remove candles and ornamentation from the churches and was pushing her to make an English translation of the

Bible available to all in England. The Archbishop wanted to use either the Coverdale Bible, which was largely based on Tyndale's work and had been dedicated to Henry and to Anne or, if his work could be speeded along, the one John Rogers had been working on, which was another version of the Coverdale Bible that Rogers was editing under an assumed name, for protection. The King had been on the verge of approving a translation, it was true, and Anne had hoped the most recent Rogers' translation might prove more to her husband's liking than the original Coverdale, or the Tyndale Bible the King had rejected, mainly because the King disapproved of William Tyndale himself. Anne believed all people should be able to read the Word of God for themselves or understand it as it was read to them. Cloaking the teachings of Christ in Latin so common people knew not what they were hearing was not beneficial to anyone. All this she agreed with, and yet she hesitated.

Anne had hardly wanted to go ahead with the dissolution of the smaller monasteries but had been convinced it was necessary and now was being pressed on other issues. Some, Anne would approve in time, but she knew for the sake of the country, for the sake of peace, she would have to stand fast on others. There had been too much change already and London was not the only place where there was unrest stirring. If the Queen wanted to avoid all-out rebellion in England, she had to slow her men down.

And now, she had to make exemptions.

"We will exclude the institutions I have already outlined from dissolution," she said to Cromwell, passing him a list of smaller monasteries and nunneries she had already decided would be saved, including the convents of Catesby and Nun Monkton. "And we will hear abbots and bishops who come to plead for the others. Let the Church know I am open to hear them."

"But, Majesty…" Cromwell eyed the paper with dismay, seeing

more houses on this first sheet alone than he would have welcomed. "My men and their investigations uncovered much that cannot be ignored. Abbots and bishops will give you only the best impression of these houses."

"As you will give me the worst, and I will weigh up what I hear." Anne stood stiff, proud, gazing at him. "Cromwell, we must save some. You and I have differed on this point before, but now I say this to you not only because it is immoral to close all these houses and take that money for the Crown with no promise it will be used for education or for the people, and that is the case now, is it not? Once we said that money would go back to the people, to support education, medicine, alms, but now it will not, for that money you say the Crown needs in order to hold the country steady or raise armies. So now, at least for a time, none of this wealth will go back to the people where it belongs."

She took a deep breath and sighed it out as she regained control over her tongue. "But for another reason, you must hear me. If all these establishments close, the people will rise against us. They may do so already, unhappy with me as Regent and angry that we have Mary imprisoned, but this would be a final reason, the last weight to tip the scales and send us sprawling into anarchy. Save some, and it will be seen that we act fairly, that we close only those drowning in ungodly ways. Hear the Church leaders on individual cases and we will gain support. Close all, hear no one, and we will be named as tyrants, and I, in this position I was not born to but was raised to by the King, I cannot afford that. It is not only what is right, Cromwell, it is what will keep my daughter and unborn child safe. You say we need money, and that I understand, but we need loyalty as well."

Cromwell stared at her a while, his expression and those dark eyes unreadable, but slowly he nodded. "I understand, Majesty."

"Send out word then, that Church leaders may come to the palace and put their cases to me for houses to be saved," she said. "And send that list out publicly as a proclamation of houses which will be saved by the Crown, so the people know we are not bent on rampant dissolution. Those houses will be upheld as models of virtue, for they were reported even by your men as being without fault or being small of fault. Let the people know we are on their side, that this reform we undertake is good and honest, and make it clear the King was in favour of closing *all* the houses, and that we have decided to save some."

Cromwell lifted his eyebrows. "You would have the people think badly of the King, my lady?"

Anne drew herself up. "The King would want his children to have every protection. If we can make it clear that this regency will be one to surpass even His Majesty's reign in virtue, it will make me and my children safe. The people must have hope, Cromwell. The King would not object to that." She paused. "Think not that order does not pain me. I want the King remembered only well, but everything I can do for my children, I will do."

"I understand, Majesty."

"Is there any news of Tyndale and if he may be released?"

Cromwell nodded slowly, still pondering on his losses. "The Emperor may be willing, but only if his cousin is released."

"I will not trade Mary for Tyndale, he must know that." Anne paused as Cranmer was announced at the door, and she waved him inside. "But if we come close to a time when Mary may be about to be returned to court, then we could bargain for Tyndale in such a way."

"If we were about to release the Lady Mary in any case, you mean, Majesty?"

"Indeed. In the meantime, try to keep Chapuys and the

Emperor negotiating on the issue at least. It may buy Tyndale some time."

"I will do all I can, Majesty."

Anne nodded. "Is there word from my sister in Calais?"

Cromwell rolled up the list Anne had given him, wondering if he could burn it without her noticing. "Your sister sent word, Majesty, that for the moment she intends to remain in Calais. There has been much talk of hostile French ships attacking English ones and she fears the journey. I have instructed Ambassador Gardiner to protest these attacks at the French court."

Anne sipped ale, brought to her by her mother who had also quietly entered the chamber. It tasted of grief, as everything did now. "I am not sure I want Gardiner in France any longer. I worry more and more about his hostility towards me, and it makes me fear he is more likely to rile the French into all-out invasion than to secure our safety."

"I understand, Majesty, and yet keeping him there means he is not here."

Anne smiled at Cromwell's quip. "I suppose you mean, he is not here to oppose us."

"That is also true, but as you know, Majesty, you are not the only one who finds the Bishop annoying, and his voice is most grating."

"That is true enough." Anne chuckled a little at Cromwell's dry tone.

"Gardiner, whilst I agree is more conservative of nature than evangelical, has represented us ably in France," Cranmer pointed out. "He did write the rather stirring and I thought intelligent answer to the Pope's bull against the King. Gardiner defended the supremacy. *De Vera Obedientia* was a powerful work, a boon for our side, and the Bishop does seem to be persuading the French that marriage with one of your

Majesty's daughters, should you have two, would be beneficial. Although as I thought, they would want Elizabeth wed to their Dauphin so he might become England's King, and Norfolk, who wants the same bride for his grandson may have got wind of the negotiations, so I hear." Cranmer glanced at Cromwell who nodded.

"We will come to that, Eminence. But what of my sister, Cromwell? Will she be safe in Calais?"

"I have persuaded Lord Lisle, the Lord Deputy of Calais, and his wife to take your sister, as well as her husband and children into their household, so she has better protection."

"And Lord Lisle remains a friend to the Crown?" Anne pressed.

"At the moment, it would seem so. Conservative of faith he might be, but Lisle was entirely loyal to his nephew, your husband. Bastard stock though he is, Lisle remains faithful to his family."

Anne felt her heart beat a little slower to think of her sister safe. "Good. Then I am happy now to talk of marriages, gentlemen. Have we heard officially from Norfolk on the subject of the marriage proposed between my daughter and his grandson? Has he made a complaint? Or is all this talk of him knowing something of the French negotiations mere talk?"

Cromwell spread his hands out before him. "He seemed surprised, but noted the proposition was an honour. He was to speak with his son. He did question, rather closely, which child of Your Majesty was being proposed, exactly, which made me wonder if he knew of talks with France."

"And what did you say?"

"I said it was obviously Elizabeth we spoke of, since she is Your Majesty's only daughter. I think, however, the Duke remains somewhat suspicious that if your Majesty bears another daughter, then he might find his grandson promised to that second daughter rather than to the Queen. This is also the trouble the French are having with the proposition. They wish to know for certain they will be wedding their prince to the correct princess."

Anne played with a ring of silver and garnet on her finger. "Make it clear to Norfolk we mean Elizabeth. As you say, any engagement can be broken later. With the French, let us simply keep talking. When my child is born, we can make more certain plans with both parties."

Cromwell pursed his lips. "Gardiner is close to Norfolk. I imagine he will soon share the information with the Duke that the French are being negotiated with over your daughter's hand, Majesty, if he has not already done so."

"If Gardiner shares this, we shall recall and arrest him. As England's ambassador it is his task to act for his country, not for Norfolk, and if my uncle finds out then I shall tell him we were playing the French along to prevent hostile relations. He is arrogant enough to believe me." Anne took another sip from her cup. "I take it the Lady Mary has not sent word that she might accept your offer, as yet?"

Cromwell shook his head. "I think she will not accept, Majesty. I believe the lady thinks me too low a match."

Anne turned to the window. "Very well. Tell her again she may leave the Tower if she swears to recognise me as Regent, my children as the true heirs. If she does so, she will be welcomed to court, in honour."

"And if not?"

"Then she remains where she is."

CHAPTER TWENTY-FIVE

Robert Aske

March 1536

Lent

Yorkshire

The North of England

Aske could feel all men there in the draughty barn staring at him. It was never a comfortable place to stand, not only in a draught but with all men watching you, waiting for you to urge them to one action or another, and the actions they might take here and now were serious, might well cost lives. But sometimes things had to be done, sometimes causes were worth standing for, even if they caused conflict, or brought death. What else was a man to do? Accept all that came his way, or stand, proud and with a straight back, to say something was not right?

Aske knew the answer in his heart. The men were waiting for one from his mouth.

The barn was warm enough, despite the chill outside, a chill only deeper since they were in the north of England, where the weather always was more extreme than the cosy, soft south. Southerners were lily-livered creatures, all men of the north knew that. The clement weather bred soft courtiers who pranced about the King, or had pranced once, but there was fire in the veins of men of the north, who faced coldness, the deep snows of winter, with resolution. All the same, Aske was glad it was warm in the barn. Animals moved softly in the other room, separated by only a cloth, their balmy breath, carrying scents of hay and spittle, riding the air, heating it as much as the men's discussion of recent events was heating their spirits.

Aske inhaled before he answered the question set to him, one regarding the legality of holding Lady Mary in the Tower, an event of which the whole country now was aware. "The King may hold any person he deems a threat a prisoner, but there must be evidence and eventually a trial," he told them. "The Lady Mary is imprisoned by the Crown, by the Regent in truth, but they do not call it imprisonment, they say she is there for her protection. In some ways this may mean no evidence would need to be submitted, nor trial held, but there is another question here, good masters."

They had asked him if it were a thing legal to lock Mary away, and Aske, being a lawyer, could argue both sides of course, but he had another point to put forth.

"What is the other question, Master Aske?" asked one of the grim-faced men gathered in the barn. They had needed a quiet place, a safe place, to talk. It would not do to be overheard. The barn, owned by a friend, gave them space enough to all fit in, and there were many more there than Aske had expected, and it was far from other ears that might listen in and report them, had they held this meeting in an inn or tavern.

Even here, it was a risk.

A frozen breath of the early spring night rippled through the men. Crept under the door it had, through rotten gaps in the lower boards. There was a scent of iron on the wind, snow falling outside, the paths turned to hard, solid ice. It would be hard going, getting home again, but carrying torches they would be seen as honest men. Those up to no good carried no lights, and such men the Watch always stopped. Already the men gathered there had arranged different paths by which to reach homes in the town nearby, for those who lived there. Arrive in a group, and men of the Watch would know something was afoot. Southerners always considered men of the north ignorant, dull of wits, but they had more brains than any living in London did, and they knew how to reach this meeting as well as steal from it without being found out.

Aske rubbed his hands together for warmth and continued. "The true question here is whether the figure now sitting on the throne has the right, a true and legal right, to act for the country." His breath came out, a little cloud carrying through the air. "Queen Anne was named Regent in the event of the King's death, we were told the Princess Elizabeth and a child unborn are named the heirs to the throne, and these were laws passed by the King and by Parliament, which made them legal, but was the King right to do this? Was he quashing the rights of another, of his own daughter, a woman most of Europe recognise as the true heir to our country? What is law is not always what is right, my friends, and that is why we amend laws, to bring better, greater justice. There are other questions. Was the King in his right mind when he named Anne Boleyn regent? Did he think he would die and leave the country in the hands of Anne Boleyn, with an infant on the throne? Do the rights of Mary outweigh those of Elizabeth? I would say, as the eldest legitimate child of the King, the Princess Mary is our true heir and it should be she who leads this country, for she will take England back to Rome and back to God, and men of conscience and honesty should not allow this land to be left in the hands of a woman God never chose for this throne, who is devoid of royal blood and who will lead us only further into heresy and sin."

Aske nodded, seeing wary faces and zealous alike about him. "These are weighty matters, good masters, but we must think fast now, and well. The King is dead, the true heir a prisoner in the Tower and there is news today that our monasteries are under attack. People say the King approved this before his death, but I do not believe it. The Boleyn witch and Cromwell, with Cranmer, that devil, looking on, would strip the goods of our houses of worship away and they start with smaller houses for they know fewer people will be there within the walls to resist them, but what of the larger? Will our great abbeys come under attack? The practices of heathens and Lutherans are already amongst us, and they are spreading. If this country is to have any chance, I believe that chance is with Princess Mary."

"I heard a rumour she's being forced to wed Cromwell," hissed a man from the edge of the crowd.

"Cromwell!" The sound came from another as a bark, which ended as a low growl.

"I hear from friends that men of Lincolnshire and Lancashire will rise with us if we lead," Aske whispered. "And every man must make his own choice, for we will be but common men marching against the royal army, but if we march with God on our side, friends, I believe we can win, in the name of Princess Mary and for the good of all England."

"We have never had a woman rule over us," one mentioned.

"We have a woman ruling us now, friend," Aske pointed out, "and a woman of the nobility, not royalty she is. Mary is of the blood royal, her parents' marriage made honest because of the twenty years they spent living together if nothing else. Mary is a woman, it is true, but she is the King's heir. When the time is right, the Princess can take a husband, perhaps of Spain or France, perhaps even of England. There are families who are not strangers, aliens or foreigners to this land who carry the old blood, and why not unite Tudor blood again with them? In that way there can be a king and queen once more, two who hold royal blood in their veins going back many generations, upon the throne. The Regent, she will rule alone, you know this, for to marry would threaten her power, so I ask, which is worse, a godly, honest woman alone for a short spell on the throne, or a heretic witch for a long one? I know which I would choose."

"Aye," there was a general rumble of agreement.

Aske noted more men nodding than before. He had always been good at the art of persuasion. "But first, masters, Mary must be freed, and the monasteries must be saved."

A man at the back lifted his voice. "I hear the Regent is allowing some to be saved already, she is to hear men of the Church about ones to be exempted."

"*All* should be exempted!" Aske, never one for losing his temper, sounded as if he might. "If there is corruption, it should be investigated and better abbots or abbesses put in place to bring about better practices, but those houses are needed, friends, are they not? How many poor rely on them? Do you want to see the sick wandering the streets? The poor without a place to go? What will happen to all those turned out from those houses, can they all fit into larger ones, or will they become beggars on the streets? We have enough of that. Our villages and towns are even now overtaxed in trying to provide for the poor and needy, so what will a sudden influx of more do to us, to you? And what of education, charity, the men and women those religious houses employ or pay to bring food? This will affect the people who bring goods to the abbeys or those who buy from them, and it will affect the alms, medical care and education the abbeys are able to offer. What will happen to nuns when they are evicted? Few are jobs or housing for women, will they be forced to marry, or God forbid, to sell their bodies just to eat? Think of that, good masters. Brides of Christ forced to become whores out of fear of starvation! Reform of corruption is one thing, good friends, but this evil is something else. These people of court, they dress up the devil to trick us into thinking they do God's work, but they do none such!"

"Aye, you are right, Master Aske."

"He has a point."

"The Church should not be assaulted!"

Many more spoke out to say much the same and eventually Aske lifted his voice once more. "Then come with me now, plan with me. We must have ways to raise men quietly at first so we have enough that we cannot be put down by the local sheriffs or their guards, and then when we have enough, there will be more to do."

"What to do then, Master Aske?"

He stared into their eyes one by one. "March on London," he said. "And claim the city in the name of Princess Mary, the rightful Queen of England."

CHAPTER TWENTY-SIX

Henry Fitzroy, Duke of Richmond and Somerset
March 1536
Lent
Greenwich Palace
London

"We need to set this uprising down, immediately," Queen Anne announced to the men of the council. She looked agitated, Fitzroy thought. It was to be expected. Men of Yorkshire were on the march, gathering more supporters at each town they stopped at. No one knew how many had risen, but it was enough to alarm local sheriffs, who had sent word, calling for aid.

A man named Aske was leading at least one of the rebel armies, proclaiming that the regency was a sham, Mary should be Queen, and the closures of monastic houses should be repealed. They were demanding control of the government, for honest men to lead them, for England to be returned to the governance of Rome and for Mary to be set upon the throne in place of Anne.

It was everything the Regent had tried so hard to avoid, and now, but two months into her reign, there were men rising, threatening to march on London. Rebellion was on its way, coming fast.

"I have sent word that local lords and officers of the peace are to band together and set these gatherings down," Anne said, "but if the numbers are too great, our northern subjects will require more than this."

"Your Grace." Anne turned to Fitzroy. "You are to gather the army the late King, your good father and my beloved husband was to issue into your command for Ireland, and once gathered, it is to head to the north. His Grace the Duke of Norfolk will assist you as Lord Lieutenant of the North."

Fitzroy bowed his head in agreement. It sounded as if the Regent had decided, in the wake of his late support of her, that he was to be trusted entirely. Setting him with Norfolk was yet another gesture of this trust. In truth, she had little option. Anne could not lead men herself, so she had to put faith in others.

"Your Grace." Anne turned to Suffolk. "You are to take the bulk of our forces from London, raise men from your own lands and head into the north as one of the two overall commander of our armies." She looked to Norfolk, who was wearing an expression of plain, unadulterated disgust on his face. He was the more experienced commander, in his eyes at least, but Suffolk she trusted more to protect the Crown, and he was younger than the old Duke.

"I understand, uncle, that you are the more experienced commander in some ways," the Regent noted. "But His Grace of Suffolk has the more recent experience in France, and, like you, his family have links to the north that may aid us. You, of course, will be the other commander of our forces, and I expect you and His Grace of Suffolk will work together well, your experience complementing his. His Grace of Richmond will be second commander. Since you must raise men from different parts of England, you will split apart, then reconvene at a place convenient so you may march north together."

"I think it would be better for me to ride ahead with the forces I have gathered, Majesty, as soon as they *are* gathered," Suffolk mentioned, a frown furrowing his brow. "These other forces, which were to be raised in Wales and the west of England, if I remember the late King's plans rightly..." he glanced at Richmond, who nodded in agreement "... may take longer to bring together. Any delay in riding out to meet this rebellion could be disastrous."

"If you believe you can raise enough men to face the rebels, Your Grace, then I give you leave to advance on them." Anne hoped Suffolk and the others could not hear the insecurity in her heart. It lurked there, a hard creature, chuckling at her inexperience. She never had thought she would be in charge of directing men in warfare. Anne had no experience of it, except in books she had read and now, standing before these men, every word of every book she ever had read vanished from her mind, as well as all the wisdom derived from the discussions she had held in private with her brother George and her father in preparation for this meeting only an hour before. She felt like a child.

"When the western forces are gathered, they will reinforce those of the Duke of Suffolk," she continued. "In the meantime, my Lord Rochford, as Lord Warden of the Cinque Ports, is to ensure the Cinque Ports are rallied and ready to repel any foreign invasion in case anyone should think to use this time to move against us from France or Spain." Anne indicated to her brother, who bowed his head, then she turned to her father. "My lord, the Earl of Wiltshire, as Lord Privy Seal will be needed here and will be placed in charge of the security of the royal household during this time of strife."

Anne had to restrain herself from sighing out loud in relief as she saw Suffolk nod in agreement with regards to the last few orders she had issued. At least he approved of something she had said.

"I hear many monks and nuns have joined the northern rebels, Your Majesty," Audley noted. "Many are there in support of Lady Mary as Queen, but there are plenty who are disaffected over the proposed closures of the smaller religious houses."

The closures had begun, Fitzroy had heard of them and of monks turning out with clubs in hand to attempt to save their homes and houses of worship from the men sent by Cromwell. Only a few had gone ahead, the worst of the houses. Fear over the others that would close, however, had led to the inhabitants of other small houses joining this rebellion.

Anne ran her hands over her white skirts. "I understand, and we have sent men out to preach to those who do not understand that we are not aiming to close all the smaller houses. I have issued lists of the establishments to be saved which are being proclaimed even now, so men may inform people who are listening to fearful, inflamed gossip, that it is not all smaller houses that will close, but only those with practices abhorrent which cannot be salvaged. Those acting in accordance with their vows, or who can be redeemed, will be saved from the purge we make now, for the good of God."

For the good of your purse, thought Norfolk, grimacing as he rubbed his belly, another pain, and he always had so many, troubling him. He shifted in his seat, wishing this dull meeting held by this witless niece of his to be over so he could leave and fart loudly in private, as his belly desired.

"Once our forces are gathered, you, Your Grace…" Anne nodded to Richmond, "will return to London in order to keep the council appraised of the army's plans."

Fitzroy hesitated. "Your Majesty, would it not be better for me to stay with my men? A messenger could be sent just as easily with dispatches."

"And yet could not grant us a full and comprehensive appraisal of the situation." She smiled at the young man. "You are a fit, hale man, Richmond. Your father often boasted of your virility with great pride, so I am sure you can, as he once did, take on such a journey and tire many horses before you yourself grow weary."

And I want to have you here, reporting to me so Norfolk gets no ideas, she thought. Norfolk had said nothing about the betrothal offer. That was a thing strange. Of course, there was this trouble in the north, and that was high in everyone's minds, but still, something jangled in her soul about his silence.

Anne needed Fitzroy to gather men, Fitzroy knew that. Already Cromwell, Wiltshire and others would have assured her he would be capable of gathering many more than others could. He had thought this a gesture of her faith in him, but clearly Anne did not entirely trust Norfolk and Fitzroy away together in the north. Anne's mistrust stung a little, and he resented it.

As they filed out of the council chamber, Norfolk raised one eyebrow at his son-in-law. They both understood: the Regent suspected them. From a certain glint growing in Norfolk's eye, Fitzroy was starting to think there was good reason for that.

CHAPTER TWENTY-SEVEN

Katherine Willoughby, Duchess of Suffolk

2nd of April 1536

Passion Sunday

Suffolk Place

Southwark

"And what am I to do as you run off north and betray the Crown?" Katherine stared in horror at her husband of three years. She was seventeen, he fifty-two, but at that moment Katherine felt she possessed more wisdom, sense and reason than he did. Perhaps it was fitting it was Passion Sunday, for she felt her passions, not to mention her fear of being arrested and executed, rise.

"It is not a betrayal of the Crown, but a restoration of the true line," Suffolk insisted, his cheeks afire.

"I am sure the Regent's guards will accept that excuse when to my gate they come and arrest me as an accomplice for what you are about to do, lord husband."

Charles walked to her, setting a hand on her waist. Something long left sorrowful and lonely in Katherine quivered. Once she had loved this man, she remembered, when she was growing up in his house as his ward, when she had seen him with his first wife, the King's sister, Mary. Once she had thought him romantic and exciting. Since they had been married, and it was not so very long, she had encountered fewer of these feelings but still he could make her feel an echo of them, when he touched her with a gentle hand, when he stared into her eyes as he was doing now. "You will come with me," he said. "Though the army is not place for a woman, the Poles tell me they have a plan and mean to move Princess Mary to Warwick Castle. There, you will be safe, and you will be with Mary, whom you knew as a girl."

Sometimes Katherine wondered if she should have stayed a girl. Fourteen she had been when wed to Charles, and she had thought herself indeed in love and he in love with her, until later, when she found he had been ruinously in debt and needed her grand inheritance to stem the bleeding of his account books. Since then… it was a thing strange to be wed to a man who professed with his mouth he loved her yet never seemed to want to be around her, unless it was to show off his prize at court or bed her. Much had been easier when she was a girl, living in the household of Charles Brandon and his wife Mary Tudor, who had been a kind woman, a fine replacement for her own mother, whose household she had left, as many noble children did to learn courtly graces in that of another.

She tried not to roll her eyes. Charles did not *think*. "And what of my mother? Are we to leave her in London to be arrested by the Regent? And our son, Charles, what am I to do with him? And your other children? What am I to say to Frances and Eleanor? Are their husbands in this plot with you, or will you send notes to them to let them know they are in danger? And how are you to explain to the Regent that you march out of London, on your way to deal with rebels no less, with your wife, child and mother-in-law as part of the party? Will you dress us as men or issue us halberds so we might pretend we are soldiers? It will make no sense you are taking us to war, and she will know something dark is afoot!"

Charles looked flummoxed for a moment, and Katherine realised he had not thought of this, of how it would look. Charles was often a creature of the immediate moment, not one for grand forethought, unless it was in battle and even then she had the impression he relied more on audacious daring, which required little planning, than preparation. Katherine sighed in exasperation.

"You will go with the army, as planned," she said, her quick mind working fast. "I will go to my mother and tell her all. Mother and I will take little Henry and make for the estates of my Willoughby ancestors in Lincolnshire, to Grimsthorpe Castle. It is old and not in good shape yet, since our renovations have only just begun, but it will be safe enough. I will excuse myself from court, say I am ill, and I will escape London with our family. Then I will wait for you to tell me it is safe to ride for Warwick. Your daughters you must send word to, or better yet, go yourself so they can make plans, for if not and they are left knowing nothing they surely will be arrested and used against you. And you must not declare what you are up to, Charles, you must not announce yourself for Mary's cause until I send word that we are free of the city and safe. Do you understand, Charles? You must wait!"

"I will wait." He sounded like a sulking child.

They spoke little more, for he had men to gather, and she had plans to make too. Katherine went to her son's nursey. Henry, not a year old yet, was asleep, having fed from his wet nurse. The nurse would have to come too, Katherine knew, for her own milk had dried up in the first month of her son's life, aided by cabbage leaves bound to her breasts. The wet nurse had been chosen with care. She had clear skin, a respectable character and fair hair, so Katherine's child would receive only the purest milk, and the wet nurse had herself birthed a boy. Charles believed in the old superstition that if the wet nurse had a girl of her own yet nursed a boy, that boy would grow up to be weak and docile. Katherine was not so sure of this, but her husband had insisted, just as he had about Katherine herself ceasing to feed her child.

Noble women were not permitted to suckle their children, it impaired conception, and Charles wanted more sons, as many as possible, his obsession rather akin to that of the late King. Her husband's first son, another Henry, child of Mary Tudor, had died not long after Katherine had married Charles. Katherine had been supposed to wed that Henry, not his father, but Charles had come to her, professing endless, devoted love and like a fool she had believed him. He had been so proud of their son, though, little Henry, named for his dead brother and for the King. In that at least she believed he was honest.

She looked down on her son's small, sweet face. *What a time to be born into,* she thought, for his father was about to either make their fortunes rise or bring them crashing to the ground.

CHAPTER TWENTY-EIGHT

Magpye Grey

18th of April 1536

The King's Arms Inn

Southwark

London

Magpye was not even sure how it had started. One moment the inn had been as normal. Well, normal for now, tempers were always a little fractious these days, and the next there was uproar. It was the day after Easter Monday. From Passion Sunday to Easter Sunday, Queen Anne's preachers had been out, surrounded by guards carrying pikes and halberds, telling all at court and beyond of the righteousness of the new regime. In the inn, people had come that day to speak of it, and of the trouble in the north.

At first, it had seemed as if all the panic at the beginning of the month had been for nothing. Local sheriffs and lords of Yorkshire had ridden out with their men, stopped gatherings, made arrests, carried out bloody, brutal punishments, and they had managed to subdue the uprising in their county. Their quick response and ruthless methods had caused the men marching to hesitate. Some rebel groups had broken apart and men had made a dash for home, not wanting to end up as a head upon a spike. But then, just as it seemed the rebellion had died, suddenly into life it flared again. A week ago, there came word that men of Yorkshire had gathered together again, in greater numbers this time, and men of Lancashire were rising now too, bent on rebellion. They were being led by a man called Aske, and he was a great speaker, it was said, inspiring many to join his growing army, which was calling for Mary to be freed and named Queen.

Norfolk and Richmond had ridden a week ago for the west of England, their leaving delayed at first as rumours had flown that the trouble in the north had died down. Suffolk too had left. Not three days ago he had taken the bulk of the royal guards within London and marched north, aiming to raise more men on the way. The tales were that all these dukes were to come together, with their forces, and stamp on the rebels in the north of England.

But in truth unrest was everywhere, in the streets, in the mouths of people, in minds. Each day as Lent had come to a close had seemed more fractious than the last, until that day, when it erupted.

In the inn, one group of people had started arguing with another, about something overheard, and a fight had broken out. That wasn't unusual. Magpye's pa had to break up fights all the time, yet usually it was but one or two people and this time it seemed it was the whole inn, all at once. There was a shout, heated words and then it seemed as if everyone was on their feet, fighting.

Magpye ducked and ran, dodging legs running her way and fists flying overhead, running for Ma's voice which she could hear over the shouting, calling her name over and over. On, on, she ran on her little legs until she reached the safety of her mother's arms, outstretched and waiting for her. The fight had spilled into the street by then and like a tinder sparking, suddenly the street was aflame but not with fire, with men fighting, with doors being broken in, and with noise.

The noise was the worst thing, Magpye thought as she and Ma ran up the stairs and locked themselves in their family room, as Pa had told them to, screaming at them to run as he grabbed his club and his dagger and, with some loyal regulars, friends of his of old from service in France, started to throw people out and attempt to defend the inn. Upstairs, cowering on the other side of Ma and Pa's bed which was next to her little one, Magpye covered her ears, but the noise wouldn't stop. The more she covered her ears, the more it seemed to grow louder, as if the noise was not outside at all but was inside her head, and that was where the fight was too, her own thoughts wrestling each other. There were women screaming in the distance, children crying and ringing over all that din were men bellowing at each other and the grunts of those falling in the street. Like a wind born of chaos it grew in the skies, a storm of summer breaking over them all, and it got louder and louder until she thought her head might burst.

Then it was gone.

Magpye unclasped her hands a little from her head, then a little more. There were shouts still, but most of the noise had moved on down the street, along with the people making it. "Joan!" Pa was at the door, knocking with his reddened knuckles. Magpye could see them now even though he was outside the room, and she was inside. They were hairy, rough. She'd always found them funny, tracing the hairs with her fingertips until her pa laughed, saying it tickled him. "Are you and Mag alright?"

Ma went to the door, having released Magpye from the close, tight embrace she had been holding her in. "We're alright, John." She opened the door, the big key turning in the lock. It was a good lock. Pa had always said they needed it, as you never knew who might stay overnight at the inn. You could hope all those taking a bed on the straw for a night were honest, but as

Pa said, sometimes honest faces were the best disguises liars and cheats had. He had wanted his ladies safe, he said.

Pa pulled Ma to him, a fast, relieved embrace. There was blood on his head. "You're hurt." Joan's voice was distraught, high with fear as her fingers traced the wound.

"A scratch, I'm fine." He hugged her again, then took Magpye in his arms and lifted her up so she sat on his side, her legs dangling in the air, his big, strong arm about her waist, holding her aloft as if she was nothing more than a little sack of rye flour.

"Have they gone?" Ma sounded as if she'd been running, her breathing coming hard.

He nodded. "Easier sport up the street. They've gone for the shops up there, perhaps the merchant houses if they're feeling bold enough. There will be looting tonight."

"What happened?"

"It was Tom Makepeace, arguing aloud about the Queen and her men taking control of the city and how she didn't deserve to be in power. Another jumped in, saying the little Queen Elizabeth was the only true blood of the King until his boy is born, and they called Makepeace a traitor. There was a scuffle, and others joined in. Now all this fuss, it's not about the regency or anything else. People have been riled for days, boxed in their houses during these early curfews, feeling fractious. Things aren't normal, people feel trapped, like animals, and it's spilled out. They'll riot and loot, and then the Watch will set them down."

"You think it will be over soon?"

"Not soon enough for some, but I think so."

"Is there much damage?"

"Broken stools, tables. Will, old man Llewellyn and young Ned, Baxter's son, helped me get them out and keep them out. The money's safe."

Joan took Magpye by the hand and they went downstairs. Magpye heard the shouting still, distant now, but it rang in Magpye's ears. There were bells ringing too, those of St Mary Overie were sounding in warning. Magpye hoped the priory was safe. She loved the church, with its high spire and lofty ceilings.

The inn was a mess, cups on the floor, ale pooling, blood too, here and there, splattered on the walls in little, bright flecks. Tables were overturned, stools broken, but Pa was right, it was superficial, Magpye could see that. They would set it right.

It took most of the day. Pa mended as they tidied. Joan washed the floor with water and vinegar and swept the water out with her great brush, pausing at the door every now and then to listen to the far-off sounds of the riot still occurring. Neighbours wandered past, asking what had happened, offering aid. One woman gave Ma a pie, warm from the bakehouse up the road, and they ate that as they worked. There were rumours that St Thomas's Hospital had been attacked and though the hospital had a dubious reputation it was still a place which tended to the poor. St Katherine's, near the Tower, too, was said to be overrun.

"You had trouble here, good Master Grey," a voice seemed to float on the wind and Magpye looked up. The owner of the voice had deep black eyes. She supposed they were brown in truth, but black they looked, like his skin. *A Moor*, she thought, marvelling at his beautiful eyes. There were many Moors in the neighbourhood as well as Flemings and other strangers or aliens as people called them; people whose ancestors had come from another land far away and had settled here in London. Some had been there for many generations. She supposed she was the same, in a way. Ma's ma had come from Wales. That was far away.

Pa glanced up and laughed a little, struck out a hand and pulled the man into an embrace he reserved only for friends. "Good to see you, Thomas," he said. "And as usual you describe much with understatement."

He pulled the man about. "Joan… Thomas, this is my wife," in excitement he spoke to both at the same time. "Mistress Joan Grey, this is Master Thomas Blanke, the friend from the market I said about."

"And a friend from France, long ago." The man bowed low to Joan, who giggled a little at the most courteous gesture.

"I'm not a lady of court, Master Blanke," she said almost shyly.

"But a lady all the same," he said, kissing her cheek as she came forth to kiss him, as was the custom in England, "and another little lady just here." He stared down at Magpye.

"Our Mags, we call her Magpye."

"Well met, Mistress Magpye." He bowed again, making Magpye titter.

"You served in France, Master Blanke?" Joan asked.

"In the King's army, an archer, like your fine husband here."

"The man saved my life, Joan, long before we met. Had he not been here, we might never have married." Pa grinned wide at Thomas, then at Joan.

"Then I am grateful to you, good Master Blanke," she said. "I would not have wanted to marry another but John."

Thomas smoothed his black coat. "John, being a man to never speak in his own praise, has probably not told you that he saved me too, Mistress Grey. To be a soldier is a thing most dangerous. It is good to know someone is there, watching out for you in hard and troubled times, and we were lads when we served, unprepared for much we encountered. We owe much to each other, in truth."

"I think your actions outweighed mine, Thomas." Magpye's pa smiled, but his eyes were serious.

Joan narrowed her eyes at her husband, then turned to Thomas. "John indeed did not tell me enough, clearly, Master Blanke, of his time in the King's army, although he has spoken of you, of course, but why do we not see you here, at the inn?"

Thomas smiled. "I am not one to partake of the ale," he said. "Although I am a Christian, my father was raised in a religion which forbade the drink and I was ever denied it as a child and young man. For a short time, when first he came here, my father still honoured, in private, the faith of his father, but as the years passed he converted, as did his children. The faith I hold now permits me to partake, but I find I have no stomach for it, and no temper for the kind of trouble it can cause."

"Aye, sometimes I think I should have taken on another profession," Pa said, rue in his voice as he gazed about the damaged inn.

"A good man must run an inn, my friend, or bad men will."

"But why have we not met before?" Joan pressed.

"Thomas is not often in London and when here, only in passing," Pa explained. "It was sheer luck I saw him at the market the other day. He is a well-respected merchant, a finder of valuable things, and often, when in London, he is passing here and there to the houses of great men and women, giving them the items they tasked him to find."

"Business, my good lady, sadly keeps me on the move," said Thomas, glancing at Magpye's pa with affection and amusement for the grand way he had described Thomas's life. "Such is the life of a small merchant. Your husband flatters me by saying I work only for the rich, but in truth I work for many people, high and low. We smaller merchants, we must be ever on the move to outdo the larger ones, who can undercut us. But when I heard there was trouble in this quarter, and knowing your inn was here, I made haste to come and see that you were alright." He indicated to a few men, milling outside. Their faces were pale and weatherbeaten, indicating they had been travelling long in the sun and wind, and they had active eyes, watchful, as if ready for trouble. "I have men, John, usually I use them to protect the passage of my wagons, but they are at your disposal if you have need of them to defend the inn."

"I think the riot's moved on." Pa wiped a hand over his sweaty forehead. "They made a mess, but they didn't get our money, nor did they cause too much harm."

"They are moved on, indeed," said Thomas. "But they may come back. I hear apprentices are running wild and even the aldermen and guilds cannot keep control."

"Apprentices always run wild, whenever there is any excuse to do so. I am sure it will settle soon, and if not, I have my club, my dagger, and good neighbours here. We'll set something up for the street, our own watch of men, to ensure we're not attacked again."

"Englishmen are the bravest I ever met, and I have met men of every land," observed Thomas.

"Are you not an Englishman, Master Blanke?" Magpye asked, her voice piping in. Thomas sounded English, to her ear, but there was a subtle undercurrent of an accent she could not quite place. Was it Portuguese? She did not think it Flemish or French. Southwark was full of accents. Magpye had a game she played sometimes, trying to place them.

Thomas turned to smile at her. "I am an Englishman, and a proud one," he explained. "I was born here, Mistress Magpye, just as your father was, but as I said, my father hailed from another land, one much hotter than this, far to the south of this lovely isle in the sea. Some of my ancestors, my mother's kin, are of England, as some hail from many other lands. In some ways, just as I know I am English, I also consider myself bonded to all the places my ancestors have called home. We used to travel, my family and I, about the world, and I still do as I trade and sell my goods. Look in the background of any man and you will find he is English, and Irish, and Welsh or comes of the Empire, and perhaps he even has ancestors from lands you never have heard of. That is the magic of this world, that we may be of one place, and all others. That this whole world is our home."

"I wish I could see such places." Magpye's eyes felt bright in her face at the thought of these lands so far away, at the idea of belonging to more than one land. Was Wales hers also, because of Ma? Perhaps it was so, but never had she seen anywhere but London.

"There are wonders in every country, Mistress Magpye. But more to be found in the sanctum of the family."

Magpye beamed. She liked the way Thomas talked; it was like poetry, like the psalms Pa softly spoke over her when she was drifting off to sleep.

"Let my men aid you in clearing up," Thomas offered. "It is the least we can do. I am bound for Dover and with all the trouble London is in now, I think it a good time to be back on the road, but I can spare a day for my men to help you."

"We'd welcome the help, Master Blanke," said Joan. "There are some larger broken parts of the tables which are beyond help and must be chopped up and stacked out the back, in the garden."

The rioters hadn't reached the garden, or the pig or chickens, which was a good thing as they needed them for eggs and for meat when November came around and it was time to slaughter the pig. Magpye was always sad when that year's pig died but she knew, because Pa had told her, that you didn't keep a pig for any other reason than to eat it and their pigs had a fine life, getting fat on the trenchers from the inn and snorting in their hut or basking in the sunshine when it was warm. Ma was an expert at smoking and pickling so their garden's food always went far, but it wouldn't have stretched to feed everyone at the inn each night, even a simple dish of pottage such as they served, with bread from the bake house up the road. Joan and Magpye would make the loaves at home, then Magpye took them to the bakehouse. Everyone did the same, and everyone had their own special mark on their bread so no one got each other's loaves. Their cabbage, Alexanders and turnip harvest usually did well, and some went in the pot for the inn most nights, they bought dried peas from the market to bulk out the evening's offering, and oats too, but the meat, usually mutton, for the food served at the inn, Ma had from a butcher who gave her a goodly deal for she was a regular customer and the fishmongers did the same, for she always had a smile and a jest for them. People liked Ma, as she was kind and pretty and nice to everyone. Men at the inn were always saying had John not wed her, they would have, and Joan always replied, just as she had to Thomas, that she never would have wed another but her John. Magpye's heart shone like the sun to know her parents loved one another. Plenty of couples about Southwark seemed to loathe one another only more as every year rolled on, but not her parents.

"Then I will set my men to moving all you wish moved, under your direction, good lady," Thomas said.

Magpye watched Thomas as he continued talking to Pa after directing his men to be commanded by Joan in the art of cleaning up. His tunic and coat were finer than Pa's, made of dark cloth, black, which was an expensive dye, but it was a little faded and Magpye suspected he had bought it of a fripperer, a merchant who sold second-hand clothes, often finery discarded by the wealthy. Fine clothes often passed from lord or lady as a gift to their servants, then to children or to be sold on. Some cloth, colours or fur was not to be worn by lesser people, the sumptuary laws forbade it, but sometimes if a cloth or fur was worn enough, it was hard to tell what it had started out as and people got away with wearing fabrics they were not supposed to. Magpye had heard great ladies of court often defied sumptuary laws by claiming they wore a certain fabric because their father's rank was high enough, even if their husband's was not. Only lately had the King become stricter about clothing laws, trying to stop Katherine and Mary from demonstrating their professed status as Queen and Princess by the clothes they wore.

Magpye marvelled at Thomas's garments, though, because even second-hand or third, Thomas's clothing, because of the colour, would have been expensive. Black was a costly dye, but oddly it was a colour not so restricted by the sumptuary laws. Merchants favoured it because it could demonstrate their wealth, and therefore their success in business. That was why he wore it, she understood, to show his clients that he was a man of money, to be trusted. His cap was dark too, with a bright white feather sticking out of it.

Thomas moved with a grace she found a little fascinating, and spoke with a soft, but firm tone. Suddenly she realised that since he had spoken, she hadn't heard the noise of the rioters so much, they had faded into the background. There was something calming about his presence, something comforting. She was glad Pa had friends like Thomas, glad they had been archers together in the King's army and even more glad Thomas had saved Pa's life. If Pa had never been here, she would not have been either, and then, how lonely Ma would be, she thought, to be alone without either one of them at her side.

CHAPTER TWENTY-NINE

Queen Anne Boleyn
25th of April 1536
St Mark's Day
Richmond Palace
London

Anne jumped as someone screamed in the corridor outside. There was a sound of racing feet, guards shouting, trying to keep order. The panic which had flooded court in the last hour was now wildly out of control. No matter what Anne ordered, people were not listening.

"It is time to go, now!" her brother shouted at her. "We cannot delay any longer, there are people almost at the very gates, a horde of them!"

"He is right, Majesty," said Norris, his servant George Constantine hovering close at his elbow, looking nervous. "You have delayed escape in order to bolster the spirit of the guards and the city long enough. We must preserve you now."

Anne felt as if she walked in a dream. The night before she had dreamed of her beloved dog, Purkoy, who she had lost two years ago as he fell from an open window. In her dream he had come, as often he did when she was sad, and nestled his small, wet nose into her hand, nudging until his soft head lay under her palm. In her dream she had stroked him and known that all would be well, for he was there and even if many hated her, Purkoy loved her. In the worst of times, when she had felt broken, shattered by a miscarriage and Henry's infidelity, her hound had been there, offering love, offering solace. In her dream Anne had sighed, feeling a sense of peace flow through her veins.

Then she had woken, to this.

The riots which had broken out in the city had lulled overnight then exploded the next morn, in many parts of London, so many, too many. Over the days that followed they had become more intense, better followed, more organised. Men seemed to teem out of woodwork and wall to join the rioters, who fast were becoming a rebellion. Some were shouting the name of the Lady Mary in the streets.

Anne had sent out men to make barricades, to hold streets, to fight back, but the Watch and the royal guards, those who remained left to her after Suffolk had marched out with so many, could barely keep control. They found themselves outmanoeuvred and outnumbered, and as the days had passed some of the rioters were being reported as being suspiciously well armed, as if someone had aided them, someone with power and resources. They had grown in number every day and seemed to have a plan now too, not just concentrating on attacking shops and inns or houses of the poorer people of London, as usually happened in times of unrest, but attacks on the houses of the rich had been reported, and all of those houses which had been targeted belonged to her supporters. People had flooded to court, begging her to shelter them. From Greenwich the court had shifted to Richmond, being further out of the main city it was thought safer. But now rioters or rebels were on the march, heading for Richmond, for her. It was reported their numbers had swollen. Two thousand, so it was claimed, were on their way to Richmond, and other bands of thousands were heading for Whitehall, Westminster, for the gates of London's walls, to take control of all of the city.

London was fast falling to chaos.

Anne thought of another dream, not the one of the night before. Katherine had shown her, had she not? Shown her London burning. *"When the Tower is white, and another place green, then shall be burned two or three bishops and a Queen, and after all this be passed, we shall have a merry world again."* That was what Katherine had said. Were the people coming here to murder Anne? Would she burn this day?

"Majesty!" George's voice shocked her out of her daydreams of death.

"We should shift to the Tower of London," Anne said. "It can be fortified, held well."

"We cannot." Her father's face was harried, grey. "The river down that way is full of boats claimed by rioters. London Bridge has been swamped by men looting the shops there and the Tower itself is surrounded. I hear the guards of the Tower are holding out well, but we will not get to it. It is not safe to try."

"Where, then?"

"Windsor," he said. "A farther journey, but the castle can be secured. It is not so far out of London that we cannot issue orders from there, yet not so close as to cause issues of security for you and the children. Elizabeth must be kept safe."

Anne stared at him. Did he think she did not know this? "Elizabeth *will* be safe, Father," she said firmly. "As long as she is with me, no man will get close enough to harm her." She drew herself up. "Very well, we make for Windsor. Tell the court they are to evacuate in an orderly manner, panic aids no one. Father, get Elizabeth and bring her to me. Mother too, she was resting in her chambers. We will have a party of guards with us at all times."

Her father rushed away, and Anne turned to George. "George... Jane. I sent her to your rooms to gather her belongings, but there is no time."

"I will get her." He ran off.

"Norris," she said. "Stay with me. I fear much, but with you beside me I fear less."

"I am here, Anne," he said quietly. "No man will come near you as long as I am here."

Anne stared about the chamber, her wandering eyes taking in cushions and hangings she herself had embroidered. Emblems of acorns, honeysuckle, of roses and bulls filled the rooms. Would the rioters come here and burn all of this? Would they strip this palace of all she had made, of all the signs and symbols she had created of Henry, of her, of them together, of their marriage? Would she have nothing left but her memories?

From a table she snatched up a book. It was an illuminated manuscript of the writings of Jacques Lefèvre d'Étaples. George had had it made for her, years ago, when she had lost her child before it was born and had become lost in lowness. The book had helped her then and she found that now it was the item she most wanted to save if all else she was to lose.

"What will come of this, Norris?" she asked, her voice dry in her throat as she clasped the book to her breast. "And who is helping the people to rise up? Someone is behind this, something else is behind it. There is a purpose, this is not just rebellion. I can feel it."

"Whoever they are, and whatever they do now, they will pay for it," he said.

Anne hoped he was right, for she had an awful feeling it might not be these conspirators, whoever they were, who would pay, but her.

CHAPTER THIRTY

George Boleyn, Viscount Rochford

25th of April 1536

St Mark's Day

Richmond Palace

London

"George!"

Jane cried out as her husband entered their chambers, her face pale and worried yet resolute, he noted. She was commanding her servants like a general as they raced about, packing cases.

George looked about at the cases of half-packed clothes, books and jewels. "We must leave, Jane. All this, we must leave it. There are men almost at the gates. It is time to flee the palace."

Jane froze a moment, staring at the finery in the chamber, at her dresses, her jewel case, the tapestry on the walls and the hangings on the bed, then she turned her back on it. "Very well." Twisting about to face her servants she held up a hand, and they stopped immediately, looking to her with anxious eyes. "Leave it, leave it all," she said. "What matters is our lives."

She turned to George. "There is a plan?"

"We all make for Windsor, all who can. There are barges and boats gathering to take everyone."

She nodded. "Make for the water, get on whatever boat you

can," she said to her servants. "And God save you all."

They bobbed to bow and curtsey, then hurried from the door. "The situation is that grave?" she asked.

He nodded. "We are overcome. London is fallen to riots and the guards cannot keep control. The bulk of them marched with Suffolk, so we were weakened before the fight even began! It is as if it was planned. Someone is behind this, I think. The rioters barely seem like rioters. They are armed, organised. I think there is a plot here we are unaware of."

Briefly George's thoughts flitted to Cromwell. They always did when he was thinking of something underhanded. Could Cromwell be behind this? Playing friend to Anne at court and working behind her back? The man had many connections in London, enough wealth to finance much too. Before the King had died, George had thought Cromwell was moving to switch factions at court, for he had been seen with Chapuys often enough, Gertrude Courtenay too. Was it possible it was him?

Jane stared at him a while. "The Tower," she said.

George shook his head. "It is surrounded; we cannot go there."

"No, I mean, I think the Tower, Mary, they are the focus."

George paled a little. His wife had always been clever, he had known that from the first. He had thought the objective of the riots would be to reach Anne and Elizabeth, take them prisoner and perhaps kill them. It had not occurred to him that Mary would be the object, and what the rioters wanted would be her freedom. Again he thought of Cromwell. There had been rumour abroad that Cromwell had tried to persuade the King to legitimize Mary, to improve relations with Spain, and all knew Cromwell wanted England friends with the Empire for they were the stronger partner in Europe, the best ally for trade and for war. Anne had told George to trust Cromwell, he was working for her, so she said. George wondered if his clever sister could be being played for a fool.

"The rioters cannot claim the streets forever," Jane went on. "But what if this was just a distraction, so a plan to let Mary escape could be put in place?"

George's throat was dry as a scalded pot. "There are soldiers at the Tower."

"Once before in history the Tower fell, and once only. My father told me of it, part of his studies. Richard II went out to meet the rebels who assailed him, and the gates were left open. There is no King inside now, but what if the soldiers at the Tower are not loyal to your sister, but to Mary?"

"All of them?"

"It would not need to be all of them. There would just need to be enough."

"How do you know this? Are you still in contact with those who support Mary?"

Jane flinched visibly. Her shoulders began to fall as George reminded her that once she had stood with those who supported the former princess, that she had protested in favour of Mary. Yet she had gone along with those people in order to find out who supported Mary, who might be a danger to Anne. Jane had thought it a clever move at the time, but it had earnt her the suspicion of her Boleyn family, who were never sure, after that, if her loyalty truly was theirs. "I know nothing," she said, her voice tight. "I suspect much. There was a time I sympathised with the Lady Mary, part of my heart probably always will. I think her a daughter treated not well by her father, and sometimes by your sister, too. But my loyalty is bound to you. I tried to find out who supported Mary so we could protect Anne. This, I told you."

"But still, you have a knowledge of the minds of such people."

"So do you. Think what you would do for your sister, and then you will know what those devoted to Mary's cause would do for her. If your sister were in the Tower of London and you were free, would you not move heaven and earth to achieve her liberty?"

George scowled. There was nothing to be done about the Tower now. Guards in the streets were being overrun as it was, they could not be spared to reinforce the Tower, even if they could get to it. Even his suspicions about Cromwell had to wait. "We have to get away," he said. "God keep the soldiers at the Tower loyal to the true line of the Crown!"

He took her hand and they raced down the corridors. Courtiers were flying in different directions, some in groups, some in pairs, some with their hands full of plate and gold and clothes. Somewhere behind them, on the stairs someone fell, bashing into others. There was shouting, screaming, the sound of people tumbling, out of control, down the steps. George and Jane ran on, not looking back.

Outside, a cool blast of air hit their faces and to George it was like nectar. Feeling that coolness settle on the sweat heavy on his skin was bliss and brought his mind clarity for a moment. People were everywhere; voices raised all around them. He glanced about. Most people were heading for the water but some for the stables, for horses, hoping to ride out into the park and escape that way. Jane and George raced for the water steps. Anne's royal barge was waiting, guards pushing back panicked people trying to get on board, but with a nod, Sir Thomas Burgh, Anne's Chamberlain, let George and his wife through. Onto it they climbed. As he helped his wife onto the boat, George clasped her hand tight, the warmth of her skin comforting him.

As they went to find Anne and Elizabeth, as a shout rang out that they were on board and the boat began to travel through the water, oars moving fast, he found he was still clinging to Jane's hand, as if he never meant to let her go.

CHAPTER THIRTY-ONE

Eustace Chapuys, Imperial Ambassador
25th of April 1536
St Mark's Day
The Tower of London

He had never liked the River Thames, Chapuys thought as nervously he waited on his barge hovering off the Water Gate of the Tower. It was so grey and choppy, even on a good day when one could see the fish swimming beneath the water, it still seemed an angry river, dark of mood and ominous of intent. It was not a river that would flood often, it was true, not one to rush into the city, but still, there always seemed something resentful about it, a simmering rage kept captive just under the lapping skin of the water, as if something buried there long ago had not died but haunted the river, waiting for a chance to return.

He might have cause to thank it, this day, however, if they achieved what they wanted.

The rioters had been easy to approach, simple to guide. Some fell for talk of loyalty, some for coin, some for hope. Shouts for Mary and her freedom had already been heard in the streets, so the men of Montagu and the Countess, and those sent by Carew, they just had to find such men and drop the idea of the plan into their heads. Then had come the weapons, unveiled in many houses of new loyalists to the cause of Mary along the city streets, so hopefully it appeared as if it were a coincidence that men rose in many parts of London at almost the same moment, then the drink to make them bolder had been distributed. By the end of two days, they had a mass of thousands marching angrily on the Tower to set Mary free, another section looting the streets and keeping the royal guard and watchmen busy, and a last advancing on the palace of Richmond where the court had fled after trouble broke first at Greenwich. That section of their new army had gone to distract the Queen.

But the last obstacle had been to gain the guards at the Tower itself, sway them to their cause. They had been got to by Gertrude Blount and Geoffrey Pole. Some were paid; some were already sold on the belief Mary was the true Queen and needed little persuasion. Enough of them to tip the scale, so they hoped. Enough to gain control of the portcullis and gate, enough to fight within the streets of the Tower complex. Surprise would be their ally. With that on their side they did not need great numbers. Soon enough he would know if this last part of the plan had worked. If it had not, he would order his men to row on, make as if he was escaping the city as was his privilege and mission as a foreign ambassador. If it had worked, however, he would soon have a passenger.

It was the creaking of the gates, of the portcullis, the shouts that echoed in the London streets not far away which gave his heart the first reason to leap, then the sounds of fighting. Of course, not all the soldiers manning the Tower walls had been bought. But it seemed enough had.

"There is noise within, my lord," whispered one of the men on the oars, and Chapuys nodded. He could hear it too, a roar which began at the gated moat of the Tower and was gathering pace within.

There was the sound of shouting from the guards on the walls, confused orders. The bells of the Bell Tower began to ring in warning and then swift as they started, they stopped. Sound of swords and halberds clashing and screams of men followed as guard turned on guard, butchering their brothers-in-arms as they stood at post, and all the time the din grew louder, more insistent, as a wave it seemed to rise inside the Tower itself, cresting, falling, crashing.

The Water Gate opened suddenly, gates creaking as they yawned into the river itself and inside, on the slipway, a figure stood in a cloak in the shadows, her maid by her side. Clearly they had been running. A pale face looked up, the light of the waning sun reaching her skin, her frightened eyes. It was Mary. "Get to her, quickly!" Chapuys shouted to the men on the oars.

Their boat hit the slipway just a little too hard, and jolted, but Mary was on board all the same, quick as a flash, not waiting for anyone to help her, her hands scrambling to meet the sides of the boat. His men pulled her aboard, her maid too. Guards standing at the Water Gate, ready to hold off men Chapuys could see fighting and struggling in the streets beyond, within the Tower, had swords drawn, one with a halberd in hand. "Get yourselves to safety," the Princess called to them. "And God bless you!"

"God speed, Your Majesty," one said, as several men pushed the boat off, so into the water it rocked.

"Get down, Majesty," Chapuys said, throwing a blanket over her. "They must not see you." He hoped the archers on the walls had been taken care of. That had been one of the first orders given. Considering the lack of arrows flying their way, he supposed the Regent's archers were dead, slumped at post on those walls, their throats slit.

"Pomegranate," Mary laughed, sounding a trifle hysterical as she draped the blanket over her head, pulling it too over her maid. "They burst into my rooms, shouting pomegranate! I thought I was to die when I heard the riot, and then they were there and then through the Tower we ran. Men fell before my eyes, Chapuys, men died, but I am here. The men who came, they protected me, brought me to you."

"We have friends, *you* have friends, Majesty."

"You took the Tower," she said in amazement. "For me, you have made the impossible, possible."

"Few things are truly impossible, Majesty. With a quick mind and money enough, there is much a man can do. We did not need to take the Tower. All we needed was enough time for the guards to be distracted so we could pull you out."

"Where do we go?" she asked, breathless, nestling at the bottom of the boat as the oarsmen pulled hard, taking them sailing along fast with the current of the water. The time had been carefully chosen to ensure a swift escape. Other boats were flying along the river too. They were but one of many now, a good disguise.

"The house of the Poles first, so we can gather more men to guard you," he said. "And then away, to the north. There is a rebellion forming there. Men already marching out, preparing to take London. They march in your favour, Majesty. At Warwick Castle we will gather your forces. Word is being sent out that you are calling England to your side, to take the Crown."

"Let us get away from the Tower first, good friend, then we will see to England and the Crown."

"Row on," he shouted. "As if your lives depend on it... which they do!"

The boat rocked through the water, speeding fast. Few noted it in the chaos as the gates of the Tower yawned wide, and every man in London, or so it seemed, rushed within. Swiftly the Tower was overcome, the streets and walls choked with men struggling, men dying. They did not know what they fought for already was gone.

If the river was busy the roads were too, people flying away from the city, trying to get out, to get anywhere now London was fallen to chaos and violence, and amongst those many fleeing was a Queen in waiting, burrowed at the bottom of a boat, trying to stop her pounding heart from beating so hard, for she was sure the Regent would hear it from wherever she was, and come for her.

CHAPTER THIRTY-TWO

Catherine Parr, Lady Latimer

25th of April 1536

St Mark's Day

Snape Castle

North Yorkshire

England

Catherine Latimer, née Parr, looked on with some amazement. She had never seen her husband so determined. John Neville, the Lord Latimer, it had often struck her, was rather a ditherer. He often tried to play both sides whenever there was an argument so ended up supporting neither, and made no friends on either side for lack of a true opinion of his own and limited courage to support one, but not now. The old man was determined. The rebels were at their gates, and he was about to let them in.

"Mary is the true Queen, and is a daughter of the true faith," he said, his page dancing about, trying to strap Latimer's old sword to his side as his master turned to Catherine, making the job harder. She wondered if Latimer had ever truly used it in combat. "The people rise to support her, this time in greater, stronger numbers and I have had word from Lord Montagu.

The true Queen will be set free soon, and I will be at her side."

"Set free of the Tower, with the Queen Regent in London, and guards all about her?" Catherine scoffed gently, then shook her head, urging herself to demonstrate patience. "Beloved, consider, what if this is but wishful thinking? Is it wise to join this rebellion now, when all we have are half-truths and scrappy pieces of information? If you join and are seen to join, and all this is talk of Mary being freed soon is untrue, the royal army will crush the common people and you will be hanged or beheaded, my love!"

My love, she thought. *How casually we use words with great meaning when we mean them not at all.* She had never really loved Latimer. They had been married more than a year now and he was a good enough husband, kind and attentive, never free with his hands. He did not scare her. It was true he did not listen to her, like now, which was frequently frustrating as although she was much younger than he, Catherine was fairly sure she had a stronger mind; but few men believed that of any woman, and Catherine was pretty, which usually meant men believed she owned even less intelligence than other women. It was not possible for a woman to be clever and attractive, so thought many a man.

Latimer was good enough to her, she had been fortunate to find an agreeable second marriage, but love there was not from her heart to his. Sometimes she felt that lack in her, like a hole inside her it gaped, the winds of the world passing through it, whistling as they flowed. Others loved her, she knew, her Parr family, Latimer's children from his first marriage. She was more fortunate than some, and yet something in Catherine wanted to be cherished, to be loved for herself and not for the role of wife she merely played, a devoted companion, a sweet thing to come to bed to. Catherine wanted more, but she knew she probably never would have it. She would end her days the wife of Latimer, enjoying a tepid affection from one heart to another. Her marriage was not a horror, but it was empty of all she wanted it to contain.

It was, however, better than her first marriage to Sir Edward Burgh where she had been housed a long time not only with her sickly, young husband but his crazed, unpredictable father, Sir Thomas Burgh. The man was Lord Chamberlain to Queen Anne Boleyn, was fiercely loyal to the Queen and to the cause of reform, but he also had a wild temper and had taken that temper out on his son, on her, on the servants. Whoever came within striking distance would do. He had had another daughter-in-law, Elizabeth Owen, who was wed to his younger son and namesake, thrown from his house and had her children bastardized. Sir Thomas's father had been declared a lunatic, and Catherine had thought the same, fell poison of madness had fallen upon her father-in-law, too.

Catherine could thank Thomas Burgh for one thing, however; that he had introduced her, opened her eyes to the reformed faith, the true faith, such as the Queen followed. It was odd that such a blunt instrument could have performed such a delicate operation as splitting her faith from the old to take up the true, but God worked in many ways mysterious.

Catherine, upon marrying Latimer, after Edward Burgh's death, had had to hide her personal beliefs which favoured the reforms of the King and even dipped towards Lutheranism. Latimer was a staunch believer in the old faith and held it as a cardinal truth that any kind of criticism of the Church was heresy. She had made this match of marriage for safety, and it was in many ways a good one, but Catherine could not be herself, not fully, in this marriage. This was another reason she felt her husband knew her not, and without being known, without being herself, how could she ever be loved as she wished to be? One cannot love someone they do not know, all they may feel is obsession, or false affection.

Her step-daughter, Margaret Neville, came to her side. Latimer's child from his first marriage, Catherine was fond of her. John too, her step-son, though he was wilder than almost anyone knew how to temper. Catherine was the only one who could reason with him, get him to behave. She had had practice with her first father-in-law and put that training to good purpose in her second marriage. He had a vicious character, John, a feral nature. Even Latimer was afraid of him, and John was only a young man, sixteen years. But with every month he grew in age, so he grew in temper. In all honesty she wondered if Latimer riding off to join the rebels did not have something, at least a little something, to do with wanting to get away from John and the necessity of trying to calm him.

"I will go and support the true Queen, *my* Queen." Latimer put his pale hand on his sword, as if he meant to fight for Mary personally. It was more likely he would sit on a hillside watching any battle that occurred.

Margaret pressed close to Catherine, and Catherine put an arm about her. The girl was only fourteen. "If you go to join them, husband, who will stay here to protect this house?"

"Snape Castle, I leave to you. It is well-fortified, can withstand a siege. There will be our guards, men to aid you, left here. Close the gates and repel the Regent's army if near they come. Welcome, feed and house any supporter of Mary. But I will march with these men, Catherine. Honour and my conscience demand it."

And with that, her husband strode off to join a rebellion.

Catherine turned to Margaret. "And we shall hold this house, as your father commands us to," she told the frightened girl. "Go find your brother. We have need of all of us working as one."

Repel the Regent's army, Catherine thought with scorn as Margaret scurried away, her crimson skirts brushing the cold floor. How was she supposed to do such a thing? In the wars of Lancaster and York she had heard of women commanding castles, holding them against the enemy, but she had few guards here and no experience.

If trouble came of that kind, Catherine would rather surrender and find herself on the side of the Regent, who was of the true faith, than on the side of all these Catholic rebels and Latimer, who had abandoned them.

CHAPTER THIRTY-THREE

Sir Thomas Wyatt
26th of April 1536
Windsor Castle
England

That, certainly, was a journey he never wanted to make again, Wyatt thought with a mingled sense of anger and relief as he strode down the busy hallway in the castle of Windsor, dodging courtiers who were milling around, trying to find rooms, food and drink or information from each other. Busy servants wearing harried expressions were running about attempting to find what their masters wanted, and they would fail for in truth what they wanted was some measure of security and that precious commodity was nowhere to be found. The castle was in chaos.

Wyatt marched on, turning the corridor, only just getting out of the way of a racing servant, Thomas Culpepper, once cupbearer to the King, who nearly had him on his arse. "Slow down, lad!" he shouted, and Culpepper called out an apology as he ran on. He tried to bow and turn whilst running, which caused him to almost collide with a maid coming the other way.

Wyatt sighed. The faithful river had carried them to Windsor. This narrower section of the River Thames had been taxing to navigate, not because of the water or currents, but because of the sheer number of boats jostling on the waterway, trying to escape. There had been shouting and screaming on the water as boats collided, and more than one smaller craft had gone over. Fortunately, the struggling people had been pulled from the water and hauled on board other boats. When Windsor had come in sight great cheers had arisen from the bedraggled courtiers, but when they arrived not all people could find horses to take them up the hill to Windsor Castle. Some had simply started walking, not daring to wait, as others had stubbornly stood by the river, refusing to arrive at the castle in such a fashion. Horses, ridden out by servants from Windsor or from estates nearby had arrived later as increasingly nervous people had hovered about the river's banks. Then there had been scuffles and fights over those horses, but most of the court had made it inside Windsor's walls by that afternoon. For those who had not been able to get on a boat and had been forced to come by road, it had not been an easy journey at any stage. They arrived much later, for the road took longer than the river and the road in question had been wet and muddy. Some horses, ridden with too much haste by frightened people, had collapsed at the side of the road and died, heaving chests failing, legs beating the ground and foam pouring from their nostrils and mouths.

Wyatt was glad he had reached the castle in one piece.

Now, he was not sure he wanted to be there. The halls were busy with bodies, with worried faces, with talk. Like a beehive Windsor hummed, and there was something of that mild threat of pain on its way which was inherent to the buzz of such insects, which rode on the collective voice of the court. Like words in a song sung far away, he could not catch the words but understood their meaning. He could hear fear and anger, distrust, disbelief in what had happened and rage that the Regent had allowed it to. Some were defending her, some attacking and all were on edge. All were muttering, too, not daring to speak loud in case someone heard them and reported their words. No one wanted to get thrown out of this sanctum they had fled to, after all. There was a feral feeling to court, and not just because of the flight they had taken. Everyone was scared of what would come next.

The castle felt reassuring, however. Windsor was an impressive fortress, built for times of trouble. The walls could take a mighty pounding and would be hard to scale or bring down. The apartments were deep within the boundaries. They were safe here, but there were other problems.

The castle had little food, as it had not been expecting the entire court, or most of it – some people had fled to their own estates – to turn up here. Rooms were not in a state to welcome anyone and furniture, which on any progress would have been brought along, palace to palace, was not there, having been left, abandoned at Richmond. Scant pieces there were about the place, so people were sitting on the floor, sleeping on makeshift pallet beds. There were rumours flying the Queen did not even have a bed, for her glorious bed had been left at Richmond. One had been sent for, taken from other rooms to be put together in her chamber, so at least their Regent and promised heir would rest safe enough this night.

"What news, Norris?" he asked of a man hurrying down the corridor in the opposite direction. Wyatt had, in truth, been walking without a destination, and had been trying to find someone who knew more than he did. He could not simply sit still and wait.

"Come with me if you want to know, Wyatt." Norris gestured to the way before him. "There is to be a meeting of all able men in the castle, all men able to ride and to raise men for the defence of the castle and the retaking of London. That includes you."

"At least there is a plan." He fell into fast step at the side of his friend. "What of the army marching north, Suffolk's men, and those Norfolk and Richmond went to gather? Has anyone sent word to them? Can they spare men to come to us, here?"

"I think we are to find that out now," Norris said as they entered the King's Presence Chamber, the ornately carved oaken doors already open. It was packed, a pungent scent of bodies ripe from riding, sweaty from fear filled the air like thick, cloying smoke. Conversation too was heavy on the chamber's breath, people talking over one another, muttering, arguing. There was not a smile in the room, all faces either grave and still, or scowling.

Wyatt looked about, spotting Doctor Butts in the crowd. The man was a fervent supporter of the Regent. Anne had placed many young men in Gonville Hall of Cambridge University and funded their educations. Most of them were men of the doctor's choosing. Beside Butts was Matthew Parker, one of Anne's chaplains and another man devoted to her. A large, powerfully built creature, with craggy, pale skin and dark eyes, Parker looked more like a warrior than a man of God, and yet he was soft-spoken and gentle of nature. Lurking at the back near a window was Mark Smeaton, one of the Queen's favourite musicians. Wyatt was somewhat surprised to see him there. Smeaton was a marvellous musician, a handsome, ambitious man, but not the most courageous of souls. Many had fled court when the trouble came. He had thought Mark might be one of them.

Another surprise was Sir William Fitzwilliam, not for the fact he was there but for what he was doing, standing near the front, telling people to be still, to wait and have patience. Though he was Treasurer of the Household and had been a great friend of the King, he was less a friend to Anne Boleyn. Fitzwilliam was an able military commander, more known for prowess on the sea than land, but still a valuable man. He had always done as the King wished, and Wyatt supposed

Fitzwilliam was doing so now. The last commands of the King had been that his heirs by Anne Boleyn were to be supported as his successors, after all, so despite any private reservations the man might have about the Regent, evidently he had decided to uphold his master's wishes. Before his death, the King had been talking about making Fitzwilliam an earl. Wyatt wondered if Fitzwilliam had been promised this again, in return for loyalty to Anne.

Not far from them stood Anne's bishops, Latimer, Shaxton and Hilsey all flocked together with their servants. John Skip was there too, murmuring words of comfort to a group of scared ladies. Wyatt could see Bishop Latimer casting his eyes about, no doubt trying to catch any words spoken against the Queen amongst the crowd. Anne's bishops would die for her, that he was sure of.

Catching sight of his sister not far away, Wyatt pulled himself through the crowd and Norris followed. Beside Margaret was Elizabeth Browne, Countess of Worcester and wife to the imprisoned Earl. Despite her husband's crimes, Anne had allowed Elizabeth to remain in her royal household, at her side, due to her affection for her. The Countess was with child, another reason for Anne to show mercy to her, although Wyatt was unsure how merciful it was to be a part of the court at this present moment.

"Margaret," Wyatt said with relief, embracing his sister. "I lost you upon the water."

"The Queen's barge made haste," she said, returning his embrace. "But we are all safe, all who were upon it."

"Is the Queen well?"

"The journey and the panic were hard on her spirits. She is tired, but she is about to appear."

Just as Margaret stated this, a blast of trumpets announced the Regent as she entered, Cromwell and Cranmer walking ahead of her to mark her way. Anne stood by her throne, and for a moment Wyatt remembered the young girl he had played with so many years ago when they both were children. He had always thought himself in love with Mary Boleyn as a lad, Anne's older sister was so sweet and pretty, always taking his gifts of flowers with a smile and thanking him, looking on him as if he were the only man in the world. The Boleyns had something about them, all of them, that could make you feel special. When they offered their attention to you, it was as if there was no one else in the world as captivating as you. It was their magic. Many people can be charismatic, but the Boleyns made *others* feel as if they were so, as long as they liked you, that was. If they didn't, they made you feel like an inconsequential, ugly dullard. It was a sorcery all their own, to raise you up or cast you down, using but their eyes or attention trained upon you.

Whilst he had, as a boy, worshipped at the feet of Mary, when he met Anne again, after she returned from the court of France, when they met by accident on a dark night as she was travelling to her family estates and her party was swept from good, true paths of Kent by creeping fog and was sent, lost, into the forest, where she had come across his hunting lodge on his father's estate which stood next to the lands of her family, that meeting, something which surely had stepped out of a tale of romance and fairies and knights, had sparked love in his heart which never had left him. How Wyatt had hoped he might win her love to join it to his, but whilst Anne had offered friendship, she never had let her guard down around him. Knowing he was married, Anne had stood back from Wyatt, offering friendship, even flirting in the way all court ladies did, playing skilfully the games of courtly love, but surrendering her true heart never. In many ways, it had made her only more captivating, the knowledge she never could be his. Sometimes Wyatt cursed games of courtly love. Indoctrinated from a young age, one came to believe the false lies they taught were true, that the love unobtainable was the one to be most valued. Wyatt had a mistress now, Elizabeth Darell. She was here, somewhere in the castle, pregnant with his child though none knew that yet. His wife and he had separated long ago, and she loathed him, though they had sons which both of them loved. *Something to show for a marriage made in hell,* he thought dully, at least there was something. His wife was not faithful to him now, either.

Yet even though he had Elizabeth, though he had children, things to make his life brighter, he never could stop that trill which enlivened his heart when Anne entered a room. He supposed where a heart had loved once it always would, that something of love remained, even if hatred had taken root there. But he had never hated Anne. He had tried, thinking it would be easier, especially when she and the King had begun their affair. Wyatt had resented that Anne was willing to become the mistress of the King and not his lover, and then he had found she had not shared herself with Henry either, that she had held out. She had asked that her value as a woman be honoured, that the King offer friendship unless he could offer marriage, and then Henry had shocked the world by offering marriage, offering to get rid of his own wife, to alter the world, just to have Anne. It was something Wyatt could understand for there was a time when, if he had been powerful enough, he would have turned the world upside down for Anne Boleyn too. Still, it had seemed unlikely Henry would succeed. When Anne became Queen, part of Wyatt had not believed it, just as part told him that with Anne Boleyn, anything was possible.

Glancing at Norris, noting the way he stared at Anne, Wyatt knew he was not alone in still loving her. Over the years and with a mistress who loved him back, Wyatt had come to realise he was in truth annoyed at Anne simply because she did not feel the way he wanted her to feel for him. That her heart was not attuned to his was not her fault. Sometimes it helped to remember this, that no one can force love, and would we want it if it were forced or tricked from the person we love? Sometimes it helped to think thus. Sometimes it did not.

That is ever the way of the heart. Sated it might be one moment, afire the next. A silly, flighty thing it often is, ungovernable and wild, and beyond the bounds of reason.

As Anne approached the throne, Wyatt noted that the infant Elizabeth was carried in behind her. The red-haired child was nodding, almost asleep until the trumpets woke her. She blinked and yawned, staring at all the people gathered there not in amazement but only with curiosity.

"We meet a time like no other," Anne announced in a loud bold voice. The crowds fell silent. She looked tired, Wyatt thought, her skin, which usually was bright and pale was dull, but her black eyes were afire with purpose. "Rebellion has fallen on London, rebellion I am told which was planned and encouraged by those who would support the bastard Mary, and fly in the face of your King's wishes for the future of his line and this country, disgracing the memory of our dead lord."

Clever, thought Wyatt. Anne could have problems rousing them to loyalty to her, of course, but if she could convince them to fight for the memory of Henry VIII, it might be different.

"It was the last wish, the command of my husband, your lord and King, that his children through our lawful and just marriage, one made without stain of incest upon it as his union with Katherine of Spain was, should be the ones to inherit this throne." She swept a hand to the throne she had not sat upon yet as if invoking the spirit of the dead King to stand with her. "The true child of the King, Elizabeth, Queen of England, and the child I carry within me, this son of England whose heart beats under mine, this last vestige of the life force of our good, lost lord of England, Henry Tudor, this last offering of his soul to the people of England, these are the children to which the King left his throne and crown, not the bastard daughter of an illegal and incestuous union! I ask, my lords, that you aid me in protecting these children, my children, the *King's* children, his true line, as others rise up to not only plunge this country into war, brother on brother, family on family, but to attempt to place a person not chosen by your King and master and not chosen by God upon the throne in place of the just and lawful line of the King!"

Anne's voice dropped low. "I am but one woman, a mother, a widow alone in this world and without protection now that my lord is gone. My heart would happily follow him to the grave and there dwell, but I gave my husband and King my promise, my lords, that should anything happen to him I would be here to protect our children, to see them live and take up the inheritance he devised for them. My lords, I cannot do this alone. Will you, for the sake of these innocent children, one not even born, and one yet a babe, for the sake of your master who loved you as you loved him, will you aid me to crush this foul rebellion, and protect our country so the true heirs of England may succeed to the throne, born of this time of chaos, rising as phoenixes into the future?"

The crowd, which had been still, erupted into cheering for the Queen. Wyatt glanced about as he clapped his hands and called out, "Yes!" with all the others. Some faces still were unconvinced, but on many, Anne had worked that magic of the Boleyns. Appealing to a sense of knightly protection for a woman and her children was clever, he had to admit, but yanking on the tender string of their grief and sorrow was even more wily.

Did he blame her for it? The manipulation? Most certainly not. She was indeed a woman alone, just as she had said, a woman fighting to protect her children. Her pregnant state made her even more vulnerable. Anne was doing all she ought to, as a mother and as a Queen.

"We are with you, Majesty!" he shouted, his voice filling a gulf in the cheering. "Let all honest men of England, let all knights of this great country uphold the wishes of their King and uphold the innocents he left in our charge. For England, for Elizabeth, for Henry!"

"For England, for Elizabeth, for Henry!" The shout was taken up by people about him. In place of fear on faces now he could see fierceness. Many there would fight.

That was good. They would need many, for their enemies were many too.

CHAPTER THIRTY-FOUR

Queen Mary Tudor

27th of April 1536

The Road to Warwick Castle

England

It was hardly a thing for a lady to admit, but Mary's arse was sore, her legs too. The chilled boat ride past screaming London and to the jetty near Thames Street had kept her blood afire so she did not feel the cold, then they had all but dashed up side streets to Elbow Lane and the house of the Countess of Salisbury, Le Herber, where into Margaret's arms Mary had flung herself, feeling battle-worn and weary. Her old governess had held her warm and tight for what felt at once like a thousand years and at the same time less than a second, before they were taken to horses. Mary's maid looked stupefied by the whole experience, and although she felt the same, Mary tried to be strong, to reassure the girl, to give comfort. Then Mary, cloaked and surrounded by men like Carew, Montagu and their retainers, fled London with the Countess, Elizabeth Grey, Chapuys and Gertrude Blount at her side.

Hard they had ridden at first, past shouting guards in the streets trying to stop them as they tried to detain everyone, not knowing who was friend and who was foe, but most of those men were distracted by others, rioters flowing through the streets like water from a broken dam. Some had heard there had been a break-out at the Tower and rumours that she, along with the Privy Councillors, past favourites of her father like Sussex and Oxford who had led the failed coup against the Regent were out and were riding for the north. How they knew where they were going, Mary knew not, but know some did, or had guessed. Since many knew there was rebellion in the north, perhaps it was a supposition easy to make that that was where freed traitors to the Crown would head. The Queen's guards, what was left of their forces in the disordered, frenzied streets, were trying to erect barricades in places, to stop people getting through, but London had so many paths, so many winding roads, it was simple enough – although a close call had more than once occurred – for them to evade the barricades, and escape north, through Cripplegate, where Montagu had paid men in advance to let them pass.

The first night they had stopped at an abbey, in guest quarters where a welcome silence had greeted them, and the women kept to their rooms, so none would see Mary. The men too had not socialised much with the abbot, not wanting to be recognised. Then before dawn they rose and headed out to the horses once more, riding north, always north. The second night they had stopped at a hunting lodge owned by Montagu, where all the women had huddled together for warmth on the same bed.

Although the Countess and Gertrude had brought plain, good clothes of wool for Mary, to both disguise her and keep her warm in this bitter spring, Mary still felt the cold skulking into her. Whenever they stopped to rest the horses she felt it upon her, like something alive, stealing into her bones and her blood, a worm making a den deep in her marrow. Perhaps the fear of death which had been upon her since she had been taken to the Tower had kept her warmer than she thought, and now, a little removed from the power of the Regent – although now if caught she was most certainly in more peril than before – the creeping hand of the cold was more able to reach her. She knew not. All Mary knew was that, by the third day of riding, she was stiff with the cold, her arse was paining her, and she was tired. All she really wanted to do was to sleep. Sleep to rest, to forget the noise and struggle she had witnessed, to forget her parents both were dead, and she was a hunted woman about to be set in charge of a rebellion.

Mary kept seeing the face of a man who had died in the Tower before her eyes, as she ran, the guards who had freed her at her side, that man had stepped out, a short sword in hand, and two of her guards had cut him down. He had died at her feet. Somehow, for she knew this path she now was on would lead to many more deaths, it was as though his blood, his body, was a portent of all who would fall in this quest to make her Queen. His blood was still on her shoes. When she urged her horse on, she would glance down and see it, a little dash, a tiny stain. It haunted her.

Yet she could not stop on this path now chosen, could not go back. Mary was more than aware that now she had broken out of the Tower, during a riot no less, and was riding off with her supporters, she had placed herself firmly on the side of rebellion against the Crown, and no matter how much those about Mary told her she was the rightful Queen, and indeed no matter how much she believed that herself, she was aware the powers that presently held the throne would not see her that way. Be caught, and she would be killed, that now was for certain where before it had been only suspicion. She had chosen, she had made her path. The only thing to do now was to follow it.

"We will reach Warwick before the sun falls?" she asked the Countess, trying not to allow her teeth to chatter as she passed a corked leather flask of ale to her maid. The poor girl looked as pale and sick as Mary felt.

"We will, Majesty," said her old governess. "And there we will have warm fires and beds waiting for you, and on the morrow, there will be much to organise."

"Let us get to safety first." Mary shifted the reins in her aching hands. The cold was in the bones of her fingers too, despite good gloves of leather. The gloves were etched with her father's arms, a pair Mary had owned before she was to Hatfield sent. Her father had given them to her one day when she was little and he had watched her shoot her bow. With pride he had told her she would a mighty huntress be one day, so she would need the gloves. They had been too big for her then and were still a little too big now. Always she had treasured them but many of her possessions had been left behind, on the King's orders, when she was shifted to Hatfield to attend upon her sister. Mary wondered where the Countess had found them. Perhaps Margaret Pole had been hanging on to them for some time, hoping to return them to her. "I like not the idea of getting ahead of ourselves. Men we have here, my lady, but not many. If the Boleyn woman's people come for us, we are undefended out here."

There were perhaps twenty men with them, not a lot compared to the royal guards which Mary, despite being reassured that those forces were busy in London still, kept expecting to see riding after her.

"All of us will ensure you escape if anything happens, Majesty." Margaret's voice was stout. "We have already agreed. None of our lives matter, only yours."

"I will not have anyone die unnecessarily for my sake. I need you all, if I am to succeed in taking the throne."

"Men ahead!" shouted Geoffrey Pole, riding back to them.

"What men?" Carew was quick to ride to the front.

"They carry the banner of Suffolk." Geoffrey's face was grim as he took his place beside Mary, drawing his sword.

But without hesitation, to Mary's surprise, Montagu and his men rode forwards, along with Henry Courtenay, Earl of Devon and his guards. Carew's men took position about Mary, there to aid her or help her fly. But as Mary listened, tensed, ready to spur on her horse, she heard laughing. Courtenay and Montagu came riding towards her, a man she knew only too well at their side on a great grey horse.

"Majesty," said Suffolk, attempting a kind of bow in the saddle. "The rest of my men are aways from here, but we have come to support your cause for the throne."

"He was sent to raise men to fight the rebellion in the north, rising for your Majesty," chuckled Montagu, "but His Grace of Suffolk has decided, on my invitation, to join the winning team and bring with him all the men he took from London, and all he has raised since."

Mary eyed Suffolk. Her father had loved Charles Brandon dearly, and even her mother had written, long after they had been separated, saying that Suffolk had treated her well and appeared to sympathise with her cause. Suffolk never would have gone against the King, she knew that, but he never had liked Anne Boleyn and once had even warned the King about Anne's reputation in France, before she came to England, saying she had been the mistress of many a man, and of Thomas Wyatt too, when to England she came. He had been banished for it.

"Did you not take the Oath of Succession, Your Grace?" Mary asked coldly.

"As did many here," Suffolk said. "But I have come to believe that His Majesty was led into error, by Anne Boleyn, who bewitched his mind and led his passions. Besides," he went on, "her children are infants, and here before us we have a grown woman of the royal line, a Tudor and a descendant of the royal houses of Spain. Once His Majesty, my great friend and King, named you his heir, my lady, and I will honour that wish. We cannot have infants on the throne, and regents and regency councils will kill us all. We must have a ruler, and we have you. Once you are married, a male heir may inherit the throne after you, at the age of eighteen."

"You would support me, until I have an heir?"

"Do you not wish to wed, have children, Majesty?"

"All this can be surely discussed, Your Grace, in a more clement, private place to hold a conversation with a young, royal maid upon the future of her line," Chapuys said, smoothly cutting in. Mary started. She had not realised he was so close, but evidently as the Duke had ridden up the ambassador had realised there would be negotiation to engage in. "For now, there is a war to be won and a country too, is there not? I am sure Her Majesty is merry to have you here, Your Grace."

Mary nodded. "I am."

Suffolk was a graceless boor at times, but he could command an army, that was true enough. Mary held out her hand for the Duke to kiss. "My mother spoke well of you, towards the end, Your Grace. She said you had been kind to her. There were sadly not many who were, so I thank you for that, and for all the love my father bore you, calling you brother more than once, I shall name you uncle for that reason and because you were wed to my aunt. I welcome you to my side."

Suffolk took her hand and kissed it, then he and his men fell in beside the others, as they rode for Warwick Castle.

As she rode, Mary could not help but wonder if Suffolk was true to his word, or if he had come as a spy, sent by the Regent, and more than that, she wondered if she ever would stop suspecting this of any who came to her side now.

But looking at Margaret, at Chapuys, at Gertrude, Elizabeth, Montagu, Carew, the Poles and Courtenays, she knew she could trust some. These people had risked everything for her, had broken her out of a prison of fear and captivity, had gambled their lives for hers. In them she would trust fully, and no others.

CHAPTER THIRTY-FIVE

Queen Anne Boleyn

30th of April 1536

May Day Eve

Windsor Castle

England

Anne sat down. Her mother rushed to help her, but Anne waved her back. It was easier to do it alone than have another person there, even if it was her mother. Elizabeth Boleyn fell back to stand with Mistress Aucher, an old servant and fine midwife, who had come with Elizabeth from Hever to aid Anne in this difficult time, and difficult pregnancy.

It was getting harder to do simple tasks at all, let alone with any grace. Anne was heavier now, the lump on her front growing bigger every day, and the child inside kicking with vigour. She was pleased to feel it, joyous each time her ribs were assailed. Often, Anne called her women to her, especially her mother and her cousins Mary and Madge Shelton, and their mother, Anne, so they could all feel the kicking, so they could tell others that the child inside her was hale and strong. Anne needed her men to believe not only that the child was alive but that it was indeed a boy. The more vigorous a child was in the womb, the more people believed it would be a boy. Boys were active, full of energy. Girls were languid, calm. That was the way people thought.

In all truth, Anne knew not what might happen if she bore another girl. It was a worry constantly on her mind and it came with guilt and resentment, for why should she have to mourn if a healthy girl child she bore? But she knew the way the world was. Some would support Elizabeth, but plenty of her present supporters were only at her side now because they hoped there was a male heir inside her. A boy, and she and Elizabeth might be secure. A girl, and what would happen? The men would think to themselves that they might as well turn to Mary, for she was a female but at least she was already grown, a woman ready to breed, unlike Elizabeth. They could marry Katherine's daughter off to a man or prince of their choosing who would get her with child, perhaps a man they wanted in power for the foreseeable future and then, when Mary's son grew up, the Tudor reign would continue unhindered, yet another man on the throne.

"Mary has escaped?" Anne asked calmly.

"All prisoners of the Tower did, Majesty," said Cromwell, "so we have been told. It was a rout. The Tower was stormed. Some of the guards, having been won to the other side, set upon their brothers-in-arms and opened the gates. They let down the drawbridge and in flowed the rioters of London. Mary was immediately snatched from her chambers. We think she was taken to the water."

"So, Sussex and Oxford, Worcester and Westmorland are with her, then? Richard Rich too?"

"We know not where any of those men are, but there is word a party rode out of London by Cripplegate, heading north. Montagu was seen, and three or four women, one wearing a deep cowl. What that most likely means is that the Poles helped Mary to escape, and they will be heading for Warwick

Castle, the best of their fortified houses."

"One of the best castles this country has," Anne noted. "I stayed there once, it is a formidable place. If they hunker in for a siege, it could last years."

"Windsor is also very secure, Majesty."

"I do not intend to sit through a siege here, Cromwell, and watch England crumble about us." Anne drummed her fingertips on the armrest of the chair. "The King said once that he feared Katherine, Mary's mother. He said that if she took it into her head to take up her daughter's part, she could easily muster a great array and engage in war against the Crown as fierce as any her mother ever waged in Spain. I think we must take the threat of Mary with as much seriousness. I doubt she will hear any men I send to try negotiation. She never accepted me as Queen." Anne paused, remembering the time she had been told, when visiting Elizabeth, that Mary had curtseyed to Anne in the chapel and Anne had not seen it. When Anne had sent one of her women to apologise for this oversight, Mary had retorted that *the Queen* could not possibly have sent such a message as *the Queen*, her mother, was far from that place, and that her curtsey had been to God her Maker, not to Madame de Pembroke, her father's mistress. Mary had been bold enough when under the power of the Crown, now that she was at liberty who knew what she might do? Anne looked up. "Suffolk was headed that way, can he be diverted to take care of them?"

There was an uncomfortable silence, and she stared at each man in turn. "What is it?"

It was Cranmer who answered. "It may be the Duke is not our ally any longer, Majesty. There was word, unconfirmed, that his men, whilst gathering together, met some of the rebels in the north of Suffolk, near the boundaries of Norfolk. Suffolk's men reportedly told the rebels that they had nothing to fear from them, for the Duke was Mary's servant, and soon all would know this for sure."

"Curse him!" she shouted, banging her hand painfully on the armrest and regretting it immediately.

"Majesty, you should not rouse yourself to such passion," her mother murmured, setting a hand on Anne's shoulder. "It is not good for the child."

Anne barked out a scornful laugh. "This child is born of passion and grief, my lady mother. My broken heart feeds him and my torn soul sustains him, and he does the same for me. Both of us are well, I promise you." Watching her mother's face fall, Anne felt contrite. Her mother was still not hale, and here Anne was, snarling at her. "I will send for Doctor Butts and have him and Mistress Aucher examine me after this meeting," she said in a gentler tone. "I will take care, Mother. I promise you I will take care."

Elizabeth Boleyn nodded, her eyes swimming with tears.

Anne turned to Cromwell again. She could not watch her mother blink more tears away, it made her want to weep. She knew her mother worried for her, for her child, for all that had been placed upon her shoulders since the King had died and in truth, to feel the weight of her mother's love for her was almost too much to bear. It was too sweet a thing for this world of sorrows. "Has it been confirmed?" she asked Cromwell. "That Suffolk is gone to the other side?"

"I have men out, trying to find the truth," Cromwell replied. "But I believe we should act as if it has been confirmed, Majesty. We have no reports of Suffolk confronting the rebels. On the contrary, their numbers are growing, and they appear to be heading for the lands of the Countess of Salisbury."

"What of Norfolk and Fitzroy? Where are they, Wales?"

Cromwell folded his hands before his body. "They were gathering men in the west but entered Ludlow not two days ago and were calling men to their banners there. As far as we know they are still there, gathering men. They were due to ride north as soon as they had a large enough force."

"Send word I want Fitzroy back here to report to us. Norfolk is to take men north to face Suffolk as soon as possible. What of our men here in the south, out gathering men of the shires?"

"Your father sends word from Kent, he and your brother have gathered a mighty force in your homelands, Majesty, some four thousand men thus far, and they hope for more. They can launch an attack on London to retake it within days, but advise that another army, coming from the other side, led by the new Earl of Southampton, William Fitzwilliam, would aid them greatly in this. Your Majesty's forces, still within London, have made some gains. The Tower is ours once more…"

"A little late," Anne noted.

"… but other royal palaces have failed to be claimed by Your Majesty's guards. The walls of London are somewhat within our control too, the north and eastern gates are ours. There is still much to be done, and the interior still runs wild."

"Do we have enough men here to march out, join with my brother and father to take London?"

"I believe so. Men hereabouts, Norris, Wyatt, Weston, Fitzwilliam and others are reporting forces which together number perhaps three thousand, so in total, not including the guards inside London, we have an army of seven thousand. Fitzwilliam is happy to lead this force, now that your Majesty has made him an earl I think he will do anything you wish. We can come from one side, Wiltshire's men from the other and as our forces march into London we will crush the rebels inside between us."

"Then send the order. I want us back in the capital, and I want it secure. You will go with Fitzwilliam, Cromwell, be his second in command. You have experience as a mercenary, use it for us."

"Majesty, I am happy to obey and be of use."

"Good."

Anne rose, pushing up with arms that felt weak as a kitten's tottering legs. The new weight she carried was heavy upon her body and her soul. The news of Suffolk turning traitor had not helped.

It was the eve of May Day. They should be out gathering boughs and flowers in the forests to decorate the halls with. They should all be preparing bonfires too, to bless the fields with smoke so the crops would be prosperous that year. Although, Anne had to admit, the fact that some in the north celebrated this night as Mischief Night seemed apt. Games and tricks were played on May Day Eve, usually by children but sometimes by others. It was said by some that on the eve of May, much like Midsummer, the boundaries between the old world and this world came tumbling down and fairies and others spirits came out to play, taking away people to dance at their festivals held in forests, tricking the lost into eating the food or drinking the wine so then never could they leave the endless dance of the old ones, the hidden folk. There seemed to her a certain logic that this night was the night chaos broke loose on the world. It certainly seemed to have happened that year.

"I want Suffolk's family arrested," she said.

Cromwell coughed a little. "It would seem the Duchess as well as her child, Suffolk's son, and her mother, Maria de Salinas, fled London as he left, so they must have known his plans. They were last seen on the Great North Road before the city fell to chaos. Lady Eleanor, however, since she was with the court as it fled, is here and can be taken into custody. Apparently Suffolk either did not care enough or did not have enough time to alert his daughter to his plans."

"And Lady Frances and her family? Where are they?"

"Unknown, at present. They were with the court at Richmond but may have made for their own estates. Many did. The Seymours all are gone too."

"I wondered where Jane was. I thought her sick, as many have fallen after the flight from Richmond," Anne said and shook her head. "Discover where they are, Lady Frances and her family. I care nothing for the Seymours, but I want leverage over the Duke. He never has seemed to care a great deal for his daughters, but we will see if they may be used. And get word to Fitzroy. I want him back here immediately, and Norfolk on the march north as soon as possible."

"I will send Wriothesley to discover the Lady Frances and her family, he is a useful man, and I will dispatch another messenger to Ludlow." Cromwell cleared his throat, stepping forwards. "Might I suggest, Majesty, that mercenaries can be bought by the Crown, and may be required, especially if Suffolk has joined the side of Mary and intends on beginning war within England. Taking London is one thing, an ongoing civil war another."

"Civil war," Anne breathed. "I remember the tales old men told me. I never thought to see it myself." She turned to him. "Find mercenaries," she commanded. "We will pay well for them. I want us as prepared as we can be to face any threat, and send word to my brother and father to be ready to march out to retake London within three days, five at the most. If our guards are fighting to claim control of our city it is time to move and aid them. Suffolk may be lost but lose London I will not."

CHAPTER THIRTY-SIX

Lady Margaret Douglas

1st of May 1536

May Day

Windsor Castle

England

Margaret shut the door behind her. Leaning against it, she breathed hard. The Queen Regent had been railing for what felt like hours about Lady Mary, about Suffolk, about the men who had released Mary from the Tower and were raising men to bring about civil war, the second in as many generations England had seen.

Margaret too remembered tales people had told of the war, the lives lost, the spell of peace, the resumption of war. No one wanted a return to those days. To her it had always seemed as if there was more than one war, first Plantagenet on Plantagenet and then Plantagenet on Tudor. Everyone spoke as if there had been but one, but she did not see it that way.

Now there was to be one again, and if Margaret had learnt anything from all those tales it was this; that in such times the normal rules of life are suspended, and much once thought impossible, becomes possible. Sometimes this was for good, but more often it was bad.

She feared the rules might be suspended and not in her favour, when the Queen found out about her marriage, about her baby.

Margaret was not going to be able to hide her pregnancy much longer. She was already showing a little when undressed. This would not be an issue normally. Panels in a gown were fashionable and yet they concealed her belly, but at night, if called to be one of the women to sleep in the Queen's bed, then it would be harder. It was not just Margaret's belly growing bigger, her face had filled out too and her breasts were following suit. Sometimes Anne liked to embrace her women at night, when it was cold. The Regent's pregnancy had often had her running hot in the first few months but as it progressed the Queen was feeling the cold, her feet especially growing chilled at night. A bed companion was there to keep the more important inhabitant of the bed warm; maids kept the ladies of court cosy as ladies of court did the same for the Queen. If Anne sought the warmth of Margaret's body in a chaste embrace of friends, and felt the lump growing on Margaret's front, she would know, and hearing all Margaret had heard the Queen say just that afternoon about Mary, her cousin, about how the old King should have shut her away or taken her head for disobedience, Margaret feared the Queen Regent.

Down the corridor she hastened, to find Thomas. He was with a group of men playing dice. Many were standing around now, waiting for their bannermen to arrive and for some position in the Regent's army to be granted to them. It was said more would be appointed after London was taken, and in that effort the Regent's father and brother were the commanders. Margaret hovered until he saw her, then they met in the gardens, away from prying ears.

"I cannot tell her," Margaret whispered after explaining all Anne had said when railing against Mary. "She thinks all who carry royal blood a threat now, she as good as said it and stared at me, Thomas. I think I will find myself disappeared, or imprisoned. The Regent will try to say our babe is a bastard and I am but your mistress."

"We are married."

"But how to find the priest now who performed our ceremony? And our witness? Mary Howard is gone to her estates. She left with Surrey's men when Richmond fell. It is unsafe to travel. We cannot bring her here. Will we be believed without a witness or priest? There is only our word that we are married. The Queen can call our babe a bastard or take us all into prison. The Tower is claimed back by our men again, I hear. Will she put me there?"

"I have been thinking…" Thomas took her hand "… that we should get to my brother, get his good word to put with ours. The Queen needs Norfolk now more than ever, if all I have heard of Suffolk defecting to Mary is true. If we have my brother on our side, perhaps all will be well."

"You would send a messenger?"

"If you are this scared of the Queen, I think we should go, put ourselves in his hands. I have men, a way out of the castle. We can go this night. We would be in Ludlow in two, perhaps three days, and once there I can put my case to my brother, and he can protect us."

"And you think he will? Our babe could threaten that of the Queen, and he is her uncle just as you are. And what if he and Fitzroy have any intentions still for the throne?"

"My brother and his son-in-law have made it plain they are loyal to the Queen. They gather men now for her cause, and it was Fitzroy himself who informed on Sussex and the other conspirators."

Margaret bit her lip. "That is true."

"My brother is close to my mother, though she be his step-mother, but you know his mother and mine were cousins, so he always has respected her. I will send word to her too, let her know what goes on here. She will lean on him, but if Norfolk is our supporter, the Queen will be less likely to act against us when she hears of our baby."

Margaret stole into his arms. "Thomas… I am afraid."

"I will make this well, Meg. No one will hurt you, or our child."

She leaned against him, thinking of last year on this day and all the merriment that had occurred. May Day was second only to Christmas for the festivities which ensued. There would be no dancing or feasting this year, no one had even tried to bring greenery in to decorate the palace, no one wore garlands of flowers. Last year she and all the maids had snuck into the gardens at first light to bathe their faces in the dew. It was said it brought beauty to the wearer for the year ahead, granted them fresh skin and long life. Each village would have its May Queen and parade her about the streets. Some places would have Maypoles and there would be dancing about them. Milkmaids would prance too and have their pails decorated by garlands of flowers. That was what should be happening. She doubted anyone was bothering this year.

Margaret remembered being told of how her uncle the King and his first wife Katherine had gone a-Maying once at Shooter's Hill, feasted in an arbour surrounded by flowers and played at being Robin Hood and his love. This year there had been little but strained silence.

Where had their world gone? Here it had been one moment and if it was not perfect there still had been times to be merry, times where joy had been welcomed and entertained.

Now, there was nothing but pain and fear and misery. What fell magic could strip away all that she knew so fast, and why would God allow this to happen to them?

CHAPTER THIRTY-SEVEN

Jane Seymour

1st of May 1536

Wulfhall

Wiltshire

The air of the courtyard was fresh, damp with the high scent of sheep not far away. Jane breathed it in, despising the smell. It was a scent of home, the sheep, the dampness, the scent of a charcoal-making fire not far away in the woodland. The wide-open skies of Wiltshire loomed above her, and she hated them too. All this time she thought she had escaped and now she was back, here, at Wulfhall.

She had never wanted to come home. Jane didn't like Wulfhall, the place where her mother dominated, and her father, John Seymour, was fast sliding into silence and obedience, his mind surrendering his body. The proud man, once a gentleman and a soldier, was swiftly turning into a child again, as far as Jane could tell. He smiled and looked confused when his children talked to him, he became a mute when his wife entered the room, as if scared of her. Jane looked into his eyes and she could not find her father there. Someone had stolen him away, left a shell of an infant behind, one which most of the time was gentle and good-natured, and sometimes screamed and lashed out. The mind of a child might be fast falling upon him, but the old man still had strength in his arm.

He had long been ailing, and the discovery by his son, Edward, of the long-standing affair of incest had not aided the collapse of their father's mind. Edward's wife, Catherine, had been bedding John Seymour all the years she was wed to Edward, playing Jane's brother for a fool. The couple had two sons, and Edward had no idea if those boys were his sons indeed, or if they were his brothers. When the affair was found out, John had entered a short slide into mental collapse and Catherine had been sent to a nunnery. Edward was separated from her now, legally. He had placed the boys with a noble family, not being able to bear to see them, always wondering if his father had sired them or if he had. They'd kept it quiet, of course. The family needed no more scandal. But it seemed Jane herself had added to their ill reputation now.

She had not wanted the role, not really, but when the King had cast eyes on Jane, all her family, her brothers most especially, had pushed her to get close to the King in the last months of his life. All of them had pushed her. Edward had said their mother knew that Jane might become the mistress of the King and approved of it. He had convinced Jane to encourage the King's passions, telling her that she might, when in his bed, speak for Lady Mary. That had made Jane think this was some kind of moral quest, this odd seduction of the King where never did she seduce him. Edward had called in a favour of her when she had resisted, and Jane had agreed to encourage the King's lust for her. Many people had urged her on, but they seemed to have forgotten this and now they acted as if she was nothing but a whore and had cheapened herself, for all of London had known she was the King's bedfellow.

Except she never had been.

"Seymour, the poxy whore," that was what they were singing in London before the trouble broke. Singing about her, calling her names, but Jane had never given anything of her body to the King. He had kissed her, but people did that in greeting, and never had he kissed her long. She had known he was the husband of another, and yet, was he? Queen Katherine had been the true Queen and Anne Boleyn nothing more than the King's mistress.

Like you, sneered a voice in her mind.

I was not his mistress, she replied.

Jane had not wanted to be a mistress, not of any kind. She had not liked the way Anne Boleyn had risen, or the way Katherine of Spain had been cast down. Never had she approved of women rising to power through the bedsheets, even if many were forced into that path by their families. And now she was one of them, and yet a virgin. A virgin whore, ruined yet intact. She had wanted to speak for Lady Mary, for Queen Katherine she had loved, and for that wish to do something good for another, she was now cast down, cast out, a harlot none wanted near them.

Jane strode out to the barn; she had liked to hide there as a child from Thomas when he teased her. She would hide there now. About her throat was a pendant made of gold, a miniature portrait of the King inside. From her neck she pulled it, snapping the ribbon which held it. For a moment Jane stared at the surface, remembering when the King had given it to her, telling her she was beautiful. Few people had ever thought her so, but the King had.

Jane hesitated a moment and then swiftly lifted her arm and threw. From her hand the pendant flew, through the air, landing in a hedge. On she strode, to the barn.

Her brothers were inside the house, arguing. Thomas saying that they should ride to join Suffolk, who everyone said had rebelled, gone to Mary's side – Mary who was now escaped from the Tower no less! – and Edward was arguing it was too soon to join any side. Henry was there too, arrived two days ago from London which he said had fallen to madness. Jane had fled with her brothers from court, taken the chance to leave when the confusion set in. What was there to stay for? Court was where the Queen Regent was always pinching Jane and finding a reason to be unkind. Anne Boleyn did not like Jane, and Jane knew it. A whore was a threat, apparently to everyone, to the wife of the man bedded, and a threat to the morality of every other person the mistress touched, even if she was no whore, even if her brothers had pushed her to bed the King to further their careers at court, to make themselves bigger men, standing on her open thighs, crushing them with booted feet to force them to gape open only wider.

Into the gloom of the barn she walked, thinking of Edward's marriage, when all the neighbourhood had turned out to see him wed to a *true* whore, the woman who had bedded their father and blackmailed Jane into remaining silent for years about it when Jane found out. Edward had been happy that night, she remembered, his new, pretty, witty wife at his side. He had been drunk, and merry. It was one of the last times Jane had seen him without that cloak of coldness he seemed always to wear now. Jane had always loved Edward more than any other member of her family, but he had altered, become dour and distant, untrusting. He had urged her just as the others had, perhaps more so, to ruin her reputation, which was really all Jane had, so his could be enhanced. He had told her she owed it to him, for she had known about Catherine, his wife, and had said nothing. Catherine had threatened Jane, and Jane then was but a foolish child and believed Catherine had the powers she claimed, to send Jane from the house in disgrace. So Jane had kept silent, and then Catherine had been found out, and then Edward found that Jane knew. Pursuing the King was her penance, but now the King was gone.

There was a thought in her head forming. Like an egg sack something seemed to split, and wings emerged. There was in Jane's mind a butterfly thought, willing and waiting to fly.

There had been word along with that which had come about Suffolk; Lady Mary was at Warwick Castle. It was far from Wulfhall, but not so far as to be impossible to reach. A good horse could make it in a day or two if ridden well and fast, and Jane was good at riding. *Ninety miles or so,* she thought, remembering the maps in her father's house; it was possible. Her brothers were arguing about which side to join, but if there was a side to join, Jane wanted to join Mary's. Mary was the true Queen, daughter of Katherine, whom Jane had loved and served when the Queen had been cast out of court. Jane wanted her family to join with Mary, but what if they did not? Would she be forced to side with her family if they went back to the Queen Regent? Edward loved the reforms of the King, and Anne Boleyn would see more done. Edward would not want Mary on the throne if she would lead England back to Rome and to the true faith. If the Seymours sided with the Queen because of religion, Jane was sure they would be picking the wrong side, and the wrong faith.

She had travelled before. Jane had gone from here to court, thence to the north with Katherine. She knew some of the roads. What if she left this place and went to Mary? It was said the roads were full of dangers, but if she was one of Mary's supporters, the rebels rising in the north would let her through to the true Queen of England, would they not? But she could not travel alone. That was too dangerous. A woman alone would not make it far. Jane needed someone to go with.

That meant making a pact with her own personal devil, someone she had abhorred since they were children, but Thomas had said it. He had said they should join Mary. Jane just needed to convince him he was right, and that she had to go with him. Jane had known Queen Katherine well, and that was a way in with Mary, surely.

Jane smiled, for she was good at convincing people. Often they did not suspect she was even trying to, and therein lay her greatest power.

CHAPTER THIRTY-EIGHT

Agnes Tilney, Dowager Duchess of Norfolk

1st of May 1536

Chesworth House

Sussex

England

"The Queen, my own step-granddaughter calls for more men, and men she will have," Agnes Tilney, Dowager Duchess of Norfolk barked at her comptroller as he attempted to inform her of delays in the gathering of their forces. "You will answer this note of Thomas Boleyn, Earl of Wiltshire, requesting further forces for the taking of London, and you will tell him of the men we can raise and when they can march. You will make them march! If Wiltshire and Rochford are having trouble in London and the forces Cromwell has dispatched from Windsor are not enough, they must have more men. It is our duty!" To add emphasis the Dowager banged her ivory-tipped walking stick on the ground, and the man made haste for the door.

As the man scampered out, looking wild about the eyes as servants who did not instantly obey the old Duchess frequently did, Agnes turned her eyes on another granddaughter. "Your playing improves, Catherine," she noted to the young maid at the virginals, as if nothing had happened, as if they were not at war and the capital of England had not fallen, as if the Regent's forces were not struggling to reclaim it, as if men were not dying every day. "The lessons I have invested in are paying off. I think soon, when all this idle fuss settles and the Queen Regent is secure on her throne once more, we should see about sending you to court as one of her maids of honour. You are of an age now."

"I should like that, Grandmother," said Catherine, pausing in her playing. *Anything to be away from here*, she thought. It was not her grandmother, though the old lady could be fractious company and sometimes hit Catherine hard with her walking stick. Catherine could stomach much in the way of chastisement. It was her music teacher, Manox. He had been touching her and kissing her, and she did not like it. Every time he took one liberty, he used that liberty against her to gain more, threatening to tell her grandmother about all of them if Catherine did not allow him to touch her small breasts, only just budding, or kiss her. Not long ago he had touched himself as he touched her, and she liked that not at all. Catherine was only twelve. She did not know how to stop Manox doing the things he was doing, and she was not wise enough to know that her grandmother, had Agnes known of this abuse, would have sent him away and protected Catherine's reputation.

Catherine did not know this, she thought she would be the one to be in trouble, just as Manox had told her she would be if she told. She might even be cast out as a whore, and so it continued, every lesson, every time she was left alone with him, the touching, the sickness in her belly, the fear he was going to take more and more from her.

Silence is a weapon, when used well.

"I suspect you would, the court is a fine place, but you will have to gain more of grace than you possess now, if you are not to let down our house when you are there." Her grandmother laughed a little at Catherine's crestfallen expression. "Not to worry, child," she cooed like a pigeon. "There are ways to learn graces, and your cousin, the Queen Regent..." Agnes's voice rang with pride for she loved Anne Boleyn "... can teach you many. She's the woman for that, for you. When all this is over..." She swept a hand out to the window and Catherine stared at the small panes twinkling there, as if she could see the rebellion in the glass, "... we'll send you and Anne, Queen Regent of England and mother of the King, or Queen, will set you to rights."

"Are we in danger here, Grandmother?"

Agnes huffed a little. "In times like these, it is never good to be complacent," she confessed. "But I believe our men loyal to our house and to the Queen. We rouse men to send to Anne, mark me, but we will keep some back, and I have set the house to being guarded. If any come here looking for trouble, I'll see they receive it, and much more besides!"

"I hear gossip the north is rising in favour of Lady Mary, Your Grace."

"Betrayers and fools." Agnes stomped with her cane to the empty stool at Catherine's side and sat heavily on it. No one had ever told Catherine what was wrong with Agnes's leg, and she never thought to ask, but it pained her grandmother, that she did know. "They will be set down. The Poles think themselves clever, but only the Countess owns intelligence amongst them. Sadly for Margaret, my old friend, her sons are dullards all, even that so-called scholar Reginald. If he knew what was good for him he would have flattered the King, not sided with the Pope against him. The Courtenays have too much pride, too, and Suffolk is like any hammer, only effective if someone wields him with skill, and the bastard Mary has not the experience for that. They will think to fight Queen Anne, but amongst each other they will fight, you just watch. Rats in a trap of their own making."

Agnes laughed a little but soon noted her granddaughter's worried face and reached a kindly hand to her soft cheek. Catherine tried not to flinch. Often her grandmother did chastise her, but Agnes did not like it if Catherine reacted with fear to her hands. This time, hers was a touch of affection, however.

"Fear not, child." Agnes patted her cheek. "I will make sure you are safe."

I am not even safe in this house, at my lessons, Catherine thought, but she smiled and nodded to her grandmother, because she knew that was what Agnes wanted her to do.

CHAPTER THIRTY-NINE

Henry Fitzroy, Duke of Richmond and Somerset

2nd of May 1536
Ludlow
The Welsh Marches
Border of England and Wales

"The time is now," Norfolk said, authority in his voice.

Fitzroy, standing at the window, looking down at the gardens of Ludlow Castle, did not say anything to begin with. He was thinking of how his father had sent Mary here, not him, when they both were children. Fitzroy had been sent to head the Northern Council, to be named Lord Lieutenant of the North. Mary had been sent to Ludlow to oversee the Council of the Marches. The position Mary had been handed had been the more prestigious. It had long been tradition that the heir of the King was dispatched to oversee Wales, training for the time they became sovereign. Fitzroy had been kept in the running, so to speak, by being given a placement of his own, but his father had never seen him as his heir. Many times, he had proved that.

Henry Tudor might well have *considered* the notion of making Fitzroy his heir many times, toyed with it, but always he had wanted a legitimate male heir. Mary was a girl so would not do, and Fitzroy was a bastard so was not worthy either. Neither was quite right. Both were lacking, imperfect. Combine their elements in one person and their father would have been delighted but as it was, with but a stained boy and a defective girl granted to him, the King must have felt as if God were teasing him, showing him parts of the one perfect child he longed for, offering titbits of his heart's desire.

His father had always kept him as an insurance policy. Oh, Fitzroy believed the King had loved him, and in some ways Fitzroy believed he was responsible for the King separating from Mary's mother. Love for Anne Boleyn had certainly been one reason, pangs of that ever-unstable conscience another, but Fitzroy was proof Henry VIII could father sons. He was proof God *would* allow the King sons, but not within the marriage he had with Katherine. Fitzroy had been his father's proof that God was waiting to reward him. He wondered if Anne Boleyn's unborn child, this brother or sister not even in the world yet, would turn out to be this dream of his father's, and if so, it would be a dream he never got to see.

Fitzroy pitied his father that. God had teased Henry Tudor yet again, played with his desires. Why would God wish to do such a thing? Perhaps God did not think this child Henry VIII had so desired would be the best thing for England? Perhaps God had another plan?

Certain people seemed to think this was so.

Men were urging Fitzroy, just as Brereton had, and Brereton was still amongst those doing the urging now, to set himself up as King, to declare his right to the throne as the only living male heir of the King. There were ways to make Fitzroy legitimate, Norfolk and others had told him. If he did as they asked, and if he won the throne, he could have parliament declare him to be whatever he wanted. Henry IX, that would be his title. *Fitzroy* no more but Rex, bastard no more, side-lined from the true royal family no more, but King, in charge of all he saw and in control of much that eyes could never comprehend.

It was tempting.

Yet something of his conscience assailed him, that was also true. He had always got on well with Queen Anne, had liked his sister, little Elizabeth, and he would be overthrowing the rights of an unborn child if he went ahead. Fitzroy had respected his father, and Fitzroy did not believe his father had ever seriously considered making him King. Not really. Half thought and shadow had comprised any kind of consideration in that vein, he was sure. His father had not wanted this.

But what of what Fitzroy wanted?

No one had ever really asked him. Fortune and titles had been heaped upon him as a baby, then as a boy and as he grew his entire life had been about making sure he did as his father wanted. Little freedom had Fitzroy had to decide for himself. He had never wanted for food or clothes or castles even, had never suffered in ways other people, poor people did, yet always he had known himself an outsider. No one ever forgot that whilst his father had been a king his mother had at best been of little importance, and some would name her a base whore. No one, especially Fitzroy, ever forgot that he owed everything, his existence, his titles and any power he would ever wield, to the goodwill of his father, a father whose wishes he was now being encouraged to disobey and dismiss.

But now he had a choice, a chance, to take something for himself, to carve out a destiny for himself. He could rise higher than simply being twice a Duke and once an Earl. He could become more than he had ever thought possible, far more than his father had thought him capable of. He could do this *himself*. It would not be a power someone had handed him, but a power he had crafted, nurtured and created himself. The throne would be his in a way his titles up until now never truly had been.

In some ways, it was already done, barely a choice anymore. Since they had come to this place, Brereton, along with Surrey and William Parr, another childhood friend, had all been out with the men marching in from the shires and counties of Wales and western England, finding out what support Fitzroy would have if he announced his intention to make war on the Regent and seize the crown. His friends claimed that four men out of every five were with him. Fitzroy wondered about that, if it was true, but as he had met more and more men from Wales, and commanders like Herbert, married to William's Parr's sister, Anne, had arrived and supported the idea, he had come to believe it was possible. In some ways it was already done. They were willing for him to be King. He simply had to announce it.

He just had to be willing to say it, to agree to wage war on a woman who had always been kind to him, to steal a throne from his sister Elizabeth, and from his sister Mary, from an unborn baby.

But he would be kind to them, would he not? They would take a place below him, his siblings, but one of honour, and he had had another thought, one about Mary, which might aid them both. He would be kind to his sisters, make them titled and important, as he had been made. If Elizabeth as well as Mary, and this unborn child, were declared bastards he, of all people, would know how to treat them well, for he had once been in their shoes.

And what of his own family, his mother and her husband, his half-brothers and sisters? They were already here, safe, Norfolk had arranged it. Mary Howard, his wife was there too, at Ludlow, secretly brought to him by Surrey's retainers. They were safe, and the Regent could not use them against him. Fitzroy could enhance their lives and fortunes too, if he rose to become King.

Now it was time to nod or to shake his head, either refuse this power or accept that he was about to make war on one side of his family, in order to save England. That was what people told him, had been telling him, over and over and over. With an infant on the throne, the country was not safe. With Mary on the throne, the kingdom would be handed back to Rome and England would no more be at liberty. With him on the throne, England would be strong, independent, free. Was that not what his father had wanted?

"Make the announcement," he said to Norfolk. "I will go before our men tonight, as they are gathered outside, and I will take their oaths, as their King."

"Your Majesty." Norfolk swept to bow, a smirk on his face, and Fitzroy could not help but think it was a trifle sardonic, as if a little boy had announced to his father he wanted to play King.

CHAPTER FORTY

Jane Seymour

4th of May 1536

Warwick Castle

Warwick

England

Jane could hardly believe they had made it, there, to the hall of Warwick Castle.

Fast horses they had stolen, their father's horse, and Edward's. The road had taken three days to travel, and poor planning had meant they had not enough money with them for a room in the inn they stopped at the first night. A pitying innkeeper's wife had let them sleep in the top of the hay barn for all the coins they had left, which, after a supper of weak pottage and hard bread for them and feed for their horses, had not been much. Jane had thought they would make it to Warwick in a day or so, but it took the best part of three, and they had spent the second night cowering in a windy hedge, wrapped in their cloaks, no food in their bellies. Thomas had been an ill companion all the way, shouting at her when it was hardly her fault they had not taken enough money with them. She did not know what food and horses cost, did she? Father or Edward or a steward had always handled those kinds of matters.

They had meant to sell their horses and buy new ones on the

second day, but they had ridden them so hard the poor things looked close to death when they went to sell them, and no man would give them what Thomas considered 'fair' money for the beasts. All his threats of what might happen to poor folk who questioned a lord such as he had fallen on, if not deaf, then certainly chortling, ears. "Oh aye," one man had drawled, adopting then a fake upper-class accent, or what the man assumed such was like. "A *proper* gentleman like you, m'lord, out without an escort and with a lady in tow, no money in yer purse. One might think you were taking h'advantage of the situation, m'lord, all this trouble brewing all over England, to steal yourself a wife from a family higher than yours. If yer cannot prove yourself to be a gentleman, we can't be risking our *honest* souls to deal with the likes of yer."

Thomas had almost drawn his sword as a gale of laughter had erupted from the crowd about them, but Jane had put her hand on his arm. "Thomas, they are too many and they all have daggers."

"I am the son of a knight," he had hissed through clenched teeth.

"But there is only one of you, brother, and many of them. Please, Thomas, if you fall, outnumbered, as any man will when alone, faced by many, then what will I do?"

"It ain't position that matters in times like these, lad," another man, more kindly than the first, had said, coming forward in a fatherly way and putting his hand on Thomas's, the one which was on his sword. Something about the way he spoke made Thomas stand down. "It's the weight of a man's purse, and yours is light. As such, men will deal with you lightly. Come, I believe you to be a man of honour. I'll find you and the lady here some horses."

"Thank you, sir," Jane breathed, adding the mark of respect out of sheer relief.

"I am but Master Brown, not a knight, my lady," he said,

laughing. "But come, we'll see you get where you want to be going. This way, m'lord."

When finally they had reached the castle, they had not been allowed into the huge camp of common men outside for some time. Eventually, even though they were looked on with grand suspicion, for their good clothes, which normally would mark them as noble without question, had been soiled and stained by the long ride there, they were allowed to talk to the guards at the gate. There too they had not been allowed to pass with ease.

Questioned at the gates, questioned inside, eventually and despite Thomas not aiding matters at all once again by shouting and blustering, the siblings had been brought inside and separated, and Jane was now standing alone, waiting for Mary. Thomas, she was not sure where they had taken him, and she did not care. He had been a means to an end, to get her here. Her dress was dirty, her face and hands felt gritty, but she was there. She only hoped Queen Mary Tudor would not look down on her as everyone else had on the ride there, and before, when they assumed she was the King's whore. Dirty, that was what people thought Jane was, yet the dirt on her skin and clothes would wash away, and she hoped, by these actions demonstrating loyalty to the true Queen, to wash away the damage done to her reputation, too.

"Majesty." Jane swept to the floor in a deep curtsey, the best she could manage after long days of hard riding. Jane was exhausted and sore, but she was where she was supposed to be, that she was sure of.

Mary stared at her father's mistress. Jane had reached out several times whilst the King was still alive and they were both still in orbit about the court, through Gertrude Blount, to let Mary know that she was the Princess's supporter. Mary had welcomed this when she had been a cast-off child of the old King, but she was less sure now that she wanted a woman near her who in truth had no influence on the future, who owned a dubious reputation and who had just run away from her family, which in many eyes would secure that reputation all the more.

Gertrude had convinced Mary to see Jane. A Queen needed women, she told Mary, and the Countess, Elizabeth Grey and Gertrude, although high enough to be Mary's chief ladies, could not fill all posts. They needed someone lower of station in the Queen's household and Mary had only brought one maid with her. Mary suspected Gertrude did not want to take on all the menial tasks which presently were her duty. Yet Gertrude had put it another way. If the new Queen was to make a grand entrance to London, she had said, it should be with women about her as well as men, and noble women they were lacking here at Warwick. Jane's reputation was suspect, it was true, but Gertrude convinced Mary that Jane had refused to bed the King. How long her virtue would have lasted, Mary knew not, but she supposed it counted for something.

Yet her father *had* intended to bed this woman and Jane *would* have surrendered. If treason thought was still treason, were not lust and adultery the same?

"Mistress Seymour," Mary said, lifting her up by touching her hand, gazing in a little horror at the dirty gown Jane wore, and the scent of her body which, although Mary had smelt worse of late considering all the sweaty men riding into her camp to profess their loyalty, she certainly had smelt better too. "I understand you have endured a hard ride and have abandoned your family, who think to stand with the false Queen, to be at my side. I understand how difficult that must have been. Your brother, Master Thomas Seymour, I am told is here also."

"My brother and I support your cause, Majesty," Jane said. "You are the true Queen, as all of England knows."

"Sadly, not all of England," Mary corrected. "My bastard brother raises his own army in Wales, calling himself King, and the heretic witch who seduced my father raises another in the south and east. Both are strong with volunteers, so I hear."

"Soon all of England will come running to Your Majesty, just as I have," Jane declared in a stout voice. "Many of us remember your mother with great love and affection, Majesty, and we know you are the true blood of this country, through your father and your blessed mother."

Mary smiled, an honest smile this time. "You served my mother well, she mentioned you in many letters."

"Then I am honoured. I loved no woman as I loved your mother, and she was kind to me, as so many never have been." Tears shone in Jane's eyes, and Mary found her heart, unwilling though it had been to warm to this woman, respond with tenderness. But she could not stop her tongue, which felt less warm towards Jane.

"And my father had affection for you, also."

Jane flushed, her pale cheeks afire. "Your father… Majesty, though gossips said much, nothing passed between us but words. Your father was a good man, a great King and when I told him I did not want to become the mistress of a man, he respected that. He said he would be my friend and my champion, and he meant it. Many would never believe that is how it was between us, but that is the truth of it. I loved and respected him, but my honour means everything to me."

Mary had been one, until that time, who would not have believed it indeed, but oddly, hearing Jane now Mary did believe and more than that, wanted to. Many thoughts had entered Mary's mind about her father over the years which had passed since he cast off Mary's mother. Much she had tried to blame Anne Boleyn for, and a great deal Mary still thought Anne entirely accountable for, yet thoughts had come to her that her father could not be so easily led, that he always had possessed such a strong will and therefore some choices which seemed cruel must in truth have come from him, therefore he could not be entirely without blame. She had tried so hard to believe it was all Anne Boleyn, but to believe that was to believe her father was weak. To believe he was culpable made him stronger, but crueller. It was, in many ways, a sweet thing to hear that her father, whilst not acting with respect or love towards Mary or her mother, had acted with respect and kindness to another. On impulse, in gratitude for this sweet remembrance of her father, Mary made a decision.

"You will remain at my side, as one of my ladies-in-waiting," she said. "We have not much of a court here, on the cusp of war there is little we might call refined in Warwick, but when we march out and when I take my throne, I will have need of loyal women. I will make you a lady of the Privy Chamber, Jane, one of my most trusted servants."

Jane fell to her knees. "Majesty, I will serve you with all my loyalty and love, until the end of my days."

"Let us hope that day is a long way off, Mistress Seymour," said Mary. "Go now with the Lady Courtenay and she will find better clothes for you."

"Thank you, Majesty."

As Jane left, Mary turned to the Countess of Salisbury, silent at her side. "What of her brother? What do you think of him?"

"A reckless sort, rather boorish," said Margaret, "but we will need some of those in the days ahead. Sometimes war rewards the reckless and sometimes God takes them only faster, but there will need to be bold charges led, risky ventures undertaken. If the lad is hungry for glory, we can give that to him, in life or in death."

Mary nodded thoughtfully. In truth she never had liked the younger Seymour much. She did not warm to men who charmed and chatted as he did. They seemed false to her. She cared little for his fate. "Have him report to Montagu. Put him in charge of some of the battalions of peasants we have marching in, nothing too important, but enough to make him feel as if he is so."

Like Sussex, Oxford and the others, she thought. Those men had arrived at Warwick a few days ago, seeking to join her side. Of course they wanted to join her, they had no other choice. The Regent would have taken their heads for treason and still might be more than willing to if catch them she could, and Fitzroy had betrayed them to Anne Boleyn. The only side left was Mary's. She did not trust them entirely, they had been willing to put her half-brother on the throne as Regent, usurping her place. Suffolk had been none too happy about their inclusion either, since they had intended to act against him. Margaret Pole had convinced her to allow them into her army, saying that more men, commanders, was a good thing, but it was causing friction in the forces already, Suffolk refusing to work with them. They had been placed in lower positions of command, as Seymour would be placed now. Commanding peasants, many of whom had marched for weeks to get to her, these men could be useful, or so she was told.

Others had come. Bishop Stokesley of London was no surprise. A great friend of Thomas More, he had never welcomed the religious changes, though he had at times crumbled and spoken in favour of them when the King leaned on him. With Stokesley had come Edmund Bonner, Archdeacon of Leicester, recently returned from the Germanic states of the Holy Roman Empire. He was another who had worked for the King, yet now proclaimed himself a true, devoted Catholic. Mary could only hope these men of God were also men of truth. She had heard, to her dismay, that Syon Abbey was in support of the Regent.

Henry Percy, Duke of Northumberland was within her faction too, though she doubted he would be for long. Mary had been unwell herself for some days on arrival at Warwick, but Percy looked so ill and frail it seemed Death might well carry him off at any moment. He loathed the Boleyn Queen, however, and that made Mary warm to him. Lord Latimer had also turned up not long ago. He was an older man who carried a great deal of enthusiasm and surprisingly little skill as far as Mary could see, but he was a devout Catholic. One surprise had been Francis Bryan. His mother was at the side of the Boleyn Queen and was still acting as governess for Elizabeth. This had saddened Mary, for Lady Bryan had once been her governess too. She knew, however, how seriously Lady Bryan took her role as governess and knew also that perhaps Lady Bryan could not escape the court now, even if she wanted to.

Francis was potentially setting his mother at risk by coming to Mary's side, but he was great friends with Carew and had fallen out with the Boleyns of late. He saw Mary's cause as having the greater potential, and he was a wild man, honouring neither religion nor good sense, which she supposed could be useful. The latest man to arrive was Bryan's opposite. Lord Morely had also been a great friend of Thomas More, and had been in the household of Mary's great-grandmother, Margaret Beaufort. His daughter was Jane Parker who now was Jane Boleyn, married to George, but whilst his daughter seemed planted firm on the Boleyn side, Morely, as he had told Mary, was her man.

Perhaps the oddest arrival had been the fools. Will Somers, her father's fool and Jane The Foole had arrived together, having escaped the court as London fell. Jane had been in service to Anne but confessed to Mary she never had liked her mistress, and Will Somers frankly detested Anne. Once, Mary had heard he had called Anne a ribald and Elizabeth a bastard, and Anne had never favoured him since that time. Neither Will nor Jane were likely to be of great use in a military sense, but they lightened the mood somewhat.

Personally, Mary thought men like Robert Aske, a humble lawyer yet a man who could inspire souls all around him with but a few words, were of more use, and she was certain of his loyalty, unlike these men of court. What troubled her more, in some ways, was how this conflict was already breaking families apart. Morely, Bryan… they had female kin on the other side and yet they had come to her, abandoning them.

"We have enough men now, so says my son." Margaret handed Mary a goblet of wine.

Mary nodded, taking a sip. The wine tasted bitter, like betrayal. "Then soon we must march. We must get to London before Fitzroy does."

CHAPTER FORTY-ONE

Magpye Grey

14th of May 1536

The King's Arms Inn

Southwark

London

"But why, John?"

"The rightful Queen of this land is Elizabeth Tudor, and her mother calls for aid to retake London," he said, fastening on his belt. "Others may think what they will, Joan, but the truth of it is that the King's first marriage was illegal, and Lady Mary is not the blessed heir people think she is. It was not her fault, but she was born of an ungodly alliance of incest and cannot be upheld as an heir for England. The King understood that and removed her from her titles. Fitzroy was not his father's legitimate heir either. The Queen Regent carries her lord's child, which may be a boy but until then Elizabeth is the heir. That is as Harry wanted it, and that is what I shall defend, the true line and the true faith. London must be retaken by the army of the true Queen, or we are all lost."

Magpye's father stood in the centre of the chamber. He had a yew bow in hand, kept from serving in the wars in France under this man he kept calling Harry, but Magpye knew it to be the King who was dead. Her father stood proud, though his eyes looked a little defeated already. He knew, all of them did, that the Queen's side was not like to win in the end. London they might win, the two forces which had come to retake the city were in the east and west, and whilst they were struggling to gain a footing it seemed impossible they would not win through in the end. But that was but one battle and it seemed there was a war coming. The Regent was facing two armies now, of course all the new claimants to the throne were, but the call had gone up for men of London to volunteer for Anne Boleyn's army as the fresh ill news had arrived.

Fitzroy, the King's son but not a prince, had turned on the Regent and announced himself King. He was in Wales, and soon he would march on London. Men of Ireland, the west and Wales were turning out for him, raising banners of greyhounds above them, calling for him to be King. Lady Mary, the other claimant, had also announced herself Queen of England and she was in the north, having escaped the Tower of London. There were, it was said, thousands of peasants and lords of the north flocking to her cause. The Duke of Suffolk was her commander as it was said Norfolk supported Fitzroy. The Regent had not a duke left by her side, but soon she would have Magpye's father.

London was still in chaos, many parts occupied by looters and rioters, but others seemed to be occupied in the name of Queen Mary. Painted banners with pictures of lions, the fleur-de-lys and a crowned pomegranate, all images taken from Mary's official arms as princess, had been thrown up in these parts of town, hanging from the houses' windows and walls, demonstrating loyalty to the King's daughter. Men from these areas seemed bent on increasing the territory they occupied, and attacks on other parts of London were still being led by them.

Guards and soldiers of the Regent were gaining back lost

ground, however. In some areas there was endless battle ongoing and in others, where there were men patrolling, people were trying to get on with life as normal. Markets had even opened for a limited time in Southwark that week, though few merchants turned out and those who did looked nervous. Still, some people had to sell goods. Merchants had to make money so they could eat, and other people had to buy from them so they could.

Magpye's street had remained relatively quiet for some days after Pa and others had mounted their own guard to patrol it each night, and the Tower was in the hands of the Regent's forces again. Since the Tower was near Southwark where they lived, just across the river, there had been a greater military presence suddenly, calming the area and putting off looters and Marian loyalists. The Mayor of London and some aldermen had returned after fleeing in the first outbreak of violence. Some said order was returning to poor old London.

But some places were still holding out, either in the name of Mary or of chaos, with small battles and skirmishes breaking out each day. Greenwich Palace had been looted, they had been told, part of it burnt down, and the servants left there abused, and Cromwell's Rolls House had been burnt down too, but word was the Earl of Wiltshire and Lord Rochford, his son George who were fighting in the east and south, had called for reinforcements which were soon to arrive. This was the force Magpye's father was about to join. Able-bodied men of London had been called upon to march to the southern gates and there to meet with the army of the Earl of Wiltshire.

"The forces sent by Cromwell, led by Fitzwilliam, from the west, didn't do well," her pa had told them, having had the news from another. "They've been seen off, but I hear what's left of them are to march about and join Wiltshire and Rochford."

Old men coming to the inn over the last days, those few,

trusted people her father had allowed in, spoke of the wars of Lancaster and York again, the civil wars, which long ago, before the Tudors had come to restore peace, had been fought, but then only two sides had faced each other. Now, there were three.

"It is a triangle, when three points are made on a map," Old Meg had told her.

Magpye liked Old Meg, Ma did too. Often, of an afternoon, Meg would stomp into their kitchen on her walking stick and help Ma with the cooking. Olive of skin and silver of hair, Meg always had a story to tell and a jest to cheer them.

Meg worked for the apothecary three doors up. People said she was more talented than he, was the brains in truth behind the business, but long ago someone had accused Meg of harmful magic. It was not illegal to be a witch, many used the power of such people and went to them, for it was known they could find lost things and bring about love between two hearts, but someone had accused Meg years ago of unleashing the evil eye, of killing cattle. She'd been tried and acquitted, which was more normal an outcome than people thought in such cases, but people had always kept an eye on Meg since. She was the widow of another apothecary and could have taken on his shop, but try to run a business herself and she might come under more scrutiny, more censure, more dangerous accusations, so she worked for another, was his housekeeper, some said his lover, and worked in his shop too. But she was the person to go to when something was unknown. Meg knew things.

Old Meg had drawn out a triangle on the floor with a stick, the dust parting. On her shoulder her pet squirrel chirruped as if offering advice on her drawing. Meg drew three points; all looked different but all, Magpye saw, were forming one shape when linked, a triangle, like half a diamond, the shape of rich people's little windowpanes.

"What goes in the middle?" Magpye asked Meg, her hand hovering over the centre, where there was a gap. The squirrel jumped on Magpye's back, had a look about, then ran back to Old Meg, where he was safe.

Old Meg had smiled in a wry way. "You have a mind on you, child," she noted with approval rich, rolling in her almost-toothless mouth like nutmeg. "Many things might go in the middle, but here and now there's only one thing in this middle of this war of the three."

War of the three, that was what people called it. Some said the three meant three claimants, some said the three were three bastards. "All the King's bastards!" a drunk man had shouted in the inn the night before. "All the King's bastards are Kings!"

"What is in the middle now?" Magpye had asked Meg, looking at her drawing in the dust.

"We are," said Meg. "All us common folk, we're in the middle of this war and like as not we'll have to reckon with that sooner than we want to."

Magpye stared at the space for a while. "Aren't we already... reckoning?" she asked.

Meg chuckled, a dark sound, without humour. "This is just the beginning. Keep safe, child."

Magpye hadn't really known what Meg meant as she hobbled off, leaning on her stick, the little red squirrel taking hold of her cap so he could balance as she stomped along, but now that Pa was packing up and going off to volunteer for the Queen's army, Magpye had a feeling she understood something of what Old Meg had meant. Consequences, that was what she meant.

"But this isn't our fight, John." Magpye's mother sounded desperate.

Her father went to her. "It *is* our fight," he said. "This is for the rightful heir and what does anything mean without the right line on the throne? God's chosen must lead us, Joan. It's for

London too, for our business, our home, my love. We can't go on with little wars raging in every side-street, and us worrying when they're going to come for us, can we? But it's more than that. London is the seat of power in this country, without it the other claimants won't have a thing, not a sure hold, and they know it. That means that whatever else they do, wherever other battles are fought, they'll come here eventually. If we have control of London proper, her walls and her gates, we might stop that. Right now, we're simply subject to whatever army gets here first, and I won't live like that, falling under the wrong master because the right one wasn't here first."

"But what if the rioters, or God forbid, one of these other armies come and you aren't here?" Southwark had been relatively safe for some time, that was why Pa was going, but Ma was right. What if trouble broke again and they were on their own?

"Then you and our Magpye must hide, Joan. That's the thing to do, don't mind anything here. You know what men get like in rebellion and war. You hide yourselves until decent men are in the streets again."

"How are we meant to tell that?" she scoffed. "How are we to know which men are decent? Devils don't wear horns, John."

"When you see me come marching at the head of them, then you'll know." He grinned, grabbing her to kiss her but she turned her face away and he sighed, letting her go. "But I'll try with all I have in me to make sure that they don't get here. Retaking London is the best chance we have. Close up the inn for now, go stay with your sister in Bankside. It's not far."

"I'll have nothing for our keep, and for how long? She can't support us forever."

"There's the money in the tin which will last a while, and you can brew ale there and sell it. Magpye can do her cleaning for her. You'll be a help to her and her husband. Jack's a good man and he can't join this fight, not with that leg. They'll look after you." He kissed the top of her head. "Until I'm back and then I'll look after you."

"I've never needed looking after a day in my life," snapped Joan. "It's me who's taken care of you these last eight years and don't you forget that, John Grey."

"I don't forget it," he said softly. "And I love you, Joan."

"I love you, and I don't want you to go. Stay here, care for us, protect London if you must, but stay here."

He sighed. "I can't. I want to join and fight; it's the right thing to do and I can't rest unless I am doing that right thing."

"The right thing is to care for your wife and child."

"I am doing so, by going, by fighting for the true Queen."

"You'll fight for the baby of another woman but not for your own Magpye?"

Joan pointed at Magpye, and that made her uncomfortable. Quickly she left, heading out to a stool outside the inn, where she sat staring at the street while her parents shouted at each other. Pa lost his temper, and Joan screamed at him. It didn't happen often, their arguments, but everyone has them.

When a silence fell her father walked out of the door and scooped her up in his arms. Kissing Magpye on the cheek he told her to be a good girl for her mother, to mind what she said now, then he put her back on the stool and walked off along the street.

Magpye's eyes lost him at the end, in the crowd of other men leaving, in the mizzle falling dove-grey from the skies. Finally, she lost him because there was a mist in her eyes too and when she put a hand to her cheek, she found they were wet with tears.

CHAPTER FORTY-TWO

Queen Mary Tudor

29th of May 1536

Ascension Day

Warwick Castle

Warwick

England

"It is an ungodly idea, perverse." Mary's stomach tripped, nauseous just thinking on it. She was only speaking to herself, no one else was in the room with her, yet it seemed important to mark her rejection with words even if there were no witnesses. No one, not even her own self, should think for a moment she considered this plan sent by her bastard half-brother.

"Perhaps the way to end this would be for us to marry, as our honoured father once thought we should. A papal dispensation was once imagined for our union, let us unite our forces and apply once more for it. The match I have with Mary of the Howards never has been consummated, therefore could be annulled..."

A messenger wearing Richmond livery had come that morning, bringing this unwelcome letter to her hands. Her bastard brother was not only seeking to place himself on the throne in his own right, but now was seeking to compound his crimes, wanted to wed her and thereby steal her claim too, through marriage. Obviously, he knew full well the flaws of his own position and was seeking to bolster his false claim with her true one.

Fitzroy, she had always accepted him as a brother, as the child her father had sired on Bessie Blount, one of her mother's own serving women and a woman of small noble blood as it was, no matter her beauty, a feeble, worldly quality all had lauded at court which had led to Bessie being more respected than she should have been. Accept Fitzroy as a brother and the bastard son of her father Mary always had, but as a claimant to the throne, as a husband? Never!

Something disturbed Mary perhaps even more. This mention here, that once marriage between them had been what their father had wanted – could that be true? She hoped it was indeed a lie. Her father could not have wanted something so ungodly as to match brother and sister, no matter that they were half-blood rather than full, could he? But then, her father had done many things which had shocked her. He was not the man she had once though him to be. Not in the end.

But Mary did not want to believe this of him, not *this*. That he could have fallen so low as to think it would be a good idea to mate his children, one legitimate and one not, together so he might solve his crisis of the succession?

She had been in church that morning, celebrating Ascension Day, perhaps the holiest of days. To receive this news most ungodly just after that seemed perverse. People would be out this day, beating the bounds, marking the traditional boundaries of a parish, sometimes a village or town, by beating way markers, prominent trees and marker stones, with long canes. They would stop at points along the way, to pray, to hear a sermon, to take refreshment. Priests would have blessed the fields in the days before her father had tried to prevent all so-called popish customs. They probably still did. It was often a day of festival, but it was important too, marking a distinction of territory belonging to a certain parish. Perhaps it was fitting in some ways she had this message, offering to extend a moral boundary, to open up one set of territories to another, on this day. Mary would never accept; she would beat her own bounds with words of rejection on this day her half-brother had chosen to attempt to invade her domains.

"Did you ever hear of this demonic plan? Did my father say aught of it to you?" she demanded of Margaret of Salisbury, as the Countess entered the room, having hurried there at Mary's call. Mary thrust the letter at her.

Margaret read and lifted her eyebrows. When she looked up, there was a light in her eyes Mary liked not. "It is true? He asked for this? A dispensation to wed me to Fitzroy?"

Margaret shook her head. "Not exactly, but it was proposed, Majesty. Campeggio, the Cardinal who came to oversee the trial of your parents' marriage, I believe he was the one to raise the notion, although it might well have been the Pope's idea. The thought was to offer this solution to your father so that your mother could remain Queen, and he could have a male heir, as he wanted, or thought he wanted. The suggestion did not come from your father, and as I always understood it, he rejected it outright, thinking the idea ungodly."

"Thank God," breathed Mary. The relief was so immense, she had to hold on to the back of a chair to steady herself.

"And yet here, Fitzroy would bring it up again." Margaret sounded thoughtful.

Mary's eyes flashed up. "You think I should consider it?"

Margaret smiled. "Not for a moment, but it is interesting. I would say this means he is not as sure as his proclamation asserting his right to the throne would make him out to be. Perhaps he knows in his heart, as we all do, that you are the true Queen of England."

"That is what I thought, he seeks to bolster his feeble claim with mine."

"Indeed, Majesty. And perhaps it demonstrates something else."

"What does it demonstrate?"

"That he feels uncomfortable about this position he has accepted."

Mary snorted. "His proclamation from Ludlow – Ludlow of all places, how symbolic! – does not sound unsure."

"I am certain Norfolk wrote most of it, with a few suggestions from that pirate Brereton. But what of Fitzroy? What truly is in his heart? Always before he was a true subject to the Crown, a good and loyal son to your father. Perhaps he has been swayed into this treachery and is unsure in truth. Knowing your father never accepted him as any kind of true heir, his heart is likely divided."

"So, you think I should write to him, in secret as this came to me, and tell him I will forgive if he will join with us?"

"You could promise to make him second to no other Duke in this realm, that he would be your commander of all forces, perhaps, and offer to arrange a royal marriage for him. There are bastard daughters in the royal houses of Europe who would make a fine match for a bastard son of England."

Mary nodded. "And we may well threaten him with much if he will not comply," she said.

"What do you mean, Majesty?"

"There is no possible way Norfolk knew of this note to me or would ever have approved of it. His entire support for Fitzroy is based on the fact that his daughter, Mary Howard, is married to Fitzroy. Norfolk never would support a bastard son unless it was directly to his benefit, you know how he feels about true blood in ancient lines, and the throne is the most important of all! If Norfolk finds out Fitzroy was angling for marriage to me and trying to set aside his daughter, he would remove his support. Norfolk upholds old blood, legitimate claims. Fitzroy is none of those things. Without marriage to Mary Howard, Fitzroy is nothing but an upstart to Norfolk."

Margaret beamed suddenly and Mary laughed a little. "Why do you smile so, my lady?"

Margaret's eyes shone with pride. "Because you are your mother's daughter, Majesty, clever, wily… a Queen in all ways."

CHAPTER FORTY-THREE

Henry Fitzroy, King of England
8th of June 1536
Pentecost
Ludlow Castle
The Welsh Marches
Border of England and Wales

"Does he know?"

Fitzroy was pacing the chamber, Brereton staring at him. It had been Brereton's man who had gone to Mary, taken the message and brought back hers two days ago, a message containing threats. Fitzroy had expected his half-sister to accept, or offer an alliance, but never had expected the venom, disgust and threats which Mary levelled, one of them being she would tell Norfolk that he had offered to set aside Mary Howard. Not long after, Norfolk had brought Mary, his daughter, to Fitzroy and announced it was time the marriage was consummated. It seemed too much a coincidence. Fitzroy was busily cursing his foolish decision to try to offer Mary a deal, to appease his conscience.

"Does Norfolk know of the offer we made to Mary?" he asked Brereton again.

"I doubt it, Majesty." Brereton had assumed a maddeningly unconcerned air. He was peeling an apple, rather a wrinkly one, clearly out of a barrel stored from the last autumn. A long, curling twist of peel was slipping smoothly from under his sharp eating knife. Fitzroy felt a little mesmerized by the slippery curl.

But as Brereton had addressed him, Fitzroy had winced internally, as he did every time someone used the title of *Majesty* for him. He was trying not to, was trying to become used to it, but in truth it pained him every time it was spoken, like a jab to the ribs, as if the ghost of his father were there at his side, poking him with a dagger forged of guilt.

"Then why this sudden insistence that I consummate the match?"

Brereton shrugged. "You are about to go to war; we are but a day or so from marching towards London. Perhaps Norfolk wants to secure seed in the belly of his daughter before that time, in case anything happens. Certainly, to get her with child would bolster your position. A king with an heir in the belly of his wife, is stronger than a king standing alone. If there is a continuance of the succession it grants power, for the common people find such a consolation. It grants them hope."

"You think that all it is?"

The peel dropped to the floor. Brereton picked it up and set it on a green-glazed plate at his side. "Even if not, even if Norfolk knows, Majesty, the fact that all he has done is insist on the union between you and Mary Howard being made legal speaks of his commitment to your cause. Where else, in truth, can he go? Lady Mary would not welcome him, and the Regent has never liked him and would never trust him again after this. She might well use him and his men, but afterwards I suspect Norfolk would find himself most swiftly housed in a very nice room in the Tower for the rest of his life, and that life might well be shorter under the rule of the Regent than he would like."

Brereton paused. "I would suggest, Majesty, never mentioning this pact you tried to make with Mary to anyone, Surrey in particular might be upset, and he is less politic than Norfolk, more likely to think with his emotions and his pride than his father."

"Norfolk has pride enough."

"Yet is a pragmatist most ruthless at heart, he would always put considerations of his life and the best chances for his family's fortunes ahead of his pride. Surrey would not." Brereton cut a slice of apple.

Fitzroy threw his hands in the air. "You were the one to tell me the plan had merit!"

The pirate glanced up, looking somewhat amused. "And it did, but that plan is quashed now, the lady not open to the idea, therefore we make a new plan. Such is the way of life. Bed your wife, Majesty. If, in the future, you wish for another wife, one born higher than the daughter of the Duke of Norfolk, I am sure we may find a way to dissolve your union. Your father found a way to rid himself of a wife he wanted not, after all, and if Mary Howard should give you a son and other heirs, keep her by all means."

Fitzroy hesitated. "She is a good woman."

"And a beauty," smiled Brereton. "Which is never a poor thing in a woman." He crunched into the apple slice, and Fitzroy seemed to hear the breaking of bones.

CHAPTER FORTY-FOUR

Mary Howard, Duchess of Richmond, Queen of England

June 1536

Ludlow Castle

The Welsh Marches

Border of England and Wales

In bed, Mary Howard rolled from her back to her side and gazed over at her husband. They had been married for some time, yet now it was a secure match, finally, due to the consummation just performed – and yet was it secure? Was anything at the moment? Due to her bond to Henry Fitzroy, Mary now had the potential to become a Queen, men were already calling her by that title, and yet there was a Queen Regent, and there was another Queen Mary. True, there was no one else claiming to be King, besides the lump of Anne Boleyn's belly, but Queens wandering about England there were aplenty. Would her husband and father win this fight and make her Queen for certain? Would they fail and make her a traitor by association, by marriage and by blood? And did she think she should be Queen? No one had ever asked her.

Just as no one had asked her if she wanted to marry Fitzroy, or if she wanted to bed him. Both had been commanded.

Her father was a brutal man, and he would not be disobeyed by anyone, least of all his children. Her mother knew well what he was like, Mary remembered the bruises on her mother's arms, her throat. It had been a daily occurrence when her father was at home that her mother would the next day appear with bruises, some she could conceal and some she could not. Norfolk never cared if people saw that he had hit her, certainly he had never cared if she made a noise, which often Mary's mother had, her screams resonating down the hallways, so harsh and loud and causing such guilt that, when they were little, Mary and her brother Henry had stuffed cloth in their ears. Nothing had truly softened the sound.

They had separated some time ago, her parents, after Norfolk had thrown Mary's mother to the floor, beaten so badly she coughed blood. Mary and her brother Henry Howard had not escaped him though. Norfolk had total control over any money they received, had ordered their attendance at court, told them to whom their alliance was due. He had control of their lives, through money, by law and by law of the Church. He still had control of their mother's life too, though they lived no more in the same houses. She lived alone, whilst Norfolk entertained his mistress, a woman the same age as Mary. That same mistress, Bess Holland, was at court with Anne Boleyn. Norfolk had abandoned her. Women were means to an end, for her father.

Mary tried to repress a sigh. Was she not the same as Bess in many ways? A convenience, a tool to be used? Commanded to marry, ordered to the bed of the man she had married, and now told to bear a child. Was that under her control? Could she bring a child into the world on command?

Mary had been told long and loud and often that men held all the power of conception, and the woman was simply earth in which seed was planted, yet it always was women who were blamed when a couple did not conceive. She did not know if she wanted to be a mother, she liked children but the notion of becoming nothing in her life, *her* life, but a brood mare, there to carry child after child until one day, her body worn and exhausted, bled to death as another baby tore through her and into the world – that did not appeal to her. And besides, this time was fragile. If Fitzroy and her father failed, did she want to be the one bearing Fitzroy's child? Would it not compound her crimes and make her more likely to be punished if another side won? Would it not be better to wait until they had won, were secure, before nurturing a seed in her belly?

Mary had had such thoughts before she came to the bed of her husband. Commanded to spread her legs she had been, commanded to bear a child if she could she had been. She had not been forbidden, however, from eating herbs before and after she came to her husband. Norfolk would not have thought it possible his daughter would do so, considering what he had ordered, but Mary had done so. She had no intention of conceiving a child in a time so dangerous. If her husband and father failed, she did not want a child of hers born and raised in exile at best, or in the Tower at worst. Everyone knew what had happened to other young claimants to the throne, the young Earl of Warwick, the princes in the Tower. They had claims to the throne that those *on* the throne had not liked, and they had died for it. Mary Howard would not bring a baby into the world only for someone to kill or imprison it, and her. If they won, when they were safe, if she was made Queen for sure, then she would bear a child. Not before.

Mary would not hand an insecure life to an innocent. Children should be born to those who can offer them all they can, who can at least offer them life, not to those who can only offer peril, and death.

So, Mary Howard had her herbs, rue, artemisia, savin, pennyroyal… whichever she could get she would dose herself with now she and Fitzroy were as man and wife. She had sworn to bed her husband and she had, she had sworn to *try* to bear a child, and she would, but Norfolk had never mentioned *when* she should bear a child. Mary could fulfil that promise when it was safe.

As for Queen, did she want to be so? Until now Mary had never thought on it. She was not of the line of succession, though she held royal blood as many of the highest of the land did. Did she think she had more right to the throne than Queen Anne? Possibly. More than Queen Mary? No, she did not think that was the case.

Did her husband have a right to the throne? Mary thought not. Not in law. Fitzroy was a bastard; Mary had been brought up to believe only the legitimate may inherit.

But that hardly mattered, did it? What she thought, what the law said was right? Many a man had made himself King by war, by battle and feats of arms and by proclaiming much and often afterwards so it made it sound as if he had a right to the throne he had stolen. Fitzroy could become one of those kings. It was possible. Henry VII's claim to the throne had been tenuous at best, and although not illegitimate himself, that King had come of a line which had been bastardized. A full bastard had sat on the throne before, the Conqueror. Men with a claim lesser than another had taken the throne, that had happened in the civil wars between Lancaster and York, over and over again, stealing from each other like birds fighting over an ancient nest.

It was up to God who won. Mary would wait and see who was to be King, or Queen.

"You march on London?" she asked Fitzroy. Mary did not dislike her husband. In truth she knew him but little, yet he was intelligent and hale, nice to look upon and he was kind to her. He had taken his time, tried not to hurt her in their so recently shared bed. It had been a painful experience, but he had tried hard to make it less painful, something many a man did not bother to do, and at least he had come to her sober. Almost every girl she had known as a child had ended up with an at least somewhat drunken husband on the first night. To Mary's mind it was the girls who could have done with more stiff drink, considering the boorish behaviour they had to put up with from men with lust in mind and too much alcohol in their blood to consider being careful with their new wives. Considering some of the experiences she had heard of, Mary had cause to wonder what was different in the marriage bed to rape? Both seemed to involve a woman being taken hard and against her will, the only difference in marriage being the man had the good will of the bride's family.

Fitzroy nodded. "Soon," he said, pulling on his linen undershirt.

"Someone could come and dress you, rather than you doing it," she pointed out.

"I know, I don't like all the fuss. Everyone fusses about me now, more so than before."

"The fuss is what marks you as the King."

She wondered at the flicker of insecurity she saw on his face as he glanced at her. Did he, too, wonder if he should be named King? It was interesting if that was the case. Most men would simply adore the notion of others worshipping them, but Fitzroy did not seem to warm to the notion, though he had accepted his new title.

"My father was better at this than I will ever be," he muttered.

She rose from the bed, walking to him unclothed. A flicker of interest rose to his unsure eyes. Mary smiled; she knew she was desirable. That was a good thing. Women had few weapons and were trained with fewer, but beauty could become a shield, even a sword, if a woman learned to wield it. "It takes time, and practice," she said, putting on her own undergarments, reaching for her gown.

He came to her, helped her put on her kirtle, then to lace her dress. His fingers fumbled over the lacings, the pins, but despite his inexperience he helped her put on her clothes well enough and did not seek to take them from her again. Clothed, she turned to him. "You are unsure about this role you have taken on." It was not a question.

He swallowed, looking away.

"I will say nothing to my father, Henry. You are my husband. Loyalty to you now supersedes that owed to Norfolk."

He inclined his head, meeting her eyes. "If my father wanted me to be his heir, would he not have named me so?"

"He thought he was about to have another child with his Queen."

"He *will* have another child with his Queen. That he is dead does not negate that the child in her belly is his. If it is a boy, will I be going against the wishes of my father, perhaps the wishes of God? At the very least I will act against my own half-brother, just as now I act against two half-sisters."

"This preys on your conscience?"

He nodded. "It does. At first, I was swept away with the arguments of men like your father, Brereton, your brother, and Parr... they all told me my father had many times considered naming me his heir and in that light the throne should be mine. Because I am a grown man, the throne should be mine, they said. But my father, though he honoured me, never once indicated to me he wanted me as his heir. I was his proof he would sire sons, I think, and I believe he loved me, but in his eyes, I always was a bastard."

"You can change the status of your birth through Parliament, if you win."

He laughed. "And yet never change the whisper in my heart, or the thought held by many, that no matter what a piece of paper or proclamation says, I am not the heir of Henry VIII, and I am not the true King." He sighed. "It has gone too far now to stop. Even if I did, the Queen Regent would never trust me again, nor Mary, my sister. Whichever won, if I pulled out now, they would execute or imprison me. To win is the only option for me now, for to fail in any way will mean I lose my freedom and my life."

"But you are unsure this is your destiny?"

"I am."

Mary touched his face. "When Henry VII won Bosworth, it was said God wanted him to be King, wanted the restoration of the Lancaster line. If you march out and win, you will know this is your destiny, you will know God wants you on the throne."

"Why would God want a bastard on the throne of England?"

She felt true affection spike in her heart for this man she had married. "Perhaps because He knows you are a good man, Henry," she said. "And perhaps doubt is part of what makes you a good man. There is humility in you. So many here and now are so sure of the way things should be, but you question, and that makes you different. If God sees this, as I believe He sees all things, then He knows you might be a king of another kind, one willing to listen to many sides, to make choices others would not."

"So, you think this may be my destiny?"

Mary stared into his earnest eyes and answered honestly. "I think it could well be, if God wants another kind of world, another kind of King, to rule us all."

CHAPTER FORTY-FIVE

Queen Mary Tudor

12th of June 1536

Corpus Christi

Warwick Castle

Warwick

England

Mary stood in a side chamber of the chapel of Warwick Castle, staring at the altar. A scent of incense filled her nose, something she had always previously associated with comfort, awe, the presence of God, and she knew the scent now would always be associated with a tinge of dread, because of this moment. "I do not even know this man," she whispered to Chapuys. "Is this not a mistake, Lord Ambassador? When Queen, I could marry into Spain or Portugal, as my mother always planned, marry a kinsman of the Emperor, a prince worthy of my blood. I could make England stronger. This match, now, it will bring nothing to England but the old blood of the Plantagenets and that I already carry, and we know not what my cousin, the Emperor, thinks of this. I fear I will lose his support."

Chapuys nervously pulled on the cuffs of his sleeves. "Yet is has been made clear, Majesty, without this marriage, you will not have the support of the Poles or the Courtenays, and that support you need, here and now."

Chapuys was none too happy about the situation either. In a recent meeting of Mary's council, the Countess, a person he had always thought of as having the highest morals, had led with an argument that Mary should wed her son Reginald Pole, and had made it clear this was a required action to secure the continued support of her house and others. Clearly this had been talked of in private between them, for Courtenay supported Margaret as did her sons. Even Suffolk backed the notion. It might even have been talked of before Mary was set free. Chapuys had always considered himself a clever man, an astute fox in the holt of English politics, and he had the uncanny and uncomfortable feeling he had, in fact, been outfoxed by an older vixen.

Reginald Pole was a deacon, many said he could have become a cardinal, but not now. He had been commanded to England to marry Mary by his mother and by the Pope himself. This third son, not even the first – though Montagu was married already of course, and the second Pole son had been married and now was dead but still, a third son! – of the Countess of Salisbury had been sent for to secure the alliance between the English nobles supporting Mary for the throne. Reginald had never been ordained, so was eligible to wed, but he was a scholar more than a man of action. Mary had met him perhaps ten years ago, when he came back to England to work for the King, her father, but they did not know each other well. Reginald had made himself unpopular with Henry VIII because he was opposed to the Boleyn marriage and had fallen out with the King for speaking against it and eventually writing against it, but they had not fully broken ties until the King had heard of his book, *In Defence of Unity,* which reportedly denounced the King's religious changes, and denied the legality of the King's second marriage. The book was on the verge of being published, and it had been said because of this that the Pope would make Pole a cardinal if the book caused the stir it was supposed to. Of course, all that had been changed by the King's death, and the apparent high necessity of marrying this son of the Poles to Mary.

The book and its reputed contents had made Reginald popular with those who supported Mary of course, but whilst Mary had respect for this man, she had no wish to marry him. Chapuys thought it an ill match too, though it had been mooted by Imperial Ambassadors before, he himself had even spoken in support of it once, but now he was not so sure. Yet the Poles and Courtenays had been gentle but insistent. The message was clear. If Mary wanted their continued support through this war of the three claimants, if she wanted the men they could bring, the connection of their blood, the arms and money they possessed, then Tudor must marry with Pole, uniting the Plantagenet and Tudor dynasties.

"Your grandfather took an English bride, one with old blood, with a family line and support that he needed in order to secure his claim," Chapuys said. "There were rumours he and Elizabeth of York did not like each other to begin with, but they came to respect each other, and eventually they forged bonds of friendship and love."

"You think I will find love here, in a marriage I am being forced into? God's eyebrows! I never thought the Countess would use such bribery upon me." Mary had been shocked and dismayed by the ultimatum. She had thought of the Countess as like a mother, and now that mother had turned on her. Mary felt used, duped, but she could see no way out of it. All her power meant so little, she realised, for if people did not support her, she had no authority, she was no Queen.

"I think you will find the support you need in this moment, Majesty, in this marriage. What will come after will come." Chapuys shifted on his feet, his mind working fast. His master, the Emperor, had not yet heard of the match and would not be pleased about it when he did, nor would he be happy the Pope had sent a dispensation for the union. Although the Emperor could hardly offer his own hand, since he was married, and his son was a little young, being nine years of age, he still would want to dictate his cousin's choice of husband. "You could refuse to bed him," he suggested. "If there was no consummation, there would be cause to dissolve the match at a later date."

Mary's mouth twisted. "You think I should become as my father, take one partner then another?"

"It would not be the same situation."

Mary twitched nervously, her hands moving at her sides. "I always thought to marry a prince," she whispered, "someone of the same rank as me."

"Fate alters, sometimes for the best. If you had married a prince of another land, you might have been taken out of England, then we would not have you here, now," Chapuys told her. "And if you had been married to a prince, it would have been to create alliance, safeguard the land of your birth. That is what you do, here and now." He sighed. "God has a plan, Majesty. Marry this man, claim your throne, and listen to the voice of God in your mind as to whether or not to secure the match."

"You think I should deceive my allies?"

"I think you have been pushed into a position you are uncomfortable with. That is no way to treat a Queen, therefore your allies are only allies on the basis of compromise and bribery, not loyalty, therefore what loyalty do you owe them?"

She smiled. "You have a lawyer's heart, Ambassador. When I hear you argue, often I think of More, and what he would have said."

"He was a good man, I liked him."

"I did too, my father once loved him more than any man, I think, then he sent him to his death." She looked far away for a moment, thinking of her father, trying to remember the last time she had seen him. Had it been when he came to see Elizabeth and she had gone to the top of the house to try to see him, for he had refused to see her whilst she still defied him and his orders to accept Anne, Elizabeth, and all else? He had taken his cap off to her, then ridden away. Was that their last interaction? Perhaps it was. That was it, the span of their relationship, which once had revolved around him coming to her chamber as a child, kissing her awake, praising her for her lessons and learning, for her grace, always telling her how he loved her, always telling her how precious she was. Then to end that with a hat being taken from a head, as if she was no more than a passing stranger. *How swift may the heart alter*, she wondered, *how fast can it change from love to hate, or indifference?* And if a heart could change one way, could it change to another? Could she learn to love this man the Poles had commanded to come to England, who the Pope had approved of and had too commanded to marry her, this man who had sailed to a country on the verge of war to wed her, arriving at King's Lynn not three days ago with a papal dispensation for their match in hand, and who had ridden straight here to see her? It demonstrated bravery, did it not? Commitment to her and her cause? Reginald Pole too was willing to set aside the life he had thought to live, in favour of one which, it was thought, would benefit others. Was this a sign of a strong character, or a weak one?

Of course, much of this bravery she noted now was self-interest, Mary knew that. He had the chance to become a king, to advance his family, and yet she could not deny Reginald had taken risks to be with her, to become her husband. Risks that perhaps showed the kind of man he was, and perhaps that kind of man was more than a mere scholar, perhaps there was a heart within him, and courage. Perhaps he was the kind of man she could wed. Mary had rarely been a pragmatist at heart, often she made decisions based on her feelings, and whilst it could be said this was a match made of pragmatism, she also listened to what her heart felt. At that moment what lifted its head in her chest was hope.

It was a holy day to be married upon. Corpus Christi, celebration of the body of Christ. Reformers wanted it gone, of course, especially since it was a festival introduced by the papacy only a few hundred years ago. Processions used to mark the day. Given the turmoil in the kingdom, that seemed less likely this year, but Mary had always honoured the festival. Was it fate that she should be brought to the altar on such a day, where the body and blood of Christ were celebrated as being truly present in the wine and bread of the Mass? Perhaps it was not a coincidence, perhaps it was a sign from God Himself, a sign of blessing and of her mission to restore England to the true faith.

She breathed in. "I am ready," she said. "Let God decide what will be."

CHAPTER FORTY-SIX

Thomas Howard, Duke of Norfolk

12th of June 1536

Corpus Christi

Ludlow Castle

The Welsh Marches

Border of England and Wales

Norfolk stared hard at his much younger half-brother. The sense of loathing in his chest threatened to rise up through his throat and choke him. Norfolk never had liked his brother. Another male heir, with the same name, and from the same family, it had always felt as if Thomas the younger was there just in case Thomas the elder suffered an accident and died. A replacement for his own self, his life, provided by his father's second wife, Agnes, an irritating woman, one of those with opinions which he still had to suffer now, even after his father's death, though she had a few uses, unlike many women.

Now here his fool of a brother was, accompanied by a wife no less, or so he claimed, here to tell his elder half-brother there was a babe inside that wife, as if this was a good thing for Norfolk. Thomas the younger wanted his protection. Thomas the elder felt like reaching out, taking hold of his brother's throat and squeezing until the light drained from his brother's eyes. What a relief that vision would be!

The wife was a woman of the royal line, and her baby was therefore too, and whilst many could say Fitzroy was a bastard with no claim to the throne, and Mary likewise, there never had been dispute that Lady Margaret Douglas was legitimate despite the annulment of her parents' marriage some years ago. It was accepted she had been born in good faith, as the saying went, and the King had always favoured her. That meant this child, his brother's child, the child brought to him, Norfolk, to protect, could be said to have a better claim to the throne than the man Norfolk was supporting.

If it was a boy, that was. No one wanted yet another woman thrown into this stew for the succession England was stirring. No one wanted to support Margaret Douglas, but a child born of her and the line of Norfolk was another matter. The Howards carried royal blood, distant it was, but it flowed in them. Margaret Douglas obviously also carried blood destined for the throne.

For a moment, Norfolk hesitated; was it worth supporting this? Supporting his brother and his child? But the child would be a babe a long time, and the claim was distant, weaker because it came through a female line. It would not hold up, and he knew it. Also, this would mean his younger brother's line would sit upon the throne, not his. The whole point of lowering himself and supporting Fitzroy, the King's bastard, was to get his own grandchild on the throne.

The Queen had offered to make his grandson a king already, of course. Perhaps. This offer of Elizabeth's hand he had also pondered over, hesitated over, but his mind had rejected it even before Gardiner wrote in secret to tell him of the talks Anne Boleyn was also holding with France. It was a game, a play. If the Regent bore a son, Norfolk's grandson would be wed to a princess, to be sure, but not to the Queen, and Norfolk had a feeling that if the Regent had another girl, he would find his grandson promised to the second daughter and not the first, excluding his line once more from the succession. He had also had a sneaking suspicion that he might well find any engagement to any of Anne's children broken along the way once his support was not so valuable. No, safer it was to support his own cause, to support Fitzroy even if the boy was of bastard blood. That way Norfolk could control who got on the throne and when, and assure himself that his line would eventually be the one to take control of England.

But now there was yet another fly in this already so tainted ointment.

"Brother," Norfolk said, trying to inject warmth into his voice. "Of course you will here be sheltered. What more can family do?" He smiled at Margaret, thinking she looked ill. His brother was a fool indeed, if he cared for the wench to have ridden her hard here to Ludlow in her condition. She might well lose the child, but then all would be fixed, would it not? It might be a good solution. He would never have to tell Fitzroy about it, if that occurred.

"You will be cared for, sister," Norfolk continued, bowing graciously. "Take Lord and Lady Howard to a chamber, have hot water and food brought up for them. Tired from their journey they must be," he commanded his men. "We will talk more later, brother, when you and your wife are rested."

"Your Grace, you are kinder than I could ever imagine," Margaret Douglas said, kissing his hand. She looked rather overawed by his graciousness.

"How now," said Norfolk, even managing to blush a little. "It will all be well soon, child."

And it will be, he thought grimly.

As they were led away, he turned to his servant, William. "Have them separated, put guards about their chambers. They are not to leave, do you understand? And they are not to see each other."

William nodded, though he looked surprised. "They are to stay here, under guard and in separate places in the castle, Your Grace?"

"They are traitors to the realm, and they endanger our King."

"I understand, Your Grace."

Norfolk strode off, to find Fitzroy. They had delayed long enough. Lords of Ireland had sent ambassadors, offering men, and this had held them up a while. Some were already at Ludlow, with their forces, but any more arriving later could simply follow. It was time to move. They would march on Windsor where his bitch of a niece was, and take her and her children prisoner, then on London and claim the capital. He heard common people were holding out for Mary there, but the army which had flocked to Fitzroy was large enough to vanquish any resistance. Twenty thousand they had now. Rumours of the Regent's forces and their pitiful numbers had made Norfolk smile, a rare occurrence. They would not be a problem.

Then they would deal with the Lady Mary, and then his daughter would sit on the throne next to that Tudor bastard, until his grandson could claim it. Norfolk would be the power behind the throne until his grandson came of age, then order would be restored to the world, with a Howard in charge of England.

And he meant it to be the elder Thomas Howard in charge, the elder with his line on the throne. His brother's child would not threaten Norfolk's design and purpose for the throne. That would never be permitted, even if it meant Thomas the younger and Margaret Douglas vanished from the world here and now.

Fleetingly he thought it was a shame a woman so pretty would disappear, but then, Norfolk thought, there were plenty of pretty women in the world. The loss of one hardly mattered.

CHAPTER FORTY-SEVEN

Magpye Grey

13th of June 1536

Bankside

Southwark

London

Magpye was asleep one moment and not the next. From dreams she never remembered was she startled awake to find her mother was there, Joan's face close to hers. "Up!" Joan all but shouted. It was a strange shout. It tried so hard to be quiet yet was alive with unimaginable strain.

Magpye was bleary-eyed, dull of mind, but sleep vanished in a second as she heard the noises downstairs. Shouting, banging. She could hear her Aunt Mary screaming. It seemed to go on forever.

"Mama…" She did not usually address her mother like a baby would, but something in her fractured, reverting to infancy as she was shaken awake, as she saw her mother's face, drawn, pale as a corpse in the small light from the moon outside. Magpye did not get to ask what was happening. There had been trouble for days, getting closer to them all the time. Fresh conflict had been breaking out all over London. There had been news of deaths, of war being raged anew in the streets near the Tower, Westminster, Greenwich, as Marian supporters tried to conquer London for the Lady Mary, and as forces led by Wiltshire marched for the Queen. Men seemed bent on destruction, but Bankside had not been a site of trouble.

Not only her mother's face but the sound of chaos outside told Magpye that time had ended.

Her mother dragged her from the chamber in her aunt's house which they had all been sharing and along the short, dark hallway. Magpye's legs seemed to tumble along the corridor, her feet tripping over themselves. There, at the back was a small window. Her mother pulled open the shutter and ripped the oiled paper away. The night air blew in. It smelt of cold and smoke and fear. Magpye looked out, seeing the opening led to a short thatched roof. "They are inside the house. Rioters, Magpye. You must run!"

Her mother lifted her and carefully pushed her out of the window. Onto the thatch Magpye fell with a thump.

"Mama!" she cried, looking up to the window, confused and chilled by the air, the moisture on the thatch. "Come! You must come too!"

But Magpye knew already Joan could not get out of the tiny window. It was too small. Joan glanced behind her, then back to Magpye, her face pale. "Run, Magpye, run for the inn. The key to the back is in the garden, in the old place Pa used to hide it. Go! I will come and find you. Keep safe." Her voice cracked as noise came from behind her. Someone, many people, they were close. Feet sounded on the stairs, alerted by her voice. "I love you. Run!"

The panic in her mother's voice commanded her. Tears blinding her, Magpye scrambled down the thatch and fell down the short drop to the garden below. Onto her aunt's leek bed she tumbled, a soft enough landing though it knocked the wind from her all the same. A high scent of human waste on the vegetable garden filled her nose for a moment as she picked herself up off the floor. Her hands were wet with the earth, with the shit mulched into it. She wiped her hands on her sides and looked about. Magpye was barefoot, only in her nightshift, no hose or warm woollen stockings, no shoes and no cap for her head. Her nightcap had fallen somewhere. It had been a cold start to summer and the night air bit her to the bone, but as she came hesitantly from the garden and turned the corner into the street, the night's chill seemed to vanish as everything about her became as fire.

People were everywhere, invading houses, shops. Smoke was billowing from somewhere, but she knew not where. She coughed, hanging back into the shadows. Shapes of darkness and vicious shades raced and ran before her. There were men struggling in the street, hitting each other, screaming. In the houses there were noises of fighting. "For Queen Mary and the Blessed Virgin!" she heard a man shout as he ran down the road with a banner in hand, a crowd of men following in his wake armed with clubs stained with blood.

Women were screaming. A child stood outside one house alone, crying loud and long, his hands balled into fists, rubbing his eyes. A fraught cry from above and behind her caught Magpye's mind and she looked up, knowing the sound of her mother's voice even in the din and confusion. Joan was gone, she had been dragged back into the house. "Mama," she whispered, but Joan was gone.

But Ma had said she would find her. She had said Magpye was to go to the inn. Even in the dark, Magpye knew the way. For a moment she stood there, watching to see if her ma came back, but then a hand came from nowhere and tried to grab her and Magpye ran.

She ran fast, her feet cut over and over on debris on the street, on the cobbles, on mud and on grit. Her poor feet bashed down, hard, as she raced and she did not feel the pounding, the blood pouring from the underside of her feet or from a gash on the side. There was pottery on the road, shards of it everywhere from broken cookware and plates thrown out of people's houses by those looting, spread by people scuffling and fighting. Magpye did not heed the pain in her feet, she felt nothing, her body alive with panic and fear and the mission; she had to get home, where Ma had told her to go.

People were busy with their own struggles; she flew past them. Just like in the inn when she had dodged people, so she did so now, ducking from a fight here, veering off to the side there. She was a falcon plummeting in the skies to catch a smaller bird, she was light itself, so fast it could not be seen arriving or vanishing.

Magpye ran so fast she thought her chest would explode, so fast she could barely see for the tears streaming down her face. She cried as she ran, wept for Ma and for how afraid she was, cried because Pa wasn't there. Magpye wept because she was alone and didn't know what to do, besides to run for home as Ma had said. She didn't know how to help her ma, she didn't know how to make the people stop fighting, which was all she wanted to do. But racing thoughts didn't stop her running. Nothing would. She was running for home. Magpye was running for the place she had been safe before. She was not safe here, no one was. Once these had been streets she had known well, ones she'd wandered down and bobbed to curtsey in greeting to neighbours. Now, they had turned in a moment from something familiar and comforting to some kind of hell, and she was trapped there. All she had known was gone and nothing was safe.

Magpye had thought nothing would change the world she knew, but she had just that hour come to an understanding that she had been wrong. It could change in a moment, all that was safe turning unsafe, all that was good becoming bad. The world had turned, and she had lost her footing.

But her feet still knew where to go.

When she reached the inn, Magpye didn't need to find the key. The front door of the inn was wide open, the insides smashed to pieces. Tables were overturned, chairs too. The windows covered in billowing cloth, roused by a cruel wind, were open, the wooden shutters torn almost from the hinges. She stood there for a moment staring, but a noise of shouting coming fast down the street, along with the sound of boots, made her move. She slipped in through the door and ducked down behind a table as the men ran past outside. For a moment their shadows loomed large on the walls of the inn, and the light of torches discarded in the street, still burning on the ground, along with the pale light of the moon made those shadows of men seem like giants. They raced past, others followed. Further down her street there was more noise, more screaming.

Not knowing what else to do, Magpye came from her first hiding place and hid behind the bar. There was a place, when trouble broke in the inn, where Pa sometimes hid her. A little alcove with a rag over it, small enough for just her. She hid herself in there and waited for her ma.

But Ma never came.

In the morning, Magpye came out. The sounds of fighting were distant again, like the last time. The inn looked worse in daylight. Out back, the pig was gone and the chickens too. One was dead, sprawled on the little path, her pretty red feathers awash with mud and blood. It looked as if she had been trampled to death.

The scent of smoke was coming from somewhere, she suspected there were people putting out fires in many places, grappling roofs to bring whole houses down before they could catch from a neighbouring house. People were supposed to keep buckets of water outside, always filled, to stop fire spreading, for if it leapt roof to roof in London, where so many houses were timber and the roofs thatch, the whole city could become an inferno quickly. With so much looting, people's homes and their cooking fires must have been disturbed, torches or rush lamps left unattended or knocked over. It was easy to make fire spread here. Magpye hoped the fire she could smell was far enough away so it would not come for her house.

She went upstairs. Finding an old shawl lined with ratty cat fur which Ma had been about to cut up for rags she put it over her cold shoulders, and an old pair of Ma's boots, far too big for her, she pulled on her cut feet. They hurt, these boots that once had been Ma's best and they were stiff, and her feet rolled about in them, but it was better than walking on the cobbles barefoot. Her feet were cut and bruised and now she was not running like a hind fleeing the hunters, Magpye could feel how her feet ached. She needed to wash them, put Ma's ointment on them, but she was unsure where to safely find fresh water or the ointment. There was a spring they usually went to, down the road, near the river, but she didn't dare go there. There would be too many people and some of them might be like the ones she had seen the last night, faces torn with desperation and anger so vicious it led to killing. The ointment she suspected Ma had with her, at her aunt's house in Bankside.

Ma hadn't come. She had said to wait for her, but Magpye didn't want to. She didn't want to be alone anymore. She had never been alone so long, and she didn't like it.

Back to the house of her aunt she went, back to Bankside. Something in her told her she shouldn't, that she wouldn't want to see what was there, but she had to see. She had to find Ma.

Magpye wandered past the apothecary shop, called out for Old Meg but there was no one there. She walked on, heading for Bankside.

Other people were wandering about, some trying to pick up goods or possessions spilled onto the street, some trying to repair broken windows with cloth or new oiled paper. Some people were trying to find others, stopping people to ask had they seen this woman, or that child? No one asked her if she was well or wished her a good day as she wandered about in her nightgown and shoes too big for her so they flapped and slapped on the cobbles. People had their own problems, just like last night. Children were running here and there, also collecting things or trying to find parents. She hadn't been the only one to hide through the night, hands on ears, trying to block out the sound of the chaos outside. Others, small as she, or smaller, had survived in the same way.

Sometimes she saw bodies, some slumped in alleyways, some in piles, pulled to the side of the road. Some were just lying there, before her, their arms splayed out, legs too. There was blood and there were eyes staring at nothing. She tried not to look at them or at the people weeping.

Magpye reached her aunt's house, and stood there a while, staring.

The house was broken. It looked as if a great storm had fallen on it. The window at the front was caved in, the oil cloth that had covered it sailing in torn fragments in the wind, like a shroud wrapped badly. Inside, when she had the courage to creep within, the big room was as broken as the inn. Her uncle Jack was on the floor, his face smashed in so she couldn't see his big brown eyes. He had had kind eyes. Her Aunt Mary was in the hallway, slumped on the floor. She was cold to Magpye's touch.

Joan was on the bed, in the room upstairs. Her skirt was hitched up about her waist and her eyes were staring at the ceiling, wide with horror, red where the white should have been. There were marks of fingers on her neck in shades of black and red, blue and yellow, there was bruising on her face. Blood was smeared on her legs, her thighs.

Magpye stood there a while and then she gently took hold of

Ma's skirts and put them back down where they should be. Where Ma had always worn them, because Ma had been a lady though she was a common woman. Ma would not want people to see her like that, so Magpye didn't leave her that way.

She crossed Ma's arms over her body, as if they were protecting her. Magpye closed her mother's eyes, so she could be sleeping. Then Magpye turned and walked out of the house.

She was in a daze, not knowing what to do. Her mind was blank. She was sure she should be sad, should be crying, but she was not. Everything in her was numb. She couldn't feel her fingers, her toes, her legs. Magpye stumbled out of the door and her feet started walking. She didn't look where she was going.

When finally she looked about, she was back at the inn, standing outside. She didn't know how she got there. She walked inside and found some clothes. Magpye only had one dress, but she had two kirtles, and a kirtle could be used as a dress when a woman had nothing more. It laced at the front, and usually Ma helped her to do it, but Magpye had laced herself before. She did the best she could, making sure she laced it the way Ma told her, making horizontal lines of lacing rather than crosses, for ladies of the night laced their gowns with crosses. Straight-laced was the more respectable way to wear a gown, it was the way Ma had worn her gown.

Magpye kept Ma's shoes, for that was all she had. Then she went to the floor near her parents' bed and prised up the loose board. It was where Pa kept his precious things. There was a small purse of money there, mostly groats and half groats, and his copy of the New Testament. The one he had taught her to read with. It was in a box, to keep it safe and Magpye would keep it safe. She would not let men steal it, and she would not let men burn it. Magpye had failed to protect her mother, but this she would see safe back to Pa.

She took the wooden box into her hands and wandered outside again. She was hungry and she was thirsty, and more than that she wasn't sure what to do, nor was she sure how long she stood there, staring at the ruins of her home, until she heard a voice.

"Mistress Magpye?"

A deep voice, one she knew, sounded over her. Magpye turned and stared at Thomas. "They killed Ma," she told him calmly, her voice as numb as her body.

He stared at her a moment, his brow creased with pain, then he clasped her shoulder and went to walk into the inn.

"She's not here, she's at my aunt's house. She's dead too, and Uncle Jack."

Thomas ducked to one knee. His voice was the gentlest thing she had heard in what felt like a long time. "Your father, Mistress Magpye? Where is he?"

"He went to help the Queen."

Thomas nodded. He breathed in, looked at the floor and then up, into her eyes. "Then you must come with me, Mistress Magpye, together we'll find your father."

He waved a hand to one side of the street. Exhausted, Magpye looked. There was a horse without a rider, his men on other horses nearby, a small cart near them. She frowned. "What are you doing here, sir? I thought you left London?"

Thomas felt as if he had been punched in the gut by something sweet, something precious to the world, something which hurt him and filled him with awe at the same moment. Even in the midst of this horror and sorrow, here the child was, addressing him with respect and politeness as a social superior. He supposed, as a merchant, he was above John and his family, who ran an inn, but never had he considered himself above his friend, and it was more than that. This child, with her brown eyes so darkly haunted by all she had witnessed, with blood drying on her face and her brown hair torn by wind and God only knew what else, and still she kept to her manners as if it was a normal day. His chest ached with admiration, regret, and sorrow.

"I did leave, Mistress. In truth, I would not have come back here at all had I not wanted to check your father and your family were safe. When I reached a ship at Dover, I heard London was in turmoil and my conscience would not allow me to board. My men are trained well, they are good companions to have in times of trouble. I thought we could escort all of you out of London. I brought a cart to take anything you cared for, too, but clearly, I came too late. With us you will be safe, but you must come now. You cannot stay here."

"What if Pa comes back here?"

Thomas nodded. "We'll leave him a note, Mistress Magpye."

"Can I not stay here, Master Blanke? It is my home."

Thomas regarded her, then looked to the ruined face of the inn. Far off, but not far enough for comfort, there was shouting. On the other side of the river smoke was pluming from a house, the roof on fire. "There is nothing left here, Magpye," he said. "The streets are dangerous everywhere now. Rioters are out of control, forces supporting Mary are gaining ground and the Regent's army is even now marching into the east of London. There will be more fighting today, and tonight." He sighed. "The best thing we can do is flee, for a time at least. When it is safe, we can come back, we can find your father."

"How will you leave a note, Master Blanke? We have no paper here, not being rich folk."

Thomas set his hand on her arm. "I will carve a message into the bar of the inn," he said. "Your Pa will find it, and know I am with you, and you are safe."

"You'll tell him about Ma?"

Thomas nodded again and swallowed hard. Was it a lump of sorrow in his throat for Ma, such as she had in hers? "Put this on, Mistress Magpye," he said, handing her a cloak, "and get in the back of the cart here, and hide."

Magpye stared at the cloak he gave her, then at him.

Thomas smiled sadly, more a grimace it was. "It might look curious to some, a man such as me, with my heritage, taking a girl clearly not related to me out of London," he explained. "People might think the worst, and yet you cannot stay here, for there is no one here to protect you."

She clasped the cape to her with one hand, holding her precious box under her arm. "But you will protect me?"

Thomas looked as if his good heart might break. "I swear to you, Mistress Magpye, as the soldier I once was and as the friend of your father I still am, I will do all I can, until we reach your father." He touched her cheek gently. "But you know, Mistress Magpye, should you ever find yourself alone again, should I fail you, you are capable of much yourself. Many died this night, you did not."

"I did not fight, sir. I ran. I hid."

He nodded, and she noted how the sun shone on his dark, curling hair, on the feather in his cap. "Sometimes, Mistress, that is what must be done, sometimes it is the only sensible thing to do. You did what was right, you lived through the battle. That is all any soldier can hope for." He patted her shoulder a little awkwardly. "Now, into the back, and hide once again, pretend to be a sack of cloth until I call for you. Do you need something to drink?"

She nodded – suddenly her throat was dryer than she could imagine. He took a leather-bound flask from one of his men and gave her a drink of small ale flavoured with herbs. Magpye had been raised properly, so she wiped her mouth before taking a drink, and thanked Thomas's servant afterwards. The ale tasted of fennel, but also salt, as if it had been brewed with tears. Thirst sated a little, she climbed into the cart, covering herself with the cloak. She put the box next to her, safe.

As the wheels turned, and they trundled through the broken city, Magpye peeked out but once and saw there were other carts trundling the same way, along with people carrying bundles, women carrying babies. Men had children on their shoulders. Many were leaving London, trying to get away. She remembered the tales Ma had told her, of the people of God leaving the lands of Egypt. Smoke plumed high above, and birds were singing merry tunes, as if they were singing the people on their way out of danger, and towards safety. Would it be safe?

Not so very long ago, Magpye had thought her world safe enough. She had thought it would not change. There would be Ma and Pa and her and Jane who washed the cups, and there would be customers and the inn, there would be bed and sleep. Everything had changed. She had nothing now, nothing but Thomas.

But Thomas was a good man, of that she was sure.

Thinking on all these things, her eyes burned too hard in the sunlight and too harsh with tears to peek anymore, so Magpye closed her eyes and imagined Ma was there, holding her. She was asleep in the arms of her mother long before they reached the fields and country roads which lay to the south of Southwark.

CHAPTER FORTY-EIGHT

Queen Mary Tudor
14th of June 1536
Warwick Castle
England

Mary's council, to a man, and woman since the Countess and Gertrude were there, were staring at her. She realised they were expecting her to tell them what to do. She swallowed, because in truth there was not much she could do, only one course of action could she see.

Her new husband, Reginald, sat at her side, he too was silent. No wonder, for she had just received another proposal of marriage from someone who clearly did not know she was wed already. That was no surprise either, for she had been married but two days. Announced to her supporters it had been, but evidently it had not reached Scotland that she was a married woman.

And a married women who had agreed to bed her husband. Chapuys had told her to listen to the word of God in her heart, and Mary had listened to that, along with other persuasions, and she had lain with Reginald. It had been awkward, for both of them, but he had seemed so straightforward and honest when she met him, sweet in a way, that she had agreed. He had talked of children, and something in Mary wanted children, wanted to raise a baby. Talking with Jane Seymour after the marriage ceremony, however, Mary had also come to the conclusion that she again had small choice about this decision.

"The Countess says there should be proof, witnesses outside the chamber," Jane had said, looking worried as she whispered in Mary's ear. Jane was looking rather odd, for the gown and hood she wore did not really fit, being Gertrude's, and had not been yet adapted by clever stitches to mould to her body or head. "They want to know that Your Majesty is truly in earnest about the match."

Thinking ruefully upon this new part of a deal she already had accepted, and considering that there could be benefits to marriage, such as a child, as well as benefits to being married to Reginald who, aside from religion, had said he was quite happy to remain out of state affairs, Mary prayed that afternoon. Then she had gone ahead. Although God had not intervened and sent a sign, she thought again on her mission to bring England back to Rome and the true faith, to ensure her mother's memory was honoured. Her mother had loved the Countess, and this was the Countess's son, and without the support of the Poles or Courtenays, Mary had no chance. She never thought to see what might happen if she called their bluff. Mary held more power than she was aware of.

The Countess had been delighted to hear of Mary's decision, however, and suddenly in place of the rather grim, demanding person Margaret had become over the last days before the marriage, she turned sweet and encouraging again. Mary had been relieved that her friend was back, rather than this other person Margaret had seemed to be. It did not occur to Mary that now she had capitulated to everything Margaret wanted, the Countess was now being her friend again, and therefore that friendship was conditional, reliant on obedience. Mary was simply happy, for the meantime, to once more be in company with people she liked.

Witnesses had been permitted to stand outside the chamber, Mary would not let them within, but the matched had been consummated, and then this morning Mary had cause to regret it.

"The King of Scots, our cousin, makes demands of us which cannot be met and will not be entertained," she announced to her council.

"And what of the threats in his letter, Majesty?" Geoffrey Pole sounded troubled, as well he might be.

Mary inclined her head. James had not only proposed marriage between them, a way to unite their claims, but something else.

"The King of Scots has announced his own claim to the English throne," she said. "This we all know, and he suggested he and I marry to unite our claims." *Like Fitzroy*, she thought. Suddenly everyone wanted to marry her. For years it had seemed as if she might die a maid and then as soon as her father died, she could not move for suitors. "We cannot consider his proposal of marriage for we are already married..." she indicated to Reginald who smiled at her "... and we will never countenance a King of Scotland upon this throne of England, which is ours, by right of birth and by right of blood. King James indeed threatens that if I do not agree to marry him, he will invade. I cannot agree to marriage with him; therefore we must prepare to counter this invasion."

James V only announces this claim now because of the mess England is in, Mary thought. If he believed he had a true right to the throne, why not announce it when her father had died? James had waited to see if the throne would hold and when it had not, when England was plunged into mayhem, then he decided to press a claim, thinking a divided country would be easier to conquer. He thought wrong.

"We were about to march for London, Majesty, yet now, with

this threat from Scotland we cannot abandon the north." Montagu was right, although Mary did feel his point was a little obvious.

"We cannot, my lord, so further north we must go, to meet this threat. I have heard good men of London are holding out against the false Queen in my name, and we will have to trust they will continue to do so. If not, we will march on London and take it after we deal with this threat from the north. We will announce to our gathered troops the direness of this situation. England is about to encounter invasion from Scotland, and as Queen of England I will see it vanquished. Just as my mother saw off this same threat before me, so I will do so now. United let us go to show these invaders that our country cannot be so easily claimed, nor taken, for the hearts of brave Englishmen will always win through in a battle for their homeland."

"Hear, hear!"

There were calls of support, men thumping their fists on the table. Suffolk stood from his chair. "All hail Queen Mary!" he shouted.

One by one they rose, her council, many of them now her family, and added their voices to his.

Mary straightened her back. "We march north, my lords, and I will march at the head of my army. Let us show my cousin of Scots what happens to those who seek to steal my throne, and as England watches its true Queen see off this threat, I have no doubt many more will come flocking to our banner, allowing us to see off not only this threat, here and now, but also the threat of my bastard half-brother, and the witch who calls herself Regent of England."

CHAPTER FORTY-NINE

Queen Anne Boleyn

15th of June 1536
London

Riding into London, Anne wanted to bow her head in shame. The city was wretched, broken. Blood was on the streets and bodies were piled like heaps of hay in alleyways. Carts creaked in the backstreets, carrying people away to pits dug in the graveyards, mass pits, as if this were a time of pestilence, but the only pestilence upon them was war.

This was supposed to be a triumphant return for her to the seat of power, but it was nothing of the kind. Her procession of courtiers, lords and soldiers marched on, trumpets blaring, drums beating like some ancient heartbeat of the world, but Anne's heart fell only more with each step her horse took. Riding through crowds comprised of the people of London, many of whom had turned out to cheer her and her army, Anne saw people who had fought for days, for weeks against the armed insurgents inside the walls of London. Her people had reclaimed the city, cries of, "For England, for Elizabeth, for Henry!" on their lips, and their voices had clashed against those shouting, "For Queen Mary and the Blessed Virgin!" just their bodies had clashed in combat. Anne felt humbled before them, ashamed.

Anne saw many men bandaged and bleeding, women and children too, nursing broken limbs, wounds. There were people missing limbs and eyes bound, which could only mean they had sacrificed sight in this battle for London. Each new hurt, each new wound weighed heavily on her heart. Soon the weight was so great she could not bear it.

She called the procession to a halt. Anne's father rushed to her side, shocked and worried, thinking it trouble with her baby, caused by the rigours of this journey which many had called on her not to make, telling her to stay at Windsor until the baby was born, which could now be any day. She should have been in isolation, should have been in her lying-in chambers, but Anne knew she could not carry on as if all was normal. Anne had wanted to go to London. King and Queen she was now, and whilst a queen heavily pregnant could usually stay at home, a king had to ride with his men. Isabella of Castile had been pregnant when she had ridden out with her troops. Anne Boleyn would do no less.

"I am well," she said when Wiltshire came to her side. "Help me from my horse."

A step had to be brought. She was too heavy to climb up or down by herself. People had tried to put her in a litter, but Anne knew she had to be seen by the people, and she was a good horsewoman, she could make her horse walk slow enough. But now she needed to be closer still to the people. Anne came from her saddle with the aid of John Dudley, her Master of Horse. Thomas Culpepper, her cupbearer and her father supported her other side. "Stay close," she said, walking towards a group of people.

"You should not go amongst them, it could be dangerous," Wiltshire hissed.

"Just as dangerous to not," she told him. "Here and now, we have a chance to win them to us, Father. It is a chance I will take."

"Truly, you are Esther born again, Majesty," Cranmer, there too now, murmured.

"You flatter me, Eminence. For myself, I claim no such thing, but I will do what I can," Anne replied.

Anne motioned to her women to bring purses, and to Cromwell and his guards to stay at her side. Bess Holland stepped forth first, eager to be seen to be serving, and Anne nodded to her. Ever since word had come about Norfolk and Fitzroy, people had been telling her to place Bess under arrest. They would have had her do the same with Elizabeth Browne and Margaret Bryan. Elizabeth's husband and Margaret's son were marching alongside Mary, it was said. Cromwell had declared they were a risk and should be detained, but Anne would not do so and not only for the fact that Elizabeth was heavily pregnant, just as Anne was. These women were *her* women, no matter what their menfolk were up to.

Bess had paled to hear about Norfolk. Anne knew, the moment she had looked at Bess that Bess had had no idea what her lover had plotted. Bess also knew she had been abandoned by Norfolk. They had always been affectionate friends, Anne and Bess, and Anne swore to her friend, as she had to Elizabeth Browne, that any crimes of their kinsmen would not reflect on them. As for Margaret Bryan, the lady governess had stood stiffly before Anne when news of Francis had come. Margaret had offered to resign her post, but Anne had refused.

"Are you still loyal to me, and to your charge?" Anne had asked.

Lady Bryan drew herself up proudly. "I am, Majesty. My son goes his own way, but I undertook the care of the royal household of your daughter with a promise of loyalty and devotion, and nothing has changed."

"Then you will not resign, Lady Bryan. You will remain."

This conflict had already broken too many families asunder,

and the true war had not even begun yet. Even Anne's own family were divided. James Boleyn, her uncle, had gone to Mary. Norfolk was against Anne and Thomas Howard the younger, along with Margaret Douglas, had vanished from Windsor. Anne could only suppose they had gone to join another side, but nothing had been heard of them. The loss of Margaret hurt her heart. Anne had loved the girl.

Despite many Howards abandoning her, Agnes Tilney, Dowager Duchess of Norfolk, Anne's step-grandmother, had declared for Anne, as had Sir Edward Bayntun, Anne's vice-chamberlain and his wife Isabella Leigh, who was a half-sister to another Howard branch, the children of Edmund Howard, but Lord Morely, her sister-in-law's father, now rode with Mary. England was a mess, that was plain enough, but Anne would set it right.

And that began here, with these people.

With two heavy purses in hand, Anne went to the people. "Take this, a small offering for all you have suffered," she said, pressing a silver coin into the hand of a woman whose face was bruised across one side. The woman burst into tears and fell to her knees.

"Take this, for your suffering," Anne said to each, moving along the line pressing coins into the hands of all the people she could see. The crowd tried to swell towards her, but men at the front, not guards or soldiers, but ordinary men who had fought when her brother or father or the bishops had called upon them, held them back.

"Stand back, for the Queen Regent!" a man shouted. "She who came to save London when all others deserted us!"

Anne thought, a touch wryly, that she too had abandoned London, but she was not about to disagree with the man, especially since others took up his cry and shared it through the crowd. Coming to the end of the line, to the end of the coins her women had, and her men too when those of her women had been exhausted, she walked to the centre of the square.

"Queen Anne, the saviour of London!" a man with one leg, supporting himself on wooden crutches, shouted as she stood before them.

"Good Queen Anne!"

"The unborn King's mother!"

"All others abandoned us to chaos, but Queen Anne did not!"

"Queen Anne, the liberator of London!"

Anne liked that one the most. It was so different, she thought, to the way they had spoken of her before now. All the shouts of whore had gone, and now they thought her a saint. Women only ever seemed to be one or the other in the estimations of others, saint or sinner, virgin or whore. They never could be but human.

"Good people," she called out to them, and the crowds fell silent. "Good people of London, loyal men and women of England, for your suffering I sorrow, and for the liberation of our great city from the madness that has been upon it, I rejoice."

There was an eruption of furious cheering. Women threw flowers to her feet and Anne gathered some in her hands, holding them before her belly. "We will never see London, this place where my ancestors, humble though they were, began their journey of life, suffer so again. We will see it grow, and grow strong once more, fed on the courage of the noble people therein. For now, for your suffering, I offer coin, we will buy food for London to be brought to the markets and hospitals will be opened and set up about London so you may bring your wounded to doctors, to healers and to priests I will pay for, so we may begin this time of healing."

More cheering burst out. It was a generous offer. Many people could not afford a doctor, nor some even a healer and so many had to make do with home-made remedies. Considering the state most people's houses and businesses were in also, there was going to be little money left for anything. Food was already scarce. Gardens were starting to produce again now, but much had been trampled, large sections of the city had burned, and others had been pillaged.

Worse was to come, Anne thought. She did not wish to say that, but it was true. Now they faced not only Mary's army but Fitzroy's too. It was odd, but when the news had come that the lad had declared himself King, Anne had not been surprised exactly, but she had felt a curious sense of disappointment, even loss. Norfolk was behind it, she suspected. Fitzroy had seemed loyal to her, at least at first. She should not have allowed the two to ride off together and had been wondering for some time, suspecting for the same amount of time, that something of this kind was what was delaying him from riding back to court, and Norfolk from riding out against Mary. But yes, when the news had come, she had been disappointed in Fitzroy, as if her promise to name him son when he had unmasked the conspirators had indeed taken root in her heart. Mary, Anne could understand hating her enough to wage war on her. She had not thought the same of Henry Fitzroy.

But no matter what her heart felt for either of them, they were both her enemies now, enemies of her children too, and they would be set down, just as the rebels and rioters who had occupied London for far too long had now been vanquished.

Anne paused until the cheering subsided a little. "Though you might look upon me and see but a woman, thought by some to be weak and feeble, there beats within my body the heart of a King, *your* King, the son of your beloved lost lord, Henry VIII." There was another cheer, almost deafening and Anne shouted above it, "And your King is a King of *England!*"

The crowds erupted to wild, feverish acclaim, men beating their feet on the ground and cheering her, and women clapping their hands. All voices were raised as one, one great cry of defiance against all who would oppose or harm them. As the din faded, just a little, Anne lifted her chin once more to speak, and the crowds fell silent to hear her.

"These troubled days have tested my heart, my endurance, like no other. I know they have tested you. I see it on your faces, good people, I see the violence which has flooded these streets. Dark forces align against us, the army of the King's bastard, he who long pretended to be a dutiful son, gathers in the west. The army of the King's ungrateful daughter in the north gathers too. I, the Queen and Regent chosen by your King, I have come home to London, bringing my children with me, because we know of your loyalty, know that you, like us, have suffered. But I promise you, an oath sworn on my own family, on my own bones, that from suffering there shall come victory, and from pain there will be joy found again. In short time..." she touched her belly "... your King's legitimate son will be born. Those who have tried to steal his throne and the place his sister, my infant daughter, my innocent child, now holds, they would turn you against us, and yet seeing you here, coming forth to welcome us home, seeing the courage with which you fought to retake your city and defend your houses, I know they will not achieve their evil purposes. I know London will stand with us, with the Crown, with the true line of the King, the line he himself chose to rule over you. Together we stand until the end, when our enemies shall lie, wretched, in chains at our feet, and on that day we will rejoice for the will of our dead beloved lord and the will of God will have been done! Let all tyrants and false sovereigns who would rule us try their hand for they will fail! For England, for Elizabeth and for Henry!"

The noise was deafening. Many in the crowd already agreed with her, and even those who did not she could see turning to one another, talking fast and low. Loyalty meant a great deal. Mary and Fitzroy had not turned out to save London, people supporting Mary had, in fact, caused a great deal of the bloodshed, but Anne Boleyn and her army had come, had fought, had won London back from the brink of the chaos it had stood on for so long, and that meant something to those who had suffered long weeks of mayhem in the city, it meant a great deal to merchants who had almost lost everything, to people who had lost their homes, to those who had lost loved ones to death. Even those who did not believe Anne had any right to the throne believed in something else; safety, and right now she was their greatest chance at achieving that.

Rumours that the rioters who first had broken upon the city had been paid to do so by the Poles, who rode with Mary, were rife about the city, and whilst many might have supported the Princess being freed, they never would have supported the violence done to them these past weeks. All this had started when men stormed the Tower to free Mary. Was one life, *her* life, worth all the blood that had been spilt since? Was it fair that a child of the King should have found liberty through men taking the lives of so many other children? The Marian rebels let loose upon the city after had acted without honour, many indistinguishable from looters and murderers, and that too stained the reputation of their leader, Lady Mary. The people of London wanted no more of Mary's chaos.

But Anne Boleyn had shown honour. She had come to save them, had ridden with her men, whilst heavy with child no less. She had been the one to restore order. That was the action of a brave soul, a Queen in spirit even if she had not been born a Queen. Many Londoners had not supported her at first, but now they would. There was a debt to be repaid. None other had turned out to save London, but she had.

Some in the crowd told each other of the days before this, when Anne had instructed her chaplains Latimer, Skip and Shaxton to set up welfare for the poor, to provide standard orders of money for the needy, and of when she had commanded the prompt handling of petitions so that all who needed to speak could be heard. She and her ladies had done much sewing for the poor, women whispered to men, the Queen had supported many young men in education, and even had sent money to Wolsey's bastard, Thomas Winter, when no one else would.

There was a time all of this would have been ignored, or people would have accused Anne of only doing charitable acts to try to emulate Katherine, but not now. Just as when people decide you are wicked, so they will find more and more evidence to confirm your wickedness, in a like way, when people have decided to support and love you, they seek more reasons to do so. Everyone likes to be right, after all. Many now would see all that was good about Anne and excuse the bad, as once they had done with Katherine.

"Long live the Queen Regent and long live the true line of the King!" a man shouted, and people echoed him. "Long live Elizabeth! Long live our little Harry!"

"For England, for Elizabeth, for Henry!" There came the rallying cry again, and many took it up. The call sounded upon the earth and rose, echoing in the heavens above.

Anne stood there a long while, smiling, tears in her eyes. Her brother George stood behind her. Many of the court had come from their horses and they stood too with Anne. George watched his sister, watched the love raining upon her, and as he did, he put an arm about his wife. Jane leaned against him and put her hand to her own belly. She was not sure, and did not want to say yet, but she believed at Windsor she had conceived. Before he left to fight for Anne in London, George had come to his wife night after night seeking comfort. In times of peace, Jane had lost many children, and this one, forged in a time of chaos and violence should not have more call to live than they, but somehow she felt it would live, that this child, conceived in a time of war, was stronger than her other babes had been. In the time of their coupling, George had been tender, loving. Perhaps this child was made of love, and that was why Jane felt it would survive where the others, conceived in times of hatred, had not.

Anne held out her hands to the people of London, and the people cheered her as she had never thought they would. *Finally they welcome me, Henry,* she said in her mind. *As you always wanted.*

Cromwell came to her side. "They adore you, Majesty."

"Let us hope it remains that way," she said, still smiling, waving to the people. "You have news?"

"You read me well."

"It is that grim face, my friend. It speaks to me plain as the day's light."

He smiled a little. "We must move fast to secure the city. Fitzroy has started the march from Ludlow."

"We will be ready." She felt his hesitation. "What more is there?"

"There was word today, from a spy I sent to Mary's camp, Majesty. She was ready too to march but has been detained."

"By what?"

"By two things. The first is that Reginald Pole has been snuck into England, and as part of her pact with the Poles, Mary has married him. The Emperor, I understand, is in a rage about this, that his cousin married without consulting him, but the deed is done and consummated, so I hear. Poles and Tudors now are one family."

Anne shook her head. "The old wars, Cromwell, they never died, did they? Plantagenets again would tear England asunder."

"They are not alone, sadly, Majesty."

"Then what more?"

"The King of Scots, James V, has announced a claim to the throne, proclaiming all others, Mary, Fitzroy and your children to be bastards, and himself the true heir. He proposed marriage to Mary, as I understand, to secure their alliance. She refused. He now marches on the north of England. Mary is gone to meet him in battle."

Anne paused, her hand faltering for a moment in the air, but then she nodded, and lifted it anew, to fresh cheers. "One crisis, and one claimant at a time, Cromwell," she said. "Let us prepare for Fitzroy and Norfolk. Mary and James can war amongst each other, and we will see what comes of that."

And we will see if George is correct about you, Anne thought. Before he had left for Kent to gather forces with their father, her brother had come to her side, worries on his mind and lips which he had spilled. George thought Cromwell might well be playing for Mary's side rather than Anne's, and unwilling though she was to believe it, Anne had to pay attention to her brother's concerns. It was not impossible Cromwell had worked for Mary, had engineered the fall of the Tower, though many said that was the work of the Poles and Courtenays, but it was also true he had served Anne so well, especially of late.

Cromwell had advised her ably, had brought men to London to fight under his command, was rousing mercenaries for their cause and yet George still worried despite all this show of loyalty that Cromwell was not loyal. It was possible that there was a long game being played here and Cromwell might have helped them retake London only to hand it to Mary at the opportune moment. Anne could not deny Cromwell was capable of such. He could be serving her only as long as she seemed to be winning, and yet she had hardly been winning until now. Was the man trustworthy? Was he not? In truth, Anne did not know. She had evidence of his loyalty aplenty, but it was possible he could turn on her. So many had.

"One crisis at a time, Majesty, as you say." Cromwell bowed.

"Who knows?" she asked, turning to him with a smile. "Perhaps the two cousins, one of England, one of Scotland, will destroy each other?"

Anne stepped forward once more, and as she did so the people of London erupted anew into deafening applause. Anne stood before them, one hand on her swollen belly, the other in the air and about her the skies were filled with the din of the people of England cheering for her, and with flowers thrown by women in the crowd, raining down upon the Regent as if all the stars of the night sky were falling from heaven itself.

Far behind her, a figure sloughed off from the crowd, away from his company of archers, walking away from the raining flowers and the cheering. John, father to Magpye, was marching fast for home, eager to take his wife and child into his arms.

Here ends All the King's Bastards, book one of

A Succession of Chaos.

In book two, A Son of England, war will rage between the claimants

to the crown, as common people

struggle to survive in a landscape torn by war.

AUTHOR'S NOTES

The idea for this book came from an email conversation I had with one of my readers. Speaking of the great "what ifs" of history, I said that I considered the question of what might have happened had Henry VIII died in the jousting accident of January 1536 to be a fascinating one. Anne Boleyn was still alive and was pregnant, Henry Fitzroy too was still alive and was a grown man, Mary Tudor was young and still reeling from her mother's death and her father's actions against the Church, yet there was more than this, for the dissolution of the monasteries had not yet occurred, Anne and Cromwell had not fallen out quite yet (though they were regarding each other with suspicion) and James V of Scotland was not yet married, but certainly had ambition. There was great potential for chaos and for England to have taken a different path from the one which unfolded in history.

At the time, when the reader told me I should write the story, I said I didn't really write speculative historical fiction (although, of course, all writers of historical fiction have to speculate a little), and yet the idea kept coming back to me. I started making notes and then I started writing, and what came from it was this book.

I am not the first to write speculative fiction about this period. Other authors have tackled this idea in various forms, imagining what would have happened if Anne Boleyn had survived, or if she had given Henry a son, or what if Henry had died in 1536 rather than Anne? At first this put me off a little. I started thinking that since other people had written about this, perhaps I should not, since it was not an original idea, but then I came to consider that plenty of authors have written novels about the real lives of Anne Boleyn, Jane Seymour, Henry VIII etc, and this did not deter me from also writing historical fiction about these people, so why should I shy away from writing my own version of this great "what if" of history? Perhaps I had something else to add, another version of events, another way of imagining what could have unfolded?

I went ahead, and I do hope you enjoyed it. As I was writing, I decided it was too big a story for one book and intend now to write a series. My regular readers will probably smile at this, as it's hardly an unusual path for me to take. I always think it is hard to sum up a life in just one book and there are many lives in this story. I will, as usual, provide a bibliography at the end of the last book in the series.

I would like to note a few things that might bother people with a good understanding of historical events. The first is that Anne Boleyn suffered a tragic miscarriage in 1536, on the day of Katherine of Aragon's funeral, which led, in many ways, to Anne's own downfall and death for if she had not "miscarried of her saviour" as Chapuys put it, then the King would not have sent her to the block. In this book she does not lose her child and instead carries the baby to term.

It is likely that Henry's jousting accident (where in real life he was unconscious for some time but then recovered) was partly to blame for Anne's miscarriage. It was obviously an event which caused a great deal of stress to her mind and body. Anne had also lost one, or perhaps two, children before this, and many historians have speculated there could well have been a medical complication (affecting either Henry or his wives) which explains why Anne, and indeed Katherine of Aragon, suffered so many miscarriages. For this book, however, I chose to take Anne's explanation of events into account. Anne stated that the reason she had miscarried was because she had seen Jane Seymour sitting on Henry's lap, in an embrace of some kind, and this had upset her so much that she had lost the child. In this book, Henry dies in the jousting accident, so that event with Jane Seymour never happens. I chose to follow this line of events, and therefore Anne remains pregnant.

Another pregnancy in the book is that of Margaret Douglas. In the summer of 1536, Henry VIII found out that she and Thomas Howard the younger had formed a relationship. There were rumours they were engaged and even that they had married in secret. Margaret and Thomas were arrested and sent to the Tower of London. There, Thomas was condemned to death, but the sentence was not carried out and he died, still a prisoner in the Tower, in 1537, apparently of some kind of fever, although there were rumours he was poisoned. Margaret became ill whilst imprisoned and was moved from the Tower to Syon Abbey. There were reports and rumours at the time that her illness was due to a pregnancy. She was released in October 1537 just days before Thomas died. Nothing was ever said about a child, if there was one, and so either she was not pregnant and the reports were just gossip, or she lost the child, or perhaps a child was born, and it was taken away from her. I decided to follow the idea that she was pregnant at this time, and she and Thomas had secretly married. It certainly seemed that she loved Thomas Howard, and he felt the same for her.

Most of the people in this book are characters from history, but Magpye, John and Joan Grey, and Thomas Blanke are my inventions. I have wanted for some time to write about people who weren't people of court in Tudor times, and so Magpye and her family came to be. John Grey, I made a reformer who supports Anne Boleyn. It is noted in the book that it is unusual that a man of his station should be able to read, but I thought since he came from a merchant family, who had come from money, it was not impossible. His travels, as a young man, lead him to embrace reform and Lutheran thought, which in turn lead to his support of Henry VIII's reforms and Anne as Queen Regent. It is often easy to suppose that all common people of the time would have rejected the ideas behind the reformation, but ideas of reform had, in fact, proved exceedingly popular amongst poorer people in Europe and some in England supported the changes in religion too. Just as people at court were divided on the subject of faith, so common people were as well and many famous reformers, Protestants and Lutherans came from non-noble backgrounds.

Magpye just seemed to wander into the book, as if she had decided she should be there, and who was I to argue? Her name, which some might think odd, comes from the fact that many birds in England once had first, or common names: Jackdaw, Robin Redbreast, Tom Tit, Jenny Wren, etc. Some of them have lost their first names, for instance we tend to leave out "Jenny" when we say "wren" nowadays, but some birds absorbed their first name into their name, such as jackdaw and magpie. "Pye" or "pie" is the old name for the magpie, some say because of its piebald (black and white) colouring but another theory is because "pie" is an old word for a chattering noise, so magpie, in some respects, might mean something akin to "chattering Margaret". "Talebearer" was another name for these birds, again most likely because of the noise they make and Magpye gains her name because she's good at gathering information, because of her eyes and because her first name is, of course, Margaret.

Some may note Thomas Blanke's name, as I have taken his surname from a famous black musician of African heritage who worked at the court of Henry VII and his son, and was probably one of the trumpeters depicted in the Westminster Tournament Roll of 1511, an illuminated manuscript that was produced to celebrate the birth of Henry, Duke of Cornwall, the short-lived son of Katherine of Aragon and Henry VIII. The dates of the Tournament Roll and Blanke's service at court certainly fit. John Blanke played at the funeral of Henry VII and the coronation of Henry VIII and was a highly successful and well-paid court musician. It has been speculated that he came to England with the entourage of Katherine of Aragon, and his appearance in the Tournament Rolls make him one of the earliest black people recorded in England after the Roman period. I named Thomas after him because John Blanke is an important historical figure I wish more people knew about, but I was not intending that the two men be seen as related.

There remains a cultural assumption, which still exists today despite extensive research presented by historians, that either there were no people of colour in Tudor England, and everyone was white, which is false, or that all people of colour in Tudor England were servants. Whilst being a servant was a common occupation, (for everyone, actually, from the very top of society to the bottom, since the royal family were served by dukes or duchesses, and ladies or lords, and they were in turn served by people of a lower rank, and so on) during the Tudor period there are records of black ambassadors, merchants, shop keepers, artisans, divers, seamstresses, brewers and sailors, some of whom emigrated to England and some of whom were born there. They made up a smaller percentage of the population than white people, but they certainly existed. Black people, often of African descent, had been present in England (and indeed the other countries of what would eventually become the UK) since at least Roman times, and whilst it is true many did work as servants in Tudor England, their occupations were more varied than this one role and they were paid for their work. They were not, as some assume, slaves.

Britain played a vast and shameful part in the slave trade, there is no denying that (and that role, which too often is swept under the carpet, should be highlighted more, in my opinion, in school and in our country's general awareness), but whilst there were individuals who traded in enslaved people in the 1500's, the large-scale involvement of Britain as a country in the slave trade did not begin until later, in the 1560's. This increased after 1640, and by the 1700's Britain had become the largest slave-trading nation in the world.

Many people still suppose, however, that any people of colour living in England during any point of the Tudor period (or indeed before the Tudor period) would have been slaves, or they would have been occupying only the lowest positions in society, and this is untrue. During the period this book is set in, people of colour were accepted as citizens in England, they were baptised, were married and buried under the rites of the English Church and operated at various levels of society. That is not to say there was no prejudice or racism, this period was obviously not some utopia of equality, but free, not to mention prosperous, people of colour were living in England at this time, particularly in London, Northampton, Plymouth and Bristol, frequently occupying positions of respect and authority, and some families had been there for generations.

I would recommend two excellent books at this point, *Black Tudors, the Untold Story* by Miranda Kaufmann and *Blackamoores: Africans in Tudor England, their Presence, Status and Origins* by Onyeka Nubia, if you would like to read further on the subject. There are many other books on black British history, and I simply recommend these as ones which concentrate on the Tudor period, and which I particularly enjoyed.

Magpye describes Thomas as a Moor, which, if this were exact terminology, means he should come from Northern Africa or the Iberian Peninsula, but in reality, throughout the medieval and early modern period the term "Moor" was a general one applied to any Muslim or person of colour. It did not necessarily denote a country or area of origin. I chose to use this term since it is historically accurate and I didn't want to describe Thomas as African, since he is English, but I apologise if this term upsets or offends any readers.

The family alliances and politics which unfold in the story, which house aligned with which claimant, was something

I spent some time planning out and although there may be some surprises, Norfolk supporting a bastard claimant for the throne, for example, I hope most readers with an understanding of the period would agree with my choices. My proofreader mentioned that this kind of book required "mental gymnastics" and when I read that comment I laughed, because it was true. Trying to fathom out what people would have done and how the timeline would have unfolded really was a challenge, and I hope it was one you enjoyed. The Wars of the Roses, the Anarchy and the English Civil War provided some inspiration as to how a civil war at this time would have torn not only the country apart but families too, so brother would be fighting brother, and wives might find their sons fighting on opposite sides to their fathers. Civil war is never a pleasant thing, no war is, and in many ways people might well have seen this as a fight for the soul of England, as with Mary there would be a return to the Catholic Church and with Anne there would be a turn towards further reform, just as with Fitzroy there would be a return to conventional male rule, and with either of the women there would be a situation unprecedented, where the first Queen Regnant of England might arise.

I hope you enjoyed this book and will go on to read the rest of the series.

Gemma Lawrence

Wales, 2025

THANK YOU

...to so many people for helping me make this book possible... to my proofreader, Julia Gibbs, who gave me her time, her wonderful guidance and also her encouragement. To my family for their ongoing love and support. To my friend Petra. To my friend Nessa for her support and affection, and to another friend, Anne, who has done so much for me. To Sue and Annette, more friends who read my books and cheer me on. To Terry for getting me into writing and indie publishing in the first place. To Katie and Jooles, Macer, Pip, Linda, Fe, Pete and Heather, people there in times of trial. And to all my wonderful readers, who took a chance on an unknown author, and have followed my career and books since.

To those who have left reviews or contacted me by email or on social media, I give great thanks, as you have shown support for my career as an author and enabled me to continue writing. Thank you for allowing me to live my dream.

Thank you to all of you; you'll never know how much you've helped me, but I know what I owe to you.

Gemma Lawrence
Wales
2025

ABOUT THE AUTHOR

I find people talking about themselves in the third person to be entirely unsettling, so, since this section is written by me, I will use my own voice rather than try to make you believe that another person is writing about me in order to make me sound terribly important.

I am an independent author, publishing my books by myself, with the help of my lovely proofreader. I left my day job in 2016 and am now a fully-fledged, full-time author, and proud to be so.

My passion for history began early in life. As a child I lived in Croydon, near London, and my schools were lucky enough to be close to such glorious places as Hampton Court and the Tower of London, allowing field trips to take us to those castles. I write historical fiction for the main part, but I also have a fascination with ghost stories and fantasy, and I hope this book was one you enjoyed. I want to divert you as readers, to please you with my writing and to have you join me on these adventures.

A book is nothing without a reader.

As to the rest of me, I am in my forties and live in Wales with a rescued cat (who often sits on my lap when I write, which can make typing more of a challenge). I studied Literature at

University after I fell in love with books as a small child. When I was little, I could often be found nestled halfway up the stairs with a pile of books in my lap and my head lost in another world. There is nothing more satisfying to me than finding a new book I adore, to place next to the multitudes I own and love... and nothing more disappointing to me to find a book I am willing to never open again. I do hope that this book was not a disappointment to you. I loved writing it and I hope that showed through the pages.

If you would like to contact me, please do so. I can be found in quite a few places!

On Twitter, (I am not calling it X) I am @TudorTweep.

You can also find me on Instagram as tudorgram1500, on Mastodon as G. Lawrence Tudor Tooter, @TudorTweep@mastodonapp.uk, and Counter Social as TudorSocial1500.

On Facebook my page is just simply G. Lawrence, and on TikTok and Threads I am tudorgram1500, the same as Instagram. I've joined Bluesky as G. Lawrence too. Often, I have a picture of the young Elizabeth I as my avatar, or there's me leaning up against a wall in Pembroke Castle.

I publish on Substack, where my account is called G. Lawrence in the Book Nook. On there I publish articles, reviews, poetry, advice for other writers and I'm publishing a book there chapter by chapter each week. Join me there!

Via email, I am tudortweep@gmail.com a dedicated email account for my readers to reach me on. I'll try and reply within a few days.

Thank you for taking a risk with an unknown author and reading my book. I do hope now that you've read one, you'll want to read more. If you'd like to leave me a review, that would be very much appreciated also!

Gemma Lawrence
Wales
2025

Printed in Dunstable, United Kingdom